I0817862

STORM HAVEN

Vol. IV

of

THE STEWARD

M.D. IRONZ

Published in the United States of America

Professorial Holdings

professorialholdings@gmail.com

Also by M.D. Ironz

The Steward

The Steward, The Box Set, Vols. 1, 2, 3

THE STEWARD

Domaine Delafaire

Realms Of Possibility

Alas, The Best Laid Plans

Storm Haven

The Expanded Box Set, Vol. 1, 2, 3, 4

Standalone

Dire Covenants

CH 1

ELLEN FOUND THE DELAFAIRE Farm kitchen abuzz with constrained excitement when she and her detective escorts, Hawk and Trey, returned from the Council Realm.

At their unexpected entrance, the room plunged into sudden silence.

Locking eyes with Ellen, Madeline gasped. "Did you find them—your mother and Stacy?"

"No," Ellen muttered. "How about y'all—any news?"

Madeline shook her head. "We've heard nothing, I'm afraid—but welcome back."

Her canine guardians, the Chows, Max and Sophie, trotted to Ellen's side, their tails eagerly wagging—which, of course, earned them vigorous happy hugs and head scratches from Ellen.

She noted that the cat, Smokey, was nowhere to be seen; but, that was not unusual.

Miska rose to his feet. "Ah, Lady Ellen—oops, I mean *Miss* Ellen—welcome home!" The big man from Were looked to Ellen with relief in his eyes.

She immediately understood that it was not only for her obvious well-being; but that he was, in no small way, thankful that her arrival now spared him from the intense focus of the assembled guests' well-intentioned, but nonetheless persistent, queries.

Glancing up at the people assembled in her kitchen, Ellen sensed that in her absence Miska's personal tale had indeed fascinated the waiting guests; Zack and Marie, Armand and Madeline.

A last minute inspiration before her departure for the Council meeting, Ellen had suggested that Miska play host in her absence and explain his origin within the Realm of Were. If he were to describe some of his inherent challenges as a sentient lycanthropic creature, and share his heartbreaking quest in search of his long-lost brother, his tale would no doubt enthrall her patient guests until her return.

Her gratitude was immense, eclipsed only by her sympathy for Miska. She knew all too well that throughout the evening the barrage of questions and requests for further clarification must have been relentless.

Catching the big man's eye, she mouthed a silent *thank you*.

Miska nodded and opened his palms. "All is well? Can I pour you all some wine—there is plenty left, see? Uh, but where is Mark?"

Her brow arched in wry amusement, Ellen stood, brushed a trace of dog hair from her slacks, and smiled. "You mean *Lord Mark*, the newest member of the Council of Realms, now seated upon the Chair of Man as the duly elected representative of the Realm of Man, *that* Mark?"

Stunned silence held the room in its grasp once more.

Trey chuckled, nudged Hawk, and stage-whispered, "I think she enjoyed doing that."

In the next moment, everyone seemed to be asking questions at once.

Ellen could only hold up her hands in a futile effort to stem the inquisitive tide.

A sympathetic Trey came to her rescue.

"All right, all right—hold it down," the detective sergeant said firmly as everyone quieted. "Sorry, but Hawk and I are pressed for time—so, no wine for us. I'll be brief; we didn't accomplish everything we hoped. First of all, Ellen has been officially acknowledged by the Council as the Steward; but, it didn't go quite as we anticipated. The details can wait for the moment."

He glanced to Ellen, who nodded in understanding—*after all, this was, in part, her tale to tell.*

A sense of polite, yet confused, acquiescence held sway amongst the assembled guests as murmurs of assured cooperation and appropriate congratulations circulated around the large kitchen table.

Trey raised a finger in caution. "However, we're no closer to finding Millie and Stacy; there have been no reported sightings of them since they disappeared from the fields of Delafaire Farm. We learned nothing pertinent about them in the Council Realm. Now as for Mark, he will be coming later, no doubt with more information. Ellen will explain everything. Unfortunately, Hawk and I have to go. We've got court in the morning; and, we still have some things to do tonight."

Hawk reached for Ellen's hand. "Will you be okay? I don't want to leave, but Trey's right. We have to check in, and jump on any new leads on Papa George, or anything regarding your mom and Stacy."

"I understand." She mustered a pained smile. "Go on, I'll be fine. I'll have a glass of wine and give everyone a brief synopsis of what's happened." She gave him a quick kiss on his cheek and grinned as his initial surprise faded to a chagrined blush.

Grinning in return, Hawk led his blatantly bemused partner, Trey, out of the kitchen.

Pausing before passing through the back door, Trey faced Ellen and mimed holding a phone receiver to his ear. "If Mark hasn't returned by sunup, call me."

Ellen stiffened as an involuntary chill of fear for her cousin cascaded down her spine and curdled in the pit of her stomach. She intended her reply to sound confident and hopeful—but she couldn't hide a small grimace. "I will, don't worry. And Trey? Thank you—for everything."

He smiled knowingly, bobbed his head, and slipped out the door.

MARIE STEPPED TO ELLEN'S side, pursed her lips, and in her *most concerned doctor's* voice softly asked, "How are you feeling—any nausea, dizziness, or headache?"

"I'm fine, Doctor—uh, Marie—really," Ellen assured her, carefully maintaining a neutral expression. The knot of apprehensive fear had relaxed to some degree. She forced a small smile for her doctor's benefit. "A little wine is fine, right?"

Marie relented. "A little . . . should be okay."

"Well, I, for one," Marie's husband, Zack, remarked, as he pulled out a chair for Ellen, "would appreciate a brief synopsis of this evening's events, with the emphasis on *brief.* I have an eight o'clock physics lecture to deliver tomorrow morning, and my lovely bride has rounds. So, no more wine for us; we'll need to get home soon."

"As should we," added Madeline. "I know we will want to hear all the details, but for the next few minutes I think it may be best to settle for the headlines. We can meet again tomorrow, if you like, to winnow out the specifics."

Zack and Marie bobbed their heads in agreement. Armand frowned—his wife ignored him.

Madeline reached over and patted Miska's forearm. "I fear we have already put dear Miska through quite an inquisition during your absence. He's been so kind and patient with us; we were such pests with all our questions. And I'm certain we are all a bit tired."

"Well, I'm not tired—I'm enthralled, excited, and interested," interjected her husband, refilling his glass. "This is truly remarkable—another world, populated with beings of a *lycanthropic nature!* I have so many more questions. For example, how do you—"

"Armand!" Madeline interrupted and shot him *the look*. "If I say you're tired—*you are tired.*"

Armand sighed resignedly, and shook his head, a twinkle in his eye. "Um, yes dear, of course."

Marie and Zack smiled knowingly at one another, obviously familiar with the Duprees' repartee.

Ellen smirked, accepted a glass of wine from Armand, and settled more comfortably in her chair. She noted that the dogs had taken positions on either side of the cast iron stove and lay there like furry rugs, regarding her patiently, as if prepared to listen as well. She could almost swear they were smiling at her—and that warmed her heart.

"Well, as Trey said, Mark will be home later," she began, and proceeded to describe the events of the evening.

She spoke at length, briefly describing the tiny Council Realm, the unexpected appearance at the meeting of Lady Diere as Queen Mab of the Dark Elves with the New Orleans crime lord, George "Papa George" Papadolis, in tow as a candidate for the Chair of Man, and the ensuing drama that put her cousin, Mark, in the Chair of Man. She told of the subsequent attack on Queen Mab and her consort by ensorcelled guards, electing to spare her guests the goriest of details. Lastly, she confirmed the apparent escape of George Papadolis.

Her audience was reserved, attentive, and clearly spellbound. Surprisingly, they asked fewer questions than she expected during the course of her narration.

When her remarks concluded, Ellen braced for a deluge of questions; but Marie immediately stood and curtailed any further discussion.

"All right, I'm sure we all have questions; but this is quite enough for one night," her doctor declared. "Ellen, you are still my patient, and I am directing you to get some rest. Don't worry, we can all meet again—even tomorrow, as Madeline suggested—but no more tonight."

As the guests prepared to depart, each spoke personally with Miska and thanked him profusely for sharing his heartfelt story. Ellen was touched by their genuine compassion and sincerity.

She and Miska walked them to their vehicles and bid them good night.

Staring at the dwindling taillights in the cooling night, Miska remarked softly, "Those are good people, m'lady, very smart, and very curious. I think this is a good thing that they will help you—a very good thing."

Sighing, she agreed. "Yes, I think so, too, Miska."

"M'lady, if you have no need of me, I would return to the cabin. The moon is strong and it beckons to me—a change is coming on. I would spend this night in the forest."

"Of course, Miska," she acknowledged. "Go now. I'll see you in the morning. Good night, my friend."

"Good night to you, m'lady."

ELLEN WAS RESTLESS, too keyed up to sleep. She paced around her bedroom, earning annoyed looks from the dogs, Max and Sophie, splayed out on the floor and not inclined to move. Smokey, the cat, had deigned to reappear and now lay unconcerned, curled up on the covers near the foot of the bed; of course, he ignored them all.

Mark had not yet returned. That added to Ellen's pool of escalating anxiety already brimming with concern for her mother and Stacy, both still missing. Her mind would not slow down; sleep was out of the question.

Taking the journal and the spectacles, she plopped down in the chair by the cold hearth and turned on the reading lamp. She might as well make the appropriate journal entry describing the events surrounding the Council of Realms meeting while everything was fresh in her mind.

She filled two pages with her careful script and capped her pen, her thoughts never venturing too far from her mother and Stacy. She sat quietly staring into the fireplace without really seeing it.

If there was only something I could do, somehow find them and bring them home.

As she idly fingered through the pages of the journal, she glanced down to see her Aunt Maude's delicate handwriting—a passage Ellen had not seen before. She settled the spectacles more comfortably on the bridge of her nose and began reading.

The topic seemed to be a generic commentary about finding a lost love. Ellen read for some time, and then softly closed the book. In her notes Maude had speculated that there was a way, using a blend of certain ancient and arcane thaumaturgy, to draw a lost loved one to oneself. It wasn't exactly finding someone; it was more like having someone seek and find *you.*

Maude never indicated if she had ever used such a spell; but, it was clear that she at least prepared one, a blended spell of sorts, or rather an incantation apparently set to some music. Perhaps it was meant to be sung, maybe even accompanied by musical instruments; the method of its casting was not clear. Unfortunately, the journal held no more related information, no written lyrics or melodic notations.

Ellen stared again into the empty fireplace, her mind mulling over what she had just read. Something tugged at her memories—something about music.

No—not just music . . . sheet music? Yes, handwritten sheet music, when I found the journal and the spectacles, in the trunk, in the attic!

She wasted no time in making her way to the attic, hardly giving the darkened attic stairwell or creepy cobwebs a second thought. She found the trunk easily enough, but it was locked. She'd forgotten that she'd locked the clasp. The key was on the ring with the house keys—either in her room, or possibly in the kitchen.

Sighing, she rose and trooped down the attic stairs to retrieve the key.

As she reached the second-floor landing, Max and Sophie shot past her, growling ominously as they raced down the wide staircase. She followed and found them silently staring at the front door.

Ellen sensed a transit globe forming outside on the front lawn. Her first thought was that Mark was returning—but then, why had the dogs growled?

She opened the front door and stepped out onto the porch. The dogs took up positions on either side of her. Somehow, Smokey was already there, staring balefully into the night.

In the middle of the lawn, a dark transit globe had fully formed. The atmosphere in the immediate vicinity of its event horizon crackled with small reddish sparks, as if the power forming the sphere was somehow corrupted—and barely contained.

A slender woman, sheathed in a formfitting yet elegant red and black iridescent gown, with one arm in a delicate sling, stepped forth.

Queen Mab!

Max leaned against Ellen's leg; she could feel the vibrations of his nearly inaudible low growl ratchet up incrementally. He had conveyed his feelings quite effectively. Sophie leaned slightly forward, lowered her head, and fixed her stare on this unexpected interloper, the Queen of Dark Elves.

Mab stopped several paces from the front porch steps, almost as if she was reluctant to come any closer to the house. Ellen barely had time to wonder if the wards were responsible before Mab spoke.

"Ah, Lady Ellen. Forgive my unannounced arrival, but it is imperative that I seek you out. We may be of help to each other."

"Indeed, Your Majesty? How so?"

"Firstly, I must apologize for, um, being something less than gracious earlier this evening. My dear consort, Padraic, told me of how you and your escort rendered aid when I was attacked by those foully bespelled guards. You must understand, I was severely injured—not quite myself."

Her tone was conciliatory, but nonetheless lightly tainted with a hint of condescension.

"As you know, I—oh, and the Council, of course—now seek this disloyal human, George Papadolis. I am told that you seek him, as well. I understand that he kidnapped your mother—and holds her still!"

Mab paused to adjust her sling, wincing with somewhat exaggerated gestures of frailty.

Ellen noticed that any mention of Stacy was conspicuously absent. Nor did she miss the overly dramatic display with the sling. She remained stoically unmoved by such petty theatrics.

"Please, Your Majesty, continue—if your wounds will permit, of course."

For an instant, something flared in Mab's eyes and was quickly gone.

Ellen's expression betrayed nothing.

"I shall manage," Mab muttered, soldiering on.

Ellen bit her tongue, stifling a rising retort, as the elfin queen continued.

"Now, more to the point, no one can find this man, or his victim, because he moves among realms, specifically between Were, Shadow, and an unknown realm in the *wild*. I can arrange for my warrior-elves to search for him within the realms of Were and Shadow, for both are of the Unseelie Court. But to access this unsavory realm in the *wild*, I will need your help."

"How could I possibly be of any help, um, Your Majesty?" Ellen asked, genuinely curious.

"Why, to open a portal to this untamed realm in the *wild*, of course," Mab explained. "My elves will scour that place to find both this treacherous human, and your mother. But, be warned! Time is of the essence—we must do this right away! Otherwise, there is no assurance that your mother will survive the night."

Ellen was surprised—no, stunned. Was this true? Could it be this simple? But how could she possibly trust this woman, this *Dark Elf*? This was *Diere*—the woman likely responsible for attempts upon her life—notwithstanding that she now called herself *Mab.* And if Papa George was behind the kidnapping of her mother and Stacy, how could Ellen know that Mab wasn't behind that? After all, she'd been warned that Mab did *not* want her to appear at the Council meeting; in fact, Mark speculated that Ellen had been the intended target of the kidnapping all along.

On the other hand, it certainly appeared that Papa George had turned on Mab. There was no mistaking that he had escaped, leaving behind the two ensorcelled guards who had definitely tried to kill her. Why wouldn't Mab want to find George and loose her vengeful wrath upon him? How could she not? It would certainly be in character; at least, that much seemed true.

"I still do not see why you need my help, Majesty. You seem to be quite capable of crafting transit spells. Why don't *you* open this portal into this *wild* realm?"

The surprise was plain on the queen's face.

"You really do not know?" Mab asked. "No, I can see that you do not. You still have much to learn about your Stewardship, do you not?"

"It appears that I do, Majesty. Would you care to enlighten me?" Ellen responded evenly.

"Ah, of course. Those with the necessary skills can transit between realms provided they have been there before, or are taken there by one who has previously been there. Thereafter, they can do so on their own initiative."

Mab gestured an open palm toward Ellen. "Only a Steward, such as yourself, can open a portal and transit to a realm they have not visited before—provided, of course, some idea of its location is known.

"While there were, at one time, several Stewards among the realms, there are no more—save one. *You* are the only Steward among the known realms. Now, do you see why I want your help?"

Ellen had the distinct sense that she was missing something; there was more to Mab's request than she was being told. Surely, Mab had some hidden agenda. Ellen was disinclined to cooperate, just on general principles; but, she had to be careful. Mab was a formidable entity and would be a dangerous enemy in an open confrontation.

"I understand," Ellen began carefully, "but I believe you said that George still holds my mother—is that correct? And just how would you know this . . . Your Majesty?"

Ellen sensed Mab's temper flare at such perceived impertinence; and yet, the queen replied evenly, a chill frosting her words.

"A queen has resources available to her that others do not. Let me be clear, Ellen, I *will* find this pestilent human, no matter the realms in which he may try to hide. When I do, I will *not* be having a civil conversation with him."

Leaning forward intently, Mab pointed a manicured finger at her and seethed, "Understand this, Ellen—what happens to your mother is not my concern. But, if you do as I ask, she may well be restored to you. However, if you do *not*—it is likely that you will never see her again."

Shocked at the clearly implied threat, Ellen felt her ire rising, her jaw tightening; but, she maintained her silence as the queen continued.

"There is no more time! I *will* have your answer," Mab insisted. "Come with me now, and let us try to save your mother. Or deny me, and know that her doom is upon your head—she may be lost to you forever!"

Torn and distrusting, but well aware that doing nothing was not an option, Ellen reined in her building rage and resentment.

"Very well, I will come with you, and do as you ask, for my mother—not for you."

MARK STRETCHED OUT a hand and touched Selene's shoulder as he followed her through the warren of hidden passages within the walls of the Council of Realms facility.

"Selene, I am very grateful for your help. I seriously doubt that I could have found my way to Elsbeth again—certainly not through these lonely corridors."

Without slowing her pace, the undine answered, "Oh, I think you could have found her, m'lord. However, you would have had to use the common public hallways, seeking directions and asking questions; that would *not* do. Tis far better that none know that you are personally acquainted with Elsbeth. After this meeting you two can work out your own clandestine communications procedures."

"An excellent suggestion," Mark agreed. "I completely understand the need for discretion. And now that Madam Moya has opened the Enclave of the Realm of Man for my use whenever I'm here, perhaps there is some aspect thereof that might facilitate such discreet communications? I can see that I'll have some exploring to do in my spare time."

"I would be happy to be of assistance in that regard, m'lord. You need only ask," Selene assured him.

"Thank you, Selene, I may just do that."

DEEP WITHIN THE CRAMPED storage area below the Council Library, they found the aged brownie, Elsbeth, at her diminutive desk. The unofficial archivist was sipping tea from a delicate hand-painted porcelain teacup. Mark could see that there had been some changes to the towering mounds of ephemera since his last visit. Teetering stacks of old files had been pushed aside to create a modest space where a pair of simple wooden chairs now faced the brownie's small desk.

Elsbeth smiled at her visitors and gestured to the vacant seats.

"Welcome, Lord Mark, and congratulations on your election to the Chair of Man. You see, I have had so many visitors of late that I brought out some chairs. Please, be seated."

Amused, Selene added in clarification, "Lady Ellen and her escort were the only other visitors, of course; but, within these lonely stacks, that is considered quite a crowd. Right, Elsbeth?"

The wizened brownie smiled. "True, but warm and welcome company, nonetheless. Would either of you care for tea?"

Selene accepted; Mark declined.

Getting right to business, Mark explained the purpose of his visit, and waited patiently as Elsbeth sorted through a series of piles of papers on her desk.

For a moment she seemed lost in thought, but then she looked into his eyes and spoke clearly and with conviction.

"This human, George Papadolis, was not alone; he was aided in his escape by another. My sources heard a name, *Daegon,* one that appears only once in our records. He was listed as an *alchemist* in the service of the late Queen Mab LIV of the Dark Elves. Like most of her household and staff, he was thought to have perished with her; but it now appears that he survived. We have no information in regard to his magical skills; alchemy is considered a lesser, more pedestrian pursuit. We have no way of knowing if he was responsible for this act of necromancy, or if George Papadolis was, for that matter. However, the implication is obvious."

Mark nodded in agreement. "Since there's no evidence one way or the other, I seriously doubt that George has any skill with necromancy. Ergo, I would suspect this Daegon—Occam's razor."

"Ah, the simplest solution based on available facts," observed Elsbeth, smiling once again. "I can see that you and I will no doubt have many enlightening and stimulating conversations. But, let us get back to the questions at hand.

"You did raise one other issue, the room in which Lady Ellen and her escort sought refuge during the chaotic rescue of Queen Mab and her consort, the room that does not seem to exist."

"Yes," Mark conceded, "that seems to be the case. I can offer no rational explanation."

Selene interrupted and admitted, "I know of many passages and hidden rooms, but not the one described."

The brownie said thoughtfully, "As do I, Selene, but that room is unknown to me as well."

The undine shrugged and opened her palms. "Few know as much as you do about this place; none know more, save perhaps Obe—"

Elsbeth glared at Selene.

"Who?" interrupted Mark.

"No one!" Elsbeth waved a tiny hand in dismissal. "Ah, someone thought long dead. The point is that as far as I know no one living knows the full extent of the secrets held within the walls of this facility, nor how to access them. Commonly rational explanations may not apply. It may be that Lady Ellen has some sort of special aptitude or affinity for such mysteries; I know that her predecessor, Maude, certainly did. I wish I could be of more help, but I fear I can shed no more light on the subject, at least not at this time."

"I see, thank you," said Mark. "I am grateful for your efforts. May I ask, has any new information regarding the kidnapping of the Steward's mother, Millie, and close friend, Stacy, come to your attention?"

"Yes, so it would seem," Elsbeth said somewhat cryptically. "There is someone with whom you need to speak. If you will indulge me for a moment."

Elsbeth gestured to Selene, who disappeared behind a towering stack of boxed books. Moments later, she returned, but not alone; someone followed her.

Padraic!

Mark came to his feet as the brownie said laconically, "I believe you gentlemen may know of each other but have not yet formally met. May I present Lord Padraic, Consort to the Queen of Dark Elves."

Mark bowed, but remained silent. *What is this? Why is he here?*

Padraic bowed briefly to Elsbeth and smiled at Mark.

"M'lord Mark, I apologize for not arranging a proper introduction sooner, although we have briefly spoken under more difficult circumstances. But I do know quite well who you are. I could not be more pleased to meet you."

Elsbeth gestured. "Selene, would you please see to it that we are not interrupted, or overheard?"

The undine grinned and slipped away.

Mark became aware of a noticeable increase in pressure in his ears, as if they had descended several fathoms beneath the surface of the sea.

The brownie raised her index finger. "We may now speak freely. We are within a very special, invisible, yet sound-impervious bubble of water vapor. You may have noticed its pressure. We will not be overheard.

"M'lord Padraic, if you would care to proceed?"

"Thank you, Elsbeth. We have very little time, so I shall be brief. I have reason to believe that Queen Mab is behind the kidnapping of Ellen Doyle's mother, Millie, and friend, Stacy. I believe that George Papadolis was merely her tool."

"We suspected as much," confirmed Mark, "but where are they now? Does George have them?"

Padraic shook his head, "I think not. Diere—excuse me, Queen Mab—is convinced that George has betrayed her, or will. She will no doubt slay him outright as soon as she can find him. No, I think *she* has them; and more importantly, I believe I know *where*."

"What—where?" Mark demanded.

"One moment." Padraic fumbled in his pocket and produced a topaz ring. Holding it on his flattened palm, he explained. "This bauble belongs to her, this new Queen Mab. It is capable of holding an enchantment, now nearly spent. I have seen it before—I have *used* it before. I now know that George used it, at her direction, in the course of the kidnapping.

"Containing the proper spell, it could transit one to a small and solitary place of darkness with few sources of light—a realm unto itself, unlike any other—a special, private place of *hers*. I know it well; I have been there, but only at her invitation. It is there that I believe we will find Millie and Stacy. The remnant of the spell within this gem could lead us there. I would perform this task myself, if I could, but I cannot. I need *Ellen*—I need her help, as the Steward."

"Ellen?" Mark echoed, his surprise plain, but his mind seeing the essential logic almost immediately.

Padraic merely smiled and nodded.

"May I?" Mark asked as he reached for the ring.

Holding it up, Mark thought it looked a bit dull, not at all what he expected. He was growing more skeptical by the minute; he felt his innate cynicism rise to the fore.

"Lord Padraic, with all due respect, this ring seems to be nothing special, and hardly constitutes proof—"

"Lord Mark," interrupted Elsbeth, "I can assure you that this stone was once among a dragon's hoard and is quite capable of holding a transit spell—although even I can see that only a trace of the sorcery remains. These are rare gems indeed, and only a few are known among the Council Realms. This topaz has long been in the Lady Diere's possession. And notwithstanding that she is now known as Queen Mab, the ring is still considered to be her property."

Mark considered the two earnest people before him. He allowed his newly enhanced perception to passively wash over them; he sensed no intentions to deceive.

"Very well," he conceded, handing the ring back to Padraic. "I'll accept that premise. But, here is the real question; Lord Padraic, why are you telling me this? Are you not *consort* to Queen Mab? Have you not sworn *fealty*? Are you not expected to protect *her* interests? Why should I believe you? And most important—why should I *trust* you?"

The air was dead still; the silence deafening.

Elsbeth and Padraic looked at one another, and sighed together.

At a resigned nod from Elsbeth, Padraic spoke wearily.

"Mark, what I am about to tell you will be for *your* ears only! You may speak of this to *no soul* without my expressed permission—more than lives may hang in the balance. I will have your oath on it."

Mark agreed, and swore the oath as instructed, with Elsbeth as witness.

Padraic spoke softly, yet his words were clear and articulate.

"Mark, it is true that I am now consort to Queen Mab, but I have never sworn fealty to any court or *anyone*—especially not *her!* I am sincere in my efforts to protect as many beings as I can—further details of which you do not need to know. You should believe me—and trust me—when I tell you that I will never allow any harm to come to Ellen, *for she is my daughter . . .*"

Padraic continued to speak, but Mark couldn't hear him. His mind reeled, his ears full of *white noise;* the world seemed to tilt over on its axis.

"Mark? Mark, are you all right?" Elsbeth hissed in alarm.

Daughter? Padraic is Ellen's father?

"I apologize, Mark," Padraic soothed. "I did not mean to shock you; but, it *is* the truth. I *am* her father. However, she does not know it—and that may be for the best."

Mark was speechless, as Padraic continued.

"As you may have surmised, I am no stranger to the Realm of Man. I visited there often, although I confess that I have not been back for some time."

"You are . . . Patrick Doyle?" ventured Mark.

"That is one of the names I have used."

"But you and Millie were legally married! Millie has the marriage certificate!"

Padraic had the grace to appear slightly uncomfortable as he responded, "Um, yes, I understand that is true."

"So," mused Mark aloud, considerably more confident now that he was delving into matters of a legal nature, "absent a divorce decree issued by a court of record, you are in fact *still* legally married to Millie—*my aunt.* And that, in turn, means that you are *my uncle!*"

Now it was Padraic's turn to wear a shocked expression—much to Elsbeth's delight.

"Ha-ha," she cackled. "I bet you did not see that one coming, you old rogue!"

Padraic was appropriately chagrined. He could only smile, hang his head sheepishly, and mumble, "Oh, ye gods. Yes, I suppose so."

"Well, now that we've established that this is a *family matter*," Mark cajoled, "what are we going to do about rescuing Millie, *your wife*, and Stacy, *my girlfriend*?"

"Oh, this gets more interesting by the minute," observed the amused brownie merrily clapping her tiny hands.

"Stacy is your *girlfriend?*" Padraic repeated, as Mark grinned widely and nodded affirmatively.

Arching his eyebrows, and tongue firmly in cheek, Padraic declared, "Well, that changes *everything*—now they *both* must be rescued!"

Mark had a moment of stunned confusion, but Padraic's wry smile and quick wink showed that he was not without a sense of humor.

However, Padraic's tone turned serious.

"But you must understand that we need Ellen to rescue them. Only she can craft a transit spell, making use of the remnant energy in this topaz to trace the location of this isolated and very special realm."

"But are you certain," Mark asked, "that Millie and Stacy are actually there?"

"Not completely," Padraic admitted, "but it *feels* right."

His mind racing to formulate a plan, Mark considered the possibility that Padraic's instincts were wrong. But could they afford not to investigate further?

"It seems we've no choice but to check it out. I'll have to get to Ellen; she's back at Delafaire Farm. Can you come as well, Padraic? Or will you be missed? By the way, where is Queen Mab?"

"I know not." Padraic shrugged. "She transited away hours ago. She hardly ever tells me where she goes, unless it is in her interest to do so. However, I will not likely be missed. She expects me to return to the Realm of Dark Elves and wait for her. We can go. But, one last thing . . ."

"Yes?"

"It is true that I am Ellen's father; but this is *my* truth to tell her—not yours. Only *I* shall be the one to share this with her, at the moment of *my* choosing. Remember your oath. Do we have an understanding?"

"We do," Mark replied smiling, barely resisting the temptation to add, *we do indeed, uncle.*

Elsbeth murmured a charm and Selene reappeared as the sense of increased pressure diminished. Selene wore an expression of worried concern that caught Elsbeth's attention immediately.

"Selene, what is it? What is wrong?"

Padraic and Mark stood in alarm. Padraic took Selene's arm in support. Mark scanned the area behind her; she had returned alone.

"Messages came while you were in closed conference," Selene replied. "Unconfirmed intelligence reports from *certain sources* indicate that warriors in the realms of Shadow and Were are quietly gathering in large numbers."

Elsbeth gestured for Selene to be seated. Padraic eased her into a chair that Mark held for her.

The undine took a deep breath, her eyes wide with concern.

"There have been several such reports tonight, admittedly vague; but something is assuredly happening. As you know, Shadow and Were have had strong disagreements often escalating to internecine skirmishes in the past. The Dark Elves have frequently been compelled to intervene in an effort to maintain the apparent solidarity of the Unseelie Court. But this time, it does not appear that Shadow and Were are targeting each other. Equally disturbing, the Dark Elves remain quiescent, doing nothing! None of the other Council Realms appear to be involved; our sources at the Seelie Court were unaware as well. Alas, that is all we know for the moment."

"So," mused Elsbeth aloud, her brows drawn in concern, "the Seelie Court, to include the realms of Light Elves, Dwarves, and Mer are neither involved nor aware. The Unseelie Court does not appear to be taking an active role, despite the activities of two of its member realms, Shadow and Were. And yet the leadership of the Unseelie Court, and the Dark Elves, have done nothing?"

Selene nodded. "Exactly."

Elsbeth, seemingly lost in a moment of quiet reflection, shook her head and whispered, "This does not bode well, indeed."

Padraic and Selene exchanged anxious glances in the heavy silence.

Elsbeth flattened her tiny hands upon the surface of the desk, looked up with piercingly clear eyes, and spoke in grim determination. "Nonetheless, we all have important tasks to perform. Let us be about our business this night. I wish you all fair winds and good fortune—be well, and wary."

CH 2

MARK STARTED UP THE steps of the front porch, but suddenly stopped as Padraic called out.

"Mark? If you please . . ."

Padraic had not followed. He was standing still in the moonlit front yard of Delafaire Farm.

"What's the matter? Come on," Mark pressed. "There are some lights on; Ellen must still be up."

"I cannot, Mark. I must be invited—the wards, you know." Padraic shrugged with open palms.

"Oh, that's no problem. I hereby invite you."

Padraic smiled and shook his head. "Regrettably, my young friend, the invitation must come from the Steward."

"But I *am* half owner of this house," Mark insisted. "My invitation should suffice!"

"Perhaps, but only the Steward can grant me passage through the protective wards. You will have to ask Ellen to do so. There is really no other way. Please, Mark, I will wait here."

"All right," Mark conceded. "Give me a minute; I'll be right back."

Padraic nodded in acknowledgment and spent the next few moments looking around.

It had been over a quarter century since he had last seen Domaine Delafaire. Now, silvered in the pale moonlight, it appeared no different, an argent reflection of the suspended past.

His last visit had not been particularly pleasant; Maude had been displeased with him. He had been about to leave this realm, which meant he was leaving Millie—for how long, he did not really know.

Of course, he had no idea at the time that Millie was pregnant. He wondered now if that would have really made a difference. Fairies are not burdened by much of a conscience, of course, but he was truly fond of Millie. Had he known, would he have stayed? In all honesty, it was not likely. Maude had never approved of the match in the first place, probably because she knew he would inevitably leave; and she too, was quite fond of Millie.

To his mind, it was as if Maude felt that Padraic did not *deserve* Millie—a proposition that he could never comprehend, at least not then.

SITTING AT THE PIANO with Smokey in her lap, Ellen stared at a sheet of handwritten music. So intently focused was she that she hadn't noticed the arrival of a transit globe and was surprised when Mark spoke her name.

"Ellen, I'm home. Oh, I'm sorry—I didn't mean to startle you."

"Oh Mark! I'm so glad you're back! Is everything all right—is there any news?"

"There may be. I met with Elsbeth. Wait a sec—are you all right? You look a bit pale."

"I'm not really sure . . . Queen Mab was here, and—"

"What? Mab was *here?*" he interrupted, an incredulous expression on his face.

"Yes, there's more. I think she threatened my mom—"

"Hold on," he interjected urgently. "Listen, I'm not alone. Someone you really need to talk with—about Aunt Millie and Stacy—is here. He's waiting outside. You have to invite him in, because of the wards and all. Trust me on this Ellen, please!"

"But, who?" she asked.

"Padraic."

"*Padraic* is here? He's waiting outside? But *why?*"

"He thinks he knows where your mom and Stacy are—but he needs your help to rescue them. Please, invite him in and hear him out."

She gently spilled Smokey from her lap as she rose, and went to the front door with the cat trotting at her heels.

She was a bit confused and concerned. Padraic was the Dark Elf Queen's *consort*. Did he bring some message from Mab? Could Ellen even trust him—she certainly didn't trust Mab—but what about him? Well, she could at least listen to what he had to say; where was the harm in that?

Ellen found that Max and Sophie were already on the front porch, calmly staring into the night. When she joined them, she saw Padraic standing in the yard.

"Lord Padraic," she said, "I welcome you to my home. Please, come in."

He ascended the porch steps and nodded to the dogs.

"Thank you, Lady Ellen. We have much to discuss."

"This way," she said, leading him into the house and returning to the ballroom. Smokey and the dogs silently followed.

She sat at the piano, turned and asked, "I must know; did Queen Mab send you, have you any message from her?"

"Queen Mab?" Padraic responded, clearly puzzled. "She knows nothing of my visit here—nor should she—"

"But she was *here*," Mark warned. "Ellen told me."

Padraic was alarmed, and made no effort to hide it.

"Please, m'lady, tell me of this—it could be of vital importance!"

Without quite knowing why, Ellen felt that it *was* vitally important that she share the circumstances of Mab's visit with Padraic, and of course Mark. Perhaps it was in part because the pets were so calm, so accepting of Padraic, that she relaxed as well.

So, in patient detail, she explained how Mab had insisted she needed Ellen's help in opening portals in Shadow and Were to a realm in the *wild* to facilitate the queen's search for George Papadolis, who had betrayed the queen's trust. Mab intimated that he had also kidnapped her mother. Only Ellen could open the portals to the realm in the *wild* where Mab suspected George was hiding.

Clearly finding her missing mother, Millie, was not Mab's priority. At best it was a coincidental benefit—but it was nonetheless offered, something Ellen could not ignore. So, she complied and did as Mab requested.

Ellen could see that her account left both men wide-eyed and somewhat stunned. She felt a bit self-conscious and hurried through her conclusion.

"And then she told me to transit home, and to stay here until I heard otherwise from her. To be honest, when I left Shadow and returned here, I was pretty well convinced that Mab had more or less lied—and used me. Now I don't know what to do. I've been thinking about trying to go back and closing those portals, but Mab had virtually threatened that I'd never see my mother again if I did not cooperate.

"Then I remembered this spell." Ellen picked up the page of sheet music. "Maude evidently crafted to find a loved one."

Padraic reached out. "Indeed, m'lady? May I see that?"

As Padraic examined the document, Mark anxiously queried Ellen.

"Now from what you've told us, do I understand correctly that Mab only mentioned your mother? She never said anything about Stacy?"

"No, she never did," Ellen confirmed, but then, as Mark's face fell, she quickly added, "But listen, I can sense that they are still together. I think that Mab just doesn't know *who* Stacy is, doesn't consider her important, you know what I mean?"

"Yeah . . . You're probably right," agreed Mark uneasily, yet still obviously hopeful.

"Uh, m'lady, this enchantment," began Padraic, waving the sheet music before her, "would be of little use in finding your mother. You are correct in that Maude crafted the spell; but, it is intended to draw a lost love of hers back to her. And there is a catch; he would be so drawn whether it was his will or not. It would be a compulsion he could not resist—coercion, actually. I think that is probably why Maude never used this spell; to coerce a lover is to doom the relationship."

"So," Mark speculated, "she never used it. As it is, this spell is too narrow and specific to be of any use to us in our present circumstances. Can it be altered in some way to work for us?"

"No," Padraic assured him. "It is generally very foolish to tamper with a spell cast by another. Unintended consequences are almost always the result; some can be quite severe. In any case, we may not need this enchantment. But first, I have some questions about Lady Ellen's account of her travels with Queen Mab."

"What questions?" she asked, shunting aside her disappointment with Maude's spell.

"M'lady, did you recognize this realm in the wild, or anything about it? Had you ever been there before?"

"No, I don't think so," she answered. "I know I hadn't been to Were before. When we transited from Were to this wild realm, Mab had a sort of *tracing spell*—or so she called it—to guide me in calling forth the transit globe. We arrived in a rural wooded area, and then walked for at least half a mile before transiting from there to Shadow. Mab was adamant that both portals be left open. But to answer your question, I recognized nothing familiar in the wild realm; although, I thought I saw something through the trees, something reflected in the moonlight. It looked kind of like a tall skinny windmill with long thin arms. But I could be mistaken, and I only caught a glimpse of it as we were walking."

"A *tall skinny windmill?*" Padraic repeated, his concern growing.

"Well, I thought so . . . Does that mean anything?"

"It might," he admitted, "it might very well, indeed. M'lady, you must indulge me; I must go and check on something. I promise to return promptly—with a full explanation."

Mark put a hand on Padraic's arm, saying, "Now, hold on a minute! You've got to tell Ellen about her mother and Stacy."

Padraic paused, dug in his pocket and produced the topaz ring.

"Here, Mark, take the ring. Please explain its significance to Ellen while I am gone. I shall be back as soon as I can. Much may be at stake and time is of the essence!"

He strode from the house without another word.

This time, Ellen easily sensed the formation of a transit globe on the front lawn. Then it and Padraic were gone.

"Mark, what is going on? What is that ring? Is it supposed to help us find my mother and Stacy?"

"Well, yes, I think so—with your help, that is, if I understand all this correctly," Mark responded wearily. "Let's go in the kitchen and put a pot of coffee on. I think we're going to be up for a little while."

AS SOON AS HE ARRIVED in Storm Haven, Padraic was ushered into the Guildmaster's office by the senior mage, Gallenius. An air of tension stressed the mood of the hurried meeting.

"Ah, it is good to see you, old friend," said the Guildmaster somberly, seated at his desk. "Nonetheless, it seems that dark deeds are afoot this night. You know of the mustering of troops in the realms of Were and Shadow?"

"Troops? Hmm, I do," said Padraic, "and I now suspect that Storm Haven is their intended target."

"What?" exclaimed Gallenius, clearly shocked at the notion. "What are you talking about? Do they not prepare to fight each other?"

"Despite appearances—and our usual expectations—it would not seem so," cautioned Padraic.

The Guildmaster leaned forward across his desk. "That would help to explain why the Dark Elves have apparently done nothing to stop this mobilization. But tell me, Padraic, why do you say that Storm Haven is their target? They should not even know of our existence. And, our defenses should be more than adequate to repel any assault upon our entry portal."

"True, the entry portal is not vulnerable," Padraic agreed. "Please, bear with me, for this is hard news to convey."

"What news?" insisted Gallenius impatiently.

"I suspect your defenses have already been breached by Queen Mab—through betrayal, treachery, and manipulation. And sadly, the new Steward, unknowingly duped, was the means. Let me explain," Padraic said resignedly.

He spoke quickly, and in depth. Gallenius and the Guildmaster listened in shocked silence. There was a long moment of introspection before anyone spoke. Padraic grew anxious in anticipation of their reactions.

The Guildmaster leaned back in his chair and steepled his fingers, while Gallenius began to pace worriedly back and forth.

"So, Queen Mab, the former Lady Diere, has secretly orchestrated this entire invasion, and leaves the actual assault to Were and Shadow," synopsized the Guildmaster. "And by holding the Dark Elves back, that gives her plausible deniability with the Council. It would seem she is far shrewder than I gave her credit."

"Politics aside," interjected Gallenius, who halted his pacing and stabbed a finger at Padraic. "Exactly *where* are these new entry portals, these posterns the Steward so easily opened, despite our precautionary wards?"

Padraic fixed Gallenius with an ominous stare. "It is my understanding that the portals are somewhere in a rural and moderately wooded area, in the vicinity of a windmill. And they are relatively close to each other, probably within half an hour's walk."

Stepping into Gallenius' personal space, Padraic stood nose to nose with the mage and said evenly, "And for the record, Gallenius, the Steward did not know that she had compromised the security of Storm Haven—she *still* does not know. She was tricked and coerced—her mother's *life* was threatened! If you must take umbrage with someone, take it with Mab!"

Gallenius bristled, and would have responded but for the Guildmaster's interruption.

"That is quite enough, gentlemen. Let us now do what we can to ameliorate this crisis. Gallenius, send out our scouts and spies to locate these portals, and observe what our enemies may be up to. Can the College of Mages close these portals?"

Gallenius stepped away from Padraic and straightened his robes before responding.

"Well, as you know, Guildmaster, the combined strength of the faculty and the senior students may be quite formidable in a concerted effort; however, you know how strong a portal opened by a Steward can be. Clearly, she has already defeated most of our protective wards—unknowingly or not."

He gave Padraic a scowling side-glance, and continued.

"It pains me to admit that it is not likely that we would be successful in closing these portals. There may be some containment spells we can employ against those who might come through, but even those considerable sorceries would be but temporary impediments."

"I see. Padraic, can the Steward close these portals?"

"I do not know, but I suspect so," he mused and added, "I know she entertains the notion herself, but is concerned Mab would harm her mother, as she has threatened, should Ellen attempt such closures."

"Then if her mother were not in jeopardy, she would attempt to do so, do you think?"

"Lest we forget, the Lady Stacy, the Steward's closest friend, is also being held," Padraic reminded them. "But I agree. Rescue her mother and Stacy from Mab's grasp, and the Steward would do everything in her power to protect Storm Haven—of that, I am certain."

The Guildmaster slammed a fist into his palm in determination. "Then a rescue it is! Now, what can we do to help? We have had our people looking for them—so far, to no avail. Have we any new information, any fresh ideas as to where they are being held?"

Padraic smiled for the first time during this strained meeting.

"It may be that we do; but such information must be closely kept. It would not do for Diere—Queen Mab—to discover that we have penetrated one of her darkest secrets. And, I have a plan . . . "

THE DOGS ALERTED ELLEN and Mark that Padraic had returned before he could even approach the front porch of the main house of Delafaire

Farm. As Padraic paused before ascending the porch steps, Ellen swung the door open and invited him to enter.

Ellen ushered their visitor through the house and into the kitchen.

"Well. what news, Padraic?" Mark demanded.

"Regrettably, the portals Ellen opened from Were and Shadow go into a rural area of Storm Haven, and effectively bypass that realm's defenses and wards."

"Storm Haven?" Ellen cried in anguish. "Oh no—not Storm Haven! What have I done? I had no idea! What does this mean?"

Mark put his arm around her shoulders. "Come on, El', calm down. Padraic?"

"Please," Padraic soothed, his palms open. "Try to understand. We know that you were tricked and coerced—you are not to blame. We believe that Queen Mab is behind all of this—and more."

"We?" asked Ellen.

"I have just come from a visit with the Guildmaster—Storm Haven has been warned. They will prepare to meet any threat; obviously, an invasion by Were and Shadow is expected. It is imperative that you close these portals."

"But—" Ellen began.

Padraic cut her off, clasping her hands in his own. "I know you fear for the hostages—your mother and your friend. Make no mistake, they are indeed hostages. So, we must rescue them first—this we understand. But once they are out of harm's way, you *must* close those portals."

"But what will Storm Haven do," Mark pressed, "I mean, until Ellen can close the portals?"

"Defend themselves, of course, as best they can," Padraic answered, releasing Ellen's hands. "We have no time to lose. We must rescue the hostages as soon as possible. Are you ready?"

Ellen shrugged off Mark's arm, and balled her fists. "I am!"

"Mark, I assume you have explained the significance of the topaz ring and the trace of the spell still held within?"

"I have," Mark confirmed, "but I couldn't explain *how* we're supposed to do this."

Padraic smiled and said, "A simple task, much like what Ellen has already done in using Queen Mab's tracing spell as a guide in calling forth a transit globe. Ellen, do you understand?"

"Yes, I think so. I focus on the remnant energy held in the gem as I cast a transit globe, right?"

Mark gaped. "I get it! It's like a GPS locator with the trace of an address in it—that's cool!"

Padraic nodded quizzically, his smile fading. With a resigned sigh, he raised a cautionary finger.

"I must warn you—I said it was a *simple task*, but it is not without risk or considerable potential danger. This feat can only be accomplished by the most advanced adepts, learned mages of great standing, and of course, a Steward.

"It is possible that Mab has laid wards and traps to frustrate any such attempt to access this *special place* of hers. You must be of clear intention and free from any distraction. Maintain your focus on the task at hand at all times, lest we both lose our way in the void."

"Excuse me," Mark interjected, "*both* of you? For your information, I'm going with you."

Padraic started to object, but Ellen forestalled him.

"Padraic, don't bother; you won't win an argument with Mark," she warned, with a tired smile. "He's a lawyer; he'll debate you forever—we don't have forever. Besides, there's no way you're going to keep him from Stacy."

"That's the truth," Mark insisted. "So, let's move on. What can we expect in this *special place* of Mab's?"

Padraic shrugged in resignation. "Very well. We can expect darkness, and typically a solitary cone of light. That is where I believe we will find the hostages."

"Darkness, huh?" Mark grinned. "I'll be right back."

He returned to the kitchen in a rush, carrying a pair of flashlights and a larger floodlight with a six volt battery pack.

"I learned a little something on our last trip through another realm," he asserted as he handed Ellen and Padraic the flashlights. "One can't have enough light."

Ellen was more than ready. "Let's go out front; and then show me what to do."

STANDING TOGETHER ON the moonlit front lawn, Ellen held the topaz ring in her cupped palms, closed her eyes, and let her awareness seep into the heart of the stone. With very little effort, she found the remnant of the unused portion of the spell; its energy was slowly dissipating, trickling away at a snail's pace into the metaphysical ether. She didn't draw upon or interfere with its lingering energy; she merely used it as a locus for crafting the transit globe in her mind. She imagined the globe growing more substantial, and large enough for several people to use simultaneously.

"El', it worked," whispered Mark. "Open your eyes."

The large obsidian ball appeared to float upon the grass. It seemed to comprise the very essence of primeval darkness.

"Why is it so dark?" she asked, as she returned the ring to Padraic.

"It reflects our destination. You have done well, Ellen," Padraic offered in praise. "We must be in contact with one another as we enter the sphere together. No matter what you may sense when we arrive; disorientation, falling, or severe cold—do not let go, for it will only be an illusion. It will not last for long."

Ellen set her jaw. "Let's do this."

Holding hands, they stepped into the black sphere. There was an instant of severe cold followed by a wave of nausea and disorientation. Having been forewarned, they grasped each other's hands more tightly.

As Padraic had predicted, the discomfort did not persist, but the utter darkness did.

"Ellen, are we clear of the globe? Can you close the portal?" he asked.

"Yeah, we're clear . . . and the portal is now closed," she replied. "Is everyone okay?"

"I can't see a thing," murmured Mark, shuffling his feet, "but the floor feels flat and a little uneven."

"It is smoothed stone," offered Padraic, "but from where quarried, I know not. Now, be still and listen."

They heard nothing, not even the stir of echoes. The stygian dark did not abate. But for their contact with one another, each would have been lost in an unimaginable void.

"I'm going to try the floodlight," announced Mark, "you both watch your eyes—"

"No—wait!" Ellen warned. "I don't think that's a good idea; you'll just give away our position. Let me try something."

"Oh, yeah, I get it," Mark replied. "Do your *thing*."

She let her awareness expand around them, searching outward like ripples in a pond. At first there was nothing; then she sensed something small that skittered away from the touch of her mind. She became aware of something else, several larger entities that also reacted to her probe—but these did not flee. She sensed *curiosity* and growing *interest.*

"We are *not alone!*" Ellen whispered. "Something in the dark knows we are here—more than just one thing!"

"Does anything approach?" Padraic asked.

"No, not yet, not that I can sense."

"What about Stacy and your mom?" Mark hissed impatiently.

"Nothing."

"They may be bespelled," Padraic offered. "Try again, but think of a human heartbeat."

A moment later, she exclaimed, "I have them! They're close—in this direction."

Ellen tugged the men forward a few paces, and a dim shape began to form and lighten in the near distance, a barely perceptible cone of pale shadow. It began to lighten further, eventually coalescing into a comparatively bright tapered shaft of illumination that chased the shadows away from two figures lying supine upon the grey stone.

Was that Millie and Stacy?

Rushing forward, Ellen, Mark, and Padraic converged on the cone of light and stepped within its illumination. The cone widened perceptibly as if to accommodate them.

Lingering wisps of grey fog seemed to tug at the two senseless women. Mark and Ellen would have tried to scoop them up, but Padraic suddenly grabbed Ellen's arm, preventing her from touching her mother.

"Ellen, wait! Mark, do *not* come in contact with the mist! I know not if it is safe to touch. These dissipating tendrils are remnants of this binding spell;

they may yet hold some power. At the very least, it may record a trace of our presence. Give me a moment."

Standing above the two unconscious figures, Padraic held his open hands over them, palms down. Closing his eyes, he murmured a simple incantation. The thick lingering wisps of fog and mist began to drift straight up, off the recumbent bodies, and vanish overhead. Soon all traces of the binding spell were gone.

The women stirred, and opened their eyes.

Mark had Stacy in an embrace in the next instant.

Ellen helped her mother sit up and hugged her fiercely.

"Oh, Mom," she moaned, squeezing her eyes shut, "I was so worried."

"El-Ellen?" Millie mumbled, "Where are we? What happened?"

"Mark, you're squeezing me too hard!" Stacy strained to say. "Let me breathe! Uh, no, you don't have to let go. What is going on? Where are we? Why is it so dark?"

Padraic cleared his throat. "We have to go! It would be most unwise to linger here."

At the sound of his voice, Millie frowned, pulled back from Ellen's hug, and looked around.

"Patrick?" she asked, breathlessly.

Ellen looked at Millie in complete puzzlement. Holding her mother's shoulders, she looked from her to Padraic. "Mom? Do you know him? Do you know this man?"

Millie was staring into Padraic's eyes, a wry smile stealing across her lips.

"Don't look a bit different . . . all these years," she murmured to herself.

"Mom?"

Smiling at Ellen, Millie placed her hands on either side of her daughter's face and took a deep breath. "Why, of course I know him, Ellen dear—he's your father."

"*What? My father?*" Ellen blurted out, stunned beyond comprehension.

"There is not a moment to lose—we have to be away from this place!" warned Padraic, as he reached for Millie. "Can you stand, and walk?"

Mark helped Stacy to her feet—and suddenly froze.

"Listen!" he hissed, tightly gripping Stacy's hand and fumbling for his floodlight.

Then they all heard it; a shuffling and scraping sound some distance away, but growing perceptibly more distinct, and coming closer.

"On your feet, Millie," Padraic urged, tugging her to a standing position. He then reached for Ellen, "We have to go—*now*—and only you can get us out of here! Please!"

Another set of shuffling sounds came from a different direction. These, accompanied by ominously heavy breathing, seemed much closer than the first.

Mark flicked the switch on his floodlight. The wide wash of illumination feebly brightened the nearby bleakness, but dissipated beyond several paces. There it was swallowed by pulsating stygian shadows, as if the very darkness were alive.

As Ellen stood, Padraic forced something into her hand, a soft leather pouch.

"Open it," he whispered. "Another gem lies within—it, too, holds a small spell. Do as you did before with the topaz; maintain your grasp on the pouch with one hand and on the stone in the other as you cast a transit globe—quickly, now!"

She upended the pouch and a small, bright amethyst tumbled into her open palm. She did as Padraic instructed, and a small sphere winked into existence.

She dimly heard Mark's shout of surprise and warning as something large and slimy breached the outermost reach of his floodlight's illumination. A long pair of sucker-studded tentacles probed in a twisting hypnotic dance toward the five companions.

Without conscious thought, Ellen willed the globe to instantly expand and encompass the group. They were transported in that same moment—*somewhere else.*

THEY FOUND THEMSELVES huddled in a moonlit clearing, next to a small stone building.

"Ellen!" cried Padraic urgently. "We are all here! Can you close the portal?"

"Yes," she gasped, slipping the gem back into its pouch. "It's done! Where are we?"

From somewhere above her, a somewhat familiar voice announced, "Well done, Padraic. I see you were successful. Ladies and gentlemen, welcome to Storm Haven."

Ellen looked up to see a robed figure standing on the flat roof of the building. Over his shoulder, a narrow wooden tower reached toward the cloudless, star-dappled sky. At its peak, a set of long spindly wind vanes slowly rotated in the night breeze.

"Aye, Gallenius, but twas a near thing," Padraic admitted. "Our penetration into Mab's place tripped certain wards, as I suspected might happen. Some of her guardians almost had us."

"And the portals you used?" the mage asked, as he walked down a narrow set of stone stairs that Ellen had not noticed in the moonlight.

With a small trace of pride Padraic announced, "The Lady Ellen opened and closed each with no difficulty.

"Ellen, Gallenius was kind enough to loan the amethyst. It is the property of Storm Haven's College of Mages, and must be returned."

Handing the pouch to the mage, she said, "Thank you, Gallenius. It is good to see you again; but, why are we here? I would have rather taken my mother and Stacy home."

"M'lady, had you gone directly to your realm, Mab likely would have known. Any transit globe you would have cast on your own, while in that place, may have left a traceable signature—a result of one of her protective wards, we suspect. To counter that, we crafted a set of diversionary and misdirection spells and infused both into the amethyst Padraic carried with him; they will deliberately mislead any attempt to trace your path. The pouch itself was infused with the small enchantment intended to lead you here, but it would only work if you held it and the amethyst in either hand."

Ellen nodded in understanding and asked, "The amethyst? Another gem that was once in a dragon's hoard, no doubt?"

"Quite so," Gallenius admitted.

"But the clever use of the pouch," Padraic added, "was Gallenius' idea. Well done, Magus."

"Oh, I get it," Mark mused aloud. "If it fell into the wrong hands, the pouch would most likely be overlooked—the focus would be on the jewel!"

Gallenius nodded. "That was our hope; fortunately it was an unnecessary precaution."

"So, Gallenius," probed Ellen, "when can I take my mother and Stacy home?"

"Very soon," replied the mage, "In fact, as soon as you have closed those portals you opened into the heart of Storm Haven—"

"Those portals," Padraic interjected, with a stern glance at Gallenius, "you were *tricked* into opening by Queen Mab."

"Yes, of course, those," acknowledged Gallenius with a nod to Padraic, as he pushed the door to the windmill open. "They are not far from here. If you will all come inside, I will tell you what we know, and what we do not."

LESS THAN A MILE AWAY, yet still within the rural woods of Storm Haven, moonlight bathed another clearing in tones of muted silver, giving the small gathering of diverse individuals a washed-out, yet surreal appearance.

"It isss imperative that our forcesss remain ssseparate, and operate independently," Addecus insisted, fixing Ling with an unblinking stare, his vertical pupils wide, small scales upon his sallow cheeks reflecting the pale lunar light.

"I am in agreement with you, Were Lord," confirmed Lady Leanan. The vampiress tossed her red tresses, rendered black in the argent light, over her shoulder.

Turning to her immediate subordinate, the Sidhe raised an elegant alabaster finger in warning. "Lord Tepesh, I trust you can see the wisdom of such a strategy. I will not tolerate any internecine fighting with the Were. Remember, our primary purpose here is the recovery of our *property*. Am I clear?"

"Quite clear, m'lady," answered the tall Vampire Lord. "Provided those we encounter submit; otherwise, we shall slay outright any who would dare to resist."

"Now *that* is a point upon which we *do* agree," commented Ling, smiling evilly and glancing over her shoulder where two hulking werewolves stood snickering.

The lycanthropes were to serve as *aides-de-camp* to the Were commander, Ling. Ironically, the majority of the Were troops were *not* shape-shifters, but a mélange of other beings, including human men-at-arms and a few mages. It was much the same case with the Shadow troops, where the vampires were few, only a handful of Shadow vampire nobles serving as senior officers.

"Ling," warned Addecus, "I trussst you will not lossse your focusss. It isss important that your troopsss underssstand that to replenisssh our ressspective populationsss *capture* isss preferable to *carnage.* Ssshould any within your command fail to appreciate the dissstinction, you may deal with them sssumarily asss you choossse."

"It shall be as you command, m'lord," Ling responded with bowed head.

Lady Leanan cautioned the Shadow commander. "Vlad Tepesh, see to it that your troops practice such restraint as well, to include those daylight hours when you and your officers must seek shelter. Lady Sabrina and Lord Gunther will remain and observe the campaign on behalf of the Administration of Shadow. Now, tell me, how many troops have you brought through the portal?"

"M'lady, I am told a little over five hundred troops and four nobles as officers."

"Will that be sufficient?" she asked.

"I would prefer twice that number, m'lady. But the portal is not large; only two may fit through at a time. So, the muster rate is slower than we would like," Lord Tepesh explained. "By another night's time, I feel we will be up to adequate strength."

"I see. Lord Addecus, I assume you face the same problem of the small portal opening?"

"Indeed, Lady Leanan," he replied, "and I foresssee another related isssue that will affect usss both. Asssuming our forcesss are sssuccesssful, we may have to hold captured *property* in the vicinity of the portalsss until additional troopsss are no longer arriving in thisss realm. Only then will we be able to sssend our recovered property back to our ressspective realmsss."

"We will just have to make some adjustments," she said thoughtfully. "Lord Tepesh, how many personnel can you spare to guard captives?"

"Only a handful, m'lady. Of course, I will be better able to spare more in another twenty-four to thirty-six hours."

Addecus looked to Ling, who shrugged her shoulders and nodded. The Were faced exactly the same problem.

"I know you are anxiousss to begin your ssseparate offensssivesss," remarked Addecus, "but asss our forcesss are not yet at ssstrength and are underprovisssioned, may I sssuggessst that initial operationsss be limited to ssscouting missionsss, and sssmall opportune raidsss?"

Leanan pursed her lips. "I concur, a pragmatic strategy that gives us time to build our strength and minimizes our captive issue for the time being. Let it be so."

Addecus smiled in gratitude at Leanan's support, and raised a finger to get the attention of both commanders, Ling and Vlad Tepesh.

"Very well. Pleassse coordinate your ssseparate areasss of operationsss. Lady Leanan, I know you plan on returning to your realm well before sssunrissse, but before you depart, may I trouble you for a word in private?"

THE WERE LORD AND THE Sidhe stepped away from the group and stood near the edge of the clearing. His dark robe and her sable sheath seemed to vanish in the night leaving only their faces barely visible in the argent moonlight.

"Yes, Addecus?" she whispered huskily. "Something troubles you?"

"True enough, Leanan . . . I know it would ssseem that Mab hasss offered an anssswer to our mossst ssseriousss problemsss, but my gut churnsss with dissstrussst. When you came through thisss new portal, from your realm to thisss one, did you not sssensse sssomething amisss—sssomething *old* and *unclean*?"

"Do you mean about this *place,* or the portal itself?" she asked, a twinge of recent memory struggling for recognition like a minnow striving for the surface of a hidden pool.

"The portal . . . I sssensssed sssomething—the sssubtle taint of great age and corrupt ssstrength. Yet I know thessse portalsss to be newly formed—mossst likely by the Sssteward—whether or not Mab isss to be believed."

Leanan considered his words and reviewed her own recent passage through the portal. There *had* been something—something slightly *different, almost dark,* about this new portal. But if Ellen had created these portals, as Mab had intimated—not *admitted*, of course—there should have been nothing dark about them.

"Addecus, I seriously doubt that the Steward has been compromised. More likely, she was coerced, if she is indeed responsible for these portals, as we suspect. But in truth, we do not know for certain that this is entirely the work of the Steward."

"Pray tell, who elssse?" he responded. "I know of no living mage who could do thisss. And if ssshe hasss been coerced, what of our *insssurance—Missska?* Hisss account ssservesss to prove the realmsss of Were and Ssshadow were not involved in the asssasssination of the late dark elfin queen, and even implicatesss Diere—the new Queen Mab. Do you sssupossse he isss ssstill sssafe? He isss in the Sssteward'sss care. Can you underssstand my concern?"

"Of course," she replied. "I will check on his well-being, when I find the time. But, to be candid, I think we have less to worry about with the Steward than Mab and her false *generosity*. She still intends that we maintain our silence regarding our suspicions about her involvement in the assassination. Offering us this wild realm is a bribe for our cooperation, nothing less."

"Oh, I am in complete agreement. Thisss is alssso to her advantage in sssome fassshion. I jussst cannot yet sssee how—but I ssshall. It isss bessst that we now depart thisss realm and let our minionsss conduct the campaign. I would rather monitor the activitiesss of thossse within the Adminissstration of Were asss thisss event unfoldsss."

Leanan smiled and shook her head. "Ah, politics—the intrigue never ends. I, too, have issues in my own realm to monitor. Be well, and careful, Addecus. You are the only Were Lord to earn my trust—I would not be pleased were you to come to harm."

Addecus smiled. "High praissse indeed from the mossst dreaded of the Sssid-he. Fare thee well, m'lady."

As they turned from each other and made their way toward their respective portals, they did not feel hidden eyes upon their backs.

DEEP WITHIN THE TANGLED underbrush on the edge of the clearing, the russet fox remained perfectly still for several long minutes after Addecus and Leanan had gone. As the moon waxed brightly toward the western horizon, the fox silently rose and padded away into the shadows.

THE SERIES OF SPECIFIC soft knocks on the door of the windmill brought all conversation within the small candlelit room to a shuddering halt. Gallenius stepped to the door, knocked in a deliberate pattern on the inside of the door, and received another set of knocks in response. The mage unlocked the door to admit a tall and worn man of middle years, wearing disheveled brown and green homespun, mud-stained and bracken-frayed.

"Ah, Wilhem, welcome back!" Gallenius whispered. "As you can see, Padraic has been successful. Have you a report?"

Rather than answer, Wilhem cast his eyes around the stark interior of the small room, looking directly into the eyes of each of those within. He then looked to Gallenius and arched his eyebrows in an unspoken question.

"It is quite safe, I assure you," Gallenius murmured. "All are known to us and have been *vetted*."

Wilhem did not speak, only nodded once and went outside. He returned a moment later accompanied by a petite woman wrapped in a hooded cloak of dusky auburn. Only tufts of her russet hair around her face and her light brown eyes shone from within the hood.

Stacy nudged Ellen and whispered, "I think I know them. I'm sure I've seen them both before, when I was in Shadow."

Gallenius gestured to a seat and said, "Please, Frieda, sit down and give us your report."

She made herself comfortable, but never dropped her hood.

"M'lord, we found both portals and they remain open. Shadow troops have set up an inner perimeter around the one from their realm as more soldiers and supplies arrive. They number over five hundred, and are well disciplined and alert. They have established a tight outer perimeter—it was quite difficult to slip past them. There are a few lesser mages and only a handful of vampires. Vlad Tepesh commands; Lady Sabrina and Lord Gunther are there 'to observe'.

"The Were, on the other hand, appear to be generally disorganized, although they number slightly more, over six hundred. They mill around the vicinity of their portal, but have set few guards, only a loosely maintained outer perimeter. A woman called Ling commands, and a number of shape-shifters attend her. I saw only two minor Were mages.

"Both forces intend to act independently, an effort to minimize the internecine strife to which they are mutually prone. They will initially carry out scouting missions and small raids. An organized assault will not occur until additional troops and provisions have been brought through the portals. But their intentions are clear; they are primarily slave hunting, but will eagerly slay any who resist.

"One other thing, the Were Lord Addecus and Lady Leanan of the Sidhe were there briefly to confer, and have returned to their home realms. There seems to be growing mutual trust and cooperation between those two. *Both* distrust Queen Mab of the Dark Elves, who surely has a significant but hidden hand and subsequent impact on these events."

Wilhem cast a knowing glance at his wife. Her report had been incomplete; she had mentioned nothing about what she had overheard regarding Miska.

"That concludes our report," she said, locking eyes with Wilhem in subtle confirmation that her omission had been deliberate. "I need to rest for a bit, if you don't mind."

"Of course, and thank you both," Gallenius offered. "Feel free to rest here."

TURNING TO ELLEN, GALLENIUS asked, "M'lady, how close do you need to be in order to close either portal?"

"I don't really know," she answered candidly. "I've always been pretty close when I've closed them before."

The mage looked to Frieda and spread his hands. "How close can you get her?"

Frieda shook her head. "Not close at all to the Shadow portal, but perhaps very close to that of the Were. By that I mean only her—no one else."

The room erupted in argument. None of Ellen's companions was willing to let her try something like this, especially not alone. They were understandably quite vociferous in their objections—not that it mattered.

"All right, that's enough," Ellen declared. "This is not a debate! I am going to close those portals—tonight! Gallenius, will everyone be safe here until I get back?"

"Yes, I believe so."

"Then that's it," she announced. "Everyone just sit tight! I'll be back as soon as I can. Frieda, are you ready?"

Frieda nodded. With a gesture to Wilhem and a swirl of her cloak, she was out the door.

Ellen looked back at her friends, her mother, and her *father—that was going to take some getting used to*—and smiled as confidently as she knew how. She just wished she actually felt that way.

Without another word, she, too, was gone.

WILHEM LED THE WAY through thick underbrush; the tall man could move like a ghost in the night. Ellen barely kept up, even with Frieda silently prodding from behind. Finally he stopped near the edge of a ravine, a dry watercourse choked with debris left by a past flash flood. He stood utterly still, like a tree himself.

Ellen followed his example, with Frieda presumably somewhere behind her.

Something brushed against Ellen's calf in the dark. Startled, she froze.

Holding her breath, she watched as Wilhem stooped in a patch of moonlight. He extended his hand; a fair-sized fox seemed to materialize beneath it. She watched in awe as he affectionately stroked the vixen's thick coat and scratched behind her ears.

Wilhem looked directly into Ellen's eyes. He pointed to the fox, and then to Ellen. He waggled two fingers in a walking motion, and pointed again to the fox.

Now, she understood; she was to follow the vixen.

Nodding to indicate her comprehension, she stepped forward. The fox looked into her eyes; Ellen was surprised at the depths of intelligence held in those amber orbs.

The vixen snorted softly, turned and disappeared over the lip of the ravine.

Wilhem motioned for Ellen to quickly follow; and so she did.

Following a fox through a thick forest in the moonlight is no easy task; nonetheless, Ellen managed. Of course, the vixen was very forgiving, and doubled back more than once when Ellen had lost her way.

Eventually, they came to the first of the Were sentries, a loose line of tired men-at-arms spaced about a spear's throw apart. It was no great feat to slip unnoticed between the bored soldiers.

Soon they came to a small stream. The fox sniffed the night air, urgently nudged Ellen behind a fallen tree, then dropped to its belly and lay motionless amidst a carpet of damp leaves. Something was coming from upwind of their position, following the streambed. Ellen could now detect its mildly stale stench. The smell was uncomfortably familiar; then she knew—a troll.

She was wrong. It was not *a* troll, but *two* trolls, wearing chain mail armor and carrying clubs the size of small tree trunks. Each carried a huge shield strapped to one forearm, and a murderous double-bladed ax stuffed in a bejeweled belt. One also carried the corpse of a freshly slain cow across one shoulder—no doubt some poor farmer's former source of milk.

Ellen held her breath as the two hulking forms passed within ten paces of their hiding place and continued along the streambed. She had a good look at them in the moonlight. These were not like the stupid brute she and her friends had encountered before, in the Realm of Shadow. No, these trolls appeared to be far more intelligent, and heavily armed. She heard them grunting to one another in measured low bass tones.

A language? Hmm, abbreviated grunting as some sort of secret communication? They clearly understood one another. There must be far more to these trolls than meets the eye.

The trolls turned away from the stream and stood for a moment grunting and looking into the trees. One let the cow carcass slip off his shoulder to the ground with a squishy *schlump-plop*. Then both trolls disappeared into the trees.

After a few minutes, Ellen thought it was safe to move and started to rise—but a paw on her arm froze her in place as a thick shadow ghosted past the fallen tree and slipped along the streambed.

It neared the dead cow and seemed to hover in that vicinity.

Suddenly there was a howl of rage, a high-pitched yelping whine, and booming guttural laughter.

"Ha-ho! A little puppy! See what I caught, brother!"

One of the massive trolls now stood bathed in moonlight on the edge of the stream holding one arm straight out. Dangling by the scruff of its neck, balled mercilessly in the troll's huge fist, hung a full grown werewolf, legs kicking in midair, and whining pitifully.

"Ha, brother! I did not know that you kept pets!" hailed the other troll stepping from the seclusion of the trees.

"No pet, this one—*pest* more likely! He has been following us since you broke that cow's neck."

"Oh, so *this* is what I keep smelling on our back trail when the wind changed. I thought it was a *wet dog!*"

Both trolls erupted into deep bass laughter.

The captor swung his prisoner around until they were nose to nose, and in a deep rumble of a voice, devoid of any humor, said to the werewolf, "We grant you your life—this once. Follow us again and it will be at the risk of your own pelt. Now go and steal your own food!"

With that, the troll threw the werewolf high in the air, across the stream and into the treetops. A cacophony of breaking branches, yelps of pain, and sickening thuds accompanied the lycanthrope's descent to the ground.

The trolls picked up their ill-gotten meal and continued downstream, chuckling to themselves.

Ellen was in a mild state of disbelief. She had never seen anything like this.

A cold nose against her cheek helped her to focus on the task at hand. She looked into those bright amber eyes and nodded . . . *I'm ready—let's go.*

IN ONLY A MATTER OF minutes Ellen realized that they had actually penetrated well within the Were camp. Although still heavily wooded, many trees had been felled; rustic lean-tos and small campfires dotted the scene. Ellen and the fox took shelter behind a stack of freshly cut firewood, covered with several random tarps.

Frieda had not exaggerated; disorganization was the rule. All sorts of beings wandered around wherever they would. The scene was not quite chaotic, but not ordered by any stretch of the imagination. That is, except for two distinct areas.

One was a clearing surrounded by torches, in which a tall, dark-haired woman could be seen gesturing to several individuals who would periodically rush off to carry out her orders.

The other was a smaller clearing in which pairs of soldiers seemed to be stepping into existence from nowhere. They were then directed to other areas of the camp by a hulking werewolf.

Ah, that is the portal.

Ellen could see that more than a few people wandered near the portal; however, they all gave the big werewolf a wide berth. She thought that rather wise, under the circumstances.

So, why not try and close the portal from here?

Concentrating, she sensed the energy signature of the portal. She willed it to dissipate.

Nothing happened.

That was disappointing. Evidently, she would have to get closer.

Without realizing why, she whispered to the fox, "I can't do it from here. I've got to get closer."

The vixen studied the scene, turned, and tugged on one of the roughly woven tarps with its teeth, easily pulling it off the stacked firewood. Dragging the tarp to Ellen, the fox tugged it across her shoulders, and with its front paws, rolled a couple of short lengths of firewood toward Ellen.

Ellen got the message and smiled. "An excellent idea!"

Pulling the tarp over her shoulders and her head, she improvised a sort of hooded robe that kept her features fully in shadow. Cradling pieces of firewood in her arms, she looked like any one of the multitude milling about.

Winking at the fox, Ellen whispered, "Wish me luck," and stepped from concealment.

SLOWLY SHE MADE HER way across the Were camp, carefully mimicking the seemingly aimless meander she'd seen so many others demonstrate. As she got closer to the area near the portal, she realized there was someone else with the werewolf, a small man, who had been hidden from her view by the lycanthrope's bulk. He was bald and bent with age, and judging by his robes, a mage of some standing.

Worse, he seemed to be monitoring the portal by means of a small crystal emitting a pale light in one hand, and an engraved wand in the other.

Ellen could not stop without drawing unwanted attention, so she shuffled onward. As she drew closer, she could more easily see the sphere. The darkness within the globe had its source in the Realm of Were, making it nearly impossible to discern the portal from any greater distance.

Somewhat close to the portal, a small cooking fire had died down to glowing embers, around which a few men-at-arms lay about, satiated and dozing.

With a sudden inspiration, Ellen knelt near the dying fire and stirred the embers, slowly adding a few pieces of firewood, yet keeping her face hidden by shadows.

In the hope that her current position was now close enough, she tried once more to close the portal.

At first, nothing happened; then she concentrated and renewed the attempt with an intense effort.

There was an electric crackle and the smell of ozone; but she dared not look up. Keeping her face within the shadow of her improvised hood, she stole a glance at the portal. A series of bright sparks and spindly tendrils of purple-tinted electrical charges arced over the surface of the globe in continuous waves of conflicted power.

The portal would not close—some other power, dark and oppressive, held it open and fought her efforts to dissipate the original binding of essential energy.

The men-at-arms around her had awakened and were climbing to their feet. She stood as well, carefully mimicking their hesitant confusion. For the moment, all eyes were on the flashing electrical discharges and the sharp snap of bolts snaking forth and striking the ground in the immediate vicinity of the roiling globe.

Many began to back away, including the werewolf—but not the mage.

He paced in front of the portal, just out of reach of the discharging bolts of energy, and focused intently on the crystal in his hand. In his other hand, the tip of his wand began to glow as he swung it slowly in a wide arc. It glowed brighter as it swept past her general direction.

She now intuitively knew. When she tried to close the portal she had tripped some sort of ward, something she hadn't known about, something that had been added to the portal. And this mage was trying to find the source of whatever had tripped the ward. He was hunting *her!*

He stepped between her and the globe and began turning in a complete circle, wand extended and his eyes once more intent upon the crystal.

In the heart of the now fully alert Were camp, there was nowhere to run, nowhere to hide. She was doomed.

So this is my fate . . . So be it. If it's the last thing I do, I will close that portal!

Standing firm in her resolve beneath the tarp, she balled her fists, closed her eyes, and concentrated on amassing as much ambient energy as she could. Surprisingly, there was a great deal—much of it was *fear*. She didn't care; she would use it, whatever its source. She imagined condensing and compacting this wild energy into a dense, barely constrained mass of cold fusion. When she could contain it no longer, she mentally threw it at the active globe in a final effort to close the portal.

Blinding light flashed and a thundering shudder echoed through the camp!

Ellen was flung to the ground, the wind knocked out of her. Her ears ringing, bright spots danced before her eyes. Slowly catching her breath, she remained still until her vision cleared. Carefully looking out from under the tarp, she saw that every being in the immediate vicinity had been knocked to the ground. Many of them were groaning as they tried to get up.

"What happened here?" demanded a stern female voice. "You there, soldier! On your feet! What did you see?"

Keeping the tarp over her features, Ellen slowly propped up on her elbows to see more clearly.

A tall elegant woman, a long thick braid of jet-black hair over one shoulder, wearing a formfitting mottled leotard and a low-slung weapons belt, had demanded an explanation of a confused man-at-arms.

"I-I know not, m'lady," he managed, trying to dust himself off. "We saw the mage do something—something to the portal."

"Aye, twas the mage!" repeated another man-at-arms who spat at the ground.

Clearly there was no love lost between the men-at-arms and those aloof practitioners of magic.

"The mage," she repeated. "Where is he?"

Another voice called out, "There, m'lady! Er, twas there he were standing."

Ellen rolled her head to see the speaker, another soldier not ten feet away from her. More people began to gather; she slowly regained her feet, careful to stay concealed within the growing crowd. Peering between the shoulders of two men, she saw the woman approach a blackened pile of smoking ash as indicated by the pointing soldier.

Taking a spear from a bystander, the woman probed the pile, flicking charred bits of bone and blackened teeth out of the mound. Something the size of an egg rolled out, and she stooped to examine it more closely. Taking a bit of shimmering cloth from the pouch at her belt, she carefully picked up the object and wiped it off. She then gently blew the remaining ashes off its surface—the crystal.

Ellen's breath caught—would she be discovered?

But the crystal was clearly cracked, its inner light snuffed out.

Ellen could only guess that her maximum effort to close the portal had somehow overloaded the protective ward. It had apparently lashed out in retaliation with a burst of electrical energy. However, instead of impacting her, it was drawn to the closer standing mage who was busily working his own magic—a fatal attraction, indeed.

The portal!

She eased through the crowd to get a look, and saw . . .

The portal was intact.

Her heart sank. She had failed.

The tall woman cursed loudly and dashed the broken crystal to the ground, shattering it into shards.

"Damn that meddling mage! All right, get back to your duties! Longshanks, go through the portal and have the troops begin transiting again. Tell them to send more food; we have already exhausted our initial supply. Then send a message to Lord Addecus telling him what has happened, and return to me. Now, go!"

A lanky werewolf trotted to the portal and vanished within.

PULLING THE TARP TIGHTLY around her, Ellen turned and walked away with the rest of the crowd as it dissipated. When she neared the woodpile, she caught a glimpse of russet fur; a pair of amber eyes delved into her own—her vixen guide.

I tried my best . . . but I failed . . .

It occurred to her to just keep aimlessly walking, deeper into the thicker woodland. Every now and then, she caught a glimpse of the fox in the waning moonlight, somehow leading the way. When she stumbled near the ravine, Wilhem and Frieda were waiting for her.

Frieda threw an arm around Ellen's waist and helped her up the side of the ravine. Ellen started to explain her failure, but Wilhem just shook his head sympathetically and placed a finger to his lips. Gesturing for her to follow, he led her back to her companions at the windmill.

THE NEWS OF HER FAILURE was met with sympathy and quiet disappointment.

Ellen's eyes welled with tears as she told her tale; it was evident that her spirit had been crushed.

Her mother wanted to hold her, but Ellen forestalled her, insisting that she just wanted to be left alone. She went off by herself and sat in a corner of the small space while Frieda began a more comprehensive report on the troop dispositions within the Were camp.

Gallenius was very interested in what his spy had observed, especially regarding the trolls.

"This tends to corroborate some limited information we received about a tribe of intelligent trolls who are allegedly immune from the effects of sunlight, and have recently surfaced as mercenaries. But we do not know where they are from or where they are based."

"Could they be from Were?" asked Padraic.

"Possibly, but we have seen no evidence of them there," Gallenius admitted. "Be that as it may, now I have to get this information to the Guildmaster. At any rate, no one can stay here; raiding parties will surely be drawn to this windmill."

Padraic stood and said, "Agreed, I must accompany Ellen and her group back to the Realm of Man, and return here after I take care of a few things. I shall report to the Guildmaster upon my return."

"Very well. All should depart soonest," Gallenius acknowledged. He bade them a quick goodbye, and slipped like a ghost from the windmill, disappearing with Wilhem and Frieda into the night.

Padraic knelt on one knee next to Ellen and said softly, "Ellen, it's time to take everyone home. Are you ready?"

Looking into his face, she saw a mixture of concern, sympathy, and strength; it calmed and pleased her to some small degree. Perhaps she had begun to see what her mother had seen in him.

"Yes, I'm ready . . . I'm fine. Let's go outside; there's more room."

THEY RETURNED TO DELAFAIRE Farm just before dawn.

Millie went directly to the kitchen and put on a pot of coffee. She would have commenced to prepare a full breakfast for everyone had not Padraic pulled her into the library for a private conversation.

Mark could not seem to release Stacy's hand for any length of time. They now sat huddled together at the table, talking quietly while the coffee brewer burbled on the counter.

For just a moment, Ellen felt left out—she suddenly missed Hawk terribly. Glancing at the oak-framed clock above the counter, she saw it was after six. She reached for the wall phone.

"Mmph . . . Yeah, hello?"

Drat! She'd woken him. "Hawk, it's Ellen."

"Uh, yeah . . . Is everything all right?"

She almost felt guilty about waking him; but there were things he needed to know—and she missed him. "We got my mom and Stacy back!" she blurted.

"Wh-what? Are they okay?"

"They're fine, but . . . Well, it's sort of a long story. I don't really want to go into it over the phone—you know what I mean? Can you come over?"

"Uh, yeah, sure . . . Oh wait—I can't, not right away. Have you called our office?"

"Uh, no. You're the first person I called. Is that a problem?"

"No, not really—I'll call to notify them that we can call off the search for your mom and Stacy. Are you sure you can't tell me more, over the phone, I mean?"

"No, no, it's just that . . . I can't really explain—not over the phone. Can't you come now?"

“I’m sorry, Ellen, but I have to be in court first thing this morning. I can have some patrol units respond to your location.”

This was *not* what she really wanted. “No, that’s okay. My mom and Stacy are *home*—safe and sound! So, it’s not really an emergency situation—we don’t need . . . Don’t send anybody! I just need to explain some things *to you* . . . Can’t you understand?”

“Ellen, I get it—it’s okay,” he assured her. “I understand; but you’ve gotta be a little patient with me. I’m still gonna have to figure this all out and file a report. I’ll come out there as soon I can, okay?”

“Of course, I understand . . . That’s fine.” She tried to sound upbeat—after all, her mother and Stacy were safe. But she knew he could sense the disappointment in her voice.

“Look, I’ll call you as soon as I get out of court to let you know I’m on my way, okay?”

“Yeah, that’d be great . . . Thanks, Hawk.”

“No problem. Now I gotta get up and get ready, so I gotta go.”

“Sorry to have woken you . . . I’ll see you.”

“It’s all right—the good news was worth it! Bye, now.”

“Bye.”

Replacing the receiver, she felt a modicum better—although thoroughly tired.

Despite the dichotomy of an overwhelming sense of relief for the safety of her mother and Stacy, and her despondent sense of failure with the tainted portals, she had an unexpected moment of clarity; she realized she hadn’t eaten anything in some time and was likely running on adrenaline, a scenario she knew from past experience would precipitate irrational decisions and downright stupid mistakes. She didn’t feel hungry, but she desperately needed sleep. But there was still so much to do—what about those portals? Why hadn't she been able to close them now that Millie and Stacy were out of Mab's clutches? Had Mab done something?

She realized her thinking was getting clouded. She pinched her eyes shut and rubbed frenzied fingertips in vigorous circles at her temples.

"El', are you all right?" Mark asked.

"I'm fine . . . just tired."

"Was that Hawk you called?"

"Yeah, I had to let him know that Stacy and my mom were home safe; the sheriff's department can call off their search. He was gonna send some patrol units here, but I asked him not to. So, he's coming over later; he's gotta do some report. He's got court this morning." She surrendered to a yawn.

Stacy nudged her and said, "You look exhausted; you've been up all night. Why don't you try to get some sleep until he arrives?"

"Good idea," agreed Mark. "Nobody would mind; we'll wake you when he gets here."

"But I still have to call Madeline and Marie," Ellen insisted. "I have to tell them that my mom and Stacy are home safe. They were all planning on coming over, too, remember?"

"No problem," countered Mark. "I can make those calls. They'll probably still want to come over anyway."

"But . . . I-I really should—" Ellen stammered.

"No *buts*," interrupted Mark. "Look, I know there are still things that must be done, but if you don't rest, you'll be no good to anyone. Maybe that's why you had such a hard time with that portal. So, please, rest while you can. Besides, I think Padraic and your mom need some private time to talk—I know Stacy and I do. Then I'm gonna catch a nap as well."

Feeling even more like a third wheel at the thought of her cousin and best friend snuggling, Ellen slumped and acquiesced. "Oh, all right. I'll lie down for a while. I'm too frayed to sleep. But just in case, wake me when Hawk gets here."

SMOKEY WAS THE ONE to wake her, nuzzling her neck and licking her cheek. Warm sunlight peeked past the lowered shades, casting golden bars across the bedroom floor.

It was midafternoon; they had let her sleep.

She had evidently needed it, almost six hours of deep dreamless sleep. Sitting up, she felt stiff, as if she hadn't stirred at all since she'd flopped across her bed. She stretched and decided that a shower was a minor luxury she could afford before facing any more challenges.

Half an hour later, she found everyone in the kitchen making sandwiches from a buffet of leftover cold cuts, cheeses, chips, and other snacks on the counter. The mood was quiet and subdued.

She brightened as her eyes found Hawk at the coffee urn refilling several mugs. His smile was reassuring as he passed her a steaming cup, but his eyes were shadowed with concern.

"Did you get some rest?" he asked softly. "I called earlier, but Mark said you were asleep. So, Trey and I just came over."

"I thought y'all were going to wake me?" she said scanning the faces at the table.

Trey, standing near the middle of the counter, paused in ladling mustard on his roast beef sandwich and tossed a thumb over his shoulder.

"We wanted to wake you when we got here a couple of hours ago, but your family insisted on letting you sleep."

Millie slid a plate of cinnamon rolls in front of Padraic, and then, hands on her hips, tried to scowl at Trey but wound up forcing a grin and shrugging. The general pall over the room had affected everyone; even Miska seemed subdued.

"Don't worry, Ellen," Mark assured her. "That gave us time to bring Miska, Trey, and Hawk up to speed on everything that's happened so far."

"And on what must yet be done," Padraic added, as he stood to get everyone's attention. "We have accomplished a great deal in rescuing Millie and Stacy; Queen Mab no longer has leverage over Ellen. Despite Ellen's valiant effort—at great personal risk—the open portals still threaten Storm Haven. We must find a way to close them."

"I tried my best," Ellen insisted, "but I couldn't close even one of them. I don't know why. But I am ready and willing to try again."

Padraic smiled at his daughter. "I have no doubt of that. But there are certain issues that must be addressed first, and time, as always, is of the essence."

Ellen sat at the table between Hawk and Miska, and cupped her hands around her coffee mug. Unfortunately, the modest warmth did little to lighten her spirit. And she still needed to speak privately with Hawk; she had to explain, oh, so much.

Padraic looked each person in the eye. "It is clear that these portals have been altered, or enhanced in some way. Until we understand more, it is simply too dangerous to mount another attempt at closing them. So, I ask for patience while we all do our best to solve this problem."

The room remained silent, so he continued. "You are all in possession of a series of very powerful secrets. One of which, the very existence of Storm Haven, has already been compromised—through no fault of yours, of course. Another is that Storm Haven has, for some time, operated as a comparatively sophisticated intelligence and information brokerage—a profitable commodity, information. It may be inevitable that Storm Haven's existence becomes general knowledge; however, we would prefer that its intelligence operations remain clandestine and secret.

"And finally, you now know that Ellen is my daughter. I cannot sufficiently stress how important it is that this secret is kept—otherwise her life, and that of her mother, would be in grave danger."

Ellen blanched. *He's already told them? I wanted to be the one to tell Hawk!*

She felt as if something had been taken from her—her prerogative at least! But was it hers, truly? She hadn't voiced her feelings, which were admittedly confused enough, so no one would have known she would have preferred to have shared this staggering information with Hawk in some more private or intimate way. Under the present circumstances, she knew it was rather petty—but it still stung.

"In danger from whom, exactly?" asked Hawk, oblivious to her roiling internal discomfiture.

"Aside from Queen Mab," Padraic replied, "there are many who would gladly see me come to harm. Regrettably, I do not enjoy the protections of the Faerie Courts, having never sworn fealty to either. The point is that there are some unscrupulous people who would not hesitate to harm anyone of my bloodline, or anyone I hold dear, in order to cause me pain. I would not wish that on anyone. It is true that I have had my share of transgressions—I *am* called *The Rogue,* an appellation I did not choose, but one that I no doubt deserve. However, I always take responsibility for my own actions; so, no one else should be held accountable."

He smiled at Millie reassuringly.

"I deeply regret that Millie and Stacy were put through such a trial. Had I known sooner, I would have acted more quickly to organize a rescue."

"I don't see how that was in any way your fault," Ellen objected, her tone calmly rational despite her smoldering angst. "You had nothing to do with the kidnapping. You didn't even know about my mother—*or did you?*"

The tone of her trailing question was a surprise.

Padraic winced. "I assure you, I only learned about the kidnapping after the fact. But I did learn that you were the intended victim, and only later that it was your mother who had been taken, and Stacy of course—although I doubt that Mab yet knows just who Stacy is. Although, we should also anticipate that Mab knows by now that both her hostages are gone."

"Patrick, won't she suspect you?" asked Millie.

"I doubt it." He shrugged. "She thinks of me as a trophy of sorts, someone to flaunt before the Faerie Courts as her consort. More than likely she will come to suspect that Ellen is responsible; hardly anyone other than a Steward could have penetrated her hidden and warded domain so easily. But rest assured that I will do my best to persuade her otherwise."

"You're going *back to her?*" exclaimed Ellen, shooting to her feet.

Confused, and slightly stunned, Padraic just stood there, his mouth agape.

Stepping back, she railed, "You've only just found my mother—*your wife!* How could you desert her—*us*—*again*?" Turning her back to him, she squeezed her eyes shut.

I didn't expect to feel this angry—this hurt . . . Damn it—I'm not gonna cry!

Padraic came to her side and spoke softly, "Would you join me in the library, please? I would speak with you privately."

The others, having winced at the awkwardness of the moment, tried to politely ignore them, as she followed Padraic from the room.

ELLEN STOOD SCOWLING in the library, her arms tightly folded and her chin jutting forth.

"Would you care to sit?" Padraic asked solicitously.

A shake of her head was her only response.

"As you like . . . Ellen, your mother and I . . . we've had a long talk, and suffice to say our relationship is not *your* concern. We are who we are, and do as we must. Your mother has been at peace with my, um, leaving, for some time. And the truth is that neither of us . . . we are not the same persons we were many years ago.

"If you feel you must blame me for abandoning you both—notwithstanding that I did not even know of your *existence*—then feel free to do so. But it will not change the fact that she and I parted ways, and have no intentions of being together now. Our paths are vastly different; and, for reasons you are unaware of, it is safer for both of you that way—and for Mark as well."

"What do you mean *safer?*" she asked, the hurt in her voice clearly evident.

"Please, do not ask. This is not the time, perhaps later," he answered, as a trace of his own pain stole across his face.

"Are you two going to get a *divorce?*" she asked petulantly.

"What? No, of course not," he replied, surprised. "That never even occurred to me. Why? Do you want us to?"

"No, no . . . I don't know *what* I want . . . It's just that I'm having a hard time thinking of you as my father. It's not like I'm going to start calling you *Dad* or anything."

"I understand." He chuckled. "But *do* try to remember that it *is* a secret."

She rolled her eyes in response.

"I can see you are still upset. What is it?"

"Nothing really—it's silly . . . "

"Go on, please."

"It's just that . . . I wanted to tell Hawk, that, um, you're my father. I wanted to tell him privately. See, I told you it was silly."

Padraic could not help but smile as realization dawned, and unfamiliar warmth quickened in his heart.

"Oh, I hardly think so. I can see that he is important to you. What he may think, given this revelation, matters to you—that's perfectly understandable. Having spent some time in conversation with him, I am confident you have no need for undue concern. In fact, Trey and I are in agreement that this young man is quite smitten with you."

"He is?" she echoed, unable to forestall the momentary flush of hope.

Padraic nodded, and added cautiously, "I'd be careful about letting any of our adversaries know too much about the way the two of you may feel about each other. Some might consider such attachments as weaknesses to be exploited, threatened, or manipulated. We must always strive to protect the ones we love. Promise me you will be wary—in everything."

"All right, I will." She sighed. "Now what?"

"Good question . . . Let's rejoin the others. They no doubt wonder the same thing."

CONVERSATION DWINDLED, and all eyes watched them closely as Ellen preceded Padraic into the kitchen. Ellen resumed her seat, cupped her hands around her mug, and stared blankly into her tepid coffee.

Standing near the head of the table, Padraic announced, "Ellen just asked a very pertinent question: 'Now what?' In that regard, I may have some suggestions, if not answers. For myself, I must return to the Realm of Dark Elves, and then to Storm Haven at some point.

"Mark, if I may suggest, you might consider approaching the Council to articulate Storm Haven's plight and seek relief or assistance—it will no doubt be hotly debated. I would very much like to hear what the rest of you think might be done. Anyone?"

Sipping from his coffee mug, Trey gestured with his other hand still holding a half-eaten cinnamon roll.

"Well, Hawk and I have to decide how to close out this kidnapping case. I mean we have to file a report explaining how it is that the kidnapped victims, Miss Millie and Miss Stacy, are home, safe and sound, *without* making any sort of reference to other realms.

"Also, keep in mind that in your most recent travels, you all saw not a trace of the suspected kidnapper, the crime lord, Papa George—actually, none of us have, not since his appearance at the Council meeting when Queen Mab tried to have him elected to the Chair of Man on the Council. And the only link we've got to him in this realm is a comatose driver, who survived the crash of the limo—whom the kidnapped victims never saw, and can't identify. See what I mean?"

"Why not just relate the truth?" asked Mark, which stunned everyone.

"Consider the facts; both victims were evidently drugged in some fashion and never saw their kidnappers. They were subsequently found by family members in an unnamed location pursuant to information provided by a confidential informant who has insisted on anonymity. All is absolutely true—just carefully parsed."

"You know, that's not half bad, *Counselor*," teased Hawk.

"Yeah," mused Trey aloud, "and vague enough that our case would stay *open*, pending the discovery of new evidence; unless, of course, our limo driver wakes up and gives us a full confession."

"Right!" Hawk snorted. "That'll happen."

"You know, both victims should be checked out medically," Trey pointed out, "especially if we include the suspicion that the victims may have been drugged in our report."

"Oh, that reminds me," interrupted Ellen, seemingly more focused on the tasks at hand, "Mark, did you make those calls we talked about?"

"Oh yeah," he assured her, "I did, and they're still on for this evening."

"Good," she responded, and turned to Trey. "My doctor, Marie—I meant Dr. Latrice-Johnson—is supposed to come over this evening with her husband, Zack. Can't you work out whatever medical examinations you mentioned with her?"

"Yeah," acknowledged Trey, "I think that'll work. Uh, Hawk, are you okay with this?"

"Yeah, I am. It keeps the case open, and us in the game. We can continue investigating, *and exploring*."

Smiling, Ellen leaned forward against the table, her confidence evidently refreshed.

"Sergeant, Detective, I believe you've just become members of the Middle Earth Society."

CH 3

MADELINE AND ARMAND arrived at Delafaire Farm a little after seven that evening; Zack and Marie were only a few minutes behind them.

As it happened, Ellen was spared narrating the entire tale of events since they had last spoken because Mark had provided comprehensive explanations during his phone calls earlier that afternoon. Ellen only needed to fill in a few gaps and clarify some details.

Of course, Marie needed no prompting to conduct cursory physical examinations of Millie and Stacy. They appeared to be in fine health. Nonetheless, the doctor insisted that they meet her at the hospital the next morning for more comprehensive physicals, including complete toxicology screening; which was clearly going to be an essential aspect of the police report.

Ellen stood quietly for a moment and considered the diverse group of individuals in her kitchen.

And for that matter, how is it that all my friends and family seem to naturally gravitate toward the kitchen? Well, it certainly is a warm and welcoming place; and the fact that my mom always has some sort of snack or food laid out only contributes to the ambiance. There's something good about it. It just feels right—feels like home, especially since my mom, Mark, and Stacy now reside here. It's very good.

Madeline and Marie were huddled at one end of the table with Millie and Stacy. Without really trying, Ellen could discern snatches of conversation about Padraic being her father and how her mother met Padraic, her *husband.*

At the other end of the table, Miska and Padraic answered questions from Zack and Armand of a more logistical nature regarding the other realms. At mid-table Mark, Trey, and Hawk looked on, occasionally offering a point or two of clarification.

Trey's cell phone rang. Excusing himself, he rose and stepped away from the men to take the call in private. A moment later, he gestured for Hawk to join him. Holding the phone so Hawk could hear as well, the voice of the evening dispatcher relayed a request from a patrol unit. Ellen couldn't quite hear the dispatcher, but she could hear Trey's response.

"Have those patrol units sit tight. We're on our way."

Everyone in the kitchen went quiet and looked to the detectives.

"Ellen, I'm sorry, but we have to run," Trey explained. "I know we haven't worked anything out yet here, tonight; but, we might have a small break regarding Papa George. This call was from our dispatcher; one of our patrol units answered a burglary call at Tippet's store and just took Teddy Pots, a subject we've been looking for, into custody. The subject's not real coherent and he's rambling something about Papa George."

"Not coherent and rambling? Drunk, or is he M.O. status?" Hawk probed.

Trey grimaced. "Patrol advised upon their arrival he was out of control, pretty wild, but not drunk; so, M.O. is likely. We should interview Teddy ASAP, before he gets committed for seventy-two hours."

"What's M.O. mean?" Ellen asked.

"*Mental observation*. There's a locked ward at the hospital for disturbed people," explained Hawk. "Patients typically stay for three days, so they can be examined and possibly treated."

"Oh, I understand. Will you be able to come back?"

Trey shrugged, but Hawk answered. "Don't really know. It'll depend on what we learn from him, I guess."

"And it could be a while," warned Trey. "These kinds of interviews can be very unpredictable."

"Don't worry," Hawk assured her, squeezing her hand. "I'll call you and let you know, one way or the other."

"Be careful, please."

"Always," he said, pulling her into a hug.

Smirking, Trey discreetly turned and addressed the rest of the group. "Okay, we gotta go; but we'll be in touch."

"I'll walk y'all out," Ellen offered, keeping Hawk's hand clasped in her own.

AFTER THE DETECTIVES departed, Padraic stood and pulled Mark to one side.

"Mark, it may be best if you consider returning to the Council as soon as possible. The sooner you bring Storm Haven's plight before the member realms, the better any chance, however remote, of intervention. I will accompany you back to the Council facility. There is something I must do there, a loose end to address, before I must return to the Realm of Dark Elves."

Mark hesitated, a bit reluctant to leave, now that some of the most intelligent people he knew were presently gathered here to analyze the problems they faced.

"But, I might be needed here."

"Perhaps," conceded Padraic, "but the lives of all those in an entire realm are at risk, and they need you as well. The Council will adjourn, its agenda concluded, with the setting of the moon. Only a seated Council member can raise this issue, before adjournment, for consideration and potential action by the collective of member realms. Your persuasive skills will be needed there—perhaps more than here, this night."

"Ah, I see your point," Mark acquiesced. "Then we should get going. I'll tell Ellen."

PULLING INTO THE POORLY lit parking lot in front of Tippet's General Store, Trey pointed to the marked Chantilly Parish Sheriff's Patrol car parked near the front porch.

"There's Mac and Lizzie's unit. Let's park on this side of the lot."

"Right." Hawk parked their unmarked cruiser several spaces away as Trey advised the dispatcher of their location.

A short man in a deputy sheriff's uniform, a clipboard grasped in one hand, stepped off the shadowed porch and approached the detectives as they exited their car.

"Hey there, Trey, Hawk. How y'all are? Ain't y'all on day shift?" he asked with an unconscious swipe at his thickly bristled mustache.

"Evenin', Mac. Sho'nuff, but we're workin' late," drawled Trey as he pumped patrol sergeant Ulysses McGowan's hand. "Where's your partner?"

"Lizzie's inside," Mac responded, jabbing a thumb over his shoulder. "She and Miss Carrie are havin' some *girl talk* over a cup o' tea. The field report's already done. They jes' wanted t' visit some, while we waited on y'all. Know what I mean?"

"You betcha." Trey grinned. "So, what've we got?"

Mac thumbed a small flashlight on and directed its beam into the backseat of his patrol car. Secured within, a wild-eyed, disheveled man squinted in the beam's glare and tried to fold himself into a fetal position. His hands cuffed behind him, and further restrained by the seat belt, he could only move so much. He began jabbering incomprehensibly into his knees and shaking his head.

Clearing his throat, the patrol sergeant began to speak; hardly a trace of his usually thick Cajun drawl was evident.

"The subject presently in custody voluntarily identified himself as Theodore Rasmussen, *AKA Teddy Pots.* He admits to having violated his federal parole.

We've got a hit on NCIC, but haven't made any calls to the U.S. Marshals yet. When he started babbling about Papa George, I figured y'all'd wanna talk to him first.

"Anyway, when Horace was closing up, Teddy forced his way in the front door of the store—all in a panic about being chased—and begged Horace to protect him."

"Chased? Protect him from whom, exactly?" Hawk asked, casually looking around the darkened lot.

Directing his flashlight to the report on his clipboard, Mac cleared his throat again and continued, albeit hesitantly. "Uh, maybe not *who* so much as *what*. Now, I'm quoting here: *'big-ass cats with big-ass teeth',* and something about *'cartel hitters'.* And then he said that *'Papa George was the cause of it all'*.

"That's what he told Horace and Miss Carrie. She gave him some tea and pie, which calmed him down, while Horace called 911. When we got here, he freaked at first; but we got him calmed down a bit and he repeated what I just told you. But the more he talked about it, the more agitated he got—until he flat started flipping out, and we had to restrain him and secure him in our unit. To tell the truth, I think he *wanted* to be in custody—like he's protected somehow. Anyway, acting like that, you *know* he's looking at a three-day observation at the lock-ward—even if Horace and Carrie don't want to press charges. The feds can have him whenever they want after that."

"Did he say anything more specific about Papa George, or just the generic comment about him being 'the cause of it all'?" Trey pressed.

Mac shrugged. "No, he's not real coherent. But you can try to talk to him—maybe you'll have better luck. My car's not locked—just the back doors. I'm gonna go pry Lizzie loose and then we're gonna have to transport. So, you've got a few minutes."

"Well," Trey shrugged, "we'll give it a shot."

They opened the front doors of the unit, activating the overhead dome light. Hawk sat sideways in the front passenger seat and faced the prisoner. The man was clearly frightened.

Trey eased into the driver's seat, introduced himself and Hawk, and then read aloud from his Miranda Warning card, advising Teddy of his constitutional rights.

"What all that means, Teddy, is that you don't have to talk to us, but you can if you want to, with or without a lawyer, understand? But all we want to know right now is just where Papa George is, understand? And what are you running from—what are you so afraid of? No one can protect you from whatever, if they don't know what it is. Do you follow me?"

Teddy mumbled something under his breath and his eyes slid from side to side, seemingly unfocused.

"I'm real sorry, Teddy, but I couldn't hear what you just said. Could you repeat that, please?" Trey asked reasonably.

Hunching his shoulders, Teddy whispered hoarsely, "Them! They're watching! It's not safe—we gotta leave outta here!"

"Who?" asked Hawk. "Who are we talking about here?"

Teddy wouldn't answer; he just fidgeted anxiously, his red-rimmed eyes scanning the night beyond the paltry illumination of the parking lot's sole streetlight. Suddenly he sat stock-still—staring out the window. His mouth gaped and pulsed like that of a gasping fish, and his eyes opened wider than it seemed humanly possible.

Trey closed the driver's door, effectively turning off the interior dome light, and gripped the A-pillar spotlight control. Rotating the spotlight in the direction Teddy appeared to be staring, Trey switched it on, sending a wash of light across the parking lot.

Something, a large shadow, just beyond the edge of illumination, morphed into two. Each drifted in different directions, flanking the car and coming ever closer.

"Hawk, you might want to lock your door," breathed Trey. "Those shadows are pretty damn big, and moving."

Frustratingly, the shadows stayed just beyond the reach of the spotlight; only the twin luminous reflections of bestial eyes truly betrayed their movements.

"What are those things?" asked Hawk. "Wait—now I don't see them. Where'd they go?"

"I dunno—didn't get a good look. But damn, they're big." Trey urgently tried to bring the vehicle's spotlight to bear on the area where he'd last seen movement.

Teddy swayed from side to side, moaning and whimpering, "Too late—too late—too late."

"What, Teddy? What are you mumbling about?" pressed Hawk, anxiously peering into the backseat.

Suddenly the driver's side of the car rocked with a terrific impact!

The vehicle squatted on its suspension as the roof collapsed almost six inches. The front and rear windshields shattered, but somehow hung there nearly intact, drooping within their twisted frames, like sagging sheets of fractured crystals.

Hunching down in the seat, Trey saw the spotlight had been ripped away from the outer A-pillar; he now grasped a worthless control grip.

A snuffling, sniffing sound preceded a blood-chilling snarl that cut through the night like an icy blade. The damaged vehicle was suddenly rocked from side to side like a child's toy. Hawk gripped the dashboard and headrest and fought to stay upright as he was repeatedly slammed shoulder first into the closed front passenger door.

Teddy's mouth was open in a silent scream; his bladder and bowels let go.

Trey winced at the acrid stench as he fumbled for the ignition switch—but there was no key! *Mac must have the keys!*

At the thought of the other deputies, Trey leaned on the horn. The long blast startled whatever was assaulting the car and the rocking motion abated.

Long fluorescent tubes flared to life along the front porch of the general store.

Whatever was on the roof of the car leapt off, into the surrounding darkness.

The vehicle's stressed suspension creaked and popped as the enormous weight disappeared.

The front door of the store burst open. Mac and Lizzie, guns drawn and flashlights extended at arm's length, sprinted across the porch and took up flanking positions on either side of the damaged vehicle. All they could see was the ravaged car and the pale shocked faces of the occupants.

Whatever had done this, was gone now.

Trey couldn't get his door to open, so he had to slide over and follow his partner in exiting on the passenger side. Neither he nor Hawk had been injured. However, Teddy was a blubbering basket case.

Mac blanched at the condition of his patrol unit and groaned. "What the hell, Trey?"

"Are you guys all right?" asked Lizzie, a seasoned deputy who was known for her unflappable professional demeanor and steady calm. As she waited for a reply, she panned the shadows with her flashlight and the muzzle of her handgun.

"Yeah, I think so," ventured Hawk, tugging a limp Teddy out of the rear seat, while trying not to gag from the smell.

Holding Teddy at arm's length between them, Trey and Hawk could only shrug their shoulders and shake their heads. They eased him gently into a sitting position on the ground, where he continued sobbing and mumbling incoherently.

"I'm sorry, Mac," Trey offered. "I wish I could tell you what happened, but we never got a good look at *whatever* it was. It took off when the lights came on."

"Uh, Trey, you might want to make it *two whatevers*," interrupted Hawk, pointing a small flashlight at the dusty dirt.

"Hold your light lower, Lizzie, and you can see the tracks better. Yeah, that's good. See here, there's one set, and over there, by the rear fender is another bigger set. Man, those are big pads. Hmm, I don't see any claw marks, though."

"Meaning what?" asked Lizzie, who also enjoyed a reputation for having a pretty reliable *sixth-sense* about dangerous situations. She rose and panned the beam of her light off into the night. "I'm becoming more uncomfortable by the moment. It feels like we're being watched—more like observed and assessed. I don't like it."

Hawk didn't respond immediately; instead he began to slowly walk in an ever-widening circle, sweeping the beam of his flashlight in an arc before him. Debris from the damaged vehicle littered the lot. He paused when he found the emergency lights that had been ripped from the unit's roof. Shoving the shattered light bar aside with his foot, Hawk studied the disturbed ground intently. He squatted near a set of very clear tracks and stroked his chin.

"What?" Trey probed.

"At first," Hawk offered, "I thought *bears,* maybe a large black bear sow and a big cub. They can be incredibly strong. But that sound, that *snarl*—that was no bear. And these are definitely not bear tracks. These are more like the tracks of a cat; no claw marks are the clue. They're just *way* too big!"

"You mean like a panther or cougar?" Mac asked. "You know there used to be panthers around here, but nobody's seen one for years."

"Well, almost like a panther's track, maybe a lynx by its shape, but these prints are still too big, about twice the size of the biggest cougar track I've ever seen. I used to track and hunt a lot with my grandfather years ago. I'll have to ask him about it; he knows more about animal tracks than anyone I know."

"Gentlemen, may I suggest that we go inside the store," proposed Lizzie reasonably, casting furtive glances at the surrounding dark. "We've got calls to make. We'll have to get CSI and the patrol lieutenant out here for this report. And I'm getting that creepy itch between my shoulder blades—*y' know?*"

Looking around, Mac said, "Good idea, Lizzie. I'll string some crime scene tape. Maybe you two *detectives* can transport; he's *yours* now that my unit's out of commission. *Whew*, he really *stinks!*"

Wincing, Hawk glanced to Trey and sighed, "You think maybe Horace can spare him a pair of overalls or something?"

Trying to hold his breath, Trey merely nodded.

AFTER CLEANING TEDDY up as best they could in the mudroom at the rear of the store, the detectives found that Horace did have some old clean overalls and a T-shirt for him. Still handcuffed, they had him sit in the corner of the store office while they waited for the responding units.

Now considerably more subdued and relatively calm, Teddy kept whispering to himself, ". . . big-ass cats . . . big-ass teeth . . . big-ass cats . . . big-ass teeth . . ."

PADRAIC AND MARK STOOD to one side outside the entrance to the Council Chamber, just beyond the colorful flow of returning attendees entering the domed hall. Brightly attired Light Elves walked with stoic delegates of Mer, their muted seaweed-hued robes of black and green a subtle counterpoint to the iridescent saffron and pinks of their elfin companions. A pair of vampire lords in formal evening wear passed in quiet conversation, ignoring all those around them, followed by three grumbling dwarves who scowled at the backs of the Shadow delegates.

The Council was about to go into its final session before adjournment.

"It seems our timing is fortuitous," remarked Padraic. "I must leave you now—there is something I must do. I will return shortly and check on your progress with the Council before I return to the Realm of Dark Elves. Are you ready, Mark?"

"As ready as I'll ever be, *uncle*," he replied with a grin.

Padraic winced good-naturedly and shook his head. "Mark, that is the last time you will call me that, especially in a public place—there is far too much at stake. Do you understand?"

"Of course, I apologize—I couldn't resist. But listen, I have been going over the potential arguments I might encounter or employ, and I have a question. Would Storm Haven consider Council membership? Whether offered or sought? It occurred to me that the question might come up in the course of debate."

Padraic looked around; the flow of persons entering the Council Chamber had thinned considerably. Pulling Mark into a nearby alcove, Padraic spoke in a hushed voice.

"Let me be very clear on this matter, Mark. You must understand that Storm Haven will never seek Council membership, and would refuse in no uncertain terms should it be offered. Do not even bring it up; if anyone else does, you must plead ignorance. This is something of a delicate matter that we have not the time for now; suffice to say that feelings of resentment run deep. Truthfully, we would be surprised if the Council was inclined to intervene;

but, we lose nothing in the attempt to so persuade the members. If anything, we may gain *time,* which we so desperately need."

"I see—not that I completely comprehend, of course," Mark responded cautiously.

"I must warn you, Mark; you must be very careful! You, as the representative of the Realm of Man, can be openly sympathetic to Storm Haven's present plight in the course of debate, but sympathy is all that can be openly offered. You cannot—*you must not*—be perceived as an agent provocateur or co-conspirator! That could potentially expose you to an allegation of *sedition* against the Council or its interests. The members are always concerned, if not obsessed, about the *balance of power* within the Council *and* the Faerie Courts. You must walk a delicate path within this chamber; be wary of someone twisting your remarks out of context."

Mark pursed his lips. "Well, that certainly adds an element of inherent intrigue to my original question. Nevertheless, you need not worry; I can handle myself well in any argument or debate. But I must admit, I had no idea how firmly opposed Storm Haven would be to Council membership. Perhaps, at some later time of course, you could further articulate the details of these positions?"

"Perhaps, but not now," Padraic cautioned. "I must be about my business, and you must rejoin the meeting. I will look in on you later. I wish you luck!"

"And you, as well," Mark said, squaring his shoulders. Without a backward glance, he turned and joined the last of the stragglers passing through the crystal doors.

PADRAIC WAS SURPRISED to find a pair of gargoyles standing guard outside the entrance to the Dark Elfin Enclave. There was no sign of the carnage that had occurred here so recently. He passed within unchallenged, but halfway across the courtyard, two elfin warriors, wearing the livery of the queen's elite personal household guard, stepped from a nearby building and hailed him.

"Halt! Oh, tis you, m'lord. You may pass."

Puzzled, Padraic asked, "Why are the sentinels here? And for that matter, why are members of the elite royal guards here?"

"The queen is presently in residence, m'lord," the guard responded, and then gestured toward the entrance. "The sentinels were on post, by order of the Council, when we arrived. Extra security precautions, we were told, m'lord."

"I see. How long has the queen been in residence?"

"Since midafternoon, m'lord. And I understand that she has been looking for you, m'lord. She is in her chambers," the guard advised with a knowing grin.

Padraic did not miss the implication; he stretched dramatically, sighed, and winked. "Alas, a consort's work is never done. I had best attend to my duties."

The two guards snorted and chortled, elbowing one another as Padraic assumed a smug expression and nonchalantly made his way into the annex.

Mab is here! This is not good.

Padraic had hoped to leave the topaz ring in some inconspicuous place—as if she had thrown it there—and just let it be found in its own time. Now, he wasn't certain that tactic would still work. He had no choice now but to brazen it out.

AS EXPECTED, HE FOUND her in her chambers, seated at a mirrored dressing table, a servant brushing her hair. She watched his reflection as he entered and nodded to the lady-in-waiting and the ever-present elfin bodyguard.

Gesturing to her servant, Mab said, "Leave us, and you as well, Namron. I would be alone with my consort."

The lady-in-waiting slipped out of the room, followed by the hulking bodyguard who closed the door behind him.

"Where have you been?" Mab asked icily.

"Oh, I have been around," Padraic answered lightly, feigning a blasé attitude he did not really feel.

"You have not been seen—" she began.

"Well, of course not!" he interrupted. "I have been discreet—as per our arrangement. You surely cannot expect me to sit around and do nothing while you elect to disappear for untold hours on end. I was left to my own amusements."

"A *dalliance? Here*, in the Council Realm? My, you *are* the bold one! Who was it this time?"

Smiling wickedly, he asked, "Are you certain you want to know? Would it spark the fires of jealousy to hear the libidinous details? Or would you rather take a portion of voyeuristic delight in the intimate specifics?"

"Enough! I have no interest in your trite little encounters," she exclaimed, her temper flaring and cheeks flushing crimson. "Just see to it that I am never put in an awkward or embarrassing position by your epicurean and hedonistic pursuits—that, I shall *not* forgive!"

"As you wish, Your Majesty," he said smoothly, as he bowed slightly. Taking a seat on the bed, he lounged back and remarked, "I see you have discarded the sling. Have the wounds you sustained when attacked by your bespelled guards in this very enclave healed sufficiently? No scars, I trust?"

He kept his expression neutral as she began to look deeply at the reflection of her face. His question had sufficiently distracted her attention; he knew she would not tolerate the appearance of a blemish or wrinkle. Nor did she like losing her composure, fearing it brought on lines which lingered on her complexion.

Flexing her shoulder, Mab said evenly, "The Council healers *are* first rate. I am somewhat stiff, but I am healing well enough.

"I assume there have been no developments in the search for George? Tell me, does the Council think him responsible for the necromancy—possibly to cover his escape from me?"

Padraic shook his head. "No developments, nor is there any trace of George Papadolis. As for linking him to necromancy and the attack on your person, the Council is mired in utter confusion, completely befuddled, and generally at a loss. This apparent act of necromancy has shaken them to the core. The whereabouts of your disqualified candidate for the Chair of Man is barely a concern; the Council members have apparently made no such connection in their rambling, disjointed discussions."

"Hmmph, that is no surprise—they are so inept." She scoffed. "That conniving bastard, George—I just know he is somehow involved. I will find that fool and deal with him! He must not fall into the hands of those law enforcers from the Realm of Man.

"Now make ready to depart. We should return to my palace, as soon as the Council adjourns. There is something I must attend to."

"As you wish, Your Majesty, however, it may yet be a while before the Council adjourns," he said. "This place is abuzz with rumors that Shadow and Were are mustering troops. Strangely enough, this time they are *not* at each other's throats. Rather they plan on invading some realm in the wild, and the Realm of Man has brought the issue before the Council."

"What?" the queen screamed, coming to her feet. "What has the Realm of Man to do with any of this?"

"I know not," he assured her blandly, carefully masking his delight at her obvious discomfiture. "I heard that they intend to ask for Council intervention."

"Call my servant back," she demanded, "and go make yourself presentable! We are going to attend this meeting!"

"As you wish, Majesty," he said lazily rising from the bed, and carefully palming the topaz ring in his unseen hand.

As she turned back to the mirror, he dropped the ring on the furs of the bed. Too near the edge, it slipped on the soft ermine and dropped to the polished stone floor with a soft *tinkling* sound.

She heard—and stared at Padraic in the mirror.

Ignoring her gaze, he toed the ring and remarked, "What is *this?*"

Her brow furrowed at his reflection.

Picking it up, he said, "Hmm, it looks very familiar." He held the ring out to her. "Is this not yours, Majesty? I fear I almost crushed this pretty bauble; fortunately, I believe I only kicked it."

She came to stand before him and deftly plucked the ring from his outstretched hand. Holding it up, she peered deeply into the heart of the stone, her face a study in concentration. After a moment, she seemed to relax slightly, as if somewhat satisfied with her inspection.

"Where was it?" she asked evenly.

"I seemed to have kicked it somewhere near the foot of the bed. I did not see it before that."

"Hmm, I have been looking for this, but I thought . . . Oh, never mind," she said as if distracted. "Go now—send for my lady-in-waiting."

Bowing briefly, he said, "At once, Majesty," and withdrew.

IN THE KITCHEN AT DELAFAIRE Farm, Armand Dupree sipped his coffee and remarked, "So, we don't really know just who this Daegon person is, other than that he is suspected in Papa George's escape. And he may, or may not, be involved in this act of *necromancy*. Is that correct?"

Ellen nodded. "Yes, according to what Mark was told. And I tend to believe so, since everyone agrees that Papa George had to have some help.

"But since my mother and Stacy are safely home, I'm not all that concerned with finding Papa George right now. I'm worried about these two portals I've opened into Storm Haven, the ones I can't close."

"Yes, of course, my dear," soothed Armand. "I'm simply considering who might be capable of altering or reinforcing those portals, thus preventing their closure; and it occurred to me that this Daegon may be such a person."

"Possibly," admitted Ellen, "but he, and George, were long gone when Mab had me open those portals. So, I doubt it was either of them."

"Sounds to me," offered Armand's wife, Madeline, "like the person who wanted them open in the first place is the person who would most likely do something to keep them open. Doesn't that make sense?"

"I think Madeline has it right," agreed Stacy. "This Mab or Diere—*whatever* she calls herself—is somehow responsible. I mean, *come on*—she's a Dark Elf—and she's seized a throne! You can't tell me she doesn't have *some* power. It's obvious, at least to me!"

"Okay," said Ellen, "let's assume that Mab is responsible—which really feels right to me, too, by the way. How do I overcome whatever she's done to the portals to close them? I already know I can't do it as they are now."

"Ellen," interjected her mother, Millie, "if you can't close these portals, what else could happen?"

"Good question." Ellen sighed. "I don't really know; invasion, war—"

"No, not that," Millie insisted, "I meant, are there any alternatives to *closing* the portals?"

"Wait a minute—I think Millie's on to something here," proffered Marie. "Maybe we're too focused on *closing* the portals. What else can be done with them?"

"What do you mean, Doctor—er, Marie?" asked Ellen.

"Well, I'm not really sure . . . Um, bear with me. Look, my field is medicine, so let me draw an appropriate analogy.

"Okay, we have two portals that allow a flow of invasive troops into a place where they are not wanted. You are all familiar with the concept of 'bypass surgery' where the surgeon redirects the flow of blood around a damaged vessel or artery, right? Well, if these portals are, what—*wormholes?* Can't they be redirected to flow somewhere else? Do you follow me? Zack, help me out here—this is really your area of expertise, you're the astrophysicist."

"Well, to be honest," her husband, Zack began cautiously, "I don't think we are dealing with traditional wormholes. You see, a wormhole is a theoretical portion of the space-time continuum folded in upon itself, thereby creating a *shortcut*, if you will, between two otherwise distant points in space-time within the same universe. Therein lies the rub; we are not dealing within the same universe. I believe that the facts fairly well establish that we are dealing with parallel, and more likely, multiple universes. These portals are the equivalent of energy-maintained passages in the fabric of space-time, openings at contact points, between and among an unknown number of parallel universes."

"I'm not sure I understand how this is helping me out here, my dear," Marie commented dryly. "I know Einstein proposed the concept of wormholes. I've heard you wax on about him often enough; but where are you getting the idea of multiple universes?"

"Oh, Marie, don't get him started," warned Armand. "Don't you remember his impromptu lectures on the wonderful mysteries of M-Theory? You know—Membrane Theory?"

"Quite right," Zack responded grinning. "M-Theory it is, sometimes called 'Brane Theory', a term coined by Dr. Paul Townsend of Cambridge University, based on the work of Dr. Edward Witten. Think of it as the evolution of multiple 'String Theories'. But in regard to multiple and parallel universes, considerable credit is certainly due to a host of insightful physicists who have done some brilliant work with gravity and eleven dimensions. Thus they have offered mathematical proof of the existence of multiple universes."

"So my medical analogy was faulty?" Marie asked.

"Well, yes, but only as it relates to wormholes," Zack admitted. "I know of no theoretical manipulation of wormholes. So, your 'cosmic surgeon' would have neither instruments nor method at his disposal. However, it would seem that we do have evidence of a *prima facie* case of manipulation—indeed, the *crafting*—of these energy-maintained openings or passages between parallel universes, *these portals*. And most astounding of all, Ellen seems to be able to accomplish these feats of manipulation and crafting at will, by employing the focused energy of her own mind."

"I told you before," insisted Miska, grinning broadly, "tis *magic!*"

Laughter erupted around the kitchen.

Ellen chuckled and remarked, "Hmm, *bypass surgery?* Thanks, Marie; that gives me an idea."

CHAIRPERSON SVENGARD Thorenson was moderating the debate on the issue of Storm Haven when he noticed Queen Mab and her retinue return to the Council Chamber. The chamber was quite crowded despite the lateness of the hour; there was an air of anxious anticipation. Mab settled in her seat and appeared to focus on what Lord Talbot of the Were was saying.

"Therefore, we submit that further discussion in this regard is moot, as realms in the *wild* have no standing, and are thus due no consideration before this Council."

A low murmur swept across the audience as the Were Lord resumed his seat.

Lord Thorenson spoke in a commanding voice. "Thank you, Lord Talbot. The chair now recognizes Lord Varney of Shadow. The floor is yours, m'lord."

The elder Vampire Lord stood and strode to the center of the dais.

"Thank you, Lord Thorenson . . . Lords and ladies of the Council, let me begin by saying that the Realm of Shadow is in full agreement with the remarks made by my esteemed colleague, Lord Talbot of the Were. Shadow hereby adopts their stated position in its entirety. Furthermore, we suggest that this *distraction* has needlessly detracted from the time we had hoped to spend discussing how we shall all deal with this newly revealed threat of foul *necromancy!*"

A shocked grumbling arose from the gallery, disrupting the proceedings. Lord Thorenson slammed the haft of a ceremonial ax on the floor and demanded order within the chamber.

"Order! Order! Lord Varney, you may continue."

"Of course, Lord Thorenson. I regret that my reference to the *truth* upset so many of our loyal subjects. Suffice to say, that activities conducted by *anyone* in the *wild* are of no concern of this Council. Accordingly, I move that this issue be disregarded—with prejudice—and we concentrate on the more important matters at hand."

"May I ask Lord Varney a question, m'lord?" Mark suddenly interrupted—before anyone could second the motion.

"What?" spat the elder vampire with disdain, even before Lord Thorenson could attempt to respond to the unexpected interruption.

"Since you, speaking for the Realm of Shadow, have formally adopted the position articulated by Lord Talbot on behalf of the Were, in which he asserts that this is merely the recovery of lost *property,* and he further admits that the term refers to those beings who fled his home realm—or should I say, in the interest of accuracy, fled the yoke of oppression and slavery—and furthermore, since troops of *your* home realm of Shadow intend to conduct virtually the same campaign, how will you differentiate which *such property* belongs to whom? And how will you deal with any genetic offspring of those so deemed *lost property,* those children *born in freedom*? Or do you assert that the children of slaves are irrevocably slaves as well, notwithstanding the circumstances of their births?"

This time the chamber erupted in outrage. Not all of it was on behalf of Lord Varney's stated position; many present held little regard for the arrogance of Were and Shadow.

As Lord Thorenson repeatedly demanded order, Queen Mab hastily scribbled a message on a small blank scroll, and flagged a passing administrative brownie.

"Yes, Your Majesty? How may I be of service?"

"Give this scroll to the Lady Malvana, as soon as possible," Mab insisted.

The brownie took the scroll and bowed, "At once, Your Majesty."

A moment later the scroll was in Malvana's hands. She read it briefly and looked up, her eyes seeking her queen. Their gazes locked, and Malvana dipped her head in acknowledgment.

Order slowly returned to the chamber, and Malvana rose to speak.

"Lord Thorenson, a point of order . . . "

"Yes, Lady Malvana?"

"I believe Lord Varney offered a motion—before he was so *rudely* interrupted—to the effect that this issue be disregarded for the obvious reason that what happens in the *wild* is beyond the scope of authority of this Council. At this time, I would second the motion and ask that you call a vote thereon."

"Lord Thorenson, I must object," Mark countered. "Lord Varney has yet to answer my questions—which were entered upon the record prior to the seconding of any motion."

"That may be so, Lord Mark," cautioned the Dwarven Lord, "however, your questions, and your objection, are out of order. I have been somewhat indulgent with you, as you are newly seated on this Council; but you must understand our rules—and one is that we do not interfere with what transpires beyond the scope of the member realms. I realize you feel strongly about this matter. There are likely many present who would sympathize with such a cause, but this Council will not overstep its bounds. This wild realm has not sought Council membership nor does it enjoy any Council protection; there are no grounds for intervention. I have no choice but to put the motion before us to a vote."

"Thank you for explaining this to me, Lord Thorenson," Mark said meekly. "I think I understand. But just to clarify, am I to understand that anything that happens in the *wild*, even the activities of Council member realms, in concert or in opposition, is beyond the scope of Council authority?"

Lord Thorenson paused; clearly something about the way Mark had phrased the question unsettled him. But he had little choice but to answer in the affirmative—notwithstanding a gut-felt warning that this could very likely be a moment he would come to regret.

"Ah . . . yes, that is correct."

"Thank you, Lord Thorenson. I now understand completely."

Mark smiled smugly and resumed his seat.

CH 4

LATER THAT EVENING, after the Duprees and Johnsons had departed Delafaire Farm, and Miska had announced that he would return to the cabin for the night, Ellen settled in a comfortable chair in the library, the dogs soon asleep at her feet. Smokey wandered in and curled up atop the back of the other chair near the hearth.

With her aunt's journal in her lap and Maude's blue-tinted spectacles delicately perched on the bridge of her nose, Ellen carefully opened the book and began to read. Not tired in the least, she was determined to learn as much as these handwritten entries could offer about the portals.

An hour into her studies, a soft knock on the library door broke her concentration.

Stacy poked her head in and smiled. "Can't sleep either, huh? How about some hot chocolate?"

Looking over the rim of the spectacles, Ellen saw Stacy enter with a pair of mugs on a small tray. The aroma of warm chocolate wafted through the room; she couldn't help but smile.

"Oh, that smells good! Thanks. Pretty soon it'll be too warm outside for hot cocoa; but, I almost never pass up chocolate. Did my mom make this?"

"Nope, I did," Stacy answered, carefully plumping a pillow and trying not to disturb the drowsing cat as she joined him and settled comfortably in the other armchair.

Smokey opened his eyes to mere slits, purred indulgently at Stacy, and promptly went back to sleep.

"Your mom's not the only person who knows her way around a kitchen, you know."

"Sorry—*mea culpa*," Ellen pleaded as she closed the journal. "Is she still up?"

"Uh-huh," Stacy mumbled sipping from her cup. "I made her some, too. She's in the front parlor watching the news. She really likes that big screen TV; she said it's a lot easier to see with *old eyes*. I had to laugh at that! Now what are you up to? I heard you say that you had an idea. Come on, tell me."

"All right," Ellen conceded. "I got to thinking about what else I could do about those two damned portals, since it's clear I can't close them. So, I went back to the journal. Oh, Stacy, there's so much I didn't understand—still don't, really."

"Yeah? Like what?"

"Well, whenever I opened a portal, I just sort of *felt* it, the energy and all, and just *willed* it to work; and, I always closed it right after. But those two portals I couldn't close; so, I was trying to find out *why*. And, I've been wondering about all those globes—portals, really—that we saw in the Grand Portal near the cabin, you know? *Those* seemed to be permanent, too."

"So, what did you find out?"

"A couple of things . . . First of all, I've been doing it wrong—I should have read more. All those globes we saw, they *are* permanent because they were crafted that way, by Maude and maybe even previous Stewards. But the point is that they all—each one, I mean—have a *proximity shield* so they don't come in contact with each other."

"I don't get it," Stacy admitted. "What do you mean?"

"I didn't think about it, or even notice it at the time. But don't you remember—none of those globes touched one another, right? There was always a little bit of space between them."

"Okay . . . So?"

"Look, just bear with me for a minute. I never took more than basic physics in school—shoot, my degree is in *journalism*—so this is all like *on-the-job training* for me. I have to try to figure these things out logically, and then work with whatever I come up with, okay?"

"Yeah, yeah—so, go on already."

"Now, this *space* between the globes, I think it has to do with the properties of a transit globe. They're basically directed and contained energy; and, I think the globes have *polarity,* like magnets. You know, one pole attracts and the other repels—think positive and negative—opposite charges attract and like charges repel."

"Yeah, I know about magnets. So?"

"Let's postulate that transit globes *do* have polarity, okay? Let's further assume the shielding was not consciously applied to a globe, and it was to come too close to another unshielded globe. Now they might briefly repel, but then it's possible one or both might spin until their opposite poles attracted and made contact, just like simple magnets."

"Is that bad?"

"Possibly, yeah . . . As I understand it, they could, depending on the circumstances, either cancel each other out, or meld together evolving into a single connection. I think that would mean connecting the two destinations directly, effectively eliminating the original junction points—"

"Now, hold on," interrupted Stacy. "You mean like if two globes were not shielded in the Grand Portal, they could make contact, and then either cease to exist, cancel each other out—or they'd connect directly to each other, uh, their destinations, I mean. And neither one would exist any more in the Grand Portal?"

"Yeah, I think so," Ellen agreed, "assuming they came close enough to make contact in the first place. If I understand this right, to cancel each other out, the two globes or portals would have to be going to and from the same two places—kinda like mirror images of one another.

"However, the more I think about the globes that aren't like that—you know, mirror images—those portals that might just connect, the more I think they might only *seem* to no longer exist. I mean the melded junction would probably be intact, but somehow *out of phase*—not visible or easily perceptible. So, to any observers, the two connected portals would only *appear* to no longer be there."

Stacy frowned. "So, if observers can't see or sense something, it simply doesn't effectively exist for them—I get it. But since all the globes we saw were kept from touching, the ones that Maude and *whoever* crafted, then there's no danger of that happening?"

"Evidently not," Ellen surmised. "And apparently, that's what I've been doing wrong—crafting transit globes without consciously applying any proximity shielding."

"But you closed all the unshielded portals you opened . . ." Stacy's voice trailed off as her eyes widened.

"Not all, I haven't," Ellen said softly.

"Ellen, what are you thinking? Can those two portals be moved, like closer together or close enough, I mean?"

Stroking the binding of the journal in her lap, Ellen slowly shook her head.

"No, I'm fairly certain they are fixed in place. If I understand what Zack was explaining about M-Theory, these fixed portals might be places where the membranes of two universes are in actual contact, and the energy of the portal maintains that contact. I don't understand how the energy of the portal remains consistent. Maybe it draws from the fabric of the membranes themselves, and interrupting that flow disrupts and closes the portal. I just don't know; but in my mind, it makes a kind of logical sense."

"So?" Stacy probed, setting her mug aside.

"So, if I can't *close* those two portals, because something prevents me from interrupting the flow of energy, I'm thinking that I might be able to create another set of transit globes that are unshielded and close enough to make contact and change their destinations."

"Wait a minute!" Stacy reached out and gripped Ellen's wrist. "Didn't you say that unshielded globes might just cancel each other out? Wouldn't that be dangerous—for you, I mean?"

Ellen nodded. "Possibly . . . but—"

"But nothing!" Stacy pressed, "Just how close are we talking here?"

"I don't know, pretty close, I imagine." Ellen freed her wrist and held her open hands about a foot apart. "About this close, I think.

"Listen, as for canceling each other out, remember what I said. For that to happen, I'm pretty sure they'd have to be sourced from the same membrane to the same destination—crafted from the same place to go to the same realm—you know, like duplicate globes, or maybe mirror images?"

Holding up a finger to emphasize her point, Stacy cautioned, "Oh, I get it, mirror images with reversed polarity. Maybe, but that's only theory."

"True, but it *feels* right," insisted Ellen. "But what I'm proposing is the crafting of transit globes from different sources to go to different destinations—new locations. So, you see, it's not any real duplication—no mirror images, so no canceling out—just new destinations."

"Okay, I understand that, but even if that would work, just where would you select for a new destination? All those troops coming through those portals would have to go somewhere," Stacy pointed out, spreading her open palms.

"Good question," admitted Ellen. "I have an idea in that regard; but, I'll need to talk to Gallenius.

"Gallenius? Isn't he in Storm Haven? Cool! When are we going?"

"What do you mean *we?* This could be dangerous. I'm going to—"

"Wanna bet?" Stacy exclaimed. "I'm going with you! You're not getting out of my sight!"

Before Ellen could mount an argument, Smokey leapt to the floor and into her lap, and then stared unblinking up into her face.

Stacy laughed aloud. "Ha-ha! It looks like Smokey's going, too! And we won't take *no* for an answer! So, there! When are we leaving?"

Roused by the momentary excitement in Stacy's voice, the dogs merely peered up at the women groggily, sighed heavily, and promptly went back to sleep.

"Well, we should probably go now," Ellen reasoned, "before the situation in Storm Haven gets any worse. It shouldn't take long; I only have a few questions for Gallenius. Would you mind rummaging around in the closets to find us something that can serve as cloaks. It might be better to try and stay inconspicuous."

As Stacy nodded and rose, Ellen added, "Let me tell my mother where we're going; I don't want her worrying if she found us gone without an explanation. We can go in a few minutes."

THE SECURITY HAD OBVIOUSLY been enhanced at the normal entrance to Storm Haven; a dozen heavily armed guards were stationed in the portal anteroom. Nonetheless, the black-clad troops greeted Ellen and Stacy cordially.

The Guildmaster was surprised to learn of their arrival and granted them an immediate audience. They were escorted to the austere conference room where he and Gallenius had been focused on a large map openly displayed upon the wide table.

The Guildmaster greeted them warmly. "Ah, Lady Ellen and Lady Stacy—oh, I see Smokey is with you as well. Welcome. It is good to see you all."

"It is good to see you, too, Guildmaster, Gallenius," Ellen responded with a nod. "Please accept my deepest thanks for all your efforts in effecting the rescue of my mother and Stacy. I don't know what I would have done without friends to rely upon—"

"Yeah, and I'm grateful, too, you know," interrupted Stacy, impetuously.

"Of course. We were only too glad to be of service, m'ladies. And I am most gratified that you consider us *friends*. I assure you that your friendship and support are highly regarded by all of Storm Haven."

Ellen let Smokey spill from her arms as she responded, "Thank you, Guildmaster. As to the reason for my visit, I have an idea in regard to the, uh, problematic portals."

Turning to the mage, Ellen said, "Gallenius, when you arranged for Padraic to carry an enchanted amethyst during the rescue of my mother and Stacy, you mentioned an uninhabited realm in the wild that was to have been used as both misdirection and distraction, didn't you?"

"Yes, quite so, m'lady," Gallenius acknowledged. "How might this be of help?"

"Are you certain this realm is uninhabited? And how did you learn of this place?"

Gallenius paused, and answered the second question first.

"Acolytes at the College of Mages found a reference to this realm in one of the oldest scrolls in our library. We believe it was called *Olmus* in an ancient dialect. The old scroll is not intact; in fact, it is in quite poor condition. It mentions, in part, that this realm was considered sacred to some old gods; and that none but selected priests were permitted to reside there. As far as we know, no sentient beings now inhabit that realm. That is why we selected it as appropriate for our spell casting."

"M'lady, do you find this helpful?" asked the Guildmaster.

"I believe so," Ellen mused aloud. "As you know, I cannot close the portals that plague Storm Haven, but I may be able to *redirect* their destinations. However, I have to identify a *safe* destination, one that would not expose anyone else to further danger—"

"And," interrupted Stacy, "one that wouldn't necessarily harm anyone, uh, *sent* there, either—you know?"

"Hmm, that is very wise, m'lady," the Guildmaster acknowledged. "Our current intelligence indicates that many of the troops coming from Were and Shadow are primarily reluctant *conscripts* pressed into quasi-military service. Their leadership is, of course, another matter. "

"Unfortunately, raiding parties have already struck several outlying farms and settlements," Gallenius began, but paused to glance at the Guildmaster, who nodded affirmatively. The mage acknowledged and continued.

"The Were are poorly organized, and their raiding pattern appears spontaneous and ill planned. So far, they have struck only in sparsely populated, isolated areas; all we have lost is livestock. Unfortunately, the Shadow troops appear to be more disciplined, or at least better led. Their raids have been focused on small and unprotected villages."

The Guildmaster concluded wearily, "Sadly, we were not able to completely evacuate all our people in time; some lives have been lost and most survivors taken prisoner. A few stragglers have managed to evade capture and make their way safely to fortified villages and towns."

"I was just telling the Guildmaster," Gallenius added, "that our own scouting parties have reported several skirmishes with enemy patrols."

"That's terrible news!" Ellen winced. "I am so sorry to have been in any way responsible for this disaster."

"M'lady, we know you were tricked," said the Guildmaster firmly. "We do not hold you responsible. Recrimination is a waste of time; and time is a luxury we do not have."

“I understand, and thank you,” Ellen responded sincerely. “I intend to devote all my energy to correcting my mistakes, and do so as soon as possible.”

“Wait just a minute!” blurted Stacy. “If most of the invading troops are *conscripts*, then isn't their *leadership* the real problem—*another matter*, you said, right?”

“Quite so; that is very perceptive of you, m'lady,” observed the Guildmaster. “In fact, we had been discussing a series of strategies to free the imprisoned, and isolate or eliminate the command structure of the two invading armies. Without their leaders, we think the line troops could be, ah, *persuaded* to surrender and depart. We really do not want them here—even as prisoners.”

“I understand; and I hope you are right,” Ellen said sympathetically. “Now, I must admit, altering the destinations of these portals, I am not completely certain it will work. However, I am determined to *try*.”

“I believe I can understand how you feel,” the Guildmaster said, “but it could be quite perilous to attempt this alone. Is there anything we can do to help? Our resources are spread thin, but . . .”

“No, thank you. I am grateful for the offer, but I believe this is something only I can do. However, I could use some information.”

“Of course, m'lady.” The Guildmaster opened his gloved palms. “Please, tell us what you need.”

“Gallenius, I would appreciate all the information you have on this uninhabited realm of *Olmus*. If what I have in mind works, any more troops sent here from Were or Shadow will instead find themselves in this uninhabited realm. If they try to retrace their steps by going back through the portals, they should wind up back in their home realms of Were and Shadow. Unfortunately, I cannot do anything about those who are already here—they will still be a problem.”

“Indeed, m'lady,” Gallenius acknowledged, “a problem we know we will have to deal with even if your plan works. But, begging your pardon, a question occurs to me regarding the troops who are misdirected to Olmus. Do I understand correctly that they could return to *either* Were or Shadow?"

"I hadn't thought of that," admitted Ellen. "I would effectively be creating two separate portals into Olmus, from Were and Shadow respectively. So, yes, I can see how upon departing Olmus, they could go into either realm."

"Then may I suggest, m'lady, that you place the two new portals fairly close to one another—the better to sow confusion among the invaders. That would create further consternation for the administrations of Were and Shadow, for you will have established unanticipated *back doors* into those two realms." The mage smiled, a conspiratorial gleam in his eye.

Ellen nodded. "Ah, I see your point, Gallenius. But as these will be unshielded portals, I cannot place them too close, but perhaps within view of one another. We shall see."

"*Unshielded portals?* I believe I understand, m'lady, and *within view* would likely suffice," Gallenius acknowledged. "Now, if there is nothing else, I shall gather the information you seek. Guildmaster, m'ladies, if you will excuse me?"

The Guildmaster nodded. "Of course, Gallenius."

As the mage departed, Smokey leapt upon the tabletop and seemed to study the map.

The Guildmaster sighed. "Ah, m'ladies, may I offer you refreshment while we wait?"

"Thank you, Guildmaster, but no. Once I fully understand the location of Olmus, I intend to act. I know that time is of the essence."

"Ellen, Smokey and I are going with you!" Stacy declared. "There'll be no argument! Especially since I have the strongest sense that you're going to need us—both of us! Now, just so I'm not confused, tell me again how we're going to do this."

Ellen opened her hands. "It'll be simple; we retrace my steps. We start in Were, where I opened the first portal, and go through it to the Were campsite in Storm Haven. There I craft the transit globe to Olmus without a proximity shield; the portals connect and we arrive in Olmus. There, I find a spot close, and craft another unshielded portal that'll take us from Olmus to the vicinity of the existing portal in the Shadow campsite in Storm Haven. They connect, and the portals in Storm Haven will appear to be gone. The only direct links from Shadow and Were will then only be to and from Olmus. Storm Haven will be effectively bypassed!"

"It's a little confusing at first, but does make sense," Stacy mulled. "It's kinda like hooking up a couple of extra hoses to a pair of existing garden hoses to water a distant part of a garden. That metaphor works for me. But, can it really be that easy?"

"Sure, metaphor or simile—let's do this." Ellen wished she felt as confident as she sounded.

THE GUILDMASTER WATCHED this exchange with growing appreciation. Individually, he had found each woman competent and capable; but together, they were proving to be quite formidable, indeed.

Smokey strode nonchalantly across the map and came to sit before the Guildmaster, staring unblinkingly up into the man's darkened hood, almost as a reminder that he, too, would be part of this expedition.

The Guildmaster realized that with the addition of Smokey, a description of *formidable* might be wholly inadequate. *Awesome* might be more appropriate, he thought with an unseen smile.

CLEMENT, THE APPRENTICE, was not happy.

Well into his third year of a five-year apprenticeship to Zerban, Magus Emeritus of the Were, Clement was constantly assigned petty and annoying tasks by more senior acolytes. He found such vexations demeaning and certainly beneath him. He knew he was among the brightest students at the senior Were adept's school—not that it mattered; his evident intellect only engendered resentment among the other acolytes.

Furthermore, fourth and fifth-year students were typically allowed to delegate the more disagreeable tasks to those with less seniority. Worse, it seemed that certain upperclassmen took great delight in giving him the most disgusting of delegated assignments, like his present task—cleaning the muck from the temporary enclosure erected for the giant bats.

This task had originally been given to Stellara, a comely fifth-year apprentice; but, she had quickly delegated it to Clement, thus freeing herself to disappear into the dubious privacy of a thick alder copse with a handsome young soldier she fancied.

No doubt another tryst, Clement thought; the girl was absolutely wanton and manipulated men with appalling ease. She was detested by almost all of her female classmates; but the young men, especially the adolescent boys, were still hopelessly under her spell.

Appealing this latest degradation to Zerban would do no good. The senior mage was preoccupied, in conference within the commanders' tent, and did not suffer interruptions gladly. Since there were no first or second-year students at the portal site, as the youngest apprentice present, Clement was stuck.

Zerban and a handful of acolytes had come to this lonely location in the forests of Were at the direction of the Were Administration. They were to watch over this new portal and prevent any magical tampering; that was all Clement really knew.

The senior mage had brought six of his giant pets, carnivorous bats the size of large dogs, with wingspans the width of a man's outspread arms. In fact, they acted more like a pack of wolves hunting as a coordinated group than as common solitary bats. Zerban planned to use them to guard the portal.

The bats appeared to be unswervingly loyal to Zerban; but, they barely tolerated the acolytes.

Clement had long suspected that these giants were ensorcelled. However, as a mere apprentice he dared not ask, especially since no other journeyman adept would even broach the subject, much less go near the beasts.

All the acolytes detested caring for the bats; more than one had suffered an injury working with the bad-tempered carnivores over the years. For one thing, they had to be fed live prey if they were not allowed to hunt. Pigs and vermin were the usual fare, but occasionally cattle were so sacrificed.

On this occasion, the bats would not be permitted to hunt—as if Zerban *wanted* them in a foul humor—so live pigs were to be periodically left in the enclosure. Hours later, there would be little left. But, soon enough someone had to clean out the floor of the enclosure, all the while hoping that the bats, satiated and suspended above, deposited no more droppings.

The job was foul, but it had to be done.

Once fed, the bats were free to roam about the vicinity of the portal. A spell of containment kept them from wandering off, or hunting in the vicinity. Needless to say, the hastily assembled ragtag army gave the bats, and thus the portal, a wide berth. Only when so ordered would any of the troops approach or enter the portal—provided, of course, the bats had been confined to their towering enclosure.

Even so, many people milled about, albeit most at a modest distance.

Consequently, Clement gave no particular notice to a curious pair of cloaked and hooded figures who suddenly appeared from the edge of the trees and stood briefly in the area near the portal.

He had just finished shoveling the last of the accumulated guano into a wheelbarrow when he saw Stellara and her *paramour of the moment* emerge from the shelter of the thick underbrush in the copse of alder. She was grinning, face flushed, and her robes disheveled. She gave her equally rumpled companion a quick peck on the cheek and sent him off.

Spying Clement, she smiled evilly and started walking in his direction, subtly straightening her robes and picking at small twigs and leaves in her mussed hair.

Sighing in resignation, he stepped a few paces away from the pungent load of bat excrement and bent to scraping the disgusting residue off his shovel. This time, he was determined to ignore her teasing harassment.

"Ah, *junior* apprentice," she hailed, "I see you would rather play with the tools than perform the task assigned! Our master must be informed of your laziness and typical incompetence—"

Her words were suddenly cut off with a *whoosh* and a muffled *splat!*

Sprawled face-first in the muck-laden wheelbarrow, her legs flailed helplessly.

Clement erupted in uncontrollable snorting laughter—just before he, too, was knocked to the ground in a rush of hard bodies and leathery wings.

He regained his feet in time to see the curious pair of hooded figures disappear into the portal, with one of the giant bats almost on their heels! The other bats were close behind.

Without another thought or backward glance, Clement too gave chase, disappearing into the portal.

IN HIS SLEEPING CHAMBER beneath the temple ruins in Olmus, Papa George was unceremoniously shaken by the shoulder as the remnants of a haphazard dream shredded and faded in the theater of his mind.

"Wake up, George—we have company! Wake up, now!" The voice was insistent and flushed with urgency.

He rolled over, rubbed the sleep from his eyes, and considered the two shadows at his bedside.

The taller one leaned over him and spoke softly.

"He is awake. Leave the lamp, and go prepare the scrying chamber."

The shorter shadow blinked its widely spaced and strangely luminescent eyes, and nodded its overly large head, its crown festooned with tufts of scraggly hair sprouting above long pointed ears. Deftly handing over a brass oil lamp, the misshapen servant silently withdrew from the sleeping chamber.

In the soft illumination of the pale flame, George saw Daegon's features contorted in a mask of concern and worry.

"Okay, I'm awake," George groaned as he pulled himself up and swung his stockinged feet to the cold stone floor. "What is it?"

"Someone has transited into this realm. I do not know who it is. Come with me, now."

"All right—all right, I'm coming," George grumbled as he probed the dark recesses below the sleeping pallet with the toe of one foot. "Where the hell are my shoes? Should've never worn alligator loafers. I hate sleeping in my clothes—this is an Armani suit, for crap's sake!"

Daegon ignored his complaints.

Fruitlessly smoothing crumpled wrinkles and errant creases that would not be subdued, George gave vent to his impatient irritation. "And now we've got *company?* I don't get it, Daegon—no one knows about this place, right? At least that's what you told me when we came here—of course you didn't mention the tribes of *goblins* who live here either—"

"Enough!" Daegon blurted tersely. He led the way through the warren of subterranean passages beneath the ruins of the old temple, mumbling all the while just loud enough for George to hear, "Some *apprentice*—done damned little but complain since our arrival."

The goblin servants hastened to get out of the way. Standing only waist high to a man, and perpetually slouched in a gangly stance on short bandy legs and large splayed feet, they had extremely thin arms ending in long bony hands.

Nonetheless, goblins were surprisingly nimble, and thus easily avoided Daegon and George in the men's rush to the scrying chamber.

Attired in short tunics bearing a crescent-shaped swath of arcane runic symbols, the diminutive servants had the scrying chamber lit with candles and oil lamps; but, pockets of dark shadow nonetheless flit from crevice to cranny like emboldened vermin defying the unwelcome luminosity. In the center of the room an enormous skeletal hand jutted up from the stone floor, the bony fingers supporting a large crystal orb, a multitude of reflected flames dancing across its surface.

Daegon approached the orb and held his arms out to either side of the crystal, and simply said, "Silence."

The servants froze in place, not daring to make a sound. The goblins were clearly much in awe of Daegon and his magic.

The alchemist had explained to George that these creatures had lived secretly and well hidden in this realm for untold millennia—since the time of the Old Ones, whom they had originally served.

With the passing of the old gods and their much feared priests in the dim and misty past, the goblin tribes and their distended family groups had made their homes underground, in caves, caverns, and these secret places beneath the ruins of old temples. They ventured about on the surface only when absolutely necessary, to gather food or hunt wild game.

In fact, Daegon had assured George, very few knew of the goblins' current existence.

When Daegon had stumbled upon this place, these secretive tribes were easily convinced that a priest of the Old Ones had returned. The aura of his sorcery was old indeed, and flavored with the taint of *necromancy*, which was held in goblin lore to be among the hallmarks of the Old Ones' power.

No fool, Daegon had accepted their obeisance and did nothing to correct their mistaken impression of his standing and status. They were now *his* servants, and he treated them as such. Of course, he was always careful to be as dramatic and theatrical as possible, even when performing the smallest of magics.

As he now bent over the crystal, Daegon mumbled an arcane invocation and flailed his hands about in melodramatic fashion. The crystal clouded and then began to clear, a moonlit scene depicted within.

George stepped closer for a better look.

Two hooded figures were running toward a wood fronted by a thick wall of thorn trees. Behind the runners, something large was closing quickly. They seemed to be fleeing from whatever was chasing—no, not just chasing, but *flying* after them. With a final glance over their shoulders, they made it to the tentative safety of the trees.

The pursuing creature flared its wings and pulled up short of the canopy, obviously frustrated that its prey had found shelter. Rapidly beating its wings in a hover, the creature was joined by five more similar beasts flying into the crystal's view.

"What are those things?" asked George.

"Bats, I think, very large, but bats nonetheless," offered Daegon.

"Who are they chasing?"

"I have no idea. Did you recognize them?"

"You mean those two? No—why would I? We couldn't even see their faces," George grumbled.

"No matter," Daegon muttered. "As for these interlopers, I doubt hiding amongst those trees will forestall these hunters for very long."

"No kidding. Well then, I guess the real question is who *else* knows about this place?" George made a sweeping gesture with one hand.

Daegon knit his brow. "No one living *should* know, aside from my servants, of course. As far as I know, our departure from the Council Realm left no clues. Although I have no doubt the Council will take grievous offense at the act of necromancy I used on those two elfin guards as a distraction, when *I* saved *your* life."

"I get the point," groused George, "and I'm grateful, even though *I'll* probably get blamed for *your* sorcery. But we both know we are now wanted men, for *whatever* reasons. I don't plan on spending the rest of my life here in this—"

"Nor do I," interrupted Daegon. "I have plans as well. But it would be best to enhance your knowledge, skills, and abilities before we venture out among the wild realms. And there is no better place to base our operations than *here*—provided, of course, this remains a secret."

"Well, it doesn't appear to be a secret at the moment, does it?" George asked peevishly, and then pointed into the orb. "In fact, look; someone else has shown up!"

Another figure walked into the moonlit scene and stared at the bats swirling in short swooping arcs across the treetops, rustling the canopy with great gusts from beats of their leathery wings.

Daegon stared closely into the crystal, and cursed under his breath. "Damn the gods! This is not good. Has the secret of this realm been widely compromised—or are these few interlopers the only ones so aware? Can I curtail and contain the knowledge, seal the breach, so to speak? Damn! I need more information."

Suddenly inspired, he crooked a finger at a servant.

CLEMENT WAS NEARLY out of breath. He stopped running and walked the last few yards, panting as he watched the bats pirouette gracefully in the moonlight above a dark forest. He recognized the pattern of their flight; they were hunting.

A chill ran up his spine.

He well knew that these bats hunted like a wolf pack. When their instincts took over, they would savage anything—prey or otherwise—in mindless bloodlust.

He realized, too late, that impulsively following them through that strange portal may have been a fatal mistake.

Only Zerban could control the bats during a hunt—and that took all of his skills. There was no way a third-year apprentice could hope to survive, much less control, a hunt.

He froze—if they sensed his presence, he was as good as dead. His only hope was that Zerban would come through the portal and take charge.

Surely, Stellara would notify the Master—she must! Must she not?

"ARE THEY STILL THERE?" asked Stacy, glancing up at the dense foliage above them.

Ellen closed her eyes and concentrated.

"Yeah, six of them overhead . . . Now another presence has arrived in the field we just crossed. But, this one's very different from the others—a person, a man, but young, I think."

"Is he after us, too?"

"I don't know. All I can tell is that whoever is in that field is more frightened right now than we are—and I mean *really* scared!"

"You know, those flying things looked like *bats* to me," Stacy offered, "but they're awfully *big!*"

"Yeah, I think you're right—bats," Ellen concurred. "But they're way too big to fly in here among these closely set tree trunks; it's fairly cramped in here. And those were some healthy thorn trees near the edge of these woods."

"What's to stop them from just walking in? They're the size of Dobermans—with wings!" exclaimed Stacy, as Smokey snuggled deeper into her arms, seemingly unconcerned, but nonetheless keeping an unblinking watch on the overhead canopy.

"Keep your voice down! I think they're *listening* for us; maybe even trying to find us using echolocation—you know, like regular bats. But I think the thick foliage may be shielding us for the moment. You know, there's something *unnatural* about it—the way they seem to be working together, I mean. That's just too weird to be coincidence." Ellen looked around. "The sooner we get out of here, the better!"

"You're not going to form a transit globe in here, are you? I thought you wanted to do it in the same field where the other one deposited us. You know, *close*, like Gallenius suggested, don't you?"

"I do. But I don't see how we can get back into that field with these bats hunting us."

"Wait a minute, let me think a second. Echolocation is just identifying a location or direction based on sound waves bouncing back from something, right? So, if they're listening for us, and we had a means of directing sound waves away from us, do you think that might lure the bats away?"

"Maybe. It does make sense," Ellen agreed. "What are you thinking?"

"It's just a hunch, but let me try something." Stacy handed Smokey to Ellen.

Going up to the biggest tree trunk she could see in the dimness, Stacy placed her hands on the bark of the massive oak and closed her eyes. She stayed immobile for several minutes.

Ellen did not know quite what to make of this; but, she trusted her friend. So, she remained patient, gently scratching Smokey behind his ears.

A slight rustling of leaves came from overhead. Ellen reflexively ducked, looking up apprehensively. Soon all the lower limbs and leaves of the huge tree were rhythmically moving and shaking.

Ellen could see that Stacy, eyes still closed, was smiling broadly, and that was somehow reassuring.

Stacy removed her hands from the trunk and the tree became still. Opening her eyes, she smiled at Ellen.

"It's done. Ellen, the trees will help us—don't ask, just listen. When I ask them to, the trees will create a focused noise with their limbs and leaves. It will sound like someone lumbering through an area of heavily wooded forest. It will begin here, with this grand old oak."

Her hand gently stroked its coarse bark, her smile still blissful.

"The sound will continue, moving from tree to tree, toward the far side of these woods. It should draw the bats in that direction; then we can slip back into the field where you need to craft your transit globe. I don't know how much time we'll have so you'll need to be ready, okay?"

"Uh, okay, I'm game—I think." Ellen shrugged. "But even if this works, once we're out in the field and no longer sheltered by this dense canopy, the bats can still use their echolocation to find us."

"Well, yeah," Stacy admitted. "That's why I said you'll need to be ready. We'll have to be fast! Anything else?"

"Actually, yes, there is," admitted Ellen, leaning forward and speaking softly, yet urgently. "There's something you must understand. When we transited from Were to that portal location in Storm Haven, I knew exactly where it was, and pretty much how close to come with the new portal to connect the two—mainly because I had already been to that site more than once. I also knew it was warded in some way as well, so I knew what to expect. And it worked; we were only actually in Storm Haven for a few seconds. Then we transited here as the two portals connected; although, I didn't know we would be chased from Were and into this realm."

"Okay, I get that, so?" Stacy urged.

Ellen winced and opened her palms. "Now, here's the problem; I'm not one hundred percent sure about the exact location of the other *unshielded* portal in Storm Haven, the one connected to Shadow. I've only been there once, with Mab, when I originally crafted the portal. I mean, I know *generally* where it is, pretty much; but, I'm not sure exactly how close to it we might actually arrive. I'm sure it'll be warded in some way. And the other thing is that I understand the security around the Shadow portal is very tight—probably at both ends. So, even if this works like we hope, we may still have to deal with Shadow security forces. Do you understand?"

"Now I'm beginning to understand why you wanted to try this alone." Stacy grinned. "It's a wild crapshoot! We've done well so far; but, we might be jumping from the frying pan into the fire, right?"

"Well, yeah, we might."

"So? What other choice do we have?" countered Stacy. "We certainly can't stay here! Too many people are depending on these portals being dealt with. You know we *have* to do this."

"I know," Ellen agreed, "but I want you to know all the facts—it's only fair."

"Well, consider me well informed," intoned Stacy wryly. "Come on, we're wasting time."

"All right," conceded Ellen. "Don't forget that there's someone out in that field—still there and very frightened."

"Well, I can't help with that." Stacy sighed and shrugged. "Are you ready?"

"Let's do this."

Stacy laid her hands upon the tree once more.

Just as she had described, the sound of someone lumbering haphazardly, bordering on panic, rose from the nearby trees and seemed to move off deeper into the woods. Winking at Ellen, Stacy rose and pointed in the other direction. As the focused rustling of the trees diminished in the distance, the women cautiously made their way back the way they had come.

Soon they were at the tree line; the sky appeared to be clear. The field was starkly painted in languid moon shadows as lonely clouds scudded across the bright lunar face.

"I don't see any bats or anyone in the field," offered Stacy. "Can you sense if he's still out there?"

Ellen paused a moment. "Yes, he's still there. I don't think he's moved, but I can't see him either. We can't wait any longer—we have to chance it. Let's go!"

They ran into the night. When they came within sight of the first portal, Ellen crafted another transit globe. With a last look around, they quickly passed within, leaving the two portals shimmering in reflected moonlight.

CLEMENT STOOD AGOG as the cloud shadow passed and he was once again bathed in the cool silver of lunar light. He had seen the bats move off in the far distance over the treetops, and the two figures emerge on *this* side of the wood. He was stunned—the bats never failed in a hunt!

What is happening? I can barely see those two people. Ye gods, are they looking right at me? Do they see me? What—they disappeared! What sorcery was this?

Twisting around in a complete circle, his surprise and confusion were only momentary distractions.

However, this lapse of attention was sufficient to betray him. He looked up—the sudden sight of the returning bats diving in frenzied bloodlust on his position plunged his heart into an icy well of dread.

Flooded with fear, he took a staggering step back—and felt his ankles grabbed in a vice-like gnarly grip. He pitched forward, his arms windmilling in futility, as the ground before him opened up!

The last thing he saw was a wide-eyed, pinched face, grinning evilly through putrid and corroded teeth as he was pulled into a musty maw of darkness.

THE SMALL CAVERN IN Storm Haven was cramped with the eight members of the assembled strike team. It didn't matter to Frieda and Wilhem; this fortuitous location was critical to their mission. Although the entrance faced the opposite direction, they were only a bow-shot away from the Shadow forces' camp, and the invaders' portal.

In the dank cave, the black-clad, heavily armed men were nearly invisible in the feeble light of the sole candle Wilhem held in his hand, the only light they dared risk.

Clearing his throat, he spoke softly. "Captain, we have very little time to amend the plan, and none once you and your men move into position. Have you learned anything that might alter our strategy?"

"No, nothing," the dour man replied. "Has anything changed at the target site?"

"Only that Lord Gunther still has not yet returned," answered Frieda. "He insisted upon accompanying a raiding party and has been gone most of the night. It is almost an hour until the dawn. If he does not return, he will have to soon seek out shelter from the sun. Lady Sabrina is most likely making preparations, as we speak, for her daylight repose in the designated chamber dug out below Lord Vlad's headquarters. Vlad, himself, is still in heated conference with his officers. It seems the vampire nobles are not predisposed to work together; the petty jealousies and intrigues among the noble houses further frustrate the effectiveness of Vlad's command."

"Are they still within that wooden structure, that palisade-walled tent that their troops erected?" asked the captain.

"Yes, but for Gunther, all the vampires are within the protected redoubt," Frieda responded. "Two men-at-arms now guard the entrance; but that guard will double at sunrise when the undead return to their subterranean chamber."

"They certainly are paranoid about their safety during the day," observed a sergeant. "They had that palisade wall up by the end of their second night here, and so close to the portal, too. How did you find out about the chamber they had dug out below?"

"Let us just say that we have our sources," Wilhem answered, with a small private smile for his wife.

"It does not matter, Sergeant," chastised the captain. "It will not impact your part of the mission. You and your squad will deal with the guards at the holding pen on the other side of the encampment and rescue as many of the captured civilians as possible. There are at least a score that we know of; but be thorough, look around carefully for any others. Get them moving to the south and head for the rendezvous point. The rest of us will deal with the vampire nobles and their guards. Am I clear?"

"Yes sir."

"Good. Corporal, are the diversionary devices ready?"

"Yes, sir, I'll only need a few minutes to set the charges, and then we will have one minute on the main fuse. It will not be a large explosion, but a series of three small ones—more flash and sparks than anything else. It should work as a diversion."

"Very good," acknowledged the captain. "Final gear and weapons check!"

"Captain, a word, if you please?" asked Wilhem.

The commander and Wilhem stepped near the mouth of the cave as the troops within checked their weapons; broad double-headed axes, long daggers with silver blades, the ominous short-barreled shotguns and bandoleers of spare ammunition.

"Captain, a delicate matter," Wilhem said softly. "I am sure you are aware that, in regard to my wife and me, it is critical that our existence and identities remain confidential."

"I am. Gallenius was most emphatic on that point. My men are aware as well."

Wilhem nodded. "I know your orders are to capture, if possible, the leadership of the Shadow forces. But in consideration of the inherent danger, I would urge you to consider a more permanent solution, should you experience unexpected difficulties, or in the event our identities were to be compromised. Once engaged, none must escape!"

The captain nodded solemnly.

Wilhem leaned closer. "On the other hand, should you or one of your men be captured . . ." His voice trailed off into an ominous silence.

The captain looked at Wilhem, slightly stunned at the man's words, but not exactly surprised.

"I know. I heard virtually the same ominous admonition from the Guildmaster's own lips only a few hours ago. The two of you are among Storm Haven's most highly regarded intelligence assets. Whereas, my men and I are potentially expendable. Nonetheless, I have no intention of leaving anyone behind, whether they survive this audacious mission or not."

Wilhem nodded. "Of course, I under—"

A flash of searing light illuminated the forested countryside, followed by a concussive *whump!*

Frieda and the members of the assault team burst forth from the cave, their expressions a mixture of surprise and alert determination.

"What was *that?*" she gasped, gripping her husband's arm, and staring in the direction of the Shadow camp.

"Unknown, m'lady," replied the captain, rubbing his eyes in an effort to get his night vision back, "but it came from the camp! Sergeant, ready your squad! Corporal, it seems we won't need your diversion after all. You have your assignments—move out!"

MUCH OF THE SHADOW camp was flattened, its palisade-walled headquarters a pile of broken logs.

Bodies were strewn about; soldiers, men-at-arms, and servants. All were unconscious; many bore obvious injuries. Surprisingly, none were dead.

This was puzzling for the captain and his men.

Several of the walls of the prisoner holding pen were also knocked down, as if blown by a great wind. All the prisoners within appeared to be unconscious as well.

In fact, debris was strewn about in a rather obvious radial pattern. It looked as if the massive wind had blown out from a central point near the portal, which was no longer there. Instead, a waist-high dome of luminous roiling green energy, about the size of a farm cart, now occupied the approximate spot where the portal had once been.

FRIEDA AND WILHEM STAYED back, hidden by the trees, and surveyed the site undetected.

"Such destruction," she whispered. "What could cause this?"

"Sorcery of some kind run amok," he answered softly, and pointed. "No doubt that green *thing* is a remnant of some spell gone awry."

"Perhaps, dear, but where is the portal?"

"I . . . I do not see it—tis gone! Unless that *green thing*—"

"No," Frieda interrupted. "That dome is no portal. Something of portent has happened here! Keep careful watch over the captain and his men. I must return to the Guildmaster with this news."

"As you wish," Wilhem acknowledged. "Be careful, my love—and safe."

With a quick kiss and a smile for her husband, she melted into the darkness and was swallowed by the night.

"CAPTAIN! OVER HERE, sir!" shouted the corporal, who was sifting through the jumble of shattered logs and torn canvas that, moments before, had been the vampire lord's headquarters.

Removing what wreckage they could, the members of the Storm Haven strike team found the first of the dead, Lord Vlad, impaled and nearly beheaded. The captain finished the job.

They found most of the other vampire nobles already dead, impaled, dismembered, or partially decapitated, and thus near true and final death—final even for a vampire. Any hope of an intelligence windfall was clearly moot. The few mortally wounded vampire nobles still lingering at death's door were dispatched with quick efficiency.

The sergeant approached, his face a mask of concern, and pulled the captain aside.

"Sir, the captives, we found twenty-four—but it is most unusual! They live, but all are unconscious, and most have minor injuries. Some have even been fed upon by *these.*" He spat at the decapitated vampires in disgust. "Many bleed from the nose and ears. We could rouse none of them. The medic says that there is no way we can move them without litters, and a lot more help."

The corporal approached his superiors.

"Sir, most of the Shadow troops are in much the same way as the sergeant described—except for not being fed upon. None are dead; but all are out cold. And that weird green dome near the center of the camp is making some strange *zapping* sounds. What are your orders, sir?"

"It would probably be best to avoid that which is clearly sorcery," the captain cautioned. "The vampire lord, Gunther, is still afield, and likely knows something has happened here. No one within miles of this place could have missed that flare of light. And we have yet to account for the Lady Sabrina.

"Sergeant, we have no choice. We cannot evacuate our captive people without more help, so we'll have to leave them for now. Have your men remove more of this wreckage and locate the chamber below. We still have a vampire to find here. Look lively, now!"

They found the Lady Sabrina in short order, stunned and unconscious, but otherwise unharmed. She was quickly gagged, trussed, and blindfolded before she was thrust into a black plastic body bag, one of several provided by Gallenius for just such a purpose.

"Well done, lads. Now let us be gone," said the captain as he cast a final glance over the scene. His gaze lingered for just a second on the damaged holding pen; his heart clenched at the thought of leaving the captives behind. He knew there would be another rescue attempt; he was determined to be part of it.

He saw the glowing green dome near the camp center; a chill traversed his spine. He turned and followed his men into the forest, glad to be quit of this place—for now.

ELLEN LAY ON HER BACK on the dusty ground, a dull headache throbbing at her temples. She squinted, opening one eye, only to shut it again, a wash of pale green fluorescing a sickly afterimage on her closed eyelid. Forcing both eyes open to mere slits, she saw a green tint to her hands as she brought them to her face. Rolling her head to one side, she saw Stacy, all bathed in green as well, lying beside her. Reaching out, she grasped Stacy's arm and shook it.

"Stacy! Stacy, can you hear me, are you all right?"

"Huh? What? Ellen? Where are we? Why are you all green?"

Struggling to sit up, Ellen winced as the pain in her head flared and then began to fade.

"I think . . . I think we're safe, in some sort of a *protective dome.* I can sense that it's made of energy, like a force field or something. It's green, so everything looks greenish."

"Yeah?" Stacy groaned, leaning forward. "Well, this is plain old *dirt* we're sitting on. So, where are we? I can't see past this *force field* or *whatever.*"

Ellen shook her head. "I don't . . . Wait a minute—the green is fading. Look!"

It *was* fading. The energy comprising the wall of the dome was dissipating; in seconds, it was gone. Colors regained their normal hues, inasmuch as the pale moonlight allowed.

The damage and devastation became clearly evident; something very bad had happened here.

Ellen's heart sank as she recognized where they were.

"Hey, where's Smokey?" asked Stacy, looking around.

"Huh? Smokey?" Ellen echoed.

"Yeah, I had him in my arms when . . . " Stacy's voice softened as memory came flooding back.

Ellen was now certain that they were in Storm Haven, in the camp of Shadow troops. But the portal—it was gone! What had happened? She closed her eyes and opened her awareness.

Yes! The portal was still there after all—no, not just one, *both* of them, or rather their newly melded junction—but, it was out of phase and unperceived. And something else—wards of some kind? Yes, very strong wards! Had her attempt clashed with these wards? But the two portals had connected, hadn't they? Yes, the connection felt intact. So, her plan had worked, up to a point. But all this destruction—was all this *her* fault?

"Stacy, I think it worked—connecting the portals, I mean. But all *this*—I think I may have misjudged our transit arrival point."

"Too close, huh?"

"Yeah . . . I didn't intend all *this.* And I don't think I had anything to do with that greenish thing, that protective force field or whatever—at least not *consciously.*"

"Well, don't look at *me!*" Stacy shrugged, and then added facetiously, "So then, I guess that just leaves Smokey, doesn't it?"

Matching her sarcastic tone, Ellen retorted smugly as she rubbed an aching shoulder. "Well then, when we find him, we'll just ask him, won't we? But for now though, I think we're in a bit of trouble here."

Stacy merely shrugged in reply.

Without warning, a coldly harsh voice spoke from the darkness behind them. "Now *that* is an understatement!"

Arrogantly swaggering into the moonlight, with a dozen men-at-arms arrayed at his back, strode a deathly pale figure—wearing an eye patch.

Gunther!

CH 5

"WELL, HE CERTAINLY doesn't know much at all," grumbled George as he nodded at the slumped body of Clement suspended in irons against the stained and moldy wall of the ancient dungeon.

The lowermost cavern below the temple ruins on Olmus was chill and damp; however, the chains and manacles dangling from overhead hooks showed no signs of rust or deterioration. In the spare illumination of a few torches, augmented by glowing coals nestled in an iron cauldron, ominous shadows of an ancient rack, an iron maiden, and other macabre implements of torture pulsed across the coarse stone walls.

A large number of goblin servants had eagerly attended in hopes of witnessing a prolonged session of agony during questioning of the captured prisoner; it had been a very long time since they had been so entertained.

But they were soon disappointed; Daegon had ignored the hooked blades, thumbscrews, rack, and the red-hot iron pokers burrowed amongst the coals. Instead, he had ordered the stunned prisoner clapped in irons and hung against the unforgiving stone of the rough wall. Demanding silence, he had cast a powerful truth spell upon the boy and began a slow and patient questioning.

The goblins quickly became bored—but they dared not voice their disappointment, lest they incur Daegon's wrath.

George, on the other hand, was not so inclined.

"I tell you, we're wasting our time," he complained. "He knows nothing of any value."

"On the contrary," cautioned Daegon, "I believe we have learned a great deal from this young man—and we have his *true name*. Never underestimate the significance of knowing someone's true name."

“Okay, so we know he came from Were; and he came alone, following those bats.”

“Patience, apprentice, patience. Consider what *else* we now know.”

George merely grunted as Daegon continued.

“A portal has changed its destination! How is this possible? This boy expected to arrive in a place called Storm Haven, but came here instead. To alter a portal’s destination—aye, that is a feat few can do, very few, indeed. And the two hooded figures he saw and followed here, what became of them? They *disappeared* before his eyes!”

George wisely remained silent.

“Now apprentice, consider this; if *he* came through this portal, will not others? Were troops were mustering to enter this portal; will they too arrive here unintentionally?”

That did, in fact, give George something to worry about; but Daegon ignored him and gave voice to his train of thought.

“Hmm . . . This one’s purported master, *Zerban*, will surely come in search of his bats. And since it is evident that these creatures can be controlled, I would learn more about them—and about this mage, Zerban, as well.

“But most importantly, we must recognize that our security—the very secret of this realm—has been compromised! And *that* must be corrected.”

“Yeah, right. How are we gonna do that?”

Daegon paused, stroked his chin, and admitted, “For the moment, I do not know. But rest assured I *will* find a way.”

“Well, what do we do about him?” George asked, tossing a thumb at Clement, sagging in his chains and drooling in a spell-induced stupor.

“I could give him to the goblins to dispose of. They would take great delight in that.”

George glanced around the chamber, noting the arcane torture devices and the eager leering of the assembled servants. He could not suppress an icy shudder—then he had a sudden idea.

"Daegon, listen, I don't mind telling you that your, uh, *servants* sort of *creep me out.* So, why don't we keep this kid around? He can be *my* servant. Just do a mind-wipe spell on him or something. You know what I mean?"

Daegon cocked his head to one side as he clearly considered George's proposal.

"Hmm, your idea has merit. And it may well be that we have not yet exhausted all of his knowledge; so, a mind-wipe spell would not be appropriate."

"Huh? I don't follow—what do you mean?"

The alchemist mused aloud. "I think rather a *memory-block* and an *obedience* spell would work admirably for such a purpose. Well done, apprentice; it shall be so. I will prepare the necessary spells. But first, let us return to the scrying chamber; we must arrange to keep a watch for any more *visitors.*"

THE CRYSTAL ORB IN the scrying chamber did not display good news. Two groups of armed men were depicted within, milling about, bearing torches and searching the nearby countryside. The two companies of soldiers, wearing distinctly different uniforms, stayed generally to either side of the scene and eyed each other warily as the first hint of the imminent dawn lightened the eastern horizon.

A few men, evidently officers, endeavored to keep the two groups apart. It was obvious that confusion reigned. Apparently, none of these new arrivals expected to be here, in *this* place.

As Daegon and George watched, more soldiers and supplies arrived at opposite sides of the open field—seemingly from out of nowhere. A few more ornately dressed individuals appeared and were immediately given blatant deference—mages, no doubt.

The adepts spied one another and went forward to meet in the center of the field as the first rays of the morning sun teased the treetops. After a few minutes of hurried conversation, punctuated by graphic hand waving, the mages stormed away, shaking their gem-encrusted staffs in irritation as their elaborate robes snagged on thistles and dragged in the dust on the way back to their respective troops.

But one adept lingered for a long moment, his eyes upward, searching the lightening sky.

Daegon smiled, rubbed his hands together, and announced, "Well, now we know what likely happened to the two hooded travelers. There are *two* portals; one from Were, and unless I miss my guess, one from Shadow. But I am surprised that these troops are not skirmishing, as tends to be their wont."

Stroking his chin with one hand, he pointed into the orb with the other. "But no matter, I can see the mage whom I believe to be *Zerban.* I think he should experience our *special hospitality*."

GUNTHER WAS COMING to dislike this wild realm of Storm Haven rather intensely. His foray with the raiding party had been an utter failure. Blundering through the forest for most of the night, they had found only a few dwellings obviously recently abandoned. They engaged in no fights and had taken no prisoners. And worse, upon their return they found their own camp had been attacked.

"Lord Gunther," hailed the military aide, poking his head into the hastily erected tent.

Gunther glanced up, acknowledging the unwelcome interruption, and waited.

The aide entered, bobbed his head nervously, and stammered, "Um, m'lord, uh, an emissary of the Were is here, uh, to see Lord Tepesh . . . But now, m'lord, we, uh, assume you command."

Command? Ye gods! What now?

Gunther did not care for any distractions whenever he prepared for his daylight repose; avoiding the sun was an adjustment he found most inconvenient in his *new life*. The dawn was only a handful of minutes away, and he was already preoccupied with the chaos and shambles of the damaged camp. He had no real idea what had happened here, only that the leadership, all the vampire nobles, had been slain—leaving him to deal with this. And worst of all his beloved, the Lady Sabrina, was missing!

And now, the Were show up—how *convenient*. Suddenly suspicious, he wondered why they were here. *Could they have been responsible?*

"Who is it?" the vampire lord asked irritably.

"Um, m'lord, a woman—she did not give her name. But she is accompanied by a personal guard of *mercenary trolls!*"

The aide was clearly in awe of the intelligent trolls, as were many of the Shadow troops who had heard of them, but few had actually seen them until now.

"Harrumph," coughed Gunther dismissively. He knew very well who this *emissary* most likely was—and he did not need more complications. "Very well, I shall see her in the chamber below, *alone*. Her guards can wait outside. So inform her."

"At once, m'lord," the aide replied bowing, and then hastily slipped from the tent.

Gunther took a small oil lamp and trooped down the earthen steps to the underground chamber. The solitary flame and its wisp of cloying earthy fragrance could not mask the scent of stale blood and burnt wood that lingered despite the removal of the dead and debris.

He sensed her before he heard her. Turning, he barely saw her in the dimness.

She slinked silently closer and Gunther could see that she was attired in a formfitting garment of mottled greys and ebony, a matte black belt slung low across her hips. Her long jet hair, braided in a single thick plait, hung across one shoulder and reflected the lonely flickering flame like a live predatory thing.

Facing her, he simply said, "What is it?"

Her smile feral, Ling tilted her head. "Well, greetings to you too, Gunther. What happened here?"

Still not trusting her, he replied, "You do not know?"

"Let us not play games with each other," she cautioned ominously. "I know *nothing* of this! I was on my way here when I saw a sudden flash of light and briefly heard a distant rumbling noise."

Pausing, she tilted her head. "Oh, I see—you were not here, were you? Do you even *know* what happened here?"

He considered her warily. He had only met Ling hours ago, soon after the groups had first arrived in this wild realm. The assigned commanders of the Were and Shadow forces had been presented and introduced by Lady Leanan of the Sidhe and Lord Addecus of the Were.

He felt the innate distrust and animosity toward Ling and her kind that all denizens of Shadow bore toward the Were. Ironically, that the feeling was likely mutual barely registered with him as consequential.

Nonetheless, he had too little information, no idea what had transpired here, and was most distressed that his mistress was nowhere to be found. He realized that he had little choice but to trust this *she-Were* to some degree.

Fixing his lone eye upon her balefully, he sighed. "No, I do not. I was returning from a raid when I, too, saw the great light. I found the other vampire lords slain and the Lady Sabrina missing. Many of the troops and the prisoners were injured or senseless."

Leaning into her, his jutting jaw betraying his suspicion and distrust, he asked pointedly, "But tell me, Ling, you said you were coming *here*—why?"

Without pretense, a mask of sincere concern etched upon her face, she replied, "Because our *portal* has disappeared! I suspect we—I and my troops, that is—may be trapped here. I came to discuss this with Lord Vlad Tepesh, and perhaps come to some sort of arrangement. But that is now moot, for aside from his death, *your* portal has disappeared as well."

"What?" exclaimed Gunther in shock. The portal *gone?* How could he have not noticed? When did this happen?

He spun and started for the steps, but she gripped his arm to stop him—no small feat, but her strength was prodigious. He slowed to a halt.

"Spare yourself the effort; besides, the sun is rising," she cautioned, releasing him. "Trust me, both portals are gone, and none among my staff have the ability to transit from this realm. Not even *I* can transit—something prevents it. What about you? Can you, or any of your people, transit?"

"*Without the portal?* Uh, no, I cannot; my skill level is not yet . . . No, there is no one left who can do so," he admitted. "How could the portals be gone?"

She shrugged. "I do not know."

"But what does this mean?" he whined, not completely sure he believed her.

"It means," she said crossly, as one might to an obdurate child, "that we will receive no more troops, no more supplies. We—both of us *and* our troops—are trapped here in Storm Haven, cut off from our realms!"

He was at a loss for words.

Not so was she; after a moment's thought, she waved a finger in his face.

"Listen to me, Gunther. Clearly you are now in command of this Shadow force and you must control them with a firm hand.

"As for the portals being gone, the troops should *not* learn of this; we must remain in charge of our commands. Given the opportunity, elements of our two forces would gladly shed each other's blood, as I suspect you well know. That cannot be permitted to happen. We must maintain an iron hold upon our troops, keep them focused on our respective missions—and apart. Our survival may depend upon it. I have just over six hundred; how many do you now command?"

In all honesty, he had not thought of himself as *in command*. And yet he was the only vampire lord to have survived whatever had happened here. Thus, the troops would naturally look to him for leadership. The realization was sobering; he knew nothing of commanding troops.

Before his mistress, the Lady Sabrina, had granted him the Dark Gift, he had been little more than an accomplished woodsman and hunter. Even when taken into her service he had commanded nothing as a mere *familiar*.

Nonetheless, Ling awaited an answer.

"Uh, about the same number, I think," he murmured, not really knowing for certain, and still somewhat reluctant to divulge too much information.

Ling nodded and whispered conspiratorially. "We should act as if closing the portals was a deliberate strategy—known only to the commanders, of course."

Tracing his fingertip along the length of a scar on his cheek just below the eye patch, Gunther begrudgingly conceded. "That makes sense. But it does not explain the destruction here."

Ling only shrugged. "True enough. Until we know more, let us not try."

"Fine," he groused. "What shall we do now? Continue to carry out raids?"

Absently stroking the lower plait of her braid as one might a favored pet, she said, "Yes, I think so; it is what the troops would expect. I have less than a week's worth of supplies. I trust you have the same; that is wholly insufficient. Our future raids must secure us more. We must determine how to reestablish contact with our realms somehow, and quickly!"

He grunted in agreement, easily seeing the wisdom in that, but her next question was unexpected.

"Gunther, when you returned here, to your camp, was there anything else unusual, aside from the destruction?"

"Only that I found two women here from the Realm of Man," he answered too casually. "Lady Ellen and Lady Stacy; they were unharmed."

"What?" shrieked Ling in disbelief. "The Steward is *here?* And the *portals* are gone? This cannot be a coincidence! Where is she—no, where are *both* of them—right now?"

"They are prisoners, and are held with the others," replied Gunther, surprised at Ling's reaction. "They were tending to the wounded. I have not yet decided their fate."

"Gunther, listen to me! We must separate them immediately! Lady Ellen can transit anywhere—she *is* the Steward. The Lady Stacy is her closest friend. I know—I had her in my hands briefly. But that is not important right now. I will take custody of one and you keep the other; that will keep Lady Ellen from leaving this realm. I am not yet certain how to work this to our advantage, but I will find a way!"

Clearly confused, Gunther mumbled, "I do not understand."

"Think!" she spat, all semblance of patience absent. "The Steward surely had something to do with the loss of our portals! She *created* them, albeit at the behest of Queen Mab; so, it is likely that she *closed* them. We have to compel her to reopen them—and I think I know how."

"Indeed? How would you do so?"

"Let me worry about that," she assured him. "I will assume custody of the Lady Ellen. It would be best for you to keep the Lady Stacy under close guard. Remember, we *must* keep them apart."

"You have overlooked something, Ling; I have not yet found the Lady Sabrina. Both women denied knowing anything about her or the destruction of this camp. However, the late hour curtailed further questioning. I do not believe them, of course. But, consider this; *if* they speak the truth, and they are *not* responsible, then someone else *is.* And if she lives, the Lady Sabrina may be in their hands. I would use these women as bargaining chips to find the Lady Sabrina."

Ling looked at the vampire lord with a modicum of newfound respect. "Gunther, I think *that* may well be an *excellent* idea. There is more to you than I expected."

Despite his sullen expression and darkening mood, she placed her palm along one side of his face and purred, "There now, do not brood. I will make the necessary arrangements. You need to pass the day here. In the meantime, since I and my kind are not constrained by the day, I will make inquiries in an effort to locate your Lady Sabrina. Rest now. We will speak again after the sunset. Perhaps then you will share with me how you came to wear that patch. I find it quite sensual."

Ling bestowed a Cheshire smile upon him that seemed to linger on his senses.

A moment later Gunther realized he was alone once more. He slowly collapsed on the sleeping pallet and knew only velvet darkness.

MARK RETURNED TO DELAFAIRE Farm at daybreak.

Red clouds rolling in from the southwest painted the low horizon in ominous promise, prompting the memory of an old nautical adage to float to the surface of his mind.

Red sky at morning; sailors take warning.

A storm was coming; he could almost feel it in his bones.

He found Millie already in the kitchen, anxiously puttering about, and Miska seated at the table, his large hands wrapped around a steaming mug of coffee. The dour expression of worry on the big man's face and Millie's nervous energy as they regarded Mark without speaking, immediately conveyed that all was not well.

"What is it? What's wrong?" Mark asked with growing concern.

"The girls," gasped Millie. "They didn't come home last night. Ellen told me they were going to make a 'quick trip' to Storm Haven to talk to Gallenius about something, and they wouldn't be gone long. But they didn't come home! I know something's wrong!"

"How long have they been gone?"

Millie winced. "I don't know for sure, maybe since around midnight. I went to bed, and I didn't realize until this morning that they hadn't returned. Miska arrived while I was brewing coffee and I went upstairs to see if they might be awake and want some. That's when I . . . Oh, Mark, their beds haven't even been slept in!"

"That's okay," Mark said soothingly, as he put an arm around his aunt's shoulders. "I'm sure they're all right; they can take care of themselves. They probably just lost track of time."

Glancing over at Miska, Mark could see that the big man wasn't buying it; truthfully, neither was he.

"Mark," rumbled Miska, "perhaps we should look for them. And I think it may be wise to contact Hawk, do you not?"

"Yeah, good idea. Maybe they came back, and he knows if they're around somewhere," Mark offered unconvincingly, but fished in his pocket for his cell phone nonetheless.

He caught Hawk at home, preparing to go to work, and quickly brought him up to speed, while Miska calmly assured Millie that they would do everything possible to find Ellen and Stacy and bring them safely home.

Millie's brow furrowed in concern and subtle impatience.

Ending his call, Mark announced, "Hawk will be here as soon as he can. He said he had to go by his office and pick up some gear we might find helpful. Don't ask—he didn't elaborate."

Millie stood before Mark, hands on her hips.

"And just how are you going to search for them? Can you transit like Ellen can? We both know they didn't 'come back' and they're not 'around somewhere'! They went to Storm Haven. So, please tell me just what you have in mind—and don't you dare patronize me, young man! Be honest."

Taken aback, Mark babbled, "Uh, of course. Well, actually I *can* transit, a bit, I mean in my capacity as a Council member—"

"If I may?" interrupted Miska. "It is true he can transit among the Council realms, but he will need to use the Grand Portal to access Storm Haven."

"Exactly," Mark gratefully agreed. *Assuming such a transit globe already exists.*

"We'll use the Grand Portal, go to Storm Haven, and find them. We'll go as soon as Hawk gets here. In the meantime, I need to wash up and change clothes. And I have to admit that I'm a bit hungry."

"Me, too," echoed Miska, "Can I help prepare something—some breakfast perhaps? I do not know when we will have the opportunity to eat again."

MILLIE SMILED AND SHOOK her head; their distraction tactic was almost sweet. They didn't want her to worry, and preparing breakfast would keep her busy for a while. She knew herself all too well—she'd fret anyway. But she didn't want them to worry about her while they were looking for Ellen and Stacy; so, she would let them think they'd succeeded in calming her apprehensions.

Sighing, she kept the rest of her thoughts to herself.

Men, they're so easily manipulated—especially if they think they're being clever.

"All right, breakfast it is," she declared. "Miska, you can set the table while Mark gets cleaned up. I'll do the cooking. How does this sound; pancakes with maple syrup, country sausage, and grits? Doesn't really matter—that's what I'm cooking. I've got some sourdough rolls and some gravy I can reheat, too. Okay, stop drooling and get moving!"

Midway through breakfast, Millie was encouraged to see Hawk arrive with Trey in tow. She served them warmed up pancakes and sausage. They made short work of the hot meal as Mark explained the plan to use the Grand Portal.

Eager to set out, they declined more coffee. Instead, Millie produced a pair of tall thermoses, filled with the hot brew. "Take these, for the road."

Leading the group outside, Hawk pointed to an unmarked SUV. "I thought we might as well drive to the cabin. I know the utility company and the phone company managed to get their trucks there and back when they put their lines in."

"Yeah, they did," Mark confirmed. "The passage of their trucks effectively widened the broad path that was actually an old fire road."

"Right, so we drew a special unit from the Sheriff's Department motor pool," Hawk explained.

The dark grey vehicle with heavily tinted windows looked slightly sinister under the leaden sky.

Trey laid a hand on the vehicle's fender. "We convinced our captain that this is arguably a *missing persons* case with a potential for *search and rescue*, so we arranged to borrow one of the Special Response Team vehicles. He was prepared to assign more men, but I assured him that Hawk and I would be sufficient for now. Truth is I don't know how we would've explained exactly where we might be going. Let's hope this rig is enough."

"Yeah, it should be," Hawk said confidently. "It has a lot of stowed gear that we might need; a set of six handheld radios, high-intensity lights, night-vision gear, ropes and rappelling equipment, shotguns and sub-guns, and some nonlethal tools like tasers, tear gas, and pepper spray. We threw some extra ballistic vests in there, too—you never know. Plus, this rig is four-wheel drive—and it looks like we're going to get some weather. Okay, any questions?"

There were none. Even Millie was impressed; she liked the fact that Hawk tried to be well prepared.

Miska just stared at the SUV with a huge grin splitting his broad face from ear to ear.

Mark nudged him and teased, "I'll bet it's pretty fast, too!"

"Let's go," Hawk said climbing behind the wheel, as the rest of the men piled in.

"Be careful!" called Millie.

"We will!" assured Mark. "We'll call as soon as we get back!"

DRIVING DOWN THE OLD fire road, the conversation inside the SUV was not as optimistic as it had been at breakfast.

"What do you mean we have to find the *right globe*? I don't understand," asked Trey, twisting in his seat to face Miska.

Miska held his hands open in unconscious gesticulation as he tried to explain.

"A Grand Portal holds many, many transit globes. I do not know how to find the one we seek without looking into each one, and recognizing what is seen. I have never been to Storm Haven, so I do not know what to look for—"

"Well, I have been to Storm Haven," interrupted Mark. "But, from what I remember, it looks pretty much like every other rural place I've seen—I mean, like mostly fields and forests. It was dark; we arrived with Ellen near a windmill, I think. So, I don't know how we'll be able to tell for certain."

"Maybe they left a clue?" offered Trey.

"Well, we'll know soon enough," said Hawk. "We're here."

All at once the men fell silent as the SUV eased around the standing stones and came to a stop in front of the cabin.

"Is that—" began Mark, rolling down his window.

"Smokey!" declared Miska.

The cat sat on the cabin's front porch, his tail twitching impatiently, staring intently at the strange vehicle.

"It sure looks like Smokey," Hawk observed through his open window.

"It is he," assured Miska, his eyes glazing over and his voice taking on an ethereal monotone quality. "He has been waiting for us. He will lead us. We must trust him."

"Well, ok-a-y," uttered Hawk. "Fine, but first let's select our gear, and then we'll follow our furry friend. Is that okay with you, Smokey?"

To Hawk's surprise, Smokey looked him in the eye, cocked his head and closed his eyes.

Hawk wasn't sure if he *heard* it or *thought* it, but somewhere in his mind he sensed a response.

Very well, but hurry!

Moments later, the four men, heavily laden with equipment, followed the trotting cat into the barely perceptible shimmering globe that had materialized within the standing stones, and disappeared.

CH 6

ZERBAN WAS IN A FOUL mood. He should not have had to come here, wherever *here* was. But that was now moot; he *had* to recover his bats.

He was getting too old for this sort of foolish fieldwork. He never should have left an acolyte in charge of his bats. However, summoned to an unexpected meeting of Were commanders and mages, he had consequently been left with little choice. Thus, the crisis occurred in his absence; yet, he was still held accountable.

He did not want to go through the portal. He was quite content to stay in Were and assist in guarding the entrance against sorcerous interference as Lord Addecus had asked of him. Indeed, had not the former regent asked for his help in the first place, Zerban would have continued to enjoy his semi-retirement as titular headmaster of the Were School of Mages—but no, such was not to be.

In order to find his bats, he and two senior acolytes were compelled to make preparations to venture through the portal to this so-called realm of Storm Haven. As a last-minute addition to the mass of troops and supplies, he knew his contingent's presence would be resented, and any subsequent delay in transit would engender grumbling in the ranks. However, none of the troops would dare voice a complaint, not about a mage of his stature.

Although he was loath to admit it, he knew that much of his esteemed status and standing had to do with his apparent mastery of the giant flying carnivores. He would have them back—he *must,* at any cost.

Soon after their arrival in this wild realm, it became evident to Zerban and the Were troops that something was very wrong. The location was not as they had been told; this was *not* Storm Haven.

There were a number of equally confused troops from Shadow nearby, deposited in this unknown realm by their own portal as well. Thus, a few insults and incidents of belligerent posturing were inevitable. A few minor confrontations flared that almost led to blows; but the quick thinking and stern discipline of strong-willed squad sergeants kept the situation from deteriorating into internecine warfare.

For the moment, chaos was held at bay.

Mages from the two realms met in the vacant space between the two forces. Generally opposed to cooperation, they agreed to temporarily set aside their respective differences in order to try to determine what had gone wrong.

Zerban thought they would be lucky just to keep the two distrustful and anxious armies apart, much less accomplish anything constructive with the portals in the short term. However, he kept his own counsel and remained silent; in truth, he was preoccupied with finding his *pets*.

After the meeting of mages, he sought out the ranking Were officer, Lord Novus, a minor noble of the Lupine Clan, who had taken charge of the Were contingent when they realized they were *not* in Storm Haven. Finding him seated amongst the supplies taking a rough inventory, Zerban briefly explained his problem; he needed to search for the bats, and he would require an escort.

Lord Novus was less than impressed, and disinclined to be of any assistance.

"Magus, that is not my problem. Leave me—I have real work to do."

"I see, very well, Lord Novus." Zerban sniffed haughtily, drew himself rigidly to his full imposing height, and looked down his nose at the seated noble. "I shall inform Lord Addecus of your refusal—"

"What? Lord Addecus?" Novus sputtered. "Why didn't you say so? Of course, of course, I can spare, uh, two infantrymen as escort, but only for twenty-four hours—no more."

Rather than press the issue, Zerban scowled and stormed off to collect his acolytes.

The assigned escort met the mage and his acolytes under a greying sky. The search party left the hastily erected Were base camp, staying just ahead of more leaden clouds rolling in from the horizon. Impatience fueling his resolve, Zerban insisted upon a brisk pace. Alone with his thoughts, his disposition did not improve.

The two acolytes, Stellara and Piers, recognized their master's mood and followed in relative silence for the next few miles.

HOURS INTO THE SEARCH, Zerban cast a glance over his shoulder and spied Stellara whispering flirtatiously with the young soldier assigned to escort duty.

Tired and frustrated, he cursed the girl under his breath.

Damn that wench! She shirked her responsibilities again, and then blamed Clement for the bats' disappearance. Of course, that the lad is also missing, seems of no consequence to the little tart. She obviously only looks to her own amusements. Indeed, she shamelessly entices this blushing young infantryman—right under my very nose!

"Stellara, attend me—now!" demanded the disgruntled mage with an imperious *snap* of his fingers.

"Coming, master," the girl answered, hiking her skirts and quickly stepping forward to match her teacher's pace. "Yes, master?"

For a moment Zerban said nothing, only shifting his elaborately carved wizard's staff to his other hand while maintaining his long strides. Looking askance at her, he noted that she matched his speed with ease, despite her shorter stature. He then noticed that the pack she bore on her back was less full than when they had started out from the Were base camp.

Ignoring her question and shunting his ire aside, Zerban called out to the senior infantryman leading the way several yards ahead.

"Corporal Casius, we need to stop for a moment, five minutes."

"As you wish, m'lord," replied the grizzled veteran. "Five minutes. I will scout ahead. Ansel, stay with the mage and his party."

"Aye, Corporal," answered the young man, casting furtive glances at Stellara, who managed a coy smile in return.

"Stellara, show me the contents of your pack," Zerban instructed resignedly.

Caught off guard, her eyes widened in surprise. She slipped the knapsack's straps from her shoulders and plopped the pack on the ground. Flipping open the flap, she displayed the contents for her teacher.

"That is less than half of the items I told you to bring," he observed. "Where are—"

"Oh, I brought everything, master," she interjected. "It was, um, just that it made the pack so heavy, that um, Piers, uh, he *volunteered* to carry some of the heavier items. So, you see, we have everything."

Zerban saw the other fifth-year acolyte sitting sprawled on the stony ground, his back leaning against a nearly bursting rucksack. A goat, tethered by a rope to the boy's wrist, grazed on short bristles and weedy tufts of grass.

Piers appeared to be exhausted, even though they had only been on this trek for a few hours. Upon hearing Stellara speak his name, his weary head snapped up like that of a forlorn puppy starved for affection, eager for her notice.

Sighing, Zerban crooked a finger at the lad. "Piers, please join us, and bring your pack."

Under his watchful eye, Zerban ordered the rucksack's contents redistributed between the two acolytes. In truth, there was a considerable amount; but it was essential for him to have all of the potion ingredients readily available—especially, if when found, the bats had been hunting and feeding on the wrong prey.

Zerban had many secrets; but, his mastery of the giant bats was among the most closely kept. To many in Were, the bats appeared loyal to him as a mighty mage; however, the truth was something slightly different.

Their apparent loyalty was actually the result of a combination of sorcery and addiction to a concoction of Zerban's own design. An organic mixture, primarily herbal, once blended had an intoxicating aroma and induced mild hunger sensations. Routinely fed to livestock destined to be consumed by the bats, it was an effective way to induce a mild euphoric state in the flying carnivores, making them more manageable. More importantly, this led to the bats' inevitable addiction and subsequent dependence upon Zerban.

Thus rendered into a highly suggestible state, the bats were ripe for whatever spells Zerban might employ to insure their obedience and tractability. But there was a downside; the effectiveness of the concoction was time sensitive. It had to be administered immediately after preparation to the doomed livestock, and the *food* subsequently consumed by the bats within a few hours. Even the wild hunts the bats were allowed were actually carefully managed events, the prey suitably prepared and released beforehand.

Zerban had been curious about the effects of his concoction on human beings—and even more curious what effect it might have upon the Were nobility. But this was perilous speculation indeed—perhaps even *treasonous.* No fool, he had thus far resisted the temptation to even consider further experimentation.

The worst aspect of the current situation, the one that really concerned Zerban at the moment, was that withdrawal from this addiction would be quite unpleasant. Escalating irritability, heightened aggression, and frequent eruptions of bloodthirsty rage were ultimately inevitable.

If the bats had hunted, killed, and consumed any prey that had not been fed the specially prepared concoction, Zerban could have a major problem—hence, the need of the goat and supply of specific herbs and potions.

Zerban was distracted from his musings by the return of Corporal Casius.

"M'lord, beyond this hill lay a wooded ravine and a freshwater stream that flows within. I followed it to its source, a short but difficult trek to the mouth of a narrow cave at the base of a rocky escarpment. You told us to watch for such a place, since the bats would seek such shelter during the day."

"Indeed, I did, Corporal," responded Zerban. "And you have done very well. Lead on."

"This way, m'lord. We should hurry," the corporal cautioned, looking skyward. "The clouds appear angry. I think a storm will be upon us very soon."

"Quite so," agreed the mage, "perhaps we could partake of the cave's shelter as well. Stellara, Piers, on your feet! Follow the corporal—quickly now!"

THEY MADE THEIR WAY over the crest and down the hillside with relative ease; but the thick underbrush of the choked ravine slowed their progress. Undeterred, the corporal simply stepped into the chilling stream and sloshed along in the ankle-deep water.

Everyone followed suit, swishing their way upstream, except for Stellara, who balked and just stood on the bank, frowning.

Ansel, the young infantryman, glanced back, noted her apparent reluctance, and splashed back to stand before her. A mischievous glint in his eye, he grinned and bowed.

"Ah, m'lady, might I be of some service? Perhaps you would allow me to carry you?"

A coy smile stole across her lips as her eyebrows arched seductively in response to his thinly veiled flirtatious offer.

"Stellara!" boomed the voice of the impatient mage. "Get moving—now!"

Anger flared as she pushed past the smugly smiling soldier. An ugly scowl distorted her face in a fleeting moment of resentment, and quickly disappeared—but not quite quickly enough.

Ansel had seen—that was sufficient for him to reconsider his intentions. He did not care to get involved with someone who harbored such pettiness. On the other hand, he did not really plan on any sort of long-term relationship. His current interest was in a somewhat briefer liaison.

His thoughts wandered as he mindlessly watched the play of her hips as she trod the uneven streambed before him, her lower skirts growing heavier as the wetness rose within the fabric and clung to the shape of her legs.

She stopped so suddenly, that he almost bumped into her.

"Look! Tis Clement!" she exclaimed, pointing.

A stone's throw before them, a lone figure stood in the mouth of a cave, and without word or gesture, turned and disappeared into the dark maw of the fissured rock face.

Zerban called out as he hastily splashed forward, making for the entrance. "Clement! Wait, lad! Have you found the bats? Where are you going? Wait!"

Corporal Casius was the first to reach the cave. But he did not enter; he waited for the entire party to assemble, dripping at the rocky threshold.

"Your indulgence, m'lord. You said that these bats of yours should sleep during the day. We need to know, is it safe to proceed? What would wake them?" Casius' hand unconsciously gripped the long haft of the double-bladed battle-ax strapped across his back.

Ansel immediately caught the meaning and intention of the corporal's questions. His own knuckles went white gripping the shaft of his short spear.

Zerban cleared his throat and answered succinctly. "The bats sleep quite soundly during daylight; but any loud noise might disturb them. It would be best to be as quiet as possible. It is very likely that they are here, for Clement has surely found them."

"That was who we saw, Clement, your missing acolyte?" Casius probed.

"Quite so," assured the mage, stepping into the cave. "We all saw him enter this cave. We must follow! I am certain he can lead us to the bats."

Zerban mumbled a brief incantation and brought the heel of his staff down sharply upon the rocks at his feet. A dull blue light pulsed in the air a hands-breadth above the head of his staff and grew in intensity until it was as bright as any torch.

Casius nodded in acknowledgment. "Very impressive, m'lord. However, if you do not mind, Ansel and I will prepare torches. I mean no offense, but should we get separated, we would need our own light as well."

"No offense was taken, Corporal. But please, be quick about it."

Turning to the acolytes, Zerban pointed. "Piers, tie the goat to that small tree near that overhang and leave it for now. I do not want the animal brought into the cave—not yet."

Ansel stole a lingering gaze at Stellara as she bent over to set her pack down.

Such inattention did not go unnoticed. The corporal swatted him with an open hand across the back of his head.

Ansel grinned at his superior and set to making torches.

JUST AS THE INFANTRYMEN finished the torches, a rumbling arpeggio announced the imminent arrival of the storm. Huge drops of rain began to plop like small wet eggs on the nearby rocks, staining the dusty granite with muddy splotches and splatters.

The moment they were all safely inside the cave, the storm released its full fury. Sheets of driving rain obliterated the view of the ravine. Stark flashes of cloud-enshrouded lightning illuminated the cascade in surreal cadence to bouts of bombastic thunder, a staccato clash of elementals vying for spontaneous moments of awesome dominance.

The group moved deeper within the protection of the cave, away from the chaotic weather at the entrance. The cautious corporal took the lead, his torch held high. As they probed further into the craggy depths of the rocky passage, deep shadows flowed as if alive. The precariously uneven floor, strewn with stone chips and rock dust, bore them inexorably downward. The stagnant air took on a definitive chill.

The erratic tunnel eventually opened into a small cavern studded with tall stalagmites. Its ceiling of corresponding stalactites was so far removed that no light from the torches could penetrate the murky gloom above. Even Zerban's bright azure wizard's light could no better augment the flickering flames.

"Where *is* he? Clement?" complained Stellara, a note of uneasy apprehension nervously threading through her voice.

"Quiet!" Zerban hissed. "Keep moving—quickly now!"

Casius tried to lead the distended group briskly through the maze of stalagmites, doing his best to maintain a straight course to the other side of the chamber. But moving in a straight line was virtually impossible; and soon enough, even he was disoriented.

He turned to ask the mage a question; but no one was there!

He spun about in confusion and suddenly found a hideous grinning face—with far too many teeth—inches from his own. A crushing blow to the back of his neck delivered him into darkness.

THE OTHERS, SEPARATED and disoriented, lagged so far behind that even dim echoes of the assault upon the unfortunate corporal were lost to their ears.

Nonetheless, the nerves in Piers' neck and shoulders were quivering like ants on a griddle; he *hated* being underground, or in *any* confined space for that matter. The very thought of untold tons of earth and rock above his head was almost enough to send him screaming in search of the cave entrance, *if* he could have found it.

Thoroughly confused, he knew he was essentially lost. Worse, he had very poor night vision; without the wizard's light offered by Zerban's staff he was at a serious disadvantage. He did his best to stay close to the mage. But in doing so, he somehow lost contact with Stellara; he thought she had been somewhere just behind him.

Struggling to fend off his inherent claustrophobia and rising panic, Piers did not notice in the gloom that Zerban had stopped walking; he gracelessly blundered right into the mage.

Staggered, Zerban turned to face Piers and shoved his staff toward the acolyte. The blue glow illuminated the shaken boy; his wide eyes blinking in the azure glare as he shuffled back a pace, nearly losing his balance.

"M-master . . . I am s-sorry . . . I—"

"Quiet! Stop stammering!" Looking past the boy, he added, "Where is Stellara, and the soldier?"

"Uh . . . they were right b-behind me," the boy quaked, anxiously turning his head. "I c-can not s-see the t-torchlight."

"Confound that girl! Stay right here!" Zerban fumed as he stormed back the way they had come.

"B-but, m-master, p-please, don't—"

His protest echoed in the empty darkness. He was alone—*or was he?*

The hairs on the back of his neck were standing straight up. He could see nothing in the pitch-dark void. He squeezed his eyes shut as fiercely as he could, until small bursts of multicolor lights splashed in tiny sparks at the corners of his vision.

He dared not move; the master had ordered him to *stay right here.*

He never heard them. His only warning was a foul scent in the dead air, a stale, sour, musky odor.

He knew a moment of sheer panic when gnarly clawed hands suddenly seized him, a long raspy tongue licked across his throat and cheek, and a thudding blow to his head rendered him senseless.

ZERBAN ROUNDED A THICK stalagmite and saw the low glow of a flickering torch reflected against an outcropping of basalt. He made directly for the source of the light. As he drew nearer, he heard grunting and shuffling. Then an unmistakable clash of steel was followed by a wet slicing sound, and a plaintive gurgling gasp that could have come from no human throat.

The guttering torch lay on the floor of the chamber as exaggerated shadows leapt across the rock walls in a deadly ballet. With the additional glow of his wizard's light, Zerban could see Ansel grappling in mortal combat with two hideous creatures wielding short wide-bladed swords at the end of long gangly arms. The infantryman's sword lay shattered at his feet, and his spear had broken in two. He flailed about deftly with the two half-shafts in slashing figure eights, effectively keeping his assailants momentarily at bay.

He must have given a good account of himself, for the bodies of two similar creatures lay motionless on the stony floor, thick dark liquid oozing from their fatal wounds.

Something about these creatures tugged at Zerban's memory. *Of course—goblins!*

He had personally never seen one; but, like most mages, he was familiar with the general description found in ancient lore.

A muffled scream drew his immediate attention—*Stellara!*

Sensing movement to his left, Zerban thrust the tip of his staff into a deep shadow. The azure glow revealed the comely acolyte in the grip of two more goblins. One pinned her arms to her sides in an awkward bear hug while the other clamped a scraggly hand across her mouth, and reached over her head to squeeze her nose shut.

At the sight of her master, Stellara rallied and viciously bit down on the hand across her mouth. The goblin jerked his wounded hand away, further tearing his flesh. In the throes of pain he stumbled awkwardly into the other creature trying to hold her arms, whose grip slipped.

Suddenly breaking free and shoving the momentarily surprised goblins away from her, Stellara staggered forward. She bent over, gagging, gasping for breath, and trying to spit out traces of her captor's vile blood.

The uninjured goblin reached once again for Stellara; but Zerban pointed a stiff finger at the creature and harshly muttered an arcane word of power. A bright spark leapt forth from his fingertip and slammed the stunned creature into a jagged crystalline outcrop. Sharp bloody points of quartz blossomed from the dead goblin's chest as he hung on the face of the rock like a limp trophy.

Another spark from the angry mage struck the goblin with the wounded hand senseless, slamming him into the backs of the two attacking Ansel.

As all three creatures became entangled and lost their footing, Ansel leapt among them in a final desperate rally. Flailing furiously with broken shaft and twisted spear point despite his flagging energy reserves, he managed to dispatch each in his berserker rage.

Splattered with gore, and bleeding from a multitude of wounds, Ansel staggered, his chest heaving, to a towering stalagmite. His weapons slipped from his grasp, as he slid down the jagged cone and collapsed in a semiconscious heap.

Stellara, softly sobbing into her hands, dropped to her knees and squinted through her tears at the pulsing shadows of the downed combatants.

Zerban went to her side and pulled her to her feet. Holding his glowing staff tip close to her face he saw the extent of her injuries; a set of claw marks now marred her cheek and another set had gouged her forehead. The wounds were bleeding freely, but were not life-threatening.

He knew that she would live; but, her beauty—well, she would live.

He turned his attention to Ansel. The young soldier was cut in a dozen places; and, he was exhausted. To Zerban's quick examination, the young man's injuries were many, but none were fatal.

Wedging Ansel's guttering torch into a fissure, Zerban rifled through the soldier's pack for the infantryman's aid kit, and set to cleaning their wounds.

Within minutes, Stellara's face and head were wrapped in what was left of her underskirt; only her eyes, puffy and red, were visible. Her sobbing was now reduced to small whimpers; her tears were spent, her spirit despondent.

Mercifully, Ansel was barely conscious, as Zerban tended to him. The lad soon sported wraps on both arms, his left shoulder, and across his rib cage. He had lost a good deal of blood, but would likely survive.

Zerban was so focused that he completely forgot about Piers. It was only when he remembered that he had left the acolyte alone in the dark that he looked up—and paled.

A score or more of armed goblins stood there in silence—completely surrounding the mage and his wounded comrades.

As he slowly stood up to face the horde, Zerban's thoughts were surprisingly calm; yet only one resonated with distinct clarity.

I am really getting too old for this.

"You are Zerban, are you not?" asked a clear voice from somewhere in the darkness beyond the disturbingly luminescent eyes of the leering goblins.

Puzzled, the mage hesitated to answer.

Someone knows who I am? How is that possible? I do not even know where I am. Perhaps all is not yet lost—stall for time, gather strength.

"I am so known," he offered cautiously. "And who are you?"

"Who I am is of no consequence for the moment," the voice replied casually with a trace of condescension. "Suffice to say that I am he who now holds your life, and those of your friends, in his hands."

Zerban remained silent; his thoughts on Piers and Corporal Casius.

As if his very thoughts were being read, the voice continued. "Oh yes, the other two, the soldier and the boy, are in my hands as well. I now ask for your surrender; comply and you and your companions will live. Deny me, and all your fates are sealed."

Zerban's blood stilled in his veins, not from fear, but righteous indignation. His anger smoldered in the pit of his being, building strength and gathering energy that he could feel coursing through his body and focusing within his will.

Surrender? You fool! You have no idea whom you have challenged.

"I am Zerban, Senior Mage of the Realm of Were, Headmaster of the School of Adepts. You *dare* to ask for my surrender?" he seethed, his ire barely constrained.

"Mind your temper, old man, lest you burst a blood vessel. My servants are not impressed, and would gnaw the flesh from your bones were I to permit it—mage or not!"

"Oh, really?" Zerban retorted nonchalantly, and then jabbed a finger at a line of startled goblins. A bright searing spark shot forth and instantly immolated half a dozen of the creatures, leaving only smoking piles of ash. Spinning to the other side, the mage jabbed his finger at another group of dumbfounded goblins and another great spark leapt forth—only to splatter and dissipate upon an unseen shield like water sizzling and steaming off a hot stove.

Zerban could only look on in shock.

"Oh, come now, Zerban. Did you think you were the only one with power?"

This time the voice had come from behind him. Zerban twisted and stabbed his finger in that direction—but the deadly spark arced forth striking another unseen barrier and bounced back.

Zerban ducked, but the bolt of power struck his staff, instantly numbing his hand as it tore the shaft from his grip. It clattered across the stony floor. The azure glow of the wizard light winked out, leaving only the illumination of the solitary torch wedged in the wall.

Wincing, Zerban grasped his useless hand, rubbing it until a stinging sensation began and slight flexing of his fingers was once again possible. He looked up as a man stepped forth from the shadows.

Of medium height and unremarkable features, the dark-robed man stroked his receding hairline with both hands and dropped his arms, shaking them loosely.

"Well Zerban, it seems you would rather do this the hard way." The man sighed, planting his feet.

Ignoring his throbbing hand, and mustering his righteous indignation once more, Zerban straightened to his full height. "Just who do you think—"

The man in the dark robe suddenly shoved both hands at the startled mage, sending a ball of roiling purple energy crackling across the short distance between them.

Zerban threw up his hands in an arcane defensive gesture; the vile purple energy slammed against his hastily erected shielding. The heavy blow staggered the old adept; but, he was far from defeated.

The tainted foulness of his adversary's sorcery came as a shocking surprise; this was dark magic, indeed. Mustering a retaliatory strike, Zerban added a hidden elemental twist, a potential counter to what might be expected.

DAEGON SENSED THE COMING attack and thrust his own shields up an instant before a blinding light and a massive blow of force rocked the cavern. Losing his balance, he dropped to one knee, but his shields had held—just barely.

He began to wonder if he had seriously underestimated this old wizard; the elder adept was far more skilled than he had anticipated. On the other hand, that skill would become *his*—*if* he could defeat this old man.

Regaining his feet, Daegon planned his next assault. He now knew that he would not hesitate to physically cripple his opponent. The next spell, one of the darkest he knew, would be devastating, but hopefully leave most of Zerban's mind intact. It was a calculated risk, of course, but he would take no further chances with this mage; this old man was far too dangerous.

With the long unused runes held firmly in his mind and the dark energy of this place flowing into his soul, Daegon faced Zerban and prepared to deliver the final stroke in their sorcerous duel.

He need only drop his shields and speak the forbidden words—but, he could not drop his shields!

A swirl of dust and stones rose up from the floor and twisted madly around him, melting into the very fabric of his defensive shields and solidifying into new rock.

Recognition came as an icy shock; he nearly panicked. This was a most powerful elemental spell of the earth, one he could not counter with his mind holding the ancient runes of long forbidden sorcery in check. He could not release the curse from within the cyclone of earthen elements—it would turn on him, mercilessly! He was doomed, hoist by his own petard.

Zerban's tired voice cut through Daegon's escalating anxiety and encroaching terror.

"This is how we would deal with the vile likes of you in the Realm of Were!"

Daegon gasped for breath, his fear a living thing pressing down upon him, choking the spark of life from the very depths of his being. His vision grew dim.

The muffled sound of a dull *thud* penetrated his panic. The swirling debris slowed, stopped in midair, and simply dropped with the muffled clatter of pebbles and earth. Then the waist-high wall of newly fused rock surrounding him began to crack and crumble, collapsing into dust clouds upon the stony floor.

He looked up to see George, shrugging his shoulders and flexing his hands in a two-fisted batter's grip on the wizard's staff, as he stood over the crumpled form of Zerban.

George scoffed. "Pfffft, this is how we'd deal with *you*, in the mean streets and back alleys of New Orleans!"

Banishing all runic traces of the unused dark spell from his mind and then dropping his now useless shields, Daegon straightened, tried to catch his breath, and hastily waved a hand at George.

"Hold! Do not kill him!"

"What? Why not? Oh, are *you* going to *whack* him, right here? Oh yeah, now I remember; you said you *needed* him."

"I do need him. He has . . . a vast wealth of knowledge. Uh, I will not kill him—not yet." Daegon panted, still not breathing easily. "I must modify the spell . . . not cripple him, but make him more tractable—at least for a time. Now, stand back."

George backed away, as Daegon cast an altered spell upon the unconscious and helpless Zerban. A dull wash of purple mist formed over the defeated mage and seemed to sink into his prone form.

Handing the wizard's staff to Clement, his dull-eyed new servant, George commanded, "Here, hold on to this for me; I'll keep it as a souvenir."

Clement, his bespelled mind fogged in confusion, listlessly accepted the staff, and stared expressionlessly at the young woman whose head was wrapped in makeshift bandages, as she sat silently sobbing into her hands, near the supine body of the wounded soldier.

Stepping to the woman's side, George grasped her arm and pulled her to her feet. She stood listlessly, her breath hitching in her chest, as he turned her about and ran his hands over her as one might probe livestock at auction. Satisfied that she was otherwise uninjured and apparently of sound body, he posed a question to Daegon.

"What about the rest of them?"

"What of them?" Daegon countered. "I only have need of Zerban. The rest can go to the goblins. The tribes deserve some recompense; after all, they have lost a handful or more of their own."

His declaration was met with ominous chittering and gleeful gibbering as the creatures streamed forth to seize the unconscious infantryman and reach for the girl.

George slapped their grotesque hands away. "Now, hold on," he demanded. "Not the girl; they can have the others. *I'll* take her—I can use another servant. Just do some of those *memory-block* and *obedience spells* on her, like you did before—you know, on the kid." He nodded toward Clement. "Okay?"

"Another servant?" leered Daegon. "Are you sure that is all you want her for?"

"What's it to you? Will you do it—or not?"

"Well, you *were* helpful with Zerban." He sighed, his ego reluctantly acknowledging the enormity of George's timely, albeit unconventional, rescue from Zerban's unexpectedly potent sorcery. He rubbed the back of his neck with one hand while pinching the bridge of his nose with the other.

Daegon was stalling; his thoughts were racing as he quickly assessed the situation.

Is there potential advantage for me in granting George's request? And what of the others, does any advantage lie there? Perhaps there is, on both counts. Time will tell; and, since I am by nature a patient individual, I can easily afford to appear magnanimous.

"Very well, my apprentice," a wry grin slipped across his face, "she is yours."

Turning to the massed goblins, Daegon gestured to the wounded soldier.

"Hear me, my loyal servants. The males, this one and the two you hold in the chamber below, are yours, for your amusement. But I will ask you to leave enough of the Were soldiers intact that they may be identified. I want them found—*by Shadow troops.* Leave whatever is left of the bodies near the Shadow camp."

The goblins began chittering in anticipation, but Daegon held up a hand to forestall them.

"Also, there is a goat tethered near the entrance to this cave; it is *not* to be harmed. Take the goat back to the Were camp and leave it nearby, so it will easily be found. Oh, and stain the tether with the boy's blood."

ARRIVAL IN STORM HAVEN was not quite what the would-be rescuers had expected. From the small but brightly lit stone room, devoid of furniture and fixture, they were told by an unseen voice to proceed through the sole doorway and disarm in the next chamber. They complied under the watchful eyes of a dozen silent black-clad guards.

As they placed their gear and weapons on the smooth stone floor, Trey motioned for Hawk's attention.

"Do I see some Remington 870 pumps?"

"Yeah, and at least two Benelli M-90s. These guys mean business. Look how they're standing—no crossfire issues."

"Hmm, yeah," acknowledged Trey, with a trace of professional admiration in his voice. "Designated fields of fire."

A grey-robed figure entered the room and dropped his hood upon his spare shoulders. Mark brightened and addressed his friends as he gestured to the bearded man.

"Guys, this is Mage Gallenius. It's good to see you again, Gallenius."

"Greetings, Lord Mark. Regrettably, your visit is unexpected, and would indeed be ill-advised were you not traveling with Smokey."

"Smokey? I'm sorry, but I don't understand. What do you mean?"

Folding his arms and tucking his weathered hands within the generous sleeves of his robe, the mage explained.

"There are certain wards in place that are designed to shunt unexpected arrivals to a rather unpleasant realm in the *wild*. That is why visitors must notify us of their intentions prior to transiting. You would do well to remember this. On the other hand, for some reason, Smokey is immune to our wards and may travel where he pleases; he is, of course, always welcome here. It is fortunate that you and your party included him in your travel plans."

"Uh, yes, indeed it is," agreed Mark, somewhat chagrined. "Forgive me, my manners are lacking. Gallenius, may I introduce—"

Holding up a hand, the mage interrupted, "Sergeant Trey Bassett, Detective Connor Redhawk, of the Realm of Man, and Miska of the Ursus Clan, of the Realm of Were. We know who you are. But what is the purpose of your visit? These are not the best of times."

"We're looking for, uh, the Ladies Ellen and Stacy," Mark stated. "They came here to speak with you and, I presume, the Guildmaster. They did not return home as planned. Are they here?"

Clearly, this news surprised Gallenius and he turned to one of the guards. "Ask the Guildmaster to join us. We will be in the adjacent conference room."

As the guard disappeared, the mage motioned to the new arrivals. "Please follow me. You may leave your equipment here; the guards will see that it is not disturbed."

They followed Gallenius into a large unadorned room, furnished with a long table of smoothed planks and rough-legged chairs of ax-hewn timber with padded canvas seats.

As they took seats, the Guildmaster entered and greeted his guests.

"Please forgive our spare and cautious welcome, but these are difficult times. As you probably know, we have been invaded." He sat wearily at the head of the table and opened his gloved palms. "Now, what is this about the Ladies Ellen and Stacy being missing?"

Mark explained, as his companions stared in fascination at the Guildmaster, or more specifically, at the shimmering lights within his hood that hid his identity.

Smokey, on the other hand, simply leapt upon the table, trotted over to the Guildmaster, and promptly curled up in his lap, where he got a vigorous scratching behind his ears from his pleased host for his trouble.

As Mark concluded, the Guildmaster looked to Gallenius. "I do not recall any mention of the Ladies Ellen and Stacy returning here to the Citadel after they closed the portals, do you?"

Gallenius shook his head. "No, Guildmaster. I was under the impression they intended to return directly to the Realm of Man."

"Excuse me, Guildmaster," interjected Mark. "Did you say they *closed* the portals?"

"Well, I mean to say closed or *redirected* by Lady Ellen, in her capacity as Steward. But it appears she was successful. Our spies can find no trace of the portals, nor can the troops of Were and Shadow who are left here. Of course, they are still a problem for us, about twelve hundred strong—"

"If I may, Guildmaster," Trey interrupted. "So, we now know that Ellen and Stacy were here; we know that they were going to try to close the portals; and we know that the portals are now closed, or at least appear to be. So, the last place they might have been is the scenes of these portals—"

"Wait, a second," urged Hawk. "Do we know if the two portals were closed simultaneously?"

Gallenius glanced at the Guildmaster and shrugged his shoulders.

Holding his hands openly across the table the Guildmaster responded. "We think not. We cannot be certain, but we believe the portal used by the Were troops may have been closed first. Shortly thereafter, something happened at the portal used by the Shadow troops. We believe it was some kind of explosion. We had, uh, certain *assets* on the scene within minutes. There were many injuries in the Shadow camp—some were grievous indeed, especially to those nearest the portal site—but most appeared to be less serious. Our people took advantage of the situation and *eliminated* most of the Shadow command structure—vampires all. Our team even captured a high-ranking prisoner."

"The Shadow troops were holding prisoners as well," Gallenius added, "captured citizens of this realm. Many were injured, but none severely. Unfortunately at the time, there was no way to effectively rescue those prisoners. Our assets said there was no sign of either Lady Ellen or Lady Stacy."

"Who is the captured 'high-ranking' prisoner?" asked Miska.

"A vampiress, the Lady Sabrina," the Guildmaster answered.

Mark paled, and Gallenius noticed. "You know of her?"

Hawk grinned and nudged Trey, as Mark's mouth opened but no sound came out.

"Oh, yes," said Hawk, "Mark knows her. When we were in Shadow, and had to spend the night in Lady Leanan's castle, Sabrina tried—none too subtly I might add—to seduce and *mark* him. However, he talked so much that the rising sun almost caught her. I don't think she likes him very much."

Mark recovered his composure enough to return Hawk's grin, and offer a retort. "That's true enough I suppose. But if she was here, then her boy, Gunther, was here, too. My friend Hawk here is not held in very high esteem by that psychopath. Your people didn't happen to eliminate *him* as well, did they?"

"Sadly, no," admitted Gallenius. "We know that Lord Gunther survived whatever happened at the Shadow camp, and is still here, somewhere."

"Well, if you have Lady Sabrina," Mark warned, "and Gunther knows it, he'll stop at nothing to get her back."

"We're getting a little off point," cautioned Trey. "We'll need to interview this Sabrina, since she was at the scene when *whatever* went down. And we also need to see the scene, the last place we think Ellen and Stacy may have been."

The Guildmaster chuckled. "Sergeant, any attempt to interview our prisoner during the hours of daylight would be futile."

"Oh . . . yeah, I see," Trey admitted wryly.

"However, we may be in a better position to accommodate your other request," the Guildmaster mused aloud, and then nodded to Gallenius, who immediately understood.

The mage explained. "As it happens, we are planning a rescue of our citizens still held by the Shadow forces. Our information is that there are twenty-four being held. It has to be today, during daylight, so any remaining vampires—most especially Gunther, whom we know is here—should not be a factor. Also, a thunderstorm is brewing, which will give our team some degree of concealment.

"The Shadow forces are still in a chaotic state of disarray, and their camp has been severely damaged. They have lost nearly all of their command structure and they have not yet reorganized; but, they will. Many of their troops appear to be conscripts; but, they are closely supervised by professional men-at-arms serving as noncommissioned officers. So, we expect them to recover fairly quickly.

"However," Gallenius concluded, "right now, under cover of a storm, we believe we have our best chance of a successful rescue."

"I have some reservations; however, the circumstances may trump my reluctance," the Guildmaster admitted with a sigh.

"If you like, you may accompany the team. It may well be your only opportunity to actually see the site. Of course, your presence must in no way interfere with our intended rescue. Other than that, if there is anything we can do to assist in your search, you need only ask."

A quick glance at his companions assured Mark that this was more than acceptable.

"Yes, Guildmaster, we would very much like to accompany the team. And if you would permit another question?"

"Certainly."

"What of the Were forces? Have *they* taken any prisoners?"

The Guildmaster gestured for Gallenius to answer.

The mage shrugged once again. "Not that we are aware of. We know they took some livestock, but we have had no reports of them successfully taking any prisoners.

"Although I do understand we have a patrol in that region that is overdue by almost two hours. We have had periodic skirmishes whenever a patrol makes contact with a raiding party, but casualties have been few. And at this time, we can account for *most* of our personnel."

Trey and Hawk exchanged a glance. Hawk tapped his watch; time was going to be a significant issue.

"How soon," asked Trey, "is your team scheduled to commence the rescue operation?"

"In an hour's time, I think," Gallenius responded.

"How big is the team, and who will be in charge?"

"The captain who captured the vampiress will be in command of an eight-man team. I can arrange for you to meet with him and his team briefly, before they commence this mission."

"That'll work," Trey responded gratefully.

"Yeah," echoed Hawk. "It's very important—critical, even—to know the people we'll be working with. We brought some equipment that may be of some use."

At a nod from the Guildmaster, Gallenius stood and said, "Of course, I shall arrange it immediately. You may return, through that door, to your equipment. The captain and his team will meet you there shortly."

Placing Smokey gently upon the table, the Guildmaster rose and the rest of the company followed suit.

"Gentlemen, I must attend to my duties. I shall not see you before you depart, so I shall wish you luck now—for both the rescue and in your search. I think a great deal of the Lady Ellen and the Lady Stacy. It would grieve me greatly should something unfortunate befall either of them. Find them, please."

CH 7

THE UNRELENTING RAIN pelted the canopy of the Storm Haven forest, cascading erratically, leaf to leaf, through the foliage to splatter amidst the soaked understory and the saturated woodland floor.

The miserable weather matched Ellen's current despondency.

Coarse hemp bindings were cinched brutally tight about Ellen's wrists; her hands stung with each throb of her restricted circulation. Blindfolded by a dark cloth bag over her head, she slogged along what she sensed was a muddied forest trail, nearly falling as a sudden jerk on the line tethered to her bound hands sent her stumbling forward. She would have cried out in pain, but she was gagged as well, her muffled complaint reduced to a wincing moan.

Unseen branches laden with wet leaves whipped across her hidden face and soaking shoulders as the persistent deluge pummeled the windswept canopy. Rainwater sluiced in swift runnels across low spots on the trail, pooling in treacherous quagmires to either side of the narrow way.

Ellen's spirits were as heavy as her sodden woolen cloak, not that her captors seemed to care, pulling her along, forcing her to keep pace.

The discomfort of her predicament was nothing compared to her lingering shock and utter sense of grief. She believed Stacy was *dead*, killed by a vicious blow from one of her hulking captors, these enigmatic trolls.

WHEN SHE AND STACY were discovered by Gunther in the heart of the damaged Shadow camp in the forest of Storm Haven, they were roughly seized. Briefly questioned by the recently ascended vampire lord, they could answer none of his impatient queries, even if they had been so inclined.

Irritated and clearly distracted, he had them thrust into a holding pen with the other prisoners.

It was immediately obvious to Ellen and Stacy that many of those unfortunates had suffered injuries, and other despicable treatment. Overwhelmed with compassion, the two women ignored thoughts of escape and immediately set about rendering what aid they could under the circumstances. There was little more they could do beyond cleaning wounds with rainwater and binding them with makeshift bandages, mere strips of torn cloth.

While they were busy administering to the wounded, a voice called out Ellen's name.

Looking around, Ellen spied a tall woman in snug clothing, her long black hair plaited into a thick braid, standing at the open gate of the prisoner compound.

The woman smiled wryly at Ellen and gestured toward her. "So, *there* you are—finally, face to face. *Take her!*"

Before Ellen could react, two huge forms stepped through the open gate and strode toward her—trolls!

But these were not of the dull-witted, simple variety that she, Hawk, and Mark had dealt with in Shadow. No, these were more like the two intelligent trolls she and the red fox had seen from a place of hiding when they had first surreptitiously scouted the Were camp.

Within seconds, the hulking forms were upon her, snatching her up by either arm.

She yelped in surprise and indignation.

The trolls' only response was a rumbling chuckle of amusement.

Suddenly, one of the trolls lurched to the side as one of his knees buckled. Without releasing Ellen's arm, he dropped to his knees in the mud, his outstretched free hand keeping him from falling face-first into the muck.

Ellen twisted her head to see Stacy, gripping a stout length of broken oak, rearing back for another blow.

"Let her go—*you big lummox!*"

The felled troll uttered a low rumbling grunt, stood, and lashed out with his muddied free hand.

Stacy tried to block his swing with her improvised club, but it splintered upon impact. She took the remainder of the blow to her body. Helplessly arcing into the air, she sailed across the prisoner compound, and crumpled into a broken heap at the foot of a portion of shattered wooden palisade.

"No!" Ellen gasped; her mind could not accept what she had just seen.

Stunned with shock, she dimly heard the woman with the long braid speaking to the trolls, but did not comprehend her words—or even care. Her only thoughts were of Stacy.

Ellen's wrists were bound with rope and tethered to a length of braided leather. A length of cloth was pulled across her mouth and tied as a gag. A dark sack was pulled over her head as a blindfold. Rudely pulled forward, she was led from the prisoner compound.

Her mind reeling with the loss of Stacy, her unseen eyes flooded with tears and her breath hitched in her throat.

THUS HAD ELLEN BEEN led, mired in despondency and grief, in her listless, softly sobbing compliance. Sunken within herself, she became largely oblivious to her surroundings. The cold rain drummed upon her, lending wet weight to her saturated cloak and plastering the hooded blindfold to her skull.

She shuddered as a sobering chill began to slowly penetrate her suspended awareness, a rude awakening of sorts. Incrementally she regained a sense of purpose. She realized she needed her wits about her and fought to focus her thoughts.

She wasn't sure how long they'd been walking, but it hadn't seemed too long, nor too far.

She concentrated on expanding her awareness. With an ease that surprised her, she perceived all that was around her. With grim determination, she took stock of her situation.

There were four trolls; two walking behind her and two more in front of her, one of whom held the braided leather line tied to her wrists. They strode purposefully in single file, following the woman with the raven braid, who led several paces ahead. They moved through the soaking forest with surprising ease and little noise; only the inevitable *squishing* of their muddy footsteps betrayed their presence.

Ellen relaxed a bit and let her consciousness sort out the varied impressions of the other perceptible energy signatures. There were a number of birds and small forest creatures that went deathly silent as the party neared and passed. However, there was little else she sensed—or *was there?*

No, that's not all. There's definitely something else—a sound, in a very low register. I'm not sure if I hear it or sense it. If I focus on it, it becomes a bit more distinct. It's coming from the trolls, and it has a rhythm of sorts—a language? Haven't I heard this before? Yes! A language! These trolls have their own language, but not one that I can understand. However, I can sense discontent—no, it's a bit stronger than that. They're really not happy about something—something to do with her?

Suddenly jerked to a halt, Ellen stumbled and lost her concentration.

"Take her inside, and tie her to a chair," ordered the woman's imperious voice. "Send for a mage, and then post your brethren outside. See that we are not interrupted."

"Yes, mistress," boomed a deep voice.

No doubt one of the trolls, Ellen surmised as she was led into a tent and unceremoniously tied to a stout wooden chair. She was still blindfolded and her hands throbbed mercilessly. She extended her awareness once more and came to the realization that she was in the midst of the Were camp—and that a worried young man was hurrying to this very tent.

"Mistress," boomed the voice again, "the mage is here."

Ellen heard the *swish* of wet canvas as the tent flaps opened and closed. She sensed a new presence, and heard a new voice—no doubt addressing her haughty captor.

"Uh . . . M'lady, I am Roland, journeyman mage, at your service."

"You? You are a mage? I expected someone, um, older."

"Begging m'lady's pardon, I am a recent graduate of the Were School of Mages, a former apprentice under the tutelage of Magus Zerban, and now a full-fledged adept of the sorcerous arts. True, I am young—but I am *very* good," he assured her with a trace of pride. "Now, how may I serve you?"

"Well, you certainly do not lack confidence," the woman responded coolly. "Be careful that it does not breed arrogance."

The young mage wisely remained silent.

"Can you cast a truth spell on my guest here, Mage Roland?"

There was a long moment of silence in which Ellen felt as if a mild surge of static electricity had washed over her seated form.

"Uh, m'lady," uncertainty laced through the mage's words, "could I please speak with you, outside?"

Ellen heard no response, but she heard them depart and sensed that she was alone. *Where had they gone?* Expanding her awareness, she found them. And more surprising, she found that she could sense the gist—even the words—of their conversation. Perhaps their proximity helped—or were her powers of perception increasing?

. . . But m'lady, this is a person of some power. A truth spell, such as you ask, may not work on her, of that I am almost certain.

. . . I feared as much, even though she does not fully understand her power. Is there any way to compel truthful responses from her?

. . . M'lady, I do not think . . . No, wait, your comment gives me pause; there may be a way . . . Does this woman know that a truth spell would not likely work upon her?

. . . No, I think not. Why? What do you have in mind?

. . . Rather than focus on her, I can cast a truth spell upon the chair in which she sits. It may appear to her that the spell is upon her. Thus, if she were to expect it to work upon her, she may be compliant.

. . . I see. You impress me, Roland. Let it be done.

The *swish* of the tent flaps alerted Ellen to their return. She sensed a presence behind her, and the hooded blindfold was removed. The sudden brightness stung her reddened eyes; fresh tears welled anew. Squinting, she was increasingly able to focus on the woman standing before her.

"Lady Ellen, I am called Ling. I serve the Were. I have some questions for you. But before we begin, the Mage Roland will cast a truth spell." She leaned into Ellen's face. "To speak a falsehood would be apparent and most unpleasant. I will not waste time with lies; so, be forewarned."

Stepping back and placing her hands on her hips, Ling nodded to the eager adept.

A young man with a shock of tousled blonde hair and piercing ice-blue eyes stepped forth. Straightening his freshly minted robes of office, he folded his arms in an unconscious imitation of Zerban, his teacher, and spoke in the most formal tones he could muster.

"I am the Mage Roland of the Were. You are about to be subjected to a powerful truth spell—resistance is futile! Complete cooperation and compliance is your only path."

Slowly unfolding his arms, Roland began to recite an incantation over his open palms. As he spoke, his hands lowered slowly as if his words were tangible things, cascading from his lips, across his outstretched palms, and onto Ellen. He deftly shuffled to his left side, circumscribing a circle around her chair as he droned on in a rhythmic chant. When he had completed the circuit and his incantation, he stood before Ellen and spoke as somberly and sonorously as his youth would permit.

"I have cast a powerful truth spell. You will answer any question with the truth. Do you understand?"

Ling shot a wry glance at the young adept, sighed and stepped forward to remove the gag. "Now, answer the mage."

Ellen moistened her parched lips, stared balefully at the tall blonde youth, and uttered breathlessly, "Yes, I understand."

"Excellent!" exclaimed Ling. "Roland, you may go."

"But, m'lady, I—"

"Silence!" Ling spat. "You are to leave! If I have need of you, I will send for you."

"Of course, m'lady," Roland acquiesced, a hint of surprised fear in his voice. He deftly executed a small bow, and hastily left the tent.

Turning back to Ellen, Ling stood before her. "As I said, I will not waste time. You closed the portals—why?"

Ellen looked Ling in the eye and responded in complete sincerity, "I did not."

"What? You did not close the portals? Why do you say that?"

"Because it is true. I tried to close the portals, but I failed."

"Failed? How could you have failed? You are the *Steward*, are you not? Did you not *open* these portals?"

Ellen could feel the strange energy roiling through the chair—*the spell, no doubt.* She intuitively understood that it would have no impact whatsoever upon her responses. Nonetheless, she answered openly, cognizant that it might be best to appear to be under the influence of the truth spell.

"I *am* the Steward. I did *open* these portals, at the direction of Queen Mab."

Ling was clearly growing impatient. Leaning into Ellen's face she hissed, "So, then how is it that you cannot close that which you have opened, *Steward?*"

Ellen merely shrugged her damp shoulders. "I don't know. I don't understand it. I only know that the portals were *changed* somehow—I suspect by someone with great skill and power."

Ling stepped back and began pacing.

Ellen maintained a bland, disinterested expression; but her mind was awhirl.

Of course, as to who, I have my suspicions—quite strong suspicions. Be that as it may, for now I must appear to be under the influence of the truth spell. Perhaps I can learn something.

"Lady Ellen," the Were assassin said soothingly, laying an elegantly manicured hand on Ellen's shoulder, "I believe it may well be that some have misjudged you. Tell me, can you open a new portal from *this* realm to the Realm of Were, or perhaps Shadow?"

Appearing to be clearly confused, Ellen shook her head and said, "I don't know. I haven't tried."

Ling reached down and grasped Ellen's numb fingers. With a flick of a razor-sharp thumbnail, she sundered the hemp bonds that had held Ellen's wrists so cruelly.

Ellen winced at the pulsing pain in her hands and rubbed at her wrists as full circulation was restored.

Ling addressed the remaining ropes as deftly as the first, and then hovered at Ellen's shoulder.

As her razor-sharp nail lingered in the vicinity of Ellen's throat, Ling whispered huskily in her ear. "Then, my dear Lady Ellen, let us *try*. Open a *new* portal to the Realm of Were!"

"No."

Ling's head snapped back in surprise, and her visage clouded darkly. The solicitous tone vanished from her voice. Its timbre grated like the harsh rasp of a file on naked steel.

"This is not a request! You will do as I say—*or else!*"

Ellen turned her head until their faces were mere inches apart and kept her voice flat and devoid of emotion.

"Or else what? You'll kill me? Torture me? Go ahead. What makes you think I'd care? There is nothing you can threaten me with that will compel me to do your bidding."

"Oh, really?" Ling smirked. "You would even sacrifice your friend, the Lady Stacy?"

Ellen faced forward to hide her welling tears and murmured, "Your *thugs*—those trolls—already killed her!"

Ling was clearly startled.

Ellen immediately sensed that this came as a genuine surprise to her captor.

"Lady Ellen, you are mistaken—the Lady Stacy lives! And you may be assured she will continue to do so—*if* you cooperate. We only wish to return to our home realm, and we can only do so if you open a new portal."

Ellen kept her voice flat and emotionless. "I do not believe you."

Ling spun away, her face contorted in a silent snarl, and hissed into the empty air. She fought to maintain control and regain her composure.

Ellen easily sensed Ling's desperation—and her limited patience.

"If I were to produce the Lady Stacy—alive," Ling proposed, in a tone of calm logic and reasonable consideration, "would you then believe me?"

Ellen's heart leapt at the thought that her dearest friend may have survived. Tamping down this flush of hope, she struggled to remain placid and seemingly passive.

"I would then believe you," she murmured flatly.

"Very well," Ling cooed soothingly. "I shall have her brought here."

"Mistress, please forgive the interruption," boomed a voice, as the tent flaps swung back and the massive head of a troll poked in, "but a raiding party has returned; and, their leader has urgent news for you."

Angered at the interruption, but nonetheless curious, Ling held up a warning finger.

"*In a moment!* Ah, of course, I will see him. Have him wait for me outside."

In an apparent effort to complete the transition from *inquisitor* to *congenial hostess*, Ling said, "Lady Ellen, if you will excuse me, I shall make arrangements for the Lady Stacy to be brought to you. In the meantime, consider yourself my guest; food and drink will be provided for you."

Ellen's mind was racing. If Stacy and she were brought together, she would transit them both out of this place.

But in the interest of maintaining the façade of compelled truthfulness, she said merely, "Thank you, I am thirsty."

LING WITHDREW AND HISSED to the troll as she passed, "She does not leave this tent. No one is to enter until I return—understand?"

"Yes, mistress," rumbled the troll, standing with her under the tall tent's awning, both of them protected from the rain. "However, we must speak."

"Indeed?" she answered, mildly annoyed. "Be patient. Let me deal with this raiding-party leader, and then we shall speak. Where is he?"

"There, mistress," he pointed, "by that guards' tent."

Ling saw the man standing in the rain. As if he felt predatory eyes upon him, he looked up. He blanched and quickly averted his eyes.

She smiled to herself. Clearly she intimidated him—in fact, she intimidated most of the Were troops. Ling liked that. Only the damned trolls were blatantly indifferent and unruffled in her presence—something she found mildly disconcerting.

The man looked up again, and she motioned for him to attend her as she walked in the direction of her own tent.

He followed, and upon entering her quarters—dripping wet—executed a deep bow.

"Rise and speak."

"Forgive me, m'lady," he began, a trace of trepidation faintly laced through his voice. "I have just returned with my men. We encountered an enemy patrol, a local militia. They had laid an ambush; but, we overcame them, slaying most. We took five prisoners. We were told to notify you immediately if we took prisoners."

This was good news. Ling needed fresh intelligence; and, she had promised Gunther that she would make inquiries about the missing Lady Sabrina.

She smiled, like the predator she was; the patrol leader shrank.

"All things considered, Sergeant, you have done well," Ling condescendingly assured him. "In fact, I have another assignment for you; form another patrol and go to the Shadow Camp. Find a prisoner held there, a woman known as the Lady Stacy. She may have been injured; if so, her wounds are to be tended. I want her brought here, to me, under close guard. Do you understand?"

"The Shadow camp, m'lady?" he balked.

"Is that a problem for you, Sergeant?" she seethed ominously. "Can you not find their camp?"

"Uh, m'lady, finding the camp is not the problem. But, how am I to convince them to surrender a prisoner to me?" he whined with due deference.

"Oh, damn!" She groaned, realizing her gaff. "I see, one moment."

Turning to a small table, she hastily scribed a note on a small scroll, rolled it tightly, and sealed it with a few drops of candle wax.

"Deliver this to Lord Gunther; he now commands the Shadow troops. He will comply with my *request*."

Accepting the scroll, the sergeant's brow creased and he drew a hesitant breath, another question hovering on his tongue.

But Ling's patience was at an end. "What are you waiting for? Go!"

"Y-yes, m'lady—at once, m'lady!" He groveled, backed away, and withdrew.

She was pleased. A plan was forming in her mind and she was beginning to see how this might all work to her advantage.

Her reverie was interrupted by a rumbling voice from just outside.

"Mistress, we have to talk—now, if you please."

She stepped out to find two of the trolls standing there under the awning of her tent. She had been told their names, but she did not bother to remember.

"Very well, but be quick," she cautioned impatiently, "I have interrogations to conduct."

"It is a simple matter, mistress, our pay," rumbled one.

"And the approaching noon hour," added the other in a deep bass voice.

"What are you talking about?" demanded Ling. "Speak not in riddles!"

"Mistress, we were hired to serve for five days, but paid for three. By the terms of our contract, those three days expire at the noon hour today. If we are not paid by noon today—one gold piece each, as agreed, per each day of service—our arrangement is terminated. Pay us eight gold pieces by noon today, and we shall continue to serve you, for two more days. Beyond that time, we will renegotiate."

This caught Ling unawares. Worse, she had no gold with which to pay these mercenaries; she had received no supplies, and thus no funds, since the portals had been closed. Furthermore, she could not explain any of this to the trolls, or any of the troops, because she and Gunther had decided to let their troops think that closing the portals had been a strategic tactic.

She did not know what to do. Trying to reason or argue with these trolls was a waste of time. They prided themselves in keeping to the letter of their contracts, and were infamous for compelling others to adhere equally to the terms and conditions of their agreements.

Perhaps Gunther could loan the funds? I could send a runner to him—perhaps he could catch up with the patrol I just sent. Would it be in time? Did Gunther even have any gold?

Sudden realization washed over her like cold water—it was *daylight!* Gunther would not even be available! He could neither provide gold, nor receive the scroll she had sent with the sergeant.

Ye gods, I need an open portal!

She was coming to truly detest this mantle of command thrust upon her by Lord Addecus. He knew she preferred to work alone; she was an *assassin*, not a military strategist. As if the sheer scope of simple military logistics and support were not demanding enough, now she had to deal with this situation.

She had not been involved in the negotiations with the trolls; that had been Lord Addecus. It had been his idea to only offer a partial deposit, with the promise of full payment by noon today. Now it was *her* problem; and, for the moment, she had no answers—only frustration.

Nothing ever worked out the way she had anticipated.

Perhaps she might learn something of value from her interrogations of the newly captured prisoners—and she was in no mood to be subtle.

But first, the trolls—I have to tell them something, anything.

"I understand your concerns," she began. "I very much want to keep you in my service. You must understand that there may be some delay in arranging your pay by the noon hour, today. Circumstances beyond our control are causing unforeseen delays. I—"

"Mistress," one of the trolls interrupted, "I must remind you that any such *circumstances* are not our concern. *Delays* are not our concern. Payment on time, per the terms of our contract, is our sole concern."

"Though heavy weather may hide the face of the sun," added his huge companion, glancing up at the leaden sky, "we will know the moment of the noon hour—and that time draws nigh."

Sparks dancing in her furious eyes, Ling knew there was nothing more she could say; the trolls were intractable. Spinning on her heels, she stalked off through the rain like a storm unto herself.

As she neared the prisoner holding area, her thoughts further darkened.

The number of raiding parties must be doubled immediately! Our focus must not only be upon the acquisition of slaves, but other items of value to us as well; food and supplies, of course—and gold, as much as can be found or wrenched from these people! Surely, there must be some sort of treasury in their capital, this Citadel. Yes, that place should have all that we require, in abundance! The sooner we move on that place, the better! But first, I have prisoners to question—and now, I have far more interesting questions to ask.

STACY COULD NOT TAKE a deep breath; her ribs ached with the effort, and her head throbbed in cadence with her heartbeat. A crust of dried blood matted the hair above her right temple, but at least the scalp wound had stopped bleeding. She could feel the pain and swelling in her right cheek, and knew she'd be sporting a horrible bruise for days to come.

But she was alive, and that had to count for something.

Peering through the dense foliage of the broad elm tree, she squinted at the Were camp, a healthy *stone's throw* distant. She would have tried to get closer, but the trees had cautioned against that. Raiding parties were coming and going much more frequently and there were fewer places to hide. Here, she was well hidden and kept relatively dry. The tree was doing its best to protect her, and would warn her if anyone approached.

Of course, her real concern was Ellen. Stacy knew that Ellen was being held in the Were camp; the trees had assured her that this was so.

Wedged within the crook of several thick limbs, she was careful not to disturb any of the delicately peeling bark, curling upon itself in natural filigree. She was sore and exhausted, getting this far had not been easy.

Back in the Shadow prisoner compound, when Ellen was accosted by those two trolls, Stacy hadn't given a moment's thought to her own safety. She attacked with the first weapon she found, a broken length of oaken log from the damaged palisade wall.

Stacy grinned at the memory. She'd whacked one troll as hard as she could—a real *home-run swing*—right behind the knee; that leg collapsed like a broken promise.

Unfortunately, he didn't release Ellen, and viciously backhanded Stacy before she could hit him again.

She was barely able to get the log up to try to block the blow; sadly, that was the last thing she remembered.

Later she awoke, hurting all over, to find that some of the prisoners whom she and Ellen had helped were now tending to *her*. She was pretty well battered, but when she learned that Ellen had been taken, she was determined to follow.

Of course, first she had to *escape.*

That turned out to be easier than she anticipated.

Much of the wall surrounding the prisoner compound, like the other structures, had been seriously damaged—no doubt thanks to Ellen's slight miscalculation in their awkward arrival in Storm Haven which caused the sudden explosive energy release of the manipulated portals. Thankfully, the primary result was as intended—the portal did appear to be gone, but actually now connected Shadow directly to Olmus. Of course, the damage and injuries here in Storm Haven were unintentional.

Of the uninjured Shadow troops assigned to guard the prisoners, most had been called away to help with repairs; and the two who remained were somewhat less than conscientious since their sergeant was gone. Stacy saw that escape would be no great task, especially in the heavy rain, while the last two guards huddled around a small fire in a lean-to.

Stacy asked the prisoners why none of them had made the attempt, and learned that some had—those well enough to do so. Although many were recovering, some were still too injured to try; so, others had elected to stay and care for them. All were steadfastly optimistic and confidently hopeful that their rescue would be imminently forthcoming.

Impressed with such resolute selflessness, she was torn. She hated leaving if she could help—*but Ellen . . .*

Sensing her distress, the remaining prisoners assured her all would be well, and that it was far more important that the Steward be found and rescued.

All things considered, there was really no choice; Stacy had to find Ellen. So, after assuring the prisoners that their rescue would be a priority, she donned her muddied cloak, and under the cover of sheets of driving rain, slipped away.

As soon as she reached the forest, she collapsed against the nearest tree, fighting for breath, her ribs on fire. A tingling in her mind, a somewhat familiar probing, caught her attention—the tree had recognized her, or more specifically, sensed her nature as a *wood nymph*.

Surprised, and unaccountably hopeful, she shunted her pain aside and opened herself to the tree, and was rewarded with a wealth of information.

Trees observe a great deal, and forget nothing.

Stacy let them guide her to the Were camp, hiding whenever they warned her about approaching patrols. Her injuries were such that she could only travel slowly; but with the trees' help, she was never seen. A trek that would have taken less than thirty minutes, had taken her over an hour and a half. Her arboreal guides were extremely patient, encouraging her cautious and deliberate pace.

After all, who is more patient than a tree?

Finally, she neared the Were encampment. At the urging of the trees, she took shelter within the bounty of this magnificent elm, from which she had a relatively clear view of the camp.

While the trees were valuable allies, and told her in which tent the Were held Ellen, there was little they could do to assist in a rescue attempt. So, Stacy settled in to watch the camp and seek out its weaknesses, while the trees patiently divulged all that they had learned.

BY MID-MORNING, STORM Haven's ad hoc rescue team was in position near the Shadow camp. It had taken a great deal of skill and stealth for them to get this close.

Hawk was suitably impressed with the captain and his men. In fact, the only people who had made any discernible sounds at all in their careful trek through the forest had been Trey and Mark. They were doing their best; but, while the heavy rain all but masked their inadvertent noise, they couldn't match the woodland skills of the others. Even Miska was amazingly quiet for a man of his bulk. Of course, he would have been just as quiet in bear form, Hawk realized with a small grin.

Now they were well hidden within the thick, dripping underbrush near the edge of the trees, watching the camp carefully. As they'd been told, the encampment was in great disarray and damage was widespread.

To Hawk, it looked like an airburst bomb of some sort had gone off near the center, its characteristic damage splayed forth in an outwardly radial pattern of diminishing effects with distance.

Taking advantage of the disorder, Hawk ventured as close as adequate concealment would allow, and carefully scouted the encampment from several vantage points.

Upon his return to the rescue team, he conveyed his findings to Trey and the captain, as Mark and Miska hovered close to hear.

"There are only two places under guard; a small log and canvas structure with considerable damage, and an area where prisoners are held. There's a lot of damage everywhere. Unfortunately, I saw no trace of Ellen or Stacy. If they're being held here, they're probably under guard."

"Well, it would not be the smaller log-walled tent," offered the captain in a whisper. "That is—or rather *was*—Lord Vlad Tepesh's headquarters. It was damaged in the blast. We understand that Lord Gunther has made it his own, and ordered repairs. It also serves as the entrance to the vampires' underground *sleeping chamber* where they must hide from the day. Vampires would never hold anyone in there—not while *they* are vulnerable. If the Ladies Ellen and Stacy are being held in this camp, it would no doubt be with the other prisoners, in the other guarded area."

"That makes sense," agreed Hawk. "There's good cover near there. In this rain I think we can move a lot closer. Follow me."

They slipped silently into positions of concealment. Hawk pointed out the prisoner compound, seriously damaged but hastily repaired and essentially intact. They could see people milling about the compound entrance; a man-at-arms was apparently organizing some soldiers into work parties. The work detail formed up and began to collect various tools, leaving only a pair of guards at the entrance.

Trey tugged at the captain's sleeve. "It seems pretty disorganized. We're seeing work parties being formed by NCOs—I mean the men-at-arms—to do what, make repairs?"

"Aye," responded the captain, not taking his eyes from the scene. "First, they must cut fresh timber, *then* make repairs."

"And that means the work parties have to go into the forest," Trey mused aloud.

"What are you thinking, Trey?" asked Hawk, a smile beginning to crease his face.

"Act like you belong there, and have the authority," Trey ventured, returning Hawk's mischievous grin.

As the work detail moved off, Trey whispered, "Captain, I have an idea—it might be just bold and outrageous enough to work. Listen . . ."

THE SIX SHADOW SOLDIERS, all reluctant conscripts to this work party, resignedly followed several paces behind the man-at-arms into the soaking forest. The rain would not let up—and felling trees was dangerous enough in dry weather.

All six of them would have much rather been back in camp assigned the easy duty of standing guard at the prisoner compound. They probably would have been just as wet; but, they would not have had to work. Now they were burdened with timber axes and saws, without even their shields to fend off the rain; it would be a long wet afternoon. But one did not ignore the orders of a man-at-arms; to argue or contradict his authority was to invite a beating or worse. No, it was better to just slog along and do as one was told, no matter how miserable the duty.

When the line of unhappy men came abreast of a thick wall of drooping honeysuckle, the lower vines came alive as hands suddenly shot forth, grasping ankles and spilling the men face-first onto the muddy track. The man-at-arms spun around in a fighter's crouch, his sword hissing from its sheath.

"Freeze! Uh, don't move!" came a voice from behind him. "We mean you and your men no harm. Drop your sword—do it now!"

Instead, the man-at-arms slashed viciously behind him, but his flashing steel cleaved only open air. As he reversed his edge for a slashing return stroke, he felt a pair of bee stings in his lower back.

Zzzzap-cccrackle!

His entire body went rigid. His sword fell from his nerveless hand, and his eyes rolled up in his head as he fell to the ground in convulsive spasms. Within a few seconds, he was unconscious.

The Shadow conscripts, too stunned to react, were quickly relieved of their tools and weapons.

THE CAPTAIN OF THE Storm Haven team stared at Trey in shock. "What manner of sorcery is this?"

"No sorcery, Captain, just a taser—a stun gun, uh, *technology.* It's a battery-powered device that sort of overloads the central nervous system."

Trey's explanation met with little apparent comprehension or success.

Hawk came to his partner's rescue.

"Uh, Captain? Have you ever hit your elbow, you know, in that little special spot—your *funny bone*—and your whole arm gets all tingly? Well, this taser device does the same thing to the whole body for about eight seconds. It renders the person temporarily helpless for a few minutes. It should do no lasting harm."

"Uh, yeah, that's right, usually," agreed Trey.

Trey carefully pulled the taser darts from the prone man. Then rolling him over to get his face free of the mud, he checked to be certain that the Shadow man-at-arms was otherwise unharmed. Unconsciousness could be cause for concern; but the man groaned as raindrops pattered upon his face.

Trey sighed in relief and turned to the others. "He'll be fine. Now get their uniform tunics; and we'll secure these men."

As the team relieved their captives of their mud-stained tunics, Trey rummaged around in his pack and then handed something the color of dull silver to Hawk.

The captain, now somewhat more at ease, pointed. "And what is *this*—more *technology?*"

"Not really," replied Hawk, grinning and holding up the roll. "This is just duct tape. We'll use this to secure our *guests*, here. It, too, will do no harm. We can't have these guys interfering with our mission."

Within a few minutes, the entire work detail was trussed up in the silver-colored tape, each with a strip across his mouth as a gag. Only the dazed man-at-arms remained unencumbered.

Trey motioned to the captain. "Can you help me get this armor off him? He'll be fully aware any minute, and I'd rather have him secured before he's completely alert."

As the captain assisted, Trey remarked, "It looks like his gear will fit you—it sure won't fit me. I think you're going to have the honor of taking the lead in the next part of our plan."

The captain grinned at the implication. "Oh, be not concerned. I can fulfill that role quite convincingly."

AT THE SHADOW CAMP, the steady rain had kept the two remaining guards, Milo and Burt, close to their modest fire under an improvised lean-to. From there they could easily watch the entrance to the prisoner compound to their immediate left, its damaged gate hanging slightly askew.

In their minds, Milo and Burt considered this to be adequate execution of their duties, especially since no one had approached their post in the last few hours, and none of the prisoners dared venture too close. It was not too much of an unpleasant assignment. It could have been far worse; at least they had not been sent off on a work detail.

From out of the rain, a grey form drew closer and seemed to virtually materialize before them.

Burt cursed under his breath as he recognized the shape as a senior man-at-arms; the helmet of rank was unmistakable.

"On your feet, you lazy louts! Look alive! Where is your sergeant?" boomed the newcomer.

As they scrambled to attention, they could see a line of mud-splattered soldiers following the man-at-arms.

"Oh, just great—another work detail," hissed Milo.

"Your sergeant, fly-spawn! Where is he?" shouted the man-at-arms into Milo's face.

"Your pardon, sir. He was called to form a work detail—timber, sir."

"Damn the luck! Well, orders are orders. Very well, get those prisoners out here—they are to be put to work!"

"Sir? But we—" began Burt in protest.

"What?" exploded the man-at-arms. "You overripe lump of mule dung! Are you deaf, scum bucket?"

Burt slammed his eyes shut as he held his rigid position and prayed he wouldn't be struck.

Leaning into Burt's pinched face, the man-at-arms said ominously, "Or, do you *dare* to question my orders?"

"N-no—no, sir!" cried Burt, flinching.

"Then listen up, snot-for-brains! I will say this only once, understand? With all this rain the latrines are flooded and collapsing—new ones must be dug! That is *slave work!* So get the prisoners out here; it is past time they were put to work. Or would *you two* rather do some digging?"

"No, sir—no, sir!" Burt groveled. "We will get them for you, sir."

"Good," harrumphed the man-at-arms. "As you can see, I already have a guard detail; they will help you roust these prisoners. See to it, you men! You too, soldier!"

"Yes, sir—yes, sir," sniveled a shaken Milo. "But, the prisoners, some are injured—"

"I care not, dog-breath!" bellowed the man-at-arms. "Everybody works! Be grateful I do not add you two miserable mutts to my work detail!"

Burt and Milo scrambled to comply.

Within minutes, a long bedraggled line of disheveled prisoners shuffled out of the compound. A few leaned heavily upon the shoulders of others as they were led off into the rain by the guard detail.

THE TWO SHADOW GUARDS, Burt and Milo, feeling rather lucky to have escaped another extremely disagreeable work assignment returned to their small campfire, murmuring generic condemnations of men-at-arms.

"Ye gods, I *hate* bloody sergeants! We sure dodged an arrow that time—*digging latrines* in this weather." Burt shuddered.

"Aye, give me easy guard-duty any day—safe and simple, I always say." Milo tugged his cloak around his shoulders. "I wants nothing to do with that lot."

He spat a glob of phlegm into the mud. "I waits right here on me post, `til me own sergeant comes back. Least we know how we stand with our own bloke, eh, Burt? Not like that bad-tempered bastard—he be dangerous, that one!"

"Aye, there be no slackin' on that bloke's detail. Here now, Milo, put us some more wood on the fire. I feel a bit of *chill* comin' on."

HAWK, TREY, AND MISKA had listened gleefully over the handheld radio to the exchange between the Storm Haven captain, disguised in the Shadow man-at-arms' armor, and the two intimidated Shadow guards. The captain had a similar radio secreted in his cuirass with the transmit key taped down, thereby allowing the conversation to be overheard.

Trey chuckled as they waited for the captain and his men to lead the liberated prisoners past their location. "Oh, man! NCOs are the same everywhere! I thought I would bust out laughing!"

"Yeah," agreed Hawk. "It was too funny! I gotta admit the captain was pretty creative."

"He certainly was forceful," observed Mark, "and convincing. He sure sounded authentic!"

"Oh, I do believe," acknowledged Trey, "that our friend, the captain, may have actually worn sergeant's stripes at one time."

"You think?" teased Hawk.

Miska, standing off to one side, and cradling Smokey in his arms, was keeping watch on the faint trail. He waved an arm in caution and whispered hoarsely. "They come! We are still to follow at a distance?"

"Yeah, we're to watch their back trail and be sure they're not followed," reminded Trey. "So stay out of sight until we get where we're going."

"But, Stacy and Ellen—" began Mark.

"They'll be fine," Hawk interrupted. "The important thing is to get everybody away from here first; then we can get Ellen and Stacy out of this realm."

Miska waved them to silence as the line of prisoners shambled past their hidden position.

The captain and his team maintained the ruse of a work detail just in case they ran into any Shadow troops.

The prisoners, of course, knew no different, but they received no ill treatment. In fact, their guards seemed almost solicitous, offering to assist those who could not easily maintain the pace.

As the line entered the depths of the dripping forest, Mark grasped Hawk's arm and hissed into his ear. "I counted only sixteen; I didn't see Ellen or Stacy! Hawk, they're not here!"

Hawk grimaced. "I know—I saw. Stick to the plan; we'll question them when we get there. Let's go."

THEY WERE NOT FOLLOWED, nor did they encounter any Shadow troops. They soon arrived at an isolated windmill that appeared deserted.

Mark whispered to Hawk, "I think I've been here before, when Padraic and I rescued Millie and Stacy. Gallenius was here then, too."

Hawk nodded, but remained silent as the captain addressed the prisoners.

"People, your attention please. We are not who we appear to be; and you are no longer prisoners! You have, in fact, just been rescued by Guardsmen of Storm Haven, with some assistance from volunteers from the Realm of Man!"

Surprise, relief, and joy flowed across the faces of the bedraggled refugees as they hugged one another and profusely thanked their rescuers.

The captain and his men shucked the Shadow uniform tunics, and at Trey's request, tied them in a roll. At the captain's inquisitive look, Trey explained.

"We only borrowed these. I intend to return them; and have a little talk with the rightful owners."

"You will free them?"

"Yes, after planting some serious seeds of doubt. We did them no real harm; and such a gesture suggests a great deal of confidence on our part. That can have some long-term effects in undermining the adversary's command and control. We refer to it as psychological manipulation."

The captain smiled. "I understand. We would call it *sub rosa* suggestion—'*a rose by any other name*', I suppose."

Trey grinned and nodded. He liked this guy.

The team members retrieved a cache of food and distributed the sustenance among the liberated.

Meanwhile, Trey and Hawk took the opportunity to interview small groups of individuals. The overall response was a surprise.

"So, let me be certain I understand what you are all telling us," Trey said. "Lady Ellen was taken by *trolls,* who served a dark-haired woman. The Lady Stacy was injured, but she sufficiently recovered to escape and set out to find the Lady Ellen?"

A sea of nodding heads confirmed his synopsis.

Looking to his companions, with open palms, Trey asked, "But where? Who?"

Miska spoke up, as Smokey perched upon the big man's shoulder and growled softly in his ear. "I think that I may know where *and* who. This dark-haired woman may be Ling—a Were with whom I have had a previous disagreement."

"Wait," interjected Mark. "You mean the woman you chased from the scene of the limo accident? Isn't she a *were-panther* or *leopard,* or *something?*"

Trey and Hawk looked at each other with raised eyebrows as Miska responded.

"Indeed, I think it may be her. If so, she could only be going to the Were encampment."

"And Stacy would try to follow," finished Mark.

"Where is this camp?" asked Trey.

"It is not far; I will guide you there," the captain offered.

"But you have your own mission to complete," argued Trey, gesturing to the former captives. "You still have to get all of them safely to the Citadel."

The captain smiled and crooked a finger at Trey and his companions. "Please, come with me."

Turning on his heel, the captain led them to the stout wooden door at the base of the windmill. Pushing it open, he led them inside and lit a pair of oil lamps. "My friends, I will share a confidence with you—which you will, of course, keep secret."

With that he stepped around the huge millstones to a blank stone wall. He carefully touched a series of smoothed stones in a specific pattern, and gently pushed on a part of the wall. That section of the wall swung inward to reveal a dark unwelcoming space.

Reaching inside the darkness, the captain fumbled for a second and everyone heard the clicking of a switch. Within the space, a series of fluorescent lights began to flicker and flare to life in sequence, revealing a long low tunnel sloping gently downward and continuing as far as they could see. A thick black cable, half the width of a man's wrist, snaked along the smooth stone floor near the wall and disappeared in the distance.

The captain smiled and explained.

"This windmill, like many throughout Storm Haven, does more than merely grind grain. A small generator is housed in the uppermost section of the tower and this cable carries the electricity to a distribution point very near the Citadel. The tunnel was crafted by Dwarves, as you can see by the workmanship, primarily for the cable. But, it was thought that it might prove useful in a strategic sense, so its dimensions were slightly enlarged.

"The people we have rescued will use this tunnel to complete their journey to freedom; I will have my men accompany them. Thus, my mission will be complete and I am free to join you in your quest."

"This is *amazing*," added Mark, with a sweep of his hand. "And your selective use of certain technologies that are common in our home realm . . . I wonder . . . Did the last Steward, Maude Delafaire, have a hand in this, by any chance?"

The captain grinned. "I am not at liberty to say. Perhaps you should ask the Guildmaster? As you can see, we are not totally ignorant of the benefits of certain technologies. Although I was not familiar with your *taser*, we would no doubt welcome such nonlethal innovations. But as I said, this would best be broached with the Guildmaster."

Miska interrupted. "Forgive me, but should we not get going? Smokey is growing anxious, and I too feel a sense of urgency!"

"Quite so," agreed the captain. "If you will excuse me, I shall brief my sergeant and he will get our people on their way. I shan't be a moment."

As they filed outside into the rain, Mark squinted into the leaden sky, mumbling.

Miska nudged him. "Curse not the weather, my friend; it has proven thus far to be an unwitting ally."

"I suppose that's true," Mark admitted. "We've certainly been successful so far. The prisoners are free, and no one's been injured. I'm just anxious about Stacy and Ellen. I don't know how long our luck can hold. Don't get me wrong—I'm grateful for all the help we're getting. It's just that I have a feeling—*call it a hunch*—that we may need all the help we can get. And I have this nagging sense that we're running out of time."

Smokey nestled closer in the crook of Miska's broad arm, sheltered from the rain within the folds of the big man's robe. The inscrutable feline growled softly, as if in urgent agreement.

Miska mumbled as he absently scratched behind the cat's ears, "In truth, I cannot disagree."

A LITTLE LATER, AFTER the liberated captives had eagerly funneled into the tunnel entrance on their final trek to freedom, and the captain had led Trey, Hawk, Mark, and Miska into the dark and dripping forest toward the Were camp, a small silent figure rose from concealment high atop the windmill's capped roof.

Careful to commit what it had learned to memory, it cast its baleful gaze all around. Once certain that it was alone and unobserved, it extended and flexed a set of broad leathery wings. Turning into the wind, the diminutive gargoyle stepped off the roof, slipped between the lazy sweeps of the wind vanes, and plummeted toward the ground. Its wings flared, caught the air, and beat a rapid tattoo as it soared upward, over the onrushing treetops and disappeared into the wet night.

CH 8

WITHIN THE REALM OF Dark Elves, the windblown rain drummed against the leaded glass windows of Castle Diere as Padraic strolled through a long corridor toward the reception hall in response to a summons to attend the queen.

He was in no particular hurry. He made it a point to respond in a leisurely manner whenever she demanded his presence—a petty token of childish petulance, perhaps, but a behavior she would expect.

He was not inclined to disappoint her.

As he neared the great doors of the reception hall, the two elfin guards stiffened to attention, and then relaxed when they recognized him. Padraic enjoyed enormous popularity with the royal guards.

"Ah, Lord Padraic, a good day to you, sir," offered the nearest guard. "Begging your pardon, m'lord, but her majesty is presently meeting with a group of mages. So, if you would not mind waiting a bit, m'lord?"

"Not at all, my friend," Padraic acceded affably, as he dramatically cocked an ear at the door. "Oh my, I can hear her—she does not sound pleased. In that case, I am quite content to wait right here."

The two guards grinned. They, too, could hear Queen Mab's irate voice. The thick oaken doors muffled her words beyond recognition, but the timbre of her angry tone was unmistakable.

Moments later, the great doors swung inward and a handful of anxious elfin mages were ushered out by Tristan, the chamberlain. They hurriedly swept past the guards and walked quickly down the hall. So preoccupied were they, that they spared not a glance at Padraic.

However, the chamberlain acknowledged him with a small bow and returned to the reception hall to announce him.

"May it please your majesty, the Royal Consort, Lord Padraic."

Mab, leaning upon a pile of pillows on a wide divan, seemingly engrossed in a number of scrolls stacked on a low table to her left, glanced up, and nodded. "Excellent, you may leave us, Tristan."

The chamberlain bowed and departed, discreetly closing the great doors after him.

Padraic sauntered across the polished stone floor and paused to await her pleasure. He fully expected that she would make him wait—a petty trace of egocentric conceit that habitually tainted her otherwise unworldly beauty. So, he carefully masked his irritation with a smug leer, thus providing the apparent reaction she no doubt expected to evoke as she lounged provocatively, attired in a deep blue shimmering sheath, trimmed in silver chinchilla at the wrists, and drastically plunging décolletage.

"I want you to do something for me," she finally began without preamble. "Those *buffoons* want me to attend a *rite of execution* later this afternoon! I have absolutely no intention of doing so; I would have you attend in my stead. Go and represent me."

"A *rite of execution?*" he asked, clearly perplexed. "Ye gods, what is going on?"

As she paused, apparently sorting her thoughts, Padraic glimpsed a brief trace of fear slip across her countenance, but her voice betrayed no trepidation.

"It seems that these mages and some warriors managed to capture some sort of *resurrected* beast—a bull, I understand—that was rampaging around the countryside, somewhere in the vicinity of the late Queen Mab's castle. Of course, that is just a slag heap now!"

"Of course, Majesty. Uh, by *resurrected,* do you mean—?"

"Yes, *another* foul act of *necromancy*," she answered with a trace of shudder she could not disguise.

"The adepts are quite sure, although they think it has been some time since the foul sorcery was performed. The beast is in poor shape, significantly decomposed. I suspect its deteriorated condition is the only reason it was easily captured. Needless to say, I have no intention of going anywhere near *this,* or any other examples of necromantic creatures! That is why you must go—I simply cannot."

Padraic could see that her fear was genuine, no doubt an understandable result of her horrifying experience at the recent Council meeting, when she was attacked by her own ensorcelled guards. He too shuddered and felt a twinge of sympathy; he let it color his response.

"I completely understand; and, I will attend in your place. Do we know any more about this matter—the identity of the sorcerer, perhaps?"

"No, the adepts have not yet determined who is responsible," she shrugged, "if indeed, they ever will. Learn whatever you can at the ceremony."

"Of course, I understand."

"Oh, Padraic . . . There is another matter."

A mild sense of alarm passed through him, but he remained stoic. "Indeed, Majesty?"

Mab picked up an open scroll and handed it to him.

He started to read as she continued.

"As you can see, Queen Titania insists on a meeting, at a time of mutual convenience, yet to be determined, which she will host in her home realm, at the castle of Duke Briar."

"Duke Briar? B-but, he—" Padraic stammered.

"Put a price on your head for sullying the reputation of the duchess," she finished for him, a coy smile playing across her lips.

"Surely, you will not—" he began.

"Oh, but I *will*," she interrupted, an evil glint in her eye. "Or rather, *we will* most certainly accept her invitation and attend her meeting—in the home of Duke Briar! None would *dare* to challenge or offer harm to the consort of the Queen of Dark Elves. Did I not promise you that this would no longer be of concern for you? What better way to prove it? And I *do* so enjoy flaunting you."

"But—"

"No *buts!*" Mab declared, her eyes flaring. "I have decided! We *will* confront Titania. She has been insisting on a meeting, and I intend to learn the real reasons. I suspect it is more than just the expected reaffirmation of the Elfin Accords. Oh, do not fret; we will take appropriate precautions and the timing will be to *our* advantage.

"Now go. Prepare to deal with the mages and their rite. I have other pressing business to attend to."

"As you wish, Majesty," he replied, with a small bow. Pausing at the door, he asked, "Shall I send the chamberlain back in?"

"No, I shall retire to my chambers. Good day, Padraic."

"Good day, Majesty," he said as he closed the doors, his thoughts awhirl. *Other pressing business, you say—and, in your chambers?*

NODDING TO THE GUARDS, Padraic quickly made his way to his own chambers. Once in the privacy of his own rooms, and certain he was alone, he slipped behind a heavy baroque tapestry and pressed a series of wall stones in a specific pattern. A section of the wall opened and he stepped into the darkness. He needed no light, for his destination was only paces away. Feeling along the rough stone wall, he found the particular stone he sought. With a nudge and a twist, it swung silently to one side on a hidden hinge. He was rewarded with a view of the queen's reception chamber, albeit through a rather ancient wall hanging of threadbare silk that depicted a host of elfin heraldry.

While Padraic could not make out details, only the vague shapes of the two persons in the room, he could hear quite clearly.

"Why did you come *here?* What is the urgency?" Mab demanded.

"Becaussse only you can fix thisss—and it mussst be sssoon!"

"What do you mean? How am I supposed to fix *what?*"

"I *know* you did sssomething to the portalsss—they no longer go to Ssstorm Haven, *asss you promisssed!* Troopsss and sssuppliesss from both Were *and* Ssshadow are now deposssited in sssome unknown realm in the wild—the very sssame realm! It isss *not* Ssstorm Haven! And worssse, the sssituation hasss deteriorated; incidentsss of sssporadic fighting have broken out—troopsss of Were and Ssshadow are poisssed at each othersss throatsss!"

"First of all, I did nothing to the portals, except to ward them against being closed—which I fully expected the Steward to attempt, since I no longer have, um, certain *leverage* over her."

"Whatever you did, you mussst undo! We mussst have thessse portalsss clossed—and we mussst reopen portalsss to Ssstorm Haven! Do you not underssstand? We cannot resssupply the troopsss who *are* there, nor can we bring them home. They are underssstrength and could be lossst to the forcesss of Ssstorm Haven—that isss if they do not completely turn on one another, asss hasss already happened in thisss unknown wild realm. Did you not hear me that there have been *incidentsss?*"

"What of Leanan of Shadow? How does she feel about this?"

"Asss you know, I have little usssе for the Sssidhe. But ssshe isss in agreement, and would have come here, with me, but for the daylight. We both ssspent hoursss thisss passst night in thisss *wild* realm trying to get the belligerent possssturing and sssporadic ssscuffling between our troopsss ssstopped. Our sssuccesss hasss been limited. And worssse, neither I nor Leanan can now transssit to Ssstorm Haven to perssonally asssesss the current sssituation. Thisss plan of yoursss hasss failed! Our troopsss are cut off—and we now have portalsss that accessss our ressspective realmsss through a place in the *wild*. Thisss isss unacceptable to both Were and Ssshadow! You know thisss could lead to war! Your preciousss voting bloc in the Council would no longer exissst!"

"Enough! And just *what* would you have me do? Only the Steward can close those portals into the wild!"

"Releassse your wardingsss. Asssk the Sssteward to clossse the portalsss—you mussst!"

"And what of Storm Haven?"

"Given the opportunity, I would withdraw the Were forcesss. I sssussspect that the Lady Leanan ssharesss my opinion and would take the sssame option. Thisss plan wasss ill consssidered and isss sssimply not working. We can craft another ssstrategy, for another time. Ssstorm Haven isss no longer a sssecret—it isss not going anywhere."

"I must consider this development. Where is the Steward now?"

"We do not know at thisss time. The Lady Leanan doesss not believe that the Sssteward isss currently in her home realm."

"Indeed? I may have a way to determine her whereabouts. It seems I must confide in you—come with me. And, Addecus?"

"M'lady?"

"Remain hooded, and stay in the shadows; it would be best if you were not seen here."

They slipped quietly from the room.

PADRAIC RESEALED HIS spy-hole, chuckling to himself. He had a very good idea where Mab was going.

It hadn't taken him long in his seemingly harmless meanderings around the castle to discover a host of hidden passages, secret chambers, and the hidden room that held the scrying orb. He had recognized the crystal from his reading of ancient texts and knew it was far older—and far more dangerous—than Mab likely knew, or appreciated.

He had also discovered a chamber beneath the one in which the disembodied golden hand held the ominous crystal, a chamber that held more of that massive arm, at least to the elbow. That the arm seemed to continue down into the solid rock below, he found profoundly disconcerting.

However, Padraic had not then had the time to explore and probe into that intriguing mystery any further. It was still on his list of things to do. For now, he was satisfied to take up a position below the hidden orb room where he could eavesdrop on the muffled voices above.

"Impresssive . . . And thisss will ssshow her location? Ssscry her out?"

"Yes, it should, unless she is somehow shielded. But even then I would know where the shield is, and that will tell me at least in which realm she might be found. Now, be silent—I must concentrate. This is not without some danger."

There followed a long moment of silence, then a sudden gasp from the Queen.

"M'lady, are you all right? What hasss happened?"

"I-I am fine. I found her, or at least a glimpse of her. Something, not a shield exactly, suddenly obscured her. That was very strange, very strange indeed."

"But where?"

"Storm Haven . . . She is in Storm Haven."

"Damn the godlesss luck! Without the portalsss, we cannot now transssit to Ssstorm Haven. Both Leanan and I have tried—unsssuccesssfully!"

"Patience, Addecus. *I* do not need those portals; *I* can transit there using certain elemental powers available to me through, um, hmm, never mind. Suffice to say, I believe I can arrange to do so *with* you and Leanan. Send word to her that the both of you are to meet me, after sunset, in our usual place. I will have the necessary transit spell prepared. Then we shall go to Storm Haven, and deal once and for all with the Steward."

Padraic's blood chilled at the venom in Mab's voice.

Ye gods, no! I must get to Storm Haven before her!

THE RAIN IN STORM HAVEN was a constant companion as the captain led Trey and company, stealthily squelching their way through the soaked forest, closer and closer to the Were encampment.

Squatting silently behind the bole of a wide elm, he signaled to those behind him to gather around.

As they huddled, the captain spoke softly and gestured beyond the tree. "The Were are camped less than a bow-shot away. We may encounter sentries as we venture closer. I hope not, but if we do—"

"There's no need to kill anyone," Trey interrupted. "As you've seen with the *taser*, we can incapacitate without permanent harm."

The captain nodded in acknowledgment. In truth, he was somewhat relieved; he preferred *not* to kill whenever possible.

Miska looked as if he was about to speak when Smokey suddenly struggled to be free of the big man's cloak, and scampered up the wet trunk of the old elm. Mark and Miska stared upward, but Smokey had disappeared into the thick canopy.

Suddenly alert, Hawk, Trey, and the captain crouched—weapons at the ready—and scanned the surrounding area, trying to see what had startled the cat to flight.

Small curled bits of peeled bark drifted down like delicate grey snow, speckling Miska's beard.

Picking the pieces out of his bushy curls, he nudged Mark and mumbled, "This bark is dry?"

Looking upward once more, his face split into a huge grin, and he whispered urgently. "Look, up in the tree!"

Peering down were two faces; Smokey, purring in contentment, and Stacy! She was smiling and holding a finger to her lips, as the cat rubbed the top of his head under her dirt-smeared chin.

MOMENTS LATER, SHE was on the ground and wrapped in Mark's arms.

The others discreetly glanced away as the couple whispered urgent endearments to each other.

Miska smiled and returned Smokey to the drier folds of his cloak.

Finally Stacy pushed Mark out to arm's length and looked around. She took a deep breath and winced as her ribs throbbed in protest. Nonetheless, she began to speak urgently, her words spilling forth in an accelerating torrent.

"Everyone listen; Ellen's been taken. She's being held in a tent in that camp, and there are guards—mercenary trolls—and—"

"Now, slow down," cautioned Trey. "Are you hurt?"

Lips thinned, she shook her head. "Look, I'm okay, maybe a little sore. I gotta—"

Trey held up his hands. "Fine, now take a moment. Start at the beginning."

And so she did. Within a few minutes, she had conveyed all she knew, including that which she had learned from the trees.

"So, these mercenaries—the trolls—their contract expires at noon today?" asked Mark, looking at his watch.

Stacy nodded in the affirmative.

Mark began to smile broadly. "And you can point out the specific tent Ellen is in?"

"Yeah . . . Why? What've you got in mind?" she asked.

"Well, it's really pretty simple," he began, and explained his idea in detail.

"Do you really think that will work?" exclaimed the captain, his incredulity apparent.

"Sure it will," Mark replied confidently, "if Miska goes with me—he is from Were, so . . ."

"I get it! It's bold; but, that's been working for us lately." Trey chuckled. "Okay, but we'll be nearby, as close as we can get, but hidden."

THE TWO TROLLS STANDING outside the tent's entrance were somewhat sheltered from the constantly blowing rain by the overhanging canvas, their massive heads almost touching the high awning. One leaned forward and cast a wary eye at the thickly clouded sky and shook his head. His companion grunted in agreement and snorted.

"The noon hour is here; and we are not paid."

"Hmmph, our contract is concluded."

Two more trolls strode up and tried to stand under the awning as well; it was a tight fit.

"We left our post; no gold—no work."

As they commiserated amongst themselves, they noticed a pair of figures approaching through the mud. The larger one spoke with the common trading lilt of the Were.

"Oye! Be ye fighters for hire, good sirs?"

"Aye," rumbled the troll leader.

"Available for a contract, are ye?"

"Aye, as it happens, we are available. Be warned, we hold to the letter of our contract, and we are paid in gold."

"Then, good sirs," Miska said with a flourish, "allow me to introduce the *Counselor*, who would engage your services from this moment onward."

Mark stepped forward until he was right before the trolls. Reaching beneath his cloak, he retrieved a black leather pouch of considerable heft that jingled with the promise of bright coins. The eyes of the trolls were fixed upon the bulging leather pouch.

"Gentlemen, I understand your rates are a gold piece each for every day of service?"

"That is so . . . *Counselor*," replied the leader. "I am called *Gronk*. I lead and speak for this group."

"Very well, Gronk," said Mark, loosening the pouch straps and allowing a few gold coins to spill into his open hand. "Let us negotiate a contract. I would engage the services of you and your fellows for four days, starting now. That would be four gold coins each, paid in advance, would it not?"

"Aye, Counselor, that is our fee for four days work," agreed Gronk. "Who—or what—would you have us kill?"

Mark paused in counting out the coins and glanced up at the massive troll.

"Why, no one, Gronk. I do not even want you to *fight* anyone. I want you, all four of you, to depart this camp now, and go set up your own camp somewhere else. You do not have to do anything—no fighting, no killing. You can just relax for four days, and earn gold in the process. Of course, if I should otherwise have need of your services during that time, you would be obligated to follow my instructions. Do you understand?"

Gronk looked to each of his huge companions. All were grinning broadly, the glint of Mark's gold dancing in their eager eyes. The terms were simple; this would be the easiest pay they had ever earned. Gronk grunted in low tones and his fellow trolls answered in kind.

Facing Mark, he counted off the terms of the contract on thick fingers. "We depart now, go set up our own camp, and then do nothing for four days—no fighting, no killing—unless you call upon us."

"That is correct," assured Mark. "Do we have an accord, a contract?"

With a glance at his companions, each of whom indicated approval with a single nod, Gronk said, "Aye, Counselor, we do—upon payment."

"Of course," agreed Mark, who began placing four gold coins in each troll's outstretched palm.

When the trolls had pocketed the coins, Mark raised a finger.

"One final thing, Gronk . . . I would engage your services again in the future, if you and your fellows would be interested. Would you?"

"Yes, certainly, Counselor," agreed the troll, the weight of the newly acquired gold comfortably in his hand. "When would this be?"

"Truthfully, I do not know," replied Mark, once again loosening the pouch straps, "but I am willing to make a modest payment in advance as a retainer."

Gronk grinned. "I am not familiar with this term, *retainer*, but I think I like it. I believe we can come to an accord."

A few moments later, and all of twenty gold coins lighter, Mark and Miska stood under the awning and watched the trolls march off into the incessant rain.

IN THE MIDST OF THE camp, a thin man hurried blindly past haphazard shelters and soaked tents, his head bent and shoulders hunched while holding up the mud-splattered hem of his robes.

He never saw the troll he blundered into until he was splayed flat on his back in the queasy muck, and the troll's raucous laughter echoed in his ears.

He realized he should have been more careful, and looked where he was going, but . . .

Where are the trolls going? Weren't they supposed to be guarding something—or someone?

In a trice, he was on his feet, churning mud, trying to sprint in the direction from whence he had just come.

SHELTERED BY THE AWNING, Mark and Miska had seen the unfortunate collision of the bedraggled man and the last departing troll. It had been like watching a windblown leaf bouncing off the trunk of a mighty oak. Mark and Miska couldn't help but chuckle.

Miska leaned in close and whispered, "I have to ask—the gold coins—from the cave at Delafaire Farm?"

"Yeah, I've been planning on taking some with us whenever we go to other realms, so this time, I did. You never know when you might need local money. All right, the trolls are gone. You stay out here and keep watch—I'll slip inside and look for Ellen."

MARK DUCKED IN THROUGH a canvas flap and found that he was in a small space, and another tent flap faced him. He realized that he was in between the walls of a large double-walled tent—the outer wall treated with wax to weather the elements, and the inner wall made of thickly woven cotton-like flax, some sort of insulation, he guessed.

As he ducked in through the inner flap, the sounds of the camp and the rain diminished appreciably, but the interior was quite dim. Crates and boxes were stacked within. A sole candle flickered on a low table.

Near the center, a lone figure sat slumped and dozing in a rustic wooden chair.

Mark approached cautiously. When he was within two steps, the person's head snapped up groggily.

Ellen!

"Ellen, it's me—Mark!" Dropping to one knee before her, he anxiously asked, "Are you all right? Are you hurt? Can you walk?"

She did not immediately respond.

Standing, he gripped her hand and urged, "Come on—come with me! We have to get out of here!"

Clearly dazed, she squinted. "Who? Mark?"

"Yes! Come on—get up!"

She stood and reached out for him. "Mark! I'm so glad to see you, but—" Her voice hitched and she gasped, "B-but Stacy . . . she's—"

"Stacy? She's all right—she's gonna be fine—don't worry."

"B-but, I saw—"

"Later! Come on! I'm taking you out of here now!"

A cold voice countered, "Oh, I doubt that—I doubt that very much!"

Ling stood before them, her eyes blazing with a cruel inner light. Behind her, the mud-splattered man who had collided with the troll entered the tent through an unseen second entrance. He held the staff of a mage, its jeweled head glowing brightly.

Speaking over her shoulder, Ling jabbed a finger at Ellen. "Roland, I want her rendered senseless, but unharmed. I will *personally* deal with this fool—*slowly!*"

As Roland stepped forward and raised his staff, Mark tried to pull his cousin behind him. But Ellen was having none of it; she shoved him back, nearly losing her balance. They stumbled apart.

The sudden movement caused Roland to hesitate; but he quickly recovered, swinging his staff toward Ellen.

Mark tried to rush the mage, but Ling lashed out a vicious side kick and swept his feet from under him. Sprawled on the ground, his head twisted to his left, he barely registered the sudden flare of malignant orange light as Ellen collapsed in a heap.

Anger flared and adrenaline surged; Mark was on his feet and moving before either Roland or Ling could react. He plowed into the mage, knocking the staff from his hands, and pummeled him with his fists.

The staff's glow paled and winked out.

Roland threw his arms up in a futile effort to deflect the relentless fusillade of punches. Tripping over the muddy hem of his own robe, the mage fell back, just as a sweeping roundhouse blow caught him on the left temple and mercifully knocked him out. He never felt the brutal uppercut that broke his jaw.

Mark didn't stop until he was tired. Much of his fury spent, he stood—chest heaving, fists balled and throbbing—over the badly beaten and bloodied mage. A little surprised, and a little ashamed, he had never known such a viciously vindictive rage. He had never even thought himself capable of such *berserker* frenzy.

As his breathing began to slow, he was aware of a low vibration behind him, a guttural rumbling that rose in pitch to a definitive growl. Turning slowly to his left, Mark peered into the gloom.

There, close to the floor, two yellow slits reflected the sole candle's flame—eyes, the eyes of a predator. The dark and subtle shadow was barely discernible in the dimness. Crouched and ready to spring, its tail flicked in tense agitation.

He backed away slowly, never taking his eyes off those of the amorphous creature. *Ellen! Where was Ellen?*

He nearly stumbled over her in the gloom.

The instant he looked down, the beast—*a black panther*—sprang with a snarling shriek!

Mark ducked, instinctively shielding Ellen, and braced for the final nightmare.

With a massive *THUMP*, the cat's savage howl was abruptly cut short.

Mark sensed a huge dark form standing between him and the snarling panther, now stalking to one side. A deep rumble and a series of huffs drew his attention up the towering mass before him—a *bear,* a *very big* bear!

Miska!

The panther tried to circle the bear, but the bruin deftly lumbered from side to side, blocking the enraged feline.

Mark pulled Ellen's limp body up, and with the remainder of his adrenaline-fueled strength, hefted her over his shoulder. Sliding along the tent wall, he reached the inner flap through which he had entered.

Just as he slipped through with his burden, he heard the cat's snarling howl and the bear's rumbling roar as the combat commenced in earnest. The outer tent flap dropped closed, and the sounds of the conflict diminished, muffled by the twin tent-walls and the drumming of rain on canvas.

Mark took a few stumbling steps forward and was suddenly supported by Trey and Hawk, who gently took Ellen from him. The captain and Stacy quickly wrapped her in a cloak, but failed to rouse her from her stupor.

"Ellen! Ellen, can you hear me? Mark, what's wrong with her?" cried Hawk.

"A spell of some kind, I think," Mark grunted, as Stacy hugged him.

"Aye, this I have seen before," said the captain. "We need to get her to the Citadel! Gallenius can deal with such sorcery."

"Where's Miska?" hissed Trey, grabbing Mark's arm.

"He—he's still in the tent," gasped Mark, as he watched Stacy lead Hawk and the captain, gently carrying Ellen, into the tree-shrouded undergrowth. "He changed—he's fighting a panther! *Ling*—it's gotta be her!"

"Fighting in the tent? But we didn't hear a thing!"

Mark shrugged; he had no answers. "Who knows—the rain—maybe magic?"

"We've gotta leave now! We've got to get him out of there!" Trey declared, reaching for his sub-gun.

"Good luck—that won't work!" Mark warned. "I don't know how to get him to stop fighting her. He'll kill her or die trying!"

Smokey suddenly shot between their legs and disappeared into the tent. Mark and Trey looked at each other in shocked disbelief.

Mark shrugged, but didn't hesitate to follow the cat. "Sometimes you just gotta trust Smokey!"

TREY REACHED UNDER his robe and freed his H&K MP5 PDW from its shoulder harness. The small submachine gun might be of dubious value against a true Were creature like Ling, but it was better than nothing. He quickly entered the tent, almost running into Mark—and stood stock-still in shock.

In the dim candlelit interior stood a frozen tableau.

Trey clicked on his flashlight and let its wide beam roam, revealing details of the incredible scene.

Ling, in her panther form, was arched upon her hind legs as if about to attack, her front claws exposed and reaching, her vicious fangs glistening in her gaping mouth. Bloody furrows ran across one side of her skull, and one ear was shredded. Crimson claw marks raked down one side along her ribs.

Miska towered over her, his massive forepaws open wide, ready to crush her and rend her to shreds with his scimitar claws. His own fangs were displayed in murderous intent. Deep slashes on his forelegs bled slowly.

Between the two immobile combatants sat Smokey, calmly looking from one to the other, and licking the back of one of his front paws.

"What the hell?" breathed Trey in amazement.

"What indeed?" muttered Mark.

Smokey stood and sauntered over to Miska. He laid a paw on the bear's shaggy coat. A narrow band of tiny shimmering lights rose up like a minuscule wave and passed over the bear's body.

The great bruin shook its huge head, saw the panther poised to leap, and instantly tensed.

Smokey leapt up to Miska's shoulder and promptly batted the bear's ear. The bear turned his head, considered Smokey, and visibly relaxed. Dropping back down to all fours, he began to lick the wounds on his forelegs.

Smokey walked over to the tent flap, turned and looked over his shoulder at the men.

Meow . . .

Mark remarked, "I think Smokey is telling us it's time to leave. Miska? Miska, it's time to go."

The big bear looked up and *huffed* in acknowledgment. Wagging his great shaggy head, he ambled toward the exit.

Trey noted the intelligence deep in the bruin's eyes, and had a moment of gratitude that Miska was an ally.

Turning to follow, he panned his flashlight across the shadowed recesses of the tent, and spied someone on the ground, not moving.

"Mark! Hold on—who is this?" Leaning over the unconscious man, Trey played his light over him.

"Some mage—she called him *Roland.* He's the one who bespelled Ellen."

"Did Miska do this?" Trey asked quietly, as he probed gently and found a pulse.

Mark looked away. "No, I . . . I was angry."

"Uh-huh, right," Trey breathed slowly, looking up at Mark.

"Will he, uh, be okay?"

The beaten man uttered a pained groan.

"Yeah, I think so," Trey answered cautiously. "Someone will find him soon enough—he'll be okay. Come on, we have to get Ellen to Gallenius—she's our priority!"

AS THEY EASED AROUND the immobile panther and left the tent, neither of the men noticed that the panther's eyes followed their every movement; nor did they sense that its heart burned with resentment and festering hatred.

You damned bloody fools! You would dare to interfere? This is not over!

CH 9

"PADRAIC, YOU HAVE TAKEN a very great—and unnecessary—risk in coming here now," intoned the Guildmaster, his displeasure evident. "The Citadel is full of people, any one of whom might see you, and thus compromise your position and mission."

"I had little choice, once I learned that Ellen was here and would be in imminent danger!" The Rogue was unbowed. "I have no doubt that Mab means her harm. Little did I know that both she and Stacy were *already* in trouble."

Padraic paced, his fingers clenching into fists. Frustration hovered around him like an electric charge.

The Guildmaster leaned back in his chair and steepled his fingers.

"Calm yourself, Padraic. As I have already explained, both Ellen and Stacy are no longer in any immediate danger. It is true that Ellen is still unconscious—apparently the result of some spell; but Gallenius is working to counteract that. I have sent for him; he will join us shortly. Now please, resume your seat."

Padraic slumped into the chair like a petulant child, and flared as the Guildmaster chuckled.

"You find something amusing, Guildmaster?"

"Let us just say that I never expected that you would behave so, um, *paternally*."

That observation gave Padraic pause; he took a moment to gather his thoughts.

"In a way, I must admit I am surprised as well. I am feeling things; the urge to protect and shelter her, to see her *happy*. I have not felt this strongly about anyone before. I do not fully understand it; and yet, I worry about her."

"Welcome to parenthood, my friend," said the Guildmaster kindly.

A knock on the door announced the arrival of Gallenius. His eyes widened at the unexpected sight of Padraic and he quickly shut the door behind him.

"Guildmaster, Lord Padraic," he greeted them formally, with a slight bow. "I am at your service."

"Gallenius, no one else is to know that Padraic is here. Now, please give us a report on the Lady Ellen's condition."

"Of course. She is under the influence of a strong spell cast by a young Were mage called Roland. Our information on Roland is sparse; until last year he was a promising student of Zerban, the Senior Were Mage. By the way, Zerban is missing; we have information that he went to Olmus and somehow disappeared there. Anyway, in regard to Roland, he completed his training, earned an adept's staff, and set up his own practice. As far as we know, no Were lord took him into his household."

"Could we please focus on Ellen?" snapped Padraic irritably.

"Ah, forgive me, m'lord, but there is some relevancy here. Lady Ellen is under a *suspension of consciousness spell,* one that was cast with considerably more force than was necessary.

"Based upon what we have learned from Lord Mark, we know that the Were commander, Ling, ordered Roland to render the Lady Ellen unconscious *'but not harmed'*. We believe that Roland, a new mage and relatively inexperienced, overcompensated in the casting. In his haste or eagerness, he crafted too vigorous an enchantment—it was simply too strong. We have done all we can safely do to mitigate its effects. The spell will wear off as its energy dissipates. That is the safest course; we dare not meddle further."

"How long?" asked Padraic.

Gallenius shrugged. "A day at most, more likely something considerably less than that. We do not know for certain, but it will take time, at least hours from now."

"So, she will be safely watched over as she recovers," added the Guildmaster, opening his palms to Padraic.

The Rogue thinned his lips and nodded in acceptance.

The Guildmaster turned to the mage, "Tell us now of Lady Stacy, if you please."

"The Lady Stacy sustained some bruises, scrapes, and possibly a cracked rib. We have treated her as best we can, but it would be best if she were to return to her home realm for a more thorough examination and treatment. Lord Mark has been *most insistent* in that regard."

"Ah, yes. Therein lies the problem, gentlemen," observed the Guildmaster. "While some individuals can transit between some realms of their own volition—like Lord Mark and even you, Padraic, for example—only the Steward can open a portal that would allow another, or a group, to transit unaccompanied. And alas, the Steward now lays bespelled."

"What about a Grand Portal? Anyone can use that, if they have access . . . " Padraic began, but his voice trailed off as he realized the implications.

"True enough." Gallenius sighed. "However, only one Grand Portal is known to still exist, hidden in the Realm of Man. It does us no good *here,* in Storm Haven."

"So, until this spell wears off the Steward," Padraic reasoned, "all those from the Realm of Man are effectively trapped here?"

"Essentially, yes," agreed the Guildmaster, "as may be Miska, as well—I do not know. They, like the rest of our people who have taken shelter within the walls of the Citadel, are safe in the meantime."

"Perhaps, but only until sunset," Padraic warned. "Mab would be here sooner were she not inclined to wait for Leanan of the Sidhe—"

"What? Diere—I mean *Queen Mab*—is coming *here? Tonight?*" Gallenius blurted in shock.

"So we have just learned, thanks to Padraic," acknowledged the Guildmaster. "And she will be accompanied by not only Lady Leanan of Shadow, but Lord Addecus of Were. Although, just *how* she plans to accomplish this escapes and intrigues me."

Gallenius paled, but he found his voice. "This is most distressing news. Our wards are sufficient to deal with most of the sorcery we can expect from the mages of Shadow and Were—although someone the caliber of Zerban could be problematic. But the *Dark Elves?* Our protective measures have never been tested against the magic of the Dark Elves."

"Well then, we had better make some contingency plans. We still have several hours until sunset," observed the Guildmaster.

Gallenius turned toward the door.

"Hold! There is something else," ventured Padraic, "and I think you need to hear this, Gallenius."

The mage paused and glanced at the Guildmaster, who merely shrugged and gestured to a vacant chair. Gallenius sat and unconsciously smoothed his simple grey robe of office.

"Before I arrived in Storm Haven," began Padraic in a hushed voice, "I was required by Mab to attend a *rite of execution* in the Realm of the Dark Elves."

"Necromancy?" hissed Gallenius, his eyes widening in surprise.

Padraic nodded and sighed heavily. "Aye, I fear there can be no doubt. It was a bull, ensorcelled and abandoned. It was in bad shape. The elfin mages could not tell how long it had been so bespelled. They performed the rite without incident and the corpse was reduced to ashes. I was there to witness, as the queen's proxy."

"That is the *third* incident of necromancy within the last few weeks," Gallenius remarked.

"Ah, the third *known and confirmed* such incident," corrected the Guildmaster ominously, leaning back in his chair. "I do not believe these occurrences are coincidental. I believe it is far more likely than not that they are related. That may suggest that someone, or perhaps more than just one person, is ultimately responsible, but who?"

Padraic and Gallenius only shrugged. There were no answers.

The Guildmaster leaned forward, and raised his index finger. "Gallenius, please have our analysts review the reports of the incident at the Council meeting, when Mab was attacked by her ensorcelled guards. Also, have them reexamine Salidar's account of the rite of execution he witnessed in Shadow, an ensorcelled ogress, as I recall. If there is a connection with these three events, as I suspect, we must find it. Something is afoot; we cannot afford to be caught unawares."

"I shall see to it right away," the mage said rising. "If there is nothing else?"

The Guildmaster glanced at Padraic, who merely shook his head.

"No, you may proceed," the Guildmaster answered, "and waste no time. I fear that is the one resource we will need the most."

After Gallenius had taken his leave, the Guildmaster asked Padraic, "What are your plans now? You know you cannot stay here. You have a long-term role to play; that mission is too important to risk exposure."

"That reminds me," Padraic responded through pursed lips. "Queen Titania of the Light Elves has extended an invitation for Mab to meet with her at the castle of Duke Briar. The Elfin Accords and certain trade agreements are presumed to be the topics of agenda. Despite her reluctance, Mab can no longer avoid this meeting. So, she has decided to attend, and has made it very clear that I am to accompany her. I have some concerns—as you might imagine."

"I am sure you do," agreed the Guildmaster. "Duke Briar would still have your head on a pike, were he to have *his* way. Yes, we have learned of this invitation, but not of the timing for this meeting."

"The date has not yet been set, but I suspect Mab intends to manipulate the timing to her advantage. Given the option, I would really rather not attend."

The Guildmaster chuckled and shook his head.

"My friend, you have a singular skill with understatement. I am quite certain you would not attend, given the option. However, consider this; Titania surely has an ulterior agenda. She will not let Duke Briar, or anyone else, disrupt her plans. Any threat to the *consort* of the Queen of Dark Elves would be unthinkable under the circumstances. I would wager that Mab has also told you much the same, has she not?"

"True, she has," Padraic conceded, "but I do not trust Titania—or Mab for that matter."

"Nor should you. Titania has always displayed a curious—if not unhealthy—interest in you, my friend; but for what reason, I do not know. Nonetheless, this meeting will be a valuable opportunity to gather intelligence. Unfortunately, we have no assets currently within Duke Briar's household. You *must* attend."

Sighing, Padraic slumped once more in his chair and mumbled, "I suppose, but I—"

A muffled *CRASH* shocked Padraic into silence!

Desperate shouts and panicked screams echoed through the halls.

Both men were on their feet as the door burst open and Gallenius stumbled into the room.

"M'lords! We are attacked! Were troops have drawn up beyond the south wall—hidden by the rain and an unnatural mist. The sentries did not see them!"

"Have they breached the walls?" demanded the Guildmaster.

"No, they stay just out of bow-shot range, but they have siege engines with them, and—"

Another thudding impact shook the very floor upon which they stood, lending ironic emphasis to Gallenius' hurried report. Books tumbled off their shelves, and a small figurine toppled from the mantle to shatter upon the hearth.

Padraic grabbed Gallenius by the arm. "But your *wards—*"

"*Wards?* They defend against *magic!* These missiles are *rocks*—boulders of the earth—thrown by trebuchets!"

"Padraic!" the Guildmaster warned as he pried Gallenius away. "Only an earth elemental could deflect such things; we have no elementals here! These stones are often used to carry enchantments into a besieged place; our shields are designed to protect us from the sorcery!"

"Aye, tis the case here," agreed Gallenius urgently. "No spells have gotten through, but the rocks do damage enough!"

The Guildmaster spun Padraic around to face him. "Listen to me—you must go! You cannot be found—or even *seen* here!"

"But, Ellen—"

"She will be as safe as we can make her—now go!"

"But there must be *something* I can do?"

"Perhaps—but not here, not now! *Go!*"

With great reluctance, Padraic conjured a transit globe. Pausing only a moment, he realized there was nothing more to be said. He pushed into the globe and was gone.

ALONE WITH GALLENIUS, the Guildmaster spoke calmly.

"Move any wounded, and all noncombatants to the innermost chambers. Man the walls in shifts. At least half the men should get some sleep; it will no doubt be a long night. Have all our patrols returned?"

"Yes, m'lord, all but the patrol that went missing last night. Only our spies and scouts are still about in the countryside, continuing the search. Shall I recall them?"

"No, let them continue. However, their mission must be modified—we need intelligence. They are to keep searching, of course; but, they are to gather information as well. There is still no sign of the Shadow troops here at the Citadel?"

"Not yet, m'lord. They are reported to still be in and around their encampment—but come nightfall?"

"Aye, I fear then we shall be truly besieged."

Without another word, both men hurried to their tasks.

GALLENIUS HAD BARELY entered the infirmary room in which Ellen lay, surrounded by her anxious friends, when another barrage of missiles began to fall within the walls of the Citadel. Unattended carts in the courtyard were smashed to splinters. Nearby defenders scurried for shelter.

"Gallenius! What is happening?" demanded Mark. "Are we under attack?"

"Yes, I fear so. Were troops have commenced to sling heavy stones with their trebuchets. We can see that they have mangonels as well; but, the rains have soaked the ropes so they are useless—for now."

"What are *mangonels?*" asked Stacy.

"A kind of catapult that works with twisted ropes," replied Trey, who found his partner grinning at him. "What? Medieval History was a minor for a while in college."

Whatever clever retort Hawk was about to bandy died on his lips as the leaded window over his shoulder disintegrated in a shower of broken glass and splintered mullions. The gruesome missile thudded wetly against the far wall and rolled lopsidedly to the center of the room. No rock was this, rather a severed human head.

Gallenius winced in anguished recognition. Hastily covering the ghastly horror with a cloth, he turned to the shocked witnesses.

"We must move! To a better protected room—two levels above! Can you manage the Lady Ellen?"

"No problem," answered Hawk, as he and Trey scooped her up in a fireman's carry. "Lead the way!"

MOMENTS LATER, IN A well furnished room, Stacy sat on the bed, plumped the pillows and helped to tuck unconscious Ellen in. Satisfied, she stood, hands on her hips.

"This will work; that's a nice firm mattress. We should keep her warm."

Smokey seemed to agree; he curled up next to Ellen's pillow and purred soothingly.

Gallenius gestured to the only windows, which were smaller and faced the east and north respectively. "The attack comes from the south; so these windows should not be so vulnerable. We should be safer here."

"Whose rooms are these?" asked Stacy as she gazed upon the collection of stringed musical instruments displayed upon one wall.

"Why, these are my chambers," admitted Gallenius.

"They're very nice. What is above us?" she asked.

"The roof, a guard tower, and the roof garden, actually. Why do you ask?"

"I sensed something—a tree, to be honest." She shrugged and smiled.

He nodded and smiled in return.

"Ah, but there *is* a tree, a water willow. Let me explain.

"A very efficient system of drains and cisterns collects rainwater, which is then channeled into a rather deep rooftop pool. A valved drain at the base of the pool allows a sufficient gravity flow to operate pumps in a well at the basement level that in turn supplies the entire building with water pressure. Thus, gravity works the pumps to our advantage, you see?"

"I get it," Stacy assured the mage. "And the tree?"

"Ah yes, many years ago, a willow seed somehow took root on a small island in the garden pool; and, now a robust tree grows there. It is really quite beautiful."

The arrival of the Guildmaster drew everyone's immediate attention.

"Thank goodness you are all safe. Has there been any change in Lady Ellen's condition?"

"No, m'lord," answered Gallenius, "but she is resting easily. I sense that the spell is dissipating—slowly, of course, but diminishing nonetheless."

"Good. We must be patient," the Guildmaster said tiredly.

Gallenius pulled him aside and spoke softly. "Guildmaster, that last volley, in the infirmary, it was the head of—"

"I know—I saw," breathed the Guildmaster resignedly.

Gallenius winced. "I think we now know what became of our missing patrol."

Sighing heavily, the Guildmaster cautioned, "Speak no more of this, for now."

Turning back to the assembled companions, he spoke gravely.

"My friends, I am truly sorry that you are all more or less trapped here until the Steward recovers and can arrange to transit you home. Of course, it is perhaps possible that Mark and Miska may be able to transit to some degree on their own—"

"I am *not* leaving," interrupted Mark.

"Nor would I desert my friends," added Miska firmly. "And besides, I have tested my ability. I cannot transit from here on my own—something prevents it."

"The strengthened wards, no doubt," deduced the Guildmaster. "Whenever the Steward regains consciousness, and can do so, all of you must depart this realm."

"Forgive me for belaboring the obvious," said Trey, "but you are under attack! We can help. We are well armed and very skilled, in our own way."

The Guildmaster said simply, "This is not your fight."

"I beg to differ, Guildmaster," argued Mark, pointing to Ellen still unconscious on the bed. "We too have been attacked; we do not ignore such assaults."

"I see," the Guildmaster said wearily. "Then tell me, who are your enemies?"

"The troops of Were and Shadow, of course."

"Indeed? And not their leadership?"

"Yes, of course, their leadership as well," insisted Mark.

The Guildmaster eased himself into a nearby chair. "Have you not observed those who make their homes in Storm Haven? Have you not wondered where they have come from? For the most part, the majority are refugees from the realms of Were and Shadow, not much different from the conscripts who make up the bulk of the troops now squatting beyond the Citadel walls. In fact, the citizens of Storm Haven know that they very likely have relatives amongst these invading troops. Do you really think they wish them harm?"

The room was silent; the Guildmaster sighed heavily and continued.

"Sergeant, you say you are well armed, yes? Tell me, what effect your weapons would have upon the shape-shifting Were and the dark creatures of Shadow?

Or would your arms kill only those lesser beings among the conscripts, to include the humans?"

"I see your point, Guildmaster," conceded Trey. "But surely even your people would defend themselves."

"Oh yes, quite so, should it come to that," the Guildmaster agreed. "But we all know the most efficient way to kill a snake is to cut off its head."

"So, you would take out the leadership, rather than engage the troops?" proffered Hawk.

"*Take out?* Hmm, an interesting term, indeed," said the Guildmaster wryly. "I would prefer to reason with, persuade, or perhaps even disable rather than *kill*—a difficult enough task considering the nature of our adversaries. But yes, we would focus on the leadership."

"As I see it," offered Trey, "our full metal jacket 9mm ammunition for the subguns is only a sheath of copper over a lead core, and therefore not effective on a Were shape-shifter or vampire. Uh, no offense, Miska."

"None taken." The big man shrugged.

Trey nodded and continued, "But our pistol ammo is .40 caliber hollow points—"

"So," finished Hawk with growing excitement, "if we filled the cavities with silver—"

"Exactly!" Trey exclaimed. "We'd be back in the game. Now, where would we get some silver to melt down?"

"Silver is a spare commodity in Storm Haven," cautioned the Guildmaster. "Most is cast as rough shot and used in shotgun ammunition for the security forces. A modest amount is used in amulets and jewelry."

Gallenius took what resembled a small guitar down from the display wall and began removing the strings.

"These strings are fine silver wire," he explained, "I have a metalsmith make them for me. You are welcome to them."

"That is very generous of you, Gallenius," remarked Trey, "but we may need more silver than that."

Mark's mouth dropped open and he began fumbling beneath his cloak.

Miska noticed, his eyebrows rising, as Mark grinned broadly and produced a leather pouch.

"Hey guys! How about some silver coins?"

Stacy surreptitiously nudged Miska and whispered, "From the cave at home?"

Miska barely nodded; Stacy smiled smugly.

"Outstanding, Mark! That's just what we need," Trey announced, and turned to the mage.

"Gallenius, do you suppose that we can enlist the metalsmith's help in melting this silver down? I don't even know how hot we have to get it—"

"A bit over 1,600 degrees Fahrenheit for the coins, and about 1,760 degrees for fine silver," offered Mark, who smiled at the surprise on the faces of his friends. "I learned all about it when I was researching, uh, coins and collectors."

Everyone flinched as another muffled crash echoed from the floors below. Anxious shouts and the pounding of running feet followed.

The Guildmaster and Gallenius exchanged a worried glance. Stepping to the door, the mage peered down the hall and called out to a guardsman running past. After a hurried conversation, Gallenius returned to the room and assured everyone that despite the damage, it appeared that no one had been injured.

But they all knew his thoughts; no one had been injured—*this time.*

At a brief nod from the Guildmaster, the mage responded to Trey's question. "I am sure the metalsmith would help you, Sergeant, provided, of course, that the Guildmaster approves."

Facing the leader of Storm Haven, Trey opened his hands in supplication.

"Guildmaster, please . . . You know us; you know we will defend ourselves. We will help you in any way we can; we have no intention of deserting you in a time of need. We understand and basically agree with your desire to minimize any casualties; but, casualties may be inevitable."

"He is right, Guildmaster," Gallenius remarked. "We are running out of time; it will be dark in two hours."

"Sergeant, I will have your word that you will do your best to minimize any harm to the conscripts. Their leadership is, of course, another matter."

"You have my word, Guildmaster," agreed Trey. "As it happens, employing the minimum amount of force necessary is the standard operating procedure in our law enforcement trade."

"Very well," the Guildmaster acquiesced, and rose to his feet. "Make your preparations. Now, if you will excuse me, I must see to this latest damage."

With a heavy sigh, he nodded to them all and hurried away.

Miska and Stacy exchanged a knowing glance, and the big man cleared his throat.

"Ahem . . . Stacy and I will stay with Ellen. You all go with Gallenius to the metalsmith and do what you must with the silver. We will be fine here."

"That'll work. We'll be back as soon as we can," said Trey. "Please lead on, Gallenius."

WHEN THEY WERE ALONE with Ellen, Stacy asked Miska why he offered to stay with her.

"Was it because of the silver?"

"To be honest, it was—and it was not," he hedged.

"Although it is not widely known, silver is not quite as deadly to me, or the other members of the Ursus Clan, as it is to many, if not most, of the Were. You might say that our clan has built up a sort of tolerance over the generations. Silver does not burn me; I could touch it, and even hold it, but it would be *uncomfortable.* To be wounded by silver weapons is certainly painful—and dangerous—but is usually not fatal, unless the wound is very severe. However, the healing process can be quite protracted."

"I see. And you would prefer that this not become common knowledge, right?"

"Quite so, m'lady. I have no qualms about sharing this information with my closest friends, but . . . Let us just say that I am a very private person, and I like it that way. Besides, melting silver creates noxious fumes to which I am rather sensitive—it stinks!"

Stacy's nervous laughter was interrupted by another series of shuddering impacts and an arpeggio of shattering glass from a floor below them.

Miska reached out, grasped her hand, and said, "It will be all right. Let us speak of other things."

"What—to take my mind off being under attack?" She scoffed. "Ha! Good luck with that."

He could only shrug and offer a lopsided smile.

"All right," she conceded, "I know you're only trying to help. Tell me what happened when you and Trey went back and freed those Shadow soldiers who were on that work detail. All Trey said was that you all just cut `em loose."

"We did. Of course, Trey had a long talk with the man-at-arms, and then with his men, *before* we released them. Basically, he explained that we intended no harm, and only wanted to save our friends. He talked about the freedom to make choices, and to live peacefully with others.

"I do not remember everything he said, but I thought he was convincing. Then he told them where their tools and weapons were stashed, and we released them."

"Did they say anything? They didn't try to attack you, did they?" she queried.

"No, they offered us no violence—of course we were armed and they were not. But the strange thing was that they said not a word. They just walked off into the forest, in the direction of their gear."

"What could that mean? Do you suppose Trey got through to them?"

"I do not know," Miska admitted. "They just walked away. We left as soon as they were out of sight, and made our way to the windmill."

The momentary calm was shattered by another series of thudding impacts. This time, bits of spalled stone broke loose from the smooth surface of the south wall, and a lute crashed to the floor.

A guard burst through the door, clearly relieved to find that no one had been hurt. "Please forgive the intrusion, m'lord, m'lady—all are well?"

"Aye," assured Miska. "All are well for the moment; although, I fear they have found our range. Should we consider moving?"

The guard shook his head and shrugged. "There is only the roof and tower, m'lord. If you will excuse me?"

With a nod from Miska, the guard departed, closing the door tightly.

Another set of impacts rattled the instruments that still hung on the wall.

Stacy just cringed, and then gently pulled a blanket up to Ellen's chin, a token gesture of protection.

Glancing at Miska, she added ominously, "It's less than two hours until dark; it's gonna be a long night."

LEANAN AND ADDECUS arrived at Mab's special place within moments of one another.

They could see her standing in the solitary cone of light, resplendent in a shimmering crimson sheath that clung like a sanguine shadow to her svelte form. A delicate golden tiara adorned her jet-black hair, elegantly coiffed in twisted braids at the crown of her skull. Gold-capped hairpins of polished bone held the braids in place. A set of gold filigreed charms the length of a finger dangled from the small lobes of her pointed ears. The effect was dramatic and stunning, accentuating her elfin features.

Seemingly an unconscious gesture, Mab gently tugged the long sleeves at her wrists. The movement caused sparks of refracted light to dance from the large topaz ring on her left hand, and swirl about the eerie green glow emanating from an exquisite emerald ring worn on the middle finger of her right hand.

Addecus and Leanan could easily sense that the gemstones held powerful spells.

It was then that they realized that Mab was not alone.

A thin shape, hooded and stoop-shouldered, leaning heavily on a mage's staff, stepped forth from the darkness.

"Ah, good timing," remarked Mab to the strange figure. "Lord Addecus and Lady Leanan have just arrived as well. My friends, this is Gaspar, the former Magus Emeritus of the House of Hawthorn."

The elfin mage pulled his hood back, revealing his severe Patrician features beneath a sharply receding widow's peak. A beak-like nose and a dark brow over piercing dark eyes dominated his sallow face. His right cheek bore the traditional inverted crescent tattoo, the mark of a high-caste elfin adept. A livid scar creased his left cheek from temple to goateed chin like an angry scarlet worm.

Gaspar acknowledged Mab's introduction by merely cocking his head and nodding.

Arrogant conceit oozed from him like a vague and subtle stench.

Whether he was a powerful adept or not, Leanan took an instant dislike to this elfin mage, but thought it wise to remain silent, her expression stoic.

However, Addecus did not appear to feel any similar sense of cautious restraint.

"Gassspar . . . Gassspar . . . Now, why would I find that name sssomehow familiar, I wonder?"

"Perhaps," Mab offered, "because Gaspar was, at one time, the preeminent mage of Shadow. That is before my late cousin, Celeste, banished him from court—a grievous error on her part."

"Yesss—now, I remember," announced Addecus. "A mage known asss Gassspar had a disssagreement with Magusss Atrellan, a promissssing adept of the Dark Elvesss, many yearsss ago, a rather ssseriousss matter that resssulted in a wizardsss' duel. Would you be that sssame mage, Gassspar?"

Gaspar unconsciously stroked the long scar on his face as he glared in silence at the Were Lord.

"It is of no concern!" Mab declared heatedly. "I have elevated Gaspar to serve me as Magus Primus of the Dark Elves. In the last decade, he has taken upon himself the task of learning a great deal of very old and largely forgotten sorcery, arcane thaumaturgy that I have come to appreciate—as will you."

"Is Magus Gaspar to accompany us to Storm Haven, then?" asked Leanan.

"Storm Haven? Yes, I believe I may have need of his *special skills*."

Addecus and Leanan exchanged an uneasy glance, but neither elected to voice their concerns.

"If there is nothing else on your minds," Mab said acidly, "we should go. Are you both ready? Stand within the circle of light. A transit globe will be summoned, but I warn you—it will be of a very dark nature. You must not move! Let it encompass you, and the spell will take effect."

"And how do we know precisssely where we mussst go?" Addecus asked.

"*I* know!" Gaspar spoke for the first time, his voice a shrill and irritating rasp. "Now, be silent—I must concentrate."

Quickly meeting the Were Lord's yellow eyes, Leanan confirmed that he had missed neither the shocking *impertinence*, nor the blatant *gaffe;* and more importantly, that Addecus' thoughts and concerns mirrored her own.

You, Gaspar? You must concentrate? Is this not Mab's casting?

Such thoughts triggered faint alarms for the Sidhe and the Were Lord as the small black sphere appeared and began to grow. Rapid darkness overcame them, and they were gone.

CH 10

LYING MOTIONLESS UPON his bier, Gunther slowly sensed the sun slipping below the horizon. As his awareness increased, he soon realized he was not alone. Across the dimly lit underground chamber a lone figure reclined in deep shadow, just beyond the feeble reach of the solitary flickering candle.

He sensed a heartbeat and the bodily warmth of someone—or *something*—alive.

Propping himself up on one elbow he peered with his one good eye into the darkness. A pair of hauntingly luminescent eyes stared back.

"About time," came a woman's voice, tinged with impatience. "Arise, Gunther. Much has happened and there is much to do."

"Ling?" he mumbled.

"Who else?" she answered acidly, stepping forward until her thinned lips and drawn brow cast her face as a death mask in the sparse illumination.

Gunther merely grunted in greeting.

Lips curling in disgust, Ling asked pointedly, "Have you got your wits about you yet? Heed my words; your prisoners are gone—*escaped,* it appears—and that includes the Lady Stacy. Unfortunately, the Lady Ellen managed to escape from the Were camp as well. No doubt they are now *both* at the Citadel.

"Gunther, you must muster your troops for an assault on the city. I have already set my troops to besieging their walls, lobbing ensorcelled rocks and *other things* into their midst. But that amounts to little more than harassment; it will take both our forces to mount a full assault. We must act soon—tonight! Gunther, are you listening to me?"

Slowly coming to a sitting position, Gunther winced as he stretched.

"I heard you. What do you mean the prisoners are *gone?* And the Lady Ellen got away from *you?*"

"We have no time for lengthy explanations or arguments!" She spat. "Suffice to say that we no longer have our bargaining chips. And now we must plan on taking the Citadel. With the Steward no longer in my—*our* hands, there is now no other choice. At least the rain has let up. I think that may possibly work to our advantage."

"Why are you so eager to take this city? I have other concerns at the moment."

Ling seethed and flexed her hands stiffly. Her nails thickened into razor-sharp claws emerging from her fingertips, but receded as she tamped down her ire. With some difficulty, she managed to keep her voice even and its tone level.

"Need I remind you that our portals are gone? We have no supplies or reinforcements coming; what we have is all we will have! I have already lost the services of some mercenaries because my coffers are empty. And I have ascertained that you are no better off. And as for your other concerns, you should be pleased to hear that I have learned that your Lady Sabrina is *alive,* and being held prisoner in the Citadel."

"Sabrina! How do you know this? Tell me!" he insisted, shooting to his feet.

Smiling coyly, she reached out and stroked his arm. "Did I not tell you that I would make inquiries on your behalf? I have kept my word." She stepped closer to be face-to-face with him in the gloom.

"Tell me," he repeated.

Pouting coquettishly, she complied. "A patrol from the city skirmished with some of my troops. Only five from the patrol survived. I personally interrogated the captured prisoners, and thus learned that the Lady Sabrina lives, but is a captive. Now, does taking the city have more appeal for you?"

"You have a plan?" he blurted curtly.

"The basics of one, yes. Tell me, do you have water sprites—you know, nixies, undines, or the like among your troops?"

"I believe so. I know for certain that there are several urisk messengers within some of the minor nobles' retinues. I was told to expect a glaistig, as well. Why?"

Ling stood for a moment in contemplative silence, then gestured above her head.

"Come, let us get out of this musty hole and discuss our tactics and strategy above, under the clearing night sky. The rain has stopped, but much water remains. In fact, I think some flooding is inevitable."

Momentarily confused, he shrugged. "You need not worry; this chamber will not flood. It is well constructed and shielded from the elements."

Ling closed her eyes and bit her lip.

"I do not refer to your daylight retreat—I mean, I am sure that it meets your needs. No, Gunther, I was thinking more about the Citadel. Come, let us go."

BENEATH THE TEMPLE ruins on Olmus, George was rather pleased with himself. Under Daegon's tutelage, his skills, knowledge, and abilities had increased considerably. In token acknowledgment of his progress, Daegon had instructed George in the rudimentary spells necessary to view what the scrying orb might offer, and further encouraged him to spend long hours watching the crystal.

For some time there had been much to see on the plains of Olmus; and George was easily amused.

The two groups of troops had soon come to blows following the discovery of the slain Were soldiers who had been assigned as escorts to the mage, Zerban, and the subsequent discovery of the loose goat with the bloodstained tether. Violence seemed inevitable; accusations led to confrontations, and bloodshed followed.

George and Daegon found it highly entertaining, and relished in the *sub rosa* manipulation of the opposing forces. Highly entertaining, that is, until Lord Addecus and Lady Leanan arrived on the scene and put a stop to the violence, enforcing an uneasy truce. However, the Were Lord and the Sidhe did not stay.

Thereafter, it was then no great task to have the goblins surreptitiously create more mischief and bring the opponents back to the brink of confrontation. Several incidents had already precipitated a number of skirmishes. It would not take much to set off a full-scale battle.

George thought that might be great fun; however, Daegon felt it was foolhardy to let the situation escalate.

"Think, my apprentice! The goal must be to keep the two forces totally focused on each other, yet somewhat restrained. An all-out battle will only encourage each side to send for reinforcements through their respective portals—an unacceptable development. More troops will drastically increase the chances that we might be discovered. No, it is better to keep tension and tempers high, just short of losing control, a delicate balance of distrust, anger, and fear."

"Oh, all right," George muttered sullenly, "I get it."

"Good. Now I have much to do. Maintain your vigilance."

SOMETIME LATER, AS George gazed into the orb, something caught his attention. His eyes widened in alarm and he called out to his servant. "Clement, fetch Daegon—quickly!"

Staring intently into the crystal, his face paled and his breathing grew shallow. An icy chill rose up his spine and lodged at the base of his skull like a gnawing worm of fear.

“This had better be important,” warned Daegon as he strode into the chamber, the stoic Clement at his heels. “I was in a meeting with a messenger from the tribe of Red Cap goblins. They have found the bats we seek, nesting in one of their caves. Now, what is it that warrants this interruption?”

Stepping back from the crystal, George pointed to the orb. “Diere has come—and she is not alone.”

Daegon’s expression went blank. He stepped to the orb and scrutinized the moonlit scene within.

George pointed out the newcomers.

“There . . . they just appeared on that small hill. I recognize Addecus and Leanan, but I don’t know who is with them. Do you know this man?”

“Aye, tis no man—rather, an elf, and a *mage* at that,” answered Daegon. “That is Gaspar, I believe. I have not seen, nor heard anything of him for decades. He and Atrellan once fought a duel; Gaspar lost.”

“Yeah, whatever,” George said dismissively. “What are they doing here—and why now? Are they looking for us?”

“Hmm, they appear to be arguing.”

“Arguing? Well, turn up the audio.”

“What? Audio?” asked Daegon, clearly confused.

“Yeah, the *sound*,” George insisted, “turn it up so we can hear what they’re saying.”

“I do not understand,” began Daegon. “We can only *see—not hear*.”

“Oh, for crying out loud,” exclaimed George impatiently. “There’s gotta be *sound!*”

With that, George smacked the side of the crystal with his open hand!

The sibilant sound of the voice of Lord Addecus was suddenly in the room with them.

". . . wasss not what we were told. Pleassse explain thisss deviation from our plansss . . . "

Daegon's mouth dropped open in shocked surprise.

George just grinned and held one finger to his lips while he pointed with another into the crystal.

They both leaned forward to watch and listen as the scene unfolded within.

MAB COCKED HER HEAD at Addecus and smiled, but there was no warmth in her eyes.

"We have not the time for lengthy explanations, so I shall just say that it may be possible that Gaspar can exercise some control over these portals."

"Indeed? Can he close them?" asked Leanan with evident interest.

"Perhaps," acknowledged Mab. "He has made certain progress in his studies, and is willing to try. However, in the event he can do so, would it not be prudent to have your respective forces return to your home realms—*before* the portal is closed?"

"Ah, I ssseee. And asssuming he can clossse portalsss, you hope he can *open* them asss well. We could then sssend thessse troopsss where originally intended, to Ssstorm Haven. The original plan would be back in play. Isss that not what you have in mind?"

"Very good, Addecus. Yes, that is essentially what I have in mind. It may be that we will have no further need of the Steward after all."

Something in Mab's voice unsettled Leanan; there was more to Mab's plotting for certain. "What do you mean *'we will have no further need of the Steward'*?"

"Why, simply that Gaspar can do what we need done here," Mab answered.

"Here? No, I think you intend more than that," mused Leanan aloud, abandoning her usual caution. "I think you would rather usurp the Steward entirely, and take control of the Grand Portal in the Realm of Man."

"Well reasoned, my dear. I admit the idea does have a certain appeal," Mab said candidly, "but no one fully understands a Steward's power. Gaspar has delved deeply into these mysteries and probably knows more than any living mage. But it may not be enough—we shall see.

"For now, I must ask that you and Addecus take control of these troops; it is clearly evident that the discipline you imposed on your last visit is already breaking down. Get them separated and return them through their respective portals. Then we shall witness the extent of Gaspar's skills."

"Thisss will take sssome time, hoursss I ssshould think," cautioned Addecus. "I have another matter that demandsss my attention; Zerban, a sssenior mage of the Were isss ssstill missssing in thisss realm. I would know what happened to him."

"Your search will have to wait—we do not have the time to spare," Mab insisted. "Besides, is it not typical for a mage to go off on a quest, especially one of his own choosing every so often?"

"True," admitted Addecus, "but sssuch isss not the cassse with Zerban—not thisss time."

"Nonetheless," Mab responded firmly, "there is no time. You will have to come back here after we are done, to conduct a more thorough search."

Addecus considered arguing further, but Leanan caught his eye and gave him a nearly imperceptible shake of her head.

"Well then," announced the Sidhe. "If there is nothing else, I suggest we go and take command of our troops; it appears that restraint and discipline are sorely lacking."

"Please do, as quickly as possible," urged Mab. "Time is of the essence."

HUNCHED OVER THE WORKTABLE in the small room at the rear of the metalsmith's shop, Trey felt a neck cramp coming on as he carefully dribbled a trickle of molten silver from the tiny crucible into the cavity of the last .40 caliber hollow-point round. Replacing the crucible in its stand, he slid the tongs to one side and looked up as he removed the heavy leather gloves.

Hawk sat across the room stuffing twelve-gauge shotgun shells into a bandoleer while Mark reassembled a short-barreled Remington pump he had just cleaned.

"You know, this shotgun sure does point a lot faster than the skeet and trap guns my dad had, but I'm sure the range is compromised," Mark observed.

"Not as much as you might think," cautioned Hawk. "You're used to shooting low-brass target loads that don't have the reach of these buckshot loads. Even with that fourteen-inch barrel you'll get more range, and a much wider spread."

"Not to mention the, uh, modest increase in recoil," Trey interjected with a grin.

"Oh, I think I can manage," Mark replied drolly. "What percentage of the shot is silver?"

"About half," answered Hawk, "but you've only got thirty rounds; twenty-five in the bandoleer, and five for the initial loading. I'd recommend just loading the magazine tube and keep the fifth round in a pocket."

"Why? If I rack the slide and chamber a round, I can fit the fifth round in the tube."

"True," agreed Trey, "but don't underestimate the psychological impact of the unmistakable sound of a pump shotgun's action being racked. Sometimes that's all you need."

"Well, I guess that's so—in our home realm—but we're not at home, are we?"

"You just can't resist the temptation to debate, can you Counselor?" Hawk chuckled. "Have you forgotten that the guard force here also uses shotguns? Might we therefore reasonably assume that many in the realms may very well recognize that very special and authoritative sound?"

"Oh, yeah . . . Okay, I see what you mean," Mark admitted, and then deftly changed the subject. "How are you all coming with the pistol ammo?"

Trey gestured to the rounds arrayed in neat rows on the table. "All done, 176 rounds and we've even got some silver left, but no more bullets. I think they've cooled off enough to load the mags. We have fourteen magazines to load; five each for our two Glock 23s, and two each for our model 27s. You don't mind helping do you?"

"Of course not! Hey, do I get a pistol?" Mark asked as he picked up a pistol magazine and began loading rounds.

Hawk and Trey looked at each other in silence.

"Mark, have you ever fired a pistol," Trey began, "I mean one bigger than a .22? No? Well then, you'd be better off with the shotgun. It's a weapon you're familiar and comfortable with, having shot trap and skeet with your dad. Pistols are much harder to master, and we don't have the time to train you—not now. It's nothing personal, just the pragmatic application of available resources."

"Okay, I understand. Are you all willing to teach me—I mean later, of course?"

"Sure thing, Mark," Hawk said with a grin. "Why, Sgt. Bassett here is one of our finest firearms instructors, and the most brutal of range officers."

"Shut up and keep loading, rookie," Trey said sternly, but the corners of his eyes crinkled in a hidden smile.

The door suddenly opened and Gallenius stood there with a winded black-clad guardsman at his side. Without preamble he urged the guardsman to speak.

"Tell these men what you have just told me."

Nodding to the mage, the heavily breathing man composed himself and began.

"M'lords, the northwest gate has been opened—through treachery—our defenses there are overrun! Some waterborne minions of Shadow infiltrated through the sewers—flooded, they were, from the rains. Then they attacked the guards on the northwest gate. The fiends opened the gate, and now invaders from Were and Shadow run amok in the city!"

Hearing footsteps approach, Gallenius gripped the guardsman's arm. "That is enough."

Nestor, the metalsmith, entered from a back room and announced, "M'lords, the criers proclaim the city is invaded! All are warned to go to ground!"

"So we have just learned, old friend," responded Gallenius. "I trust you have made provisions?"

"Aye, suitable for myself and my family. But, what of your friends, here? I have not the room—"

"We need to get back to Ellen at the Ministry!" declared Hawk, slapping a full magazine home in the butt of his pistol.

"That you do," agreed Gallenius. "I must see to our wards—somehow they were compromised by these invaders. I will meet you back at the administration building as soon as possible. This guardsman will lead you there."

"What about your people here in the city?" Trey asked as he filled his utility pouch with full magazines, and nodded his head in Nestor's direction.

"Those not engaged in the defense of the city have places to hide—do not forget the origins of Storm Haven. This was once a community of the finest smugglers in all the realms; secret places abound here. Most residents will simply appear to have vanished. Be not concerned for them. Make your way to the Guildmaster in all haste! Be careful, I know not what you might encounter en route."

"We understand. You go on and do what you've got to do—we'll be fine," Hawk assured the mage.

With a nod to them all, Gallenius turned, left the shop, and disappeared into the dark streets.

"M'lords, I must lock up," Nestor said urgently.

"We're going, Nestor—and thank you," said Mark as he pressed the remaining silver coins into the metalsmith's hand.

"Hold on, just a second," cautioned Trey, fumbling in his pack. "Here, each of you should take a radio in case we get separated. Guardsman, what's your name—how are you called?"

"Uh, Phineas, m'lord."

"Okay, Phineas . . . I'm Trey; this is Hawk and Mark. We can talk to each other at a great distance over these radios. Just press down on this button and speak in a normal tone to be heard, and release it to hear what others say. Any questions?"

"Uh . . . No, no questions, m'lord."

"Good. Hawk, check the packs. What else do we have?"

"Flashlights with extra batteries, two night-vision monoculars, two tasers, OC spray, duct tape, plastic cuffs, a couple of tear-gas grenades, I think . . . Yeah, they're CS micro-powder softballs. Oh, here's the spotlight—now that might come in real handy."

"Oh yeah," Mark added, grinning.

"The subguns have 9mm FMJ ammo," reminded Trey, "so, depending on what we may have to deal with, they might not be that useful. We may as well keep them slung. Since Phineas knows the way, he'll take point. Mark, you've got the rear. That gives us shotguns with silver loads fore and aft. All right, stay alert. Phineas, lead on."

They soundlessly slipped into the dark street as Nestor bolted the door of his shop.

IT WAS NO LONGER RAINING; but puddles pooled everywhere. Moonlight shone through rents in the thick yet clearing overcast, rendering the scene a pale patchwork of shifting argent and impenetrable shadow. Gutters flowed freely, many awash. The eerie stillness and haunted silence were punctuated by occasional distant running footsteps and infrequent muffled shouts.

The men crept along in single file, as quietly as possible, seeing no one—and hopefully, seen by no one.

After a time, Mark began to think that he sensed something behind them, stalking them; but, he could neither see nor hear anything. He was growing increasingly apprehensive when Phineas suddenly stopped and waved everyone into a deep shadow near a wall.

Tensely anxious, they strained forward to see or hear what had alerted the guardsman. Moments later they too could hear it—a low snuffling sound, almost like a wet scrabbling and sniffling, growing louder and coming closer. It was vaguely familiar. Mark's throat tightened and he clenched his shotgun until his knuckles whitened unseen in the dark.

The sound stopped, and then resumed in a more agitated and excited way, as it seemed to creep closer still. Another sound began to overlay the snuffling, a high-pitched keening that descended into a manic gibbering and echoed off the walls of the lonely street like a cascading harbinger of demonic doom.

The four men involuntarily cringed where they crouched, sheltered only by a paltry pool of deep shadow.

From the middle of the street, a pair of indistinct shapes suddenly loomed and lunged at the hidden men.

Trey pushed away from the wall and triggered a pair of three-round bursts from his MP5 into each shape's center of mass.

The two vague forms shuddered with the impact of the bullets but they didn't stop. Hesitating for only an instant, they lunged again. Scabrous hands swiped and grabbed at Trey; horny nails raked his sleeve as he twisted violently and pulled free.

Losing his footing, his shoulders slammed against the wall and the breath *whooshed* out of him.

There was a sudden lull in the attack as the two forms pulled back—as if, like dogs, they had been called off.

Hawk pulled Trey to his feet and steadied him.

Trey struggled to bring the wavering muzzle of his weapon to bear, his lungs in spasm for want of breath.

In the street center, another pair of amorphous shapes seemed to materialize from the gloom, joining the first two. In the next instant all four forms uttered a shrieking, gibbering howl and rushed forward like an unfettered tidal wave of horror.

Mark leveled his shotgun at the attackers and pulled the trigger—but nothing happened! He had not chambered a round! Racking the slide, he tried to aim; but these things were too fast. He couldn't shoot for fear of hitting his friends. A clawed hand swiped at his head as he ducked and swept the butt of the shotgun up and into a grotesque masque of a face. The satisfying *crunch* of a jaw shattering sent a jolt down the length of his arm.

Just as his attacker faltered back a step, a searing white light exploded from the heart of the savage melee, washing over the combatants.

The attackers stumbled back in shocked confusion and began to frantically beat at the small flames that erupted in flares all about their bodies. The fires grew, quickly enveloping their tattered clothing and desiccated forms, until they shuddered and crumpled like charred and broken sticks into solitary puddles of steaming black ooze.

"Ghouls," spat Hawk, as he kept the spotlight on the foul bubbling remains.

"Is everybody all right?" asked Trey breathlessly.

Everyone mumbled assurances, staring at the putrid pools of muck.

"They hunt in packs," Hawk said softly. "We had to deal with some in Shadow."

Trey set his safety on his submachine gun and wheezed, "The 9mm had no effect."

"No, but two and a half million candlepower works just fine," responded Hawk, as he switched off the spotlight. "Whoa, that was bright! I believe it's the ultraviolet spectrum that does the trick, just like sunlight would. I think I'll need a minute for my eyes to adjust."

"Me too," agreed Mark. "I hadn't thought we'd be dealing with ghouls—not *here.*"

"Begging your pardon, m'lord," interrupted Phineas. "We could face any creature of Shadow or Were this night. We have had a number of reports of other beings, unconfirmed, for the most part, breaching our defenses."

"Hawk, about these ghouls," Mark began uncomfortably.

"Yeah?"

"We know they run and hunt in packs; but doesn't someone usually control them?"

"Yeah, you have a point there. We'd better keep an eye out—I don't think this dance is over. Maybe we should avoid the wider streets, move through alleyways and keep to the deeper shadows."

"Yeah, good idea. All right, stay alert," agreed Trey. "Let's move out."

AS THEY CREPT SILENTLY down an alley, with Phineas still in the lead, Mark asked in a hoarse whisper, "Anyone else smell smoke?"

"Aye, from the north," answered Phineas. "The market stalls are near the open gate, and we must pass close by."

"Quiet—listen!" demanded Trey. "Is that screaming?"

Standing dead-still, they could just barely hear a woman's plaintive cry for help.

"Where?" hissed Hawk.

Phineas looked around, cocked his head, and pointed. Without another word, the men started running in that direction, using the alleys for concealment.

They came to a halt at the entrance to a broad courtyard in which a number of torch-bearing troops in motley uniforms were quickly surrounding an impressive three-storied building, apparently setting up a defensive perimeter.

The screaming was much louder here; clearly, more than one woman was in great distress. It was coming from the upper floors of the surrounded building.

Keeping to the deepest shadows, Trey hissed into Phineas' ear. "Those are different uniforms—who are they?"

"Shadow troops . . . No, wait—there are Were troops as well, like those two coming from inside the school—"

"*School?* There are kids in there?" Trey spat, blanching in shock.

"No, no—not now at this hour," assured Phineas, "but there are teachers who live there, on the upper levels. I fear it is their screams we hear."

"Trey, I count twelve soldiers, that we can see," whispered Hawk. "There's no telling how many are around the back."

"These are humans, right?" asked Mark, and then added, "Remember what the Guildmaster said."

The strident screaming of one woman abruptly stopped with a gasping gurgle. A chaotic chorus of panicked cries and terrified wailing began anew.

Through gritted teeth, Trey said, "Humans outside, but we don't know who—or *what*—is inside."

"I don't see any firearms, just a couple of crossbows; the rest have spears and swords," observed Hawk. "I spotted one armored man, near the door; he acts like an NCO. What are you thinking, Trey? Draw them into something like an *L ambush*, to get `em in the crossfire?"

"Yeah, maybe—if we have to." Trey peered around the corner and studied the scene.

Mark was about to repeat his warning about the Guildmaster's wishes, when he had the sudden sensation once again that there was someone—or *something* coming up behind him.

Then he *knew*—whatever it was intended to attack!

"Behind us!" he shouted, spinning around and leveling the shotgun at where he instinctively knew the attack would come.

BLAAAMMM-M-M!

The report echoed through the alley as the twelve-gauge pump discharged. The muzzle flash illuminated the horror for only an instant; but that was enough.

The serpent was huge—its gaping maw the size of an open closet!

Right down that throat ripped the lead and silver buckshot!

The huge snake writhed in shock and pain. The massive coils of its body thrashed into the buildings on either side of the alley, smashing wooden walls, cracking mud bricks and stone masonry.

Mark felt a hand grab his shoulder and tug him violently to one side; a scaled coil smashed the spot he had just vacated. He was pulled off balance through the billowing dust and collapsing debris into a shattered opening in what had been, only a moment before, the rear wall of a building. Dragged along, he stumbled to keep up until he was pulled down near a wall facing another street.

There, Trey released him, holding his finger to his lips. The sergeant pointed to his partner.

Mark could hardly see in the dimness; but he could discern Hawk squatting at a barely opened doorway, peering through a small night-vision monocular at the street beyond.

Without taking his eyes from the street, Hawk said softly, "This side street is clear. All but four of the troops rushed for the alley. Wait—now, those four are bunched up at the doorway of the school. The man-at-arms went inside the building. Now he's coming out with another man wearing an eye patch. Oh, hell no!"

"What?" hissed Trey.

"Um, I think that's our old friend, Gunther. Yeah, it *is* him. Now the soldiers are forming up like an escort around him, and they're all moving off, to the north. They've turned a corner—I've lost visual."

"Gunther?" asked Mark, "He's *here*—already in the city?"

"So it appears," responded Trey, "another complication we don't need right now. Let's try and stay out of his way—especially you, Hawk."

"Don't worry—I have no intention of getting near him," Hawk assured his partner. "The street is clear again; all the soldiers are distracted for the moment with that serpent thing."

Phineas nodded and added, "A Were lord of some standing, I suspect."

"What?" hissed Hawk, "That's a *Were Lord?*"

They could hear the continuing commotion and the panicked shouts of the soldiers who had responded to the huge shape-shifter's mortal distress in the alley.

"Yeah, whatever." Trey scoffed. "Look, this may be our chance. Can we make it unseen to the door?"

"Yeah, I think so. They took their torches with them, so the courtyard is pretty dark," Hawk offered hopefully. "But hold on for a second, and let me check again."

"Good," Trey grunted. "Mark, are you all right? Can you run on your own? And by the way, how did you know about the snake?"

"Yeah, I-I'm fine. I don't really know how I knew. I had kind of a vague feeling, like a creepy itch between my shoulder blades, that someone—or *something*—was following us. But I didn't see or hear anything. And then, in the alley, I just *knew* that it was going to attack."

"Well, you sure did good, old buddy," Trey said grinning. "Just listen."

The cacophony in the alley had not abated one iota as the great serpent continued its death throes and the confused troops blundered about.

Hawk hissed from his position by the door, and gave Trey a thumbs-up sign.

"We need to go—now," urged Trey. "Hawk, take point. When we get to the door, we'll do a standard soft entry and clear the rooms we can on the way to the upper floors."

Hawk pointed to Mark and Phineas. "You two just follow our lead and cover our backs, okay?"

Mark nodded, and Phineas, wide-eyed and smiling, said, "Right you are, m'lords. Tis an honor to serve you, m'lords."

Trey winked at Hawk. "I think he's having fun. Let's go—now."

THEY SPRINTED ACROSS the night-shrouded courtyard and flattened themselves against the wall to either side of the door.

At a nod from Trey, Hawk reached for the latch and found it unlocked. Very slowly, he pushed it fully open.

A sole candle flickered in a wall sconce hung near the entrance to a long hall that disappeared into the darkened bowels of the building. A series of closed doors lined both sides of the hall as far as the lonely candle's light would reach.

The screaming, crying, and wailing rose to an ungodly crescendo, and suddenly ceased. The eerie silence was heavy, and hauntingly ominous.

Making hand signals to Trey, Hawk slung his MP5, drew his pistol, and activated the flashlight affixed to its frame. Slipping through the doorway, he went high-right; Trey followed, going low-left. At a wave from Trey, Mark and Phineas entered and hugged the walls.

Silently, they made their way down the dim hallway. Moving quickly they checked every room. Each had been ransacked, but was empty of occupants.

At the very end of the hall, they came to a dark stairwell. Standing back-to-back on the landing, Hawk and Trey swept their lights up and down the stairs. However, the beams only penetrated so far above or below, as if the dark itself eagerly swallowed the modest illumination.

Their lights did reflect off pools of water that had collected on the nearest individual steps, like huge wet footprints, but not nearly as distinct.

Hawk squatted down and dipped his fingertips into such a puddle. Bringing his fingers near his nose, he grimaced; the smell was sour and foul, like nothing he'd ever known or encountered before.

"This is *not* rainwater."

Hawk felt a hand on his shoulder, and looked up to see Trey cup a hand to an ear and then point a finger to the levels above. Hawk nodded and listened. The slightest muffled crying was coming from somewhere above.

As quietly as possible, the four men made their way up the stairs. On the second-floor landing, they found blood spatter on the walls and the open door. Strangely enough, there were water spots as well.

Their flashlights revealed the second floor to be a vast open space, holding a jumble of low tables and benches thrown about in disarray. No one was there; but there was more blood—a *lot* more blood, much of it diluted by the ubiquitous puddles of water.

Once they were back in the stairwell, they could no longer hear the soft crying from above. Instead, there were other small sounds, far more grisly and gruesome—smacking, cracking, and slurping.

With grim determination, the four men once more tread upward upon the wet and bloodied stairs. As they ascended, the sounds grew more distinct and harrowing—the sounds of a *feeding*.

The third-floor landing was spare, not much wider than the stairs. The lone door stood slightly ajar.

Hawk glanced over his shoulder and saw that his companions were stacked single-file behind him.

"I'll scope it out," he whispered. "Flashlights off, I don't want to be back-lit."

Retrieving his night-vision monocular, Hawk peered past the doorjamb into the room, and carefully scanned the area.

Breath stilled in his throat and his pulse pounded in his temples as he forced himself to commit what he saw to memory. He then eased back and gently pushed the door almost completely closed. Turning to his comrades he activated his flashlight, cupping its beam with his hand, and spoke breathlessly.

"Damn, it's a bad one—*old boots*, partner. Large open room, looks like half this entire floor. No humans—at least no survivors. Six perps, left to right; three werewolves, two uh, lizard-men, I guess, and one vampire, with long silver hair. At least I think it's a vampire; it was crouched over a body. All are in the same big room. Looks like a central hallway beyond the room, but too dark to be sure; poor lighting, just two candles on the floor. Phineas, I'm sorry, but it looks like they're feeding on some women's fresh corpses, four or five, I'd guess—the teachers?"

Phineas could not voice a response; he could only nod his head in resignation.

"How do we play it, Trey—hard entry and take them out?" Hawk whispered.

"I don't see any other option. Are we agreed?"

"Question," Mark hissed. "Are we sure there are no humans in there?"

Hawk shook his head. "I'm sure, Mark, no surviving humans."

Mark tensed and then shrugged. "Then, so be it."

"Phineas?" asked Trey.

"At your command, m'lord," the grim guardsman replied breathlessly.

"Okay, we go in fast—high and low—just like we've been doing," Trey murmured and activated his flashlight. "Brace yourselves for a shocking sight and don't freeze up. Target what's on your side of the room. Aim your shots. Oh, and Mark?"

"Yeah, Trey?"

"Don't forget to chamber a round," Trey teased, just enough to take the edge off Mark's obvious anxiety.

"Right—got it," Mark answered, grinning gratefully.

"Ready? Hawk, on the door. On my count," Trey whispered and held up three fingers, dropping each in succession as he silently mouthed, "*Three, two, one—GO!*"

STORMING INTO THE ROOM, they caught the occupants completely by surprise.

Flashlight beams washed over the bloodied muzzles of a pair of werewolves who had been busily ripping at a corpse. To their right, the head of a large lizard snapped up and blinked its large yellow eyes, pupils narrowing to mere slits in the confusing lights. Crouched nearby, another lizard had its entire head wedged inside the chest cavity of a brutally savaged corpse, blindly feeding, apparently oblivious to its surroundings.

For the breadth of a heartbeat, the scene seemed frozen in time. The lycanthropes appeared surprised and confused—but their befuddlement was short lived.

One of the werewolves heaved a decapitated head of a woman at Phineas.

The guardsman ducked, screamed a curse, and opened fire with his shotgun.

His companions followed suit.

Hawk felt a strange sense of calm detachment; for him, time slowed. It was almost as if he were watching the battle from afar, yet still through his own eyes.

He marveled at how easily he anticipated his target's movements, and compensated as the other werewolf leapt for Mark. Hawk sensed it was a feint—the beast twisted in midair and lunged, jaws agape, for his own throat.

Hawk carefully sent a silver-laden bullet through a lupine eye and into the hybrid brain. The beast dropped like a rock and lay unmoving.

MARK HAD FIRED ALL four of his rounds and was busily reloading when he heard Trey shout, "Mark—duck!"

Dropping to the floor and rolling onto his back, he saw something thick and long whip through the air inches above him—a scaled tail. He rolled onto his right side and saw the bloody maw of the huge lizard coming at him. He instantly rolled back to his left—the great jaws snapped shut just short of his face. The lizard lunged again; Mark knew those jaws would have him this time. So, he instinctively shoved the shotgun's muzzle into the scaly face as razor-sharp teeth clamped ferociously down on the barrel.

Mark racked the slide, chambering a round, and muttered, "Digest this!" and pulled the trigger.

The lizard's head exploded, showering Mark with disgusting shards of splintered bone and bits of wet tissue.

"You okay?" asked Trey urgently as he pulled Mark to his feet. "Man, I thought he had you!"

Wiping the muck off his face, Mark replied, "I-I'm all right. Damn, that thing was fast!"

"Yeah, but you were faster, my friend! Come on—Phineas is hurt. He took out the other lizard, but there was a werewolf we couldn't account for, until it attacked him from that hallway."

Mark could see Hawk bent over Phineas, who sat wedged against one wall, his legs splayed out before him. Hawk was busy administering to a bloody wound on the upper part of the guardsman's left shoulder, very near his neck.

"How is he?" asked Trey as he and Mark approached.

"Ah, it could be worse," replied Hawk, as he stuck out a flashlight toward Mark. "Can you hold this light? Yeah, right there, that's good. Gotta get this bleeding stopped.

"You were lucky, Phineas, an inch closer and it might have slashed your jugular. You're going to be pretty sore for a while, but at least you'll still be around."

"Hey, he was bitten by a werewolf, right?" reasoned Mark. "So does that mean that he'll—"

"Nay, m'lord," Phineas answered, grimacing with the effort and pointing with a long bloodied knife to the huge wolf's head lying nearby. "I am not cursed, for I have slain the beast that bit me. I must bring this head to the College of Mages. The curse will be sundered."

Trey's eyebrows rose as he and Hawk exchanged glances, but neither commented.

Mark held the flashlight steady while Hawk finished bandaging the guardsman's shoulder and started to fashion a sling for his arm. Squirming as he felt that uncomfortable itch begin between his shoulder blades, Mark twisted his head around, but saw nothing in the dimly lit room other than the evidence of the recent carnage.

Nonetheless, he was learning to trust his instincts. So, thinking they may have overlooked something, he gave voice to his concerns.

"Hawk, didn't you say that you saw someone else, someone that you thought was a vampire, somewhere in here, too?"

"Yeah, I saw something, at least one other, uh, *being*. I'm not really sure what it was."

"Well, I didn't see anyone—or anything—else with this group when we made our entry," Trey offered.

Hawk just shrugged as he finished fitting Phineas with a makeshift sling and helped him to his feet. Handing him his shotgun, Hawk said, "Good thing you're right-handed—can you still rack the slide?"

With a grin and a grimace, Phineas snatched the slide and jerked the shotgun, chambering a round with practiced ease.

"Uh, guys . . . I don't think we're alone," Mark cautioned, peering around in the dim room. "I think something's com—"

He never finished his warning.

Something fast and powerful erupted from the dark hallway, plowed into the men and sent them sprawling. There was a brief flash of green and silver, and the door to the stairwell landing banged open.

"The stairs!" shouted Trey. "It's headed down the stairs!"

Hawk swung his pack on his back and grabbed Mark's arm. "Listen—we got this! You help Phineas and follow us!"

"Got it—go!" urged Mark, as Trey and Hawk disappeared down the stairwell.

Mark gripped Phineas' uninjured shoulder, "You okay? Let's go!" and stepped toward the stairs.

But the guardsman balked. "M'lord, the beast's head—I must have the head!"

"Oh yeah, right," Mark responded, looking around for some means to carry the gruesome trophy. He spied a shredded bundle of fabric and hastily wrapped the bloody lupine skull, realizing too late that the cloth remnant was the remains of a woman's dress. He paled, but did not hesitate, stuffing the swaddled head into his pack.

"I'll carry it—you're down to one good arm, my friend. Let's go!"

"I shall be eternally grateful, m'lord," Phineas acknowledged as they, too, headed for the stairwell.

BELOW, TREY AND HAWK raced downward, one flight behind their quarry. As they reached the next landing, their flashlight beams caught the flash of green cloak and streaming ashen hair streaking across the landing below. The fugitive did not exit the stairwell at the first floor, but descended into the gloom of the lower levels.

Hawk would have continued to run pell-mell down the steps, but Trey grabbed his arm and hauled him to a stop on the first-floor landing.

"Wait a second, Hawk! Think! We haven't been below this level. If this is a vampire, what have we got to deal with it? My knowledge of folklore is a little bit rusty, and I'm not too sure about relying on just silver-filled hollow points, here."

"Yeah, good point—hold on."

Hawk rummaged through his pack. He straightened up, holding the spotlight and battery pack.

"The spotlight?" muttered Trey, not entirely convinced.

"I think it'll work. They can't take the ultraviolet light, just like the ghouls, well, almost, I think. I'm pretty sure that strong light works to some degree on any creature from Shadow."

"Well then," Trey reasoned, "I guess it's better than nothing. Better leave it off until we need it—I remember what it did to our night vision."

"Okay," Hawk agreed, returning it to his pack. "I can get to it pretty quick. Let's go."

They were far more careful and deliberate in their descent, relying on their pistol-mounted flashlights. There were two flights of stairs to the bottom, where they found a large expanse paved in broad flat stones.

"This reminds me of a warehouse, a big empty warehouse," whispered Trey, panning his light around.

"Yeah, doesn't it. Well, just remember what Gallenius said," Hawk grinned and mimicked the voice of the mage, *"smugglers 'R' us."*

"Oh, man, really?" Trey groaned. "That's just terrible."

Hawk grinned and played the light beam along the string of puddles to a wide waist-high wall of masonry. "Those weird splashes of stinky water are down here, too. See? They're almost like a wet path, leading off from the stairs. Hey, what's that over there, a low wall?"

Leaving Hawk to study the strange puddles, Trey moved closer until he could train his light over the lip of the wall. "It's water, and deep. I think it's a well, or maybe a cistern of some kind . . . Hawk?"

There was no answer.

Trey turned and called out again, "Hawk, where are you?"

Trey could see the beam of Hawk's light unmoving at floor level.

"Damn it, Hawk!"

He quickly headed in that direction and found Hawk's pistol lying on the stone floor. His pack and MP5 were lying some distance away near the foot of the staircase.

Trey had heard nothing, not a sound. And now, Hawk was nowhere to be found.

AS HE QUICKLY GATHERED Hawk's gear, Trey was certain he heard a soft splash and bubbling gurgle from across the vast space. He raced to the wall surrounding the well, panned his flashlight across the rippled surface of the black water, but saw nothing.

The subtle echo of footsteps descending the stairwell startled him, but he quickly recovered. Turning off his light, he moved to a better position, crouched in the darkness, and aimed his pistol at the foot of the stairs.

"Hawk! Trey! It's Mark and Phineas. Where are you guys?" hissed the voice from the stairs.

Trey activated his flashlight. "Here, Mark! I can't find Hawk. I found his guns and his pack, but he's missing! Watch yourselves!"

With the additional manpower, Trey was about to organize a comprehensive search for Hawk, but Mark pulled him aside.

"Trey, listen! It's Phineas; his wound is bleeding again and I can't stop it. We have to get him to a doctor! I need your help; I can't do it alone. We have to go while he's conscious—he's the only one who knows the way. Look, we can get some help and come back to look for Hawk."

However reluctant to abandon the search, Trey knew Mark was right—they couldn't let Phineas bleed to death.

Returning to the guardsman, who had slumped down next to the packs, Trey tried to rouse him.

"What . . . Oh, your pardon, m'lord." Phineas groaned and struggled to rise. "I am . . . a bit tired, m'lord."

"We have to get moving," Trey said helping the guardsman stand. "We'll get back to the streets and make our way to the Guildmaster's building. Can you show us the way?"

"Aye, m'lord . . . But not the streets—there, in that wall, a passage . . . Tunnels run under the city, a warren—but I know this one well . . . I-I used to visit someone here . . . But what of Lord Hawk—he is not found?"

"No, not yet," Trey answered, in grim determination, "but you can trust that he will be. Now, show us the way—there is no time to lose."

CH 11

LING WAS GROWING FRUSTRATED and angry. It was evident to her that she and Gunther were practically working at cross purposes. He was consumed with finding Lady Sabrina; she was equally focused on finding the Steward. Neither had made any real effort at collaboration; consequently, neither had been successful in their respective quests.

She was certain that the Steward was the key to getting clear of this debacle—but her logic had fallen on deaf ears. Stifling her impatience, she tried a new tack.

"Gunther, tell me, do you know any more now about Sabrina than we did when our troops first penetrated the Citadel's defenses? Have you any *clue* as to her whereabouts? Did you learn anything from the few prisoners your troops captured? Did any even survive your interrogations?"

He ignored her and pulled a pair of candles closer to the map splayed out on the table before him.

She paced behind him like a caged animal, her impatient strides swishing by his chair and causing the tapers' flames to gutter with each passing.

Their forces had commandeered this house within the city's walls as a temporary command post, having found the modest dwelling comfortably furnished, and vacant. In fact, very few people had been found by the invaders.

"You have no living prisoners, do you?" she spat. "You need not answer—I know all too well, for my own troops have done no better. Whoever is found and brought before a Were officer, does not last long. They divulge nothing of value—most likely because they know nothing of value!

"Our grand plan has collapsed! We have taken no slaves; none have survived. No matter—we could not take any to our home realms *without open portals!*"

He continued to ignore her; she continued to vent.

"Most Were of noble blood are in their animal forms; and the longer they remain so, the more susceptible to unbridled bloodlust they become. The human troops—even the men-at-arms—are avoiding their Were officers. The command structure is breaking down. I am losing control of a command I *never* wanted. And we are *still* trapped in this gods-forsaken realm!"

Glancing up from the map, Gunther interjected irritably, "Ye gods, woman, do you ever shut up?"

That did it.

Ling froze in mid-stride and ground her teeth. Fingernails thickened into claws; an unholy light flared within the depths of her narrowed eyes. Her breathing grew deep and her voice dropped to a husky rasp.

"What . . . did . . . you . . . say?"

He did not immediately respond. The sudden chill in the room may have prompted Gunther to consider that he may have spoken too candidly—and far too thoughtlessly.

Silently she stepped closer, directly behind him.

Rap-rap-rap!

The sudden brisk knock upon the only door broke the tension.

A man-at-arms, panting for breath, entered and bowed briefly.

"M'lord, m'lady, the Lady Triona has come—and she has a prisoner!"

As Ling backed off, Gunther seized the opportunity to rise and move away from her.

"A prisoner?" he echoed. "Indeed? Show her in."

The soldier nodded and withdrew.

"Who is Lady Triona?" asked Ling, her emotions once more under control and her composure intact.

"Lady Triona of the Glaistig is a noble of a waterborne clan of vampires. It was she who led the nixies, urisks, and the asrai through the flooded sewers and wells to seize a gate, thus giving our troops access to the city." Gunther leveled a finger at her. "You should remember—it was *your* idea."

"Yes, of course. It is just that I have never before heard of the Glaistig. Nor did I know just whom you sent to infiltrate the water system."

"It does not matter." He waved a hand dismissively and shrugged. "Few outside of the Shadow nobility know of the Glaistig. They are a very private clan, good hunters, and quite sensitive about their appearance."

Another sharp knock on the door announced the Lady Triona's arrival.

THE MAN-AT-ARMS ENTERED and held the door open as a woman of medium height swept into the room.

She was quite beautiful, ice-blue eyes and long ashen hair. She wore a loose floor-length robe of iridescent green, resembling a serape, trimmed in an intricate web of delicate black lace. Her gaze lingered upon Ling for a moment longer than normally considered polite; then she nodded.

Ling knew instinctively that this newcomer had taken her measure, and understood her true nature. This glaistig could be a formidable ally—or enemy.

"Ah, Lady Triona. This is Ling of the Were." Gunther nodded and placed his hands on his hips. "Now, what is this about a prisoner?"

"Gunther, you are so brusque—that was barely a polite introduction," Lady Triona said sweetly, and turned to Ling. "We must make time to get to know one another, my dear—"

"Triona, the prisoner?" interrupted Gunther.

"Oh, very well," she acceded.

Her voice hardened as she gestured to the man-at-arms. "Bring him!"

Triona waved a finger at the vampire lord. "Know this, Gunther—I had no intention of taking any prisoners! I was promised I could slay and drink my fill. This one was not drained—he still lives only because he is *marked!*"

"Marked?" repeated Gunther. "Are you certain?"

Two soldiers staggered through the door, supporting an unconscious man, his arms held across their shoulders. At Gunther's direction, they lowered him to the floor.

Ling took a candle and stooped over the supine man, carefully looking at his clothing. "He lives; but he is soaking wet. These *clothes*—this one is from the Realm of Man!"

Taking the other candle, Gunther squatted and grasped the man's jaw. Slowly rocking the prisoner's head from side to side, Gunther studied his features in the flickering light.

"This one," Triona began, her voice growing colder with each word, "actually *hunted* me! I would have gladly slain him—but for her mark."

"*Her* mark?" asked Ling, looking up. "Who?"

"The Lady Leanan of the Sidhe," answered Gunther, slowly standing, a hand unconsciously stroking his eye patch. "I know him; he is called Lord Hawk. He *is* of the Realm of Man. Furthermore, I have *unfinished business* with him."

Gunther returned the candle to the table, flexed his hands, and advanced on the unconscious man.

"Wait! Just a minute, now," Ling said placing a hand on Gunther's arm. "This can work to our advantage—assuming he is unharmed. Lady Triona, how is it that he is unconscious?"

"It was a small but necessary spell, to temporarily suspend his need for breath—for traveling purposes, so to speak. This will pass and he will fully recover. You see? He breathes normally even now. I would not have harmed him, not with her mark upon him."

Gunther scoffed. "Hmmph, I do not understand—how is this to our advantage?" A trace of angry petulance in his voice clearly betrayed the ember of revenge smoldering in his heart.

"Think about it, Gunther," Ling said smoothly, and nodded graciously to the glaistig. "Thanks to Lady Triona, I believe we have just found a significant bargaining chip, one that may restore the Lady Sabrina to you—*and* compel the cooperation of the Steward."

"But we do not know where either one is," he whined, clearly unhappy that his vengeance was to be denied—at least for now.

Placing her candle on the table, Ling gathered her thoughts, and then faced Gunther with open palms.

"We need only determine where the seat of government is—the administration of this realm. Then, with the right tactics, we can have those who are in charge bring Sabrina and the Steward to us."

Ling gestured to Hawk. "Do not underestimate the value that the Steward places on this man. I think she would go to great lengths on his behalf."

"So? How do we find this administration?" he asked, his interest growing.

"It will be housed in a well-defended building of some considerable size," Ling reasoned, and smiled at Lady Triona, "most likely conveniently located, somewhere near the heart of the city, and served by an excellent—and consistent—water source."

Triona returned Ling's feral smile. "Ah, I see. Have you any maps?"

"Indeed, we do," answered Gunther, beginning to smile and nod as well, as he gestured to the table. "Indeed, we do."

THE GUILDMASTER LEANED across his chaotically cluttered desk in a gesture of earnest sincerity.

"I am so sorry, Sergeant, but I have no one I can spare at this moment. I would willingly go with you myself, if I could. The guardsmen here in the Ministry building are the last of our reserves; all the rest are now operating in small guerrilla teams throughout the Citadel. I simply cannot strip this facility of the remaining guards. We treat the wounded here in the Ministry building—they must be protected."

Trey pressed his lips into a thin line and fought to maintain his decorum. He knew the Guildmaster was right—but he simply could not abandon Hawk, his partner.

Then Mark put it to words with a simple eloquence. "Guildmaster, we understand—truly, we do. And I'm sure you can understand that we will not desert our friend in his hour of need. We will commence our search without further taxing your hospitality or resources. There is no need to put your people in additional jeopardy. We regret that the guardsman, Phineas, was wounded while assisting us. Have you any word on his condition?"

"*I* do," announced Gallenius, as he entered the Guildmaster's office. "Please forgive the intrusion, m'lords. I am happy to report that Phineas will fully recover in time—and no, he will not suffer any ill effects from the 'curse' of the werewolf's bite."

"He told us as much," interjected Mark, "provided he brought the beast's head back to your mages. Could you further elucidate?"

Gallenius first looked to the Guildmaster for guidance, who offered a nod to signify his approval.

The mage began, "Counselor, please understand that this would not normally be the sort of information that the College of Mages would share, but under the circumstances—"

Sudden explosions, muffled by distance, interrupted. Panicked shouts from nearby halls were followed by another series of muffled explosions.

A guardsman armed with a shotgun burst into the room.

"M'lords! We are breached! The lower-level baths—water demons and soldiers! We cannot hold them; they are too many, forcing us back!"

"Gallenius, muster what mages you can," urged the Guildmaster. "Cast some barrier wards, and move everyone to the upper floors!"

Gallenius rushed from the room.

Trey grabbed the three backpacks at his feet and rummaged through their contents. He quickly selected items from each and crammed all the chosen gear into one pack.

Glancing up he said, "I believe we can be of some help, Guildmaster—but I can't assure you we won't shed anyone's blood."

"I understand," the Guildmaster responded sadly. "Please, I would wish no harm—to anyone."

"We will use only the minimum force necessary," Mark hurriedly assured him, and looked to Trey for confirmation.

"Of course," Trey agreed, as he slung the stuffed pack over one shoulder.

Mark turned to the anxious guardsman. "Can you show us?"

Racking the slide on his short-barreled shotgun, he replied, "Aye, this way, m'lords."

FOLLOWING THEIR GUIDE down a wide circular stairwell, brightly illuminated by strategically placed electric lightbulbs, Trey pressed the guardsman for more information.

"We did not see them enter, m'lord. It was as though they were just suddenly there, in the lower bath halls—at least a dozen armed men!

"There were four guards on that level; only one managed to fight free and raise the alarm. More guards responded of course, but by then the attackers had doubled in number and would not be contained on that level. Our squads engaged them in the stairwells and slowed their advance."

As they hurried on their descent, the sounds of fighting could be heard; clashing steel, shouting, screams, and the occasional *boom* of a shotgun.

"You said something about *water demons*. What did you mean?" probed Mark anxiously.

"I have not seen them; but I have been told that small, but ferocious, beings arose from the water and attacked. And that some human invaders were led by a green-clad vampiress! Also, a male vampire wearing an eye patch followed her."

"Anything else?" asked Trey, shooting Mark a meaningful glance.

"M'lord?"

"Anything *unusual?*" Trey pressed, ignoring the blatant irony, as the din of battle loomed loudly ahead.

The guardsman had to shout to be heard, "Well, aye, m'lord, one strange thing, all of them—the human troops, too—were *soaking wet!*"

They rounded the final few steps and found a scene of utter chaos; a mass of frenzied struggling bodies, slowly being pushed back, up the stairwell toward them.

Their guide shouted a battle cry and charged into the melee.

This was vicious and brutal hand-to-hand combat. Enraged and bloodied men slashed and grappled with each other on the crimson-stained stairs. Any thoughts harbored by Trey and Mark of sparing the lives of the human interlopers evaporated with the squelched scream of another victim falling beneath the slashing steel of the invaders.

The stalwart defenders were woefully outnumbered and slowly losing ground. Another mass of enemy troops—soaking wet, as well—appeared from somewhere below and swelled the ranks of those pushing their way upward.

This battle was moments away from descending into outright butchery.

Trey grabbed Mark and shouted, "They can't hold! Too many reinforcements! We need to give our guys a chance to pull back!"

Mark nodded and raised his shotgun; but, Trey pushed the muzzle down and shook his head.

"No, not like that—not yet," he insisted, rummaging in his pack.

"Here!" Trey shoved a softball-sized object into Mark's hand. "It's a CS grenade—tear gas—pull the pin, then lob it over their heads, back to where the fresh troops are coming from, got it?"

Trey retrieved another CS grenade from his pack. "Watch me—do what I do!"

Mimicking the sergeant's actions, Mark pulled the pin and sent the grenade sailing over the heads of the nearest combatants. A few seconds later, a pair of barely audible *pops* sounded over the din from the lower stairwell, followed shortly by an epidemic of coughing and gasping.

The tide of the battle did not exactly turn, but the momentum stalled, and faltered. No longer was there a constant push from below; no fresh troops surged upward. The defenders had managed to stop the advance, but stiff fighting waged on.

Trey pressed an aerosol canister into Mark's hand and shouted, "OC spray! We have to get these guys disengaged so they can pull back! It sprays in a focused stream for about ten feet—aim it so it arcs over our guys' heads. Try for the eyes of the enemy troops behind their front line, a couple rows deep; then move forward and spray the next closer group. Watch me and do the same—don't get any on our guys, okay?"

"Got it!" Mark joined Trey in spraying long streams of pepper oil extract.

The effect on most of the invaders was almost immediate; for others, it took a few moments. Soon enough, the impact was evident; soldiers pulled back, rubbing their eyes and sucking great gasps of breath. Some dropped to their knees, wailing and coughing. Within a few moments the opposing forces had fully disengaged.

Trey found the guardsman they had followed and urged him to have his comrades fall back and regroup. Of the ten men left, four were injured and had to be helped; nonetheless, they retreated up the stairs.

Mark was the last to ascend, his shotgun leveled at the steps below; however, the enemy, now blinded, gagging, and disoriented, did not follow.

At a landing some distance above the skirmish, Trey stopped the group and assessed the injuries. "Listen, some of these men need immediate medical attention. Is there a doctor—a healer—nearby?"

"Aye, m'lord, on the fourth level, two floors above us. If we continue to ascend, you shall see!"

"Just how far does this stairwell go—how high?" Mark asked.

"Why, all the way to the roof, m'lord."

"Does it stay this wide—does it get any narrower?" Trey pressed, a tone of urgency coloring his words.

"Aye, m'lord, it narrows to less than half this width beyond the fourth level. There are heavy doors at that landing, one to the ascending stairs, and the other into the infirmary. The infirmary is well guarded."

"Excellent!" exclaimed Trey. "We can make a stand there if we have to. They can only come at us a few at a time—a strategic choke point."

"Hold on," cautioned Mark. "Are there other ways up—from the baths, I mean?"

"Aye, m'lord, there is another stairwell, not as wide as this, on the other side of the building. It accesses every floor and ascends to the roof as well. Another squad was sent to guard it, but I know not how they fare."

"Damn, we could be flanked," cursed Trey. "Let's move out, and get these men to the, uh, healers. Then I'll go check on that other squad."

"You want me to stay with this group and try to secure those doors—you know, at the landing where the stairwell narrows?" asked Mark.

"Yeah, if they come—and I think they *will*—try to hold them there. Keep in mind that if they can get to the roof by the other stairwell, they could descend this one and flank you. If so, you might have to pull back into the infirmary."

"Yeah, I know," Mark acknowledged grimly.

Trey shoved his pack into Mark's arms. "I'll leave the backpack with you. There are a couple more cans of OC spray in there; use `em if you need `em. Now, let's keep moving."

Faces set in grim determination, the men started up the steps once again. They moved at a deliberate pace in consideration for their wounded, but they kept a wary eye on the steps below.

There was still no sign of pursuit—yet.

As they came to the next landing, Mark leaned into Trey and said softly, "You know, I didn't see any demons or vampires in that mess below—*and I looked*. Those troops were human—*all* of them. But, on the other hand, I don't doubt the guardsman's words either."

"Neither do I, Mark." Trey pointed to the ascending stairs. "The infirmary is only one floor up—keep these guys together and stay alert—you got this. I'm gonna go check on that other stairwell. I'll meet you at the infirmary as soon as I can."

"No problem—be careful."

GALLENIUS STRUGGLED under the weight of the wounded junior mage. The bloodied young man had been severely beaten, and was barely conscious. He could not have walked at all, much less managed the stairs, but for the senior adept's assistance.

Nor was Gallenius unscathed; a trickle of blood seeped down his forehead from a coagulating scalp wound, stinging his eyes and blurring his vision. Momentarily leaning the younger man against the wall of the landing, Gallenius wiped a singed sleeve across his own bruised brow and tried to slow his pounding pulse and gasping breath.

The sound of quick footsteps echoed through the open door of the landing. Peering down the long hall, he saw—with considerable relief—Trey hurrying toward him.

"Gallenius! You're hurt! What happened?"

"Invaders," the adept gasped, "in the building . . . came up these stairs . . . This is Aaron, a mage . . . He was starting to set up a barrier spell . . . on the stairs below when they attacked . . . Almost too late, I came to his aid . . . There was a huge fight—but we finally got the barrier up."

Trey helped to hold the wounded man upright. "I was coming to check on the guardsmen who were supposed to be holding this stairwell. So, where were they? Let's get you both to the infirmary. You can tell me the details on the way."

Shuffling forward, with the battered mage between them, Gallenius tried to explain.

"A squad of guardsmen was posted there, but they were overrun by dozens of Shadow troops. Aaron was taken and beaten. I surprised them, managed to free him, and stop most of the invaders. However, many got through to the upper levels, before we managed to invoke the barrier spell. I do not know how many guardsmen survived—a few gave chase, but most were down."

"Damn," groused Trey, "that means Mark and the other squad of guardsmen will be flanked for sure. They're setting up defenses on the fourth floor landing of the other stairwell."

"That was to be Aaron's next stop, to erect a barrier spell in that stairwell, too," Gallenius explained, as they ascended, the wounded man feebly trying to climb the steps while propped up between them.

"I gotta ask," Trey probed, "how strong are these barrier spells—will they work, and for how long?"

Gallenius glanced aside catching Trey's eye. "They will work, strongly at first; but they will wane in a matter of hours, likely less. They are temporary measures at best, buying us some time."

"I've gotta go back—warn Mark and those guardsmen," Trey insisted, then paused. "Listen, did you see any water demons? There was a report of something like that in the lower-level baths."

Gallenius paused and shook his head. "No, I did not. Generally speaking, creatures like that cannot venture too far from water. I do not discount the report—on the contrary, if true, they are likely still in the lower levels. Now, as for warning those guarding the other stairwell, it should not be you, Sergeant, but rather *me*. If you can help me get Aaron to the infirmary, I shall go to the other stairwell and cast the necessary barrier spell. That should free Mark and a few guardsmen to find those invaders who have slipped through our defenses."

"But," Trey objected, "you're injured, too."

"My wounds are superficial; but Aaron needs immediate attention. And I have to get to the Guildmaster as soon as possible—he must be warned. Furthermore, only I can now erect the barrier spell on the other stairwell, thus freeing Mark and the guardsmen. As soon as that is done, I too shall go to the infirmary. Under the circumstances, we actually have very little choice."

"Yeah, I guess you're right," agreed Trey reluctantly.

"There is something else, Sergeant," Gallenius cautioned. "Before Aaron initially passed out, he told me that among those who got through to the upper stairwell was a vampire with an eye patch, and a glaistig. He saw they had a prisoner, bound, blindfolded, and tethered with short ropes to a pair of soldiers. From the description of the man's clothing, I strongly suspect it may be Hawk!"

"Hawk? Here? But how?"

"I have no idea. Aaron did manage to tell me that his captors repeatedly demanded to know where the Lady Sabrina was being held. As you can see, Aaron did not tell them. I came upon the scene before they could do him more serious harm. We must keep moving."

ASCENDING THE STAIRS with a wounded man who could hardly walk seemed to take forever.

Trey winced at Aaron's bloodied face and slumped posture as the lad gamely clumped up the steps; he had clearly been through an ordeal. It did not escape Trey that Gallenius chose not to remark on his own actions in the rescue, but his singed sleeves, blossoming bruises, and crusting head wound spoke silent volumes.

Shaking his head in sympathetic acknowledgment, Trey said, "Aaron is a very brave young man to have kept silent under the circumstances. Unfortunately, that doesn't mean they won't beat Sabrina's location out of someone else. And that means they will likely take Hawk there—a prisoner exchange, perhaps?"

"That is my thought as well," confirmed Gallenius.

"Yeah, but where? Near where she's being held?"

"Aye, 'tis most likely. Listen, from the infirmary, make your way to the roof. There is a heavily guarded solitary tower at the northeast corner. The Lady Sabrina is held in the uppermost chamber, a windowless cell, its walls latticed with straps of silver, beneath a shielded quartz roof—easily opened to the sun at a word."

"Ah, I see—silver and sunlight," murmured Trey appreciatively. "You could hold a were-creature or a vampire there."

They crested the fourth floor's narrow landing and saw the two stout doors. Gallenius rapped upon one in a particular pattern and received a curious set of knocks in return, which he answered. The door swung inward and two black-clad guardsmen stood there with leveled shotguns.

At a nod from Gallenius, they stepped aside, allowing the three to pass, and then secured the door.

They stood at the end of a long hall, bustling with harried people moving among a series of open doors along both sides. The sense of imminent crisis loomed heavily about the entire floor.

Gallenius, the strain of the moment evident in his face, addressed Trey.

"Sergeant, these guardsmen cannot leave this post. If you will take Aaron through the second door on your left, you should find the healers. I thank you for your assistance. Now, I really must go. I will send Mark to seek you out, as soon as the barrier is in place."

"Okay. Tell him that he should wait for me with Ellen and Stacy. He'd probably go there first, anyway. Wait, Gallenius—one last question," begged Trey. "You said Aaron saw a vampire with an eye patch—no doubt Gunther—and a *glaistig,* right? Just what in hell is a *glaistig?*"

Gallenius paused, a shadow of concern passing over his face, and answered quietly. "*What in hell indeed . . .* A glaistig is a very rare and particularly insidious vampire with an unholy affinity for water, but not constantly bound to its proximity, a very capricious and dangerous being—one that it is best to avoid." The senior adept smiled sympathetically, turned, and hastened down the hall.

Trey shrugged and murmured, "Just great! I'd love to avoid all of 'em. Well, come on now, Aaron, let's get you to a healer."

STACY PULLED A BLANKET up to Ellen's chin and stared with deep concern into her friend's face. Looking across the room she found Miska's eyes upon her.

He shifted in his chair, slightly disturbing Smokey who lay obliviously napping in his lap. The big man's eyebrows rose in an unspoken question.

Stacy shrugged. "No change—she just seems to be asleep."

Smokey woke and stretched languidly. Dropping from Miska's lap to the floor, the cat stared at the door, his tail twitching.

"Someone comes," murmured Miska, gesturing at Smokey's alert stance.

A moment later, hurried footsteps could be heard approaching. An urgent knock rapped upon the door. It swung open to reveal a harried guardsman, and the Guildmaster.

"Please forgive the sudden intrusion," the Guildmaster exclaimed, as he stepped inside, "but you are all in danger! The Lady Ellen must be moved to a safer place!"

Miska was on his feet in an instant. "What has happened?"

"Elements of the invading forces have entered the building. Most have been stopped for the moment, but some got through! We do not know where they now are. I fear I have underestimated our adversaries. You must move Lady Ellen to the guard tower at the northeast corner of the roof. A squad of guards is stationed there; she would be safer in their barracks."

"Wait a second," interrupted Stacy, "we can't just leave! Mark and Trey are supposed to meet us here, in Gallenius' rooms!"

"Gallenius told me that Mark should be on his way here now; and I saw the sergeant with some of the wounded at the infirmary, when I took Gallenius there a few minutes ago."

"Wounded? They're *wounded?*" demanded Stacy, her face going pale.

"No, no—forgive me! Trey and Mark are unharmed," the Guildmaster assured her, "but Gallenius suffered a scalp wound and I insisted he go with me to the infirmary. There, I found Trey helping a wounded mage, and we spoke. Now, we must move Lady Ellen to safety. Time is of the essence!"

Stacy, her expression a mask of grim concern, spun to Miska. "Can you carry Ellen to this tower? If you get her to safety, then I can stay here and wait for Mark."

The big man nodded, but his concern was evident.

Turning to the Guildmaster, she opened her hands and asked, "But what about Trey?"

"The sergeant said that he would meet Mark here," the Guildmaster assured her.

Stacy nodded. "See? All the more reason for me to wait right here! Please, Miska, take Ellen and go!"

"As you wish," acknowledged the big man, and scooped Ellen up easily in his massive arms.

"Don't worry! When I get the *boys* together, we'll meet you at the tower," Stacy assured him, and then looked to the Guildmaster with an unspoken plea in her eyes.

"Very well, then." He sighed in resigned acquiescence. "Stacy, I expect that Gallenius may come here as well. Please tell him to find me at the tower as soon as possible."

Without waiting for acknowledgment, the Guildmaster turned and swept from the chamber, with Miska and Smokey on his heels. The departing guardsman gently closed the door.

THE ROOM FELT STRANGELY empty and somehow diminished, but Stacy did not have long to ponder the solitude. A soft, but urgent, knock was followed by Mark's voice.

"Stacy—it's me!" He pushed the door open.

They needed no words. Mark had her in his arms the instant he saw her; she buried her face in his neck and held on fiercely.

Arriving a moment later, Gallenius paused in the doorway. He smirked discreetly at their embrace, studied his toes for a moment, and then gently cleared his throat.

Stacy leaned back and saw the mage with his head wrapped in a bandage. "Gallenius! What happened to you? Are you all right?"

He grinned a bit lopsidedly. "I admit I have been better; this is but a bump on the head. Where is everyone?"

"Miska carried Ellen to the tower on the roof. And the Guildmaster wants you to find him right away; he went to the tower, too."

"Go ahead, Gallenius," urged Mark. "I've got to wait here for Trey. We'll meet you there. Stacy, you should go with Gallenius."

"Dream on, lover! I'm not leaving your side," she declared, tousling his hair. "Not ever! We'll *both* wait for Trey!"

"Very well—I shall leave you two alone." Gallenius snickered good-naturedly, and then added in a far more serious tone, "Be careful, and please join us as soon as the sergeant arrives."

"Oh, we will," Mark assured the mage with a small forced smile, as the gravity of the overall situation reasserted itself.

With a reassuring nod, Gallenius left the room.

MARK SLIPPED THE PACK off his shoulders and stowed it and his shotgun against the wall just behind the door. He stretched his arms over his head to try to relieve the tension that bunched his shoulder muscles and contributed to a dull ache at the base of his skull.

Stacy pulled him over to the bed and had him sit next to her.

"Okay, seriously now, Mark, tell me what's going on. Start with Hawk—where is he?"

"We don't know for sure; that's part of the problem." Sighing, he commenced to describe, albeit in a quickly abbreviated form, the events of the last few hours.

AS MARK CONCLUDED HIS explanation, she looked deeply into his eyes; his earnest concern was evident. She realized the stress was taking a toll on him, but she resisted the urge to press him for more information. He looked so *harried* and on edge.

Her heart reeled with empathy, and yet her mind swirled with questions. She deferred, sensing that the best thing she could do for him was to just be here, in the moment, and hold him.

A COLDLY IMPERSONAL female voice, dripping with droll sarcasm, interrupted their tender rapport.

"How sickeningly touching—where is the Steward?"

A striking woman of exotic features, wearing a formfitting, leotard-like garment of dappled greys and black, stood just inside the room. A lone coil of thickly braided jet-black hair snaked over one shoulder and dangled well below her waist. Hands on her hips, she scowled at the couple seated on the bed.

"Ye gods, I *loathe* having to repeat myself. *Where* is the Steward?"

Mark shot to his feet. "What? How did you—?" He leveled a finger at the interloper. "I know who you are—I think. You're *Ling,* of the Were!"

"Congratulations, but I have no time for this. The Steward—*now!*" she spat, advancing on him.

"Just hold on there, *Miss Thang!*" demanded Stacy as she stepped up to Ling and waved a finger in warning.

"I don't know who the hell you think you are—but you can just back off! And what do you want with the Steward, anyway?" Stacy cocked her head. "And come to think of it—why do I find you vaguely familiar?"

Her temper clearly near the breaking point, Ling leaned forward until her face was inches from Stacy's. With considerable effort to restrain herself, she seethed through clenched teeth.

"Do not *dare* to interfere. I will have the Steward—and I will have her *now!*"

"Whoa, missy," exclaimed Stacy in mock horror. "Who flipped your *bitch switch?*"

Ling lashed out with a vicious backhanded swipe that sent Stacy sprawling across the room, toppling a small desk and shattering a reading lamp.

Mark instantly dove for Ling and managed to knock her off balance as they both slammed to the floor—but she was back on her feet with cat-like agility. He quickly rose to his hands and knees only to glimpse her flashing foot an instant before it slammed into the side of his head.

Another set of crushing kicks flipped him over in midair; and a focused punch drove the wind from his chest. He found himself leaning against the bed, gasping for breath, his legs splayed out in front of him, and his vision going grey around the edges.

Sensing movement, he tried to focus.

Very slowly, a face swam into view, a rapacious visage bearing a feral grin.

It was Ling, displaying a long elegant finger, its tip mere inches from his nose. As he watched, her fingernail grew and curved into a vicious claw.

With a strange sense of detachment, he realized with an inexplicable clarity that she intended to kill him—slowly—after she extracted the information she sought.

He tried to rise, but he could barely move. He felt spent, helpless.

Bright searing pain flared across his cheek as Ling painstakingly dragged the razor sharp talon deeply through his face from ear to chin.

"Now," she breathed huskily, and licked her lips, "we will do this *my* way—and you *will* tell me *everything* I want to know."

Suddenly grabbing his chin and twisting his head to one side, Ling plunged her tongue deeply into his wound and licked the length of the bleeding gash.

Fresh agony erupted from his gaping laceration. It was as if a hot rasp had ripped through his sundered tissues and into his brain. He jerked free of her grasp.

Ling laughed, a demented cackle devoid of any semblance of humanity.

Grimacing from the pain, Mark peered through squinting eyes only to see her snarling face coming closer once again, an evil gleam in her eyes. He could smell the disturbing coppery scent of his own blood on her panting breath.

With the sudden *crash* of splintering wood, Ling's leering face disappeared from his view—it was just simply *gone!*

Straining to look up, he saw Stacy standing above him, a broken stringed instrument dangling like a shattered baseball bat from her two-fisted grip.

She tossed the damaged lute aside, grasped him under the arms, and helped him to stand.

Unsteadily regaining his feet, Mark clapped one hand on his cheek to stem the flow of blood, and pulled Stacy into a fierce hug with the other. He was still weak and disoriented, but her embrace was a welcome anchor in a sea of pain and confusion.

He felt her suddenly stiffen; and he looked over his shoulder.

Ling was rising to her feet, a set of severe burn lines freshly etched across her face. She winced in pain; her expression grew savage. Her hands flexed; more claws sprouted.

Gallenius' words echoed in Mark's memory.

. . . These strings are made from fine silver . . .

TREY ENTERED THE ROOM.

What the—?

He swung the muzzle of his submachine gun up to cover the strange, otherworldly woman with the unusual fingernails . . . *claws?*

For an instant, the moment seemed at once suspended and surreal—then chaos ensued.

Snarling an enraged challenge that could have come from no human throat, the woman leapt at the startled sergeant with deceptive speed.

He fired a three round burst at her heart—only to have the bullets tear through empty air.

Crashing into him, she batted the weapon away and slashed viciously at his face and chest as he fell backward. Her claws shredded his clothing and sliced shallow furrows on his arms as he did his best to protect his face and throat.

He fought back! Landing a solid set of punches he managed to fight her off for an instant. He tried to twist away, out of her slashing reach, but he tripped, slamming onto his back. Instinctively kicking upward with both feet, he caught her across her hips, knocking her back and off balance.

She recovered quickly and crouched to spring once more.

Trey fumbled for his pistol, but his bloodied hands weren't responding as they should—he couldn't grasp and draw the handgun.

A sustained burst of unexpected gunfire erupted, shattering the air in the room with a blistering staccato cascade. The woman flinched and shuddered under the impact of the multiple 9mm rounds, and collapsed.

The sharp tang of gunpowder hung thickly in the air and hot spent brass casings littered the floor. Trey looked up to see Stacy holding the H&K MP5, with its magazine empty, and small wisps of smoke curling up from the muzzle and open breech.

"You're bleeding," she said calmly.

Trey looked down at his shredded shirt and tried to undo the surviving buttons, but his fingers were numb and uncooperative. His head drooped; he was nearly exhausted.

STACY TOSSED THE SUB-gun on the bed and gently pushed Trey's hands aside to help him. Once his shirt was open, they could see that his ballistic vest had saved his chest and stomach from the violent slashing of Ling's claws.

"It looks like just your hands and arms got cut," Stacy concluded.

Trey grimaced as he tried to clench his fists. "Something is wrong. My hands are stiff and tingly, like I'm losing feeling. They don't want to work—this can't be right. Who was that, anyway?"

"I'm pretty sure that was Ling," answered Mark, his hand clasped to his own facial wound still oozing blood.

"Enough about her." Stacy scoffed. "You're both bleeding; first things first."

Mark started to reply, but her warning look stopped him cold.

"No arguments, you *will* do as I say," declared Stacy as she started shredding a bedsheet into makeshift bandages. "Here, Mark, hold this cloth on your cheek and keep pressure on it."

She gestured to the lamp on the nightstand. "Over there, the bed—both of you! The light's better."

As Stacy rendered first aid to Trey, he asked, "Where is everybody?"

"Miska took Ellen—she's still unconscious—to a tower on the roof. The Guildmaster insisted; he and Gallenius are there, too," Stacy explained. "Guards are stationed there; so it's supposed to be safe—well, safer than here."

"Got it," Trey assured her. "So, we head there?"

"Right, we'll go there, too, as soon as I finish patching you two up."

Mark's wounds were somewhat more difficult to address; she suspected he may have sustained some broken ribs. His facial bleeding only slowed; it would not completely stop.

"That's the best I can do. You both are going to need medical attention. Heaven knows what diseases or bacteria you may have been exposed to—"

"Hush!" whispered Mark urgently, thrusting a hand up toward Stacy. "Listen!"

"Did you hear something?" she whispered.

Mark nodded and cocked his head, straining to hear.

"I think I did, too." Trey twisted his head, scanning the dimly lit room. "What's that smell?"

There were small sounds, barely audible squishing and snapping, and a musky odor.

The hairs on the back of her neck rising, Stacy slowly slid her hand across the bed toward the H&K MP5.

Staring intently into the murky dimness, they could see that a pair of luminous reflections stared back.

A low vibration, a sort of guttural rumbling, came from within the shadows—a trilling growl that triggered an instinctive dread among any species subject to predation.

The three friends were not immune. They watched in fascinated horror as the sinuous shape slinked slowly forward, incrementally materializing from the shadows.

The large paws padded soundlessly; long stiff whiskers jutted forth from a black muzzle that bore a set of fresh burn scars. Thin obsidian lips curled to reveal the startlingly white fangs of an accomplished predator. Beastly eyes, brimming with incongruous intelligence, focused a haunting saffron stare that could immobilize prey and freeze breath in frightened lungs.

Its unholy gaze never leaving its prey, the huge panther paced slowly back and forth across the room, a study in feline grace, the supple musculature visibly rippling beneath its sable coat.

Its chosen path blocked the door—the only exit from the room.

It seemed the predatory carnivore was deliberately savoring the moment, allowing their innate fear and panic to escalate, before the inevitable.

"Can it be?" hissed Trey.

"Why not? Ling *is* of the Were," replied Mark in a harsh whisper.

"But I *shot* her!" argued Stacy, training the MP5 on the pacing cat.

"Yeah, with 9mm full metal jacket rounds," Mark said, "just lead and copper—right, Trey?"

"Yeah, I get it," Trey answered, shifting a bit on the bed. "Where is your shotgun? It's still got those *special loads* in the tube, right?"

"Yeah," Mark whispered, "but it's over behind the door."

"Great," grumbled Trey.

"I'll just shoot her again," insisted Stacy through clenched teeth, never taking her eyes off the pacing panther as she tracked the cat with the sub-gun's muzzle.

"Whoa Stacy, that gun is empty; you already shot her with a full mag," warned Trey. "Listen, can you reach my pistol? The hollow points are filled with silver."

"Yeah, I think so."

"Mark," Trey asked as he tried to flex his hands, "think you can help me get this mattress up off the bed?"

"To use like a shield, you mean? So we can maybe get to the shotgun?" Mark speculated.

"Yeah, it's worth a try. Let's all move together—slowly. Okay, easy now."

As soon as they changed positions, the panther paused and crouched.

Stacy fumbled for Trey's pistol. Its grip was tacky with coagulating blood, but she managed to get it clear of the holster, as the men got their arms under the bedding.

At a nod from Trey, they suddenly flipped the mattress up on end and slipped behind it.

The sudden movement was enough—the cat sprang.

Stacy dodged, firing two-handed as the panther leapt—but missed.

Mark and Trey shoved the mattress up to meet the cat's attack, but were toppled back under the weight of the slashing onslaught as the mattress cover was being ferociously shredded. Trey tried to wrap one end of the pad over the back of the cat, but was batted off to one side by the rapacious predator.

Stacy slipped to the other side and tried to get off another shot, but was scared she might hit one of the men. So, she stepped in and held the pistol as close as she dared to the panther's back and squeezed the trigger.

Sensing the danger, the huge cat twisted and swatted at the pistol just as Stacy fired. The gun, torn from her grasp, clattered across the floor and disappeared in the shadows.

Stacy fell back, losing her balance.

The bullet had sliced a deep furrow down the panther's side, but did little more than further enrage the beast. In that instant of distraction, Mark shoved upward and wrapped the mattress around the snarling cat. Stumbling, he dropped to one knee, but maintained his grip.

Suddenly enveloped, the panther struggled to crawl out of the bedding, and barely managed to free its head and one foreleg. Trey threw his arms around the rolled back end of the mattress to keep it closed, but his hands were unable to grasp the material for long.

Mark drove his shoulder into the front part of the mattress and tried for a better grip, but he came too close. Scimitar claws sank into his shoulder and pulled him toward the gaping, slavering jaws.

Mark was face to face with the furious feline, the angry set of parallel burn scars heightening the horror. His doom appeared to be upon him.

Suddenly, thin loops of bright wire dropped over the panther's snarling head and sank into the fur of its thick neck. As the silver wires tightened, fur singed, smoke rose, and the cat's howling scream abruptly ceased. Its eyes widened in surprise; the beast commenced to struggle even more ferociously!

His wounded arms wrapped around the other end of the rolled mattress, Trey managed to hold on for another few seconds before he was tossed aside like a rag doll.

The brutal claws ripped free of Mark's shoulder, and he collapsed to the floor.

The bloodied men gawked at Stacy—straddling the pitching and bucking mattress like a professional bull rider, straining upward with all her might on the two pieces of the broken lute gripped fiercely in either hand.

The panther's tongue protruded from its open maw. Time slowed to a crawl as the cat's futile struggles became increasingly convulsive and uncoordinated. Finally, the big predator shuddered and grew still.

Stacy, however, did not relent in her effort to garrote the beast. Her shoulders and arms vibrated with the strain, steadily increasing the tension on the fine silver wires of the lute's strings. With a soft sluicing *per-slop,* the panther's head separated wetly from its body and thudded in dull finality to the floor.

An ominous silence descended upon the room.

Trey leaned up on one elbow, peering in disbelief at the scene before him. His astonishment was mirrored in Mark's face. Neither man seemed able to speak.

Stacy slowly stood, gasping for breath, and dropped the ruined stringed instrument from her shaking fingers.

Mark painfully regained his feet and took her gently into his arms.

Trey rose to one knee, shaking his head in amazement at the chaotic scene. "What now?" he asked, deliberately flexing his fingers and grimacing.

Stacy pushed out of Mark's arms and pointed toward the door.

"We have to get to the tower. Ellen and Miska are there."

"Uh . . . Hold on a second, guys," Mark cautioned. "I think we need to take the *head* with us, to Gallenius, you know?"

"What?" asked Trey. "What the hell are you talking about?"

"Ling . . . She was a Were," Mark answered.

"Oh yeah, right . . . Did she bite you?"

"Worse," said Mark quietly. "She *licked* me—my face—in the wound, I mean."

"Hold it right there, lover!" Stacy demanded. "Are you telling me that now you're gonna turn into some kind of a beast?"

"What, you got a problem with that?"

"As if!" She laughed. "Seriously, what's gonna happen?"

"Stacy, to be perfectly honest, I don't know. Things are weird enough as it is."

Turning to the sergeant, Mark opened his hands. "Trey, remember what Phineas said about killing the werewolf that bit him, and then bringing the head to the College of Mages—something about being free of the curse? I just don't want to take the chance. And besides, she cut you up pretty bad, too."

"Yeah, but I don't think she *bit* me," Trey retorted, "and she sure as hell didn't *lick* me!"

"Oh, I see. So, everything's just fine then? Or do you really want to take that chance?" Mark argued.

"Well, when you put it like that, no—not really. I guess I don't see the harm in running this by Gallenius," Trey reasoned. "We can wrap it in some of this bedding and take it along. Where is it? And where's my pistol?"

"There's your pistol," Stacy pointed, "by that broken reading lamp."

Trey flexed his hands once more. "Hey, my hands—my fingers aren't as stiff as they were a few moments ago. Do you think Ling's death might have anything to do with it?"

"Anything's possible, I guess." Mark shrugged.

Trey stooped and recovered his pistol, wiping the grip with tatters of cloth. Activating the attached flashlight, he panned the beam across the shadowed floor. Suddenly, he gasped.

"What is it? What's wrong?" asked Mark, alarmed.

"Uh . . . Y'all might want to see this," Trey drawled breathlessly.

They stepped to his side, and stared at the floor. In the small pool of illumination, a human head stared back, the eyes wide in shocked surprise.

"It's Ling," breathed Mark.

"You mean the *late* Ling," corrected Trey.

Stacy scowled and muttered to herself—but Trey and Mark heard.

"Bitch!"

CH 12

TREY, MARK, AND STACY weren't quite sure what to expect facing the Guildmaster in the rooftop tower; they had killed after all, despite tentative assurances to the contrary. Trey's account of events, while factually accurate, was devoid of any emotion or empathy—just like a police report.

They did not know how to react to the Guildmaster's protracted silence; the moment was decidedly awkward.

Gallenius considered the gruesome trophy swaddled in bloodstained shreds of bedding displayed upon the rough-hewn table. Ling's glazed eyes stared into an unknown infinity, a macabre imitation of blasé boredom.

Clearing his throat and nodding to the seated Guildmaster, Gallenius spoke softly to the three survivors of Ling's most recent rampage standing before him.

"The taking of a life—*any life*—is always regrettable. But in this case, it was clearly necessary. You did well to bring the head. It will be helpful in counteracting the curse of the bite of a Were."

"I wasn't bitten," insisted Trey, "but Mark may have a problem."

"Nonetheless, Sergeant," cautioned the Guildmaster, speaking for the first time since hearing the tale of Ling's demise, "it would be best if the both of you were to cooperate with Gallenius. It is true that the timely slaying of a Were can most often negate its curse, but there may be some *residual effects*. Let Gallenius craft the appropriate counter-spell. Trust him, and you will both be fine."

Stacy, fidgeting and obviously anxious, interrupted, "Look, if you all don't need me, I'd really like to go check on Ellen. So, unless there's something you need me for?"

"You sustained no bleeding wound, m'lady? Your skin is unbroken?" asked Gallenius solicitously, glancing at the Guildmaster.

"Nope, no cuts—maybe a bruise or two."

The Guildmaster nodded affirmatively, and Gallenius responded with a small smile.

"Then, m'lady, you have no need for concern. You will find the Lady Ellen above us on the second level, in the barracks room; she still sleeps. Miska attends her there, as well."

Before Mark could object, Stacy was out of the room.

His anxiety apparent, Mark turned to the mage. "I should go with her. Gallenius, just how long is this *spell crafting* going to take? Aren't we in danger of being attacked at any moment?"

The Guildmaster held up a hand and addressed both Mark and Trey. "You must be patient, gentlemen—an hour, perhaps less."

"But—" Mark began.

The Guildmaster forestalled any argument with a raised finger.

"You should know that the wards on the stairwells are still holding. I am well aware that there are some invaders who got through before the barriers were in place; admittedly we do not know where they are at this moment. But I think the risk of an all-out attack is minimal—at least for now. Even in the event of an assault, we can easily withdraw."

"Withdraw? And just how?" queried Trey in astonishment. "This tower is already on the roof. Are we supposed to *fly* away?"

"Not quite, Sergeant." The Guildmaster chuckled. "This facility, like most of our buildings, has more than a few secrets. A passage within the outer walls leads down to a tunnel, which in turn leads to a series of caves. These caves come out near the old riverbed, in a thickly wooded forest below the river dam and its hidden power station."

"The caves were discovered when the river was dammed, exposed by the low water," Gallenius explained. "Dwarves explored them and declared them suitable for our needs. They then crafted the tunnel. Of course, only a few know of its existence."

"So you would abandon the Citadel rather than fight to defend it?" pressed Trey, incredulity evident in his tone.

"Sergeant, I think you misunderstand," soothed the Guildmaster. "All of our people, but for the guardsmen, a few staff, and a handful of healers, have already left and gone into hiding. They are the soul of Storm Haven, and that alone is worth defending—not these buildings. Without our people, these are but empty shells."

"I get it," offered Mark. "Trey, think of it as a tactical withdrawal in furtherance of an overall strategy—deny the enemy whatever he seeks, and just disappear in the process."

"Well put, Counselor," Gallenius said with a smile. "Of course, there are elements of our infrastructure that are critical to us and would thus merit a robust defense; but, these buildings, the Ministry—nay, even the entire Citadel—are not among them."

An urgent knock interrupted the mage; a harried guardsman entered and gestured to Gallenius.

"Ah, please forgive the intrusion, m'lords. Magus, a word with you, if you please, m'lord?"

Gallenius took the guardsman by the arm and guided him into the hallway. After a short whispered conversation, the mage returned and bent to the Guildmaster's ear.

At a nod from his superior, Gallenius left the room.

A moment later he returned; he was not alone. A tall lanky man and a petite woman followed, both dressed in the drab homespun of the common folk. The guardsman took up a post in the hall and closed the door.

"Uh, we'll step out," Mark excused himself and Trey, "to give you all privacy."

At the shake of the Guildmaster's head, Gallenius stopped them.

"No, please stay—this may concern you. This is Frieda and Wilhem. Please, listen to what they have to say."

The woman looked at the severed head upon the table and then to the Guildmaster, her eyebrows rising.

He said nothing and calmly dropped a cloth over the grotesque sight. She did not speak until he nodded.

"M'lords, the forest beneath the river dam is in the enemy's hands. Two squads of armed men from Were are encamped near the old riverbed. Several Were officers have gleefully taken to their animal forms, wolves in this case, and now prowl the forest. It appears they have abandoned their commands and prefer running with the pack.

"Senior men-at-arms have been left in charge. It is clearly apparent that they, as well as their troops, would rather avoid their *lupine officers*. Nonetheless, they remain there; and they plan on sending out patrols at daybreak."

Leaning forward, the Guildmaster asked, "They have not yet discovered the caves?"

"No, m'lord, but the wolves will surely find them eventually. The encamped men will easily see the dam come daylight."

Gallenius turned to Mark and Trey and explained, "This is a part of our infrastructure that cannot be compromised and must be defended. Do you understand?"

Trey nodded. "I believe we do. Your intelligence is impressive. But how do you plan on defending this infrastructure?"

"If I may?" offered the Guildmaster. "Mark, we are aware of the deal you struck with those mercenary trolls. Gronk, was it?"

Mark nodded and kept silent as the Guildmaster continued.

"We are also aware of the present location of their camp—the one you suggested they make, away from the conflict. As I understand it, they are now yours to command, and sometime later as well by virtue of a retainer, which you have already paid. Is that not correct?"

"That's accurate," admitted Mark. "I think I now know what you would like me to do. You want me to have the trolls rout the Were from the forest and the riverbed, right?"

"Not quite," corrected the Guildmaster. "If they were to merely move their camp to that location, I am certain the Were would give them quite a wide berth. There should be no need for unnecessary bloodshed. The trolls intimidate the Were—and that may suffice."

"If that works," Trey smiled in appreciation, "I must admit it's a pretty slick solution. Can you do it, Mark?"

"I don't see why not—"

"I fear that I *do*," warned Gallenius. "You must go through the ritual to negate the curse of the Were as soon as possible. You can go nowhere until that is accomplished."

Mark scowled. "But—"

"There may be another way," Gallenius offered. "Is not Miska known to these trolls? Was he not present during your negotiations with Gronk?"

"Uh, yeah, he was there. So, you'd send him instead—with what, *a note?*"

Frieda chuckled and offered impishly, "With *gold*, assuming, of course, you still have some to spare. I will lead Miska to their camp, and then guide him as he leads the trolls where they will need to go. Once they are in place, Miska can return here."

"You've already seen their camp, haven't you, Frieda?" observed Trey.

She only smiled and declined to answer.

"Are we in agreement?" the Guildmaster asked.

"Of course, anything we can do to help." Mark fumbled with his money pouch. "I gave Nestor most of my silver; but gold, I've got. How much will we need?"

Frieda's eyes widened at the size and heft of Mark's pouch.

"Enough to further engage their present services for a few more days—twenty pieces, I should think," reasoned the Guildmaster. "That would leave your retainer and their subsequent obligation for future service intact."

"That'll work," Mark conceded.

The Guildmaster turned to the mage. "Gallenius, please find Miska. Tell him what's expected of him, and have him join us."

When Miska arrived, Mark handed him the hefty pouch.

Frieda spoke up, "No, not that pouch; it is too fine, and holds too much. Just count out twenty gold coins on the table."

Once he did so, Frieda dropped an empty coin pouch next to the pile of gold coins.

"Use this smaller, well-worn pouch," she cautioned. "Remember, Miska will be acting as your emissary; he would have no need to flaunt such wealth."

"Oh, yeah, right," Mark acknowledged, as he put his money pouch away.

Trey scooped up the coins and let them dribble into the small pouch; a few missed and bounced from the table to the floor. Instinctively, he stooped to catch them—as did Frieda in the same instant, and their fingers entangled.

Trey instantly felt something akin to an electric shock; his eyes slammed shut and his knees went weak. He released her hand and steadied himself by grasping the edge of the table. A confused double image of Frieda flared in his mind, and he spoke without thinking.

"You're—you're a *fox!*"

Wilhem immediately bristled and took a step forward.

"Really, Trey!" chastised Mark. "That's *rude!* You've barely met this woman."

"No—no," Trey stammered. "I mean, she's a *Were!*"

"As am I, my friend," asserted Miska. "You need have no more concerns for her nature than you do mine. I vouch for her."

"As do we all, Sergeant," assured the Guildmaster. "Frieda and Wilhem are among our most skilled intelligence operatives. We have trusted them with our lives many times over. And now, both you and the Counselor are privy to one of our most closely guarded secrets—one that you must keep. Do I make myself clear?"

"Yes, Guildmaster," said Mark.

Trey looked at Wilhem and saw only the man—or did he? There was something else, like an aura, blazing with tense and alert energy—but only a singular aura. When he looked again at Frieda, he could sense a duality about her—a double aura of sorts, calm and controlled.

"Forgive me, please—the shock was a bit overwhelming," he admitted. "Of course, I understand the need for secrecy. I apologize for my outburst. But I don't know how I know about Frieda." Turning to her companion, he added, "Or that Wilhem, here, is not a Were, but rather a normal human."

A long moment of silence ensued, as Trey looked at everyone in turn, his palms open.

Finally, Gallenius spoke in a considered, deliberate tone, "It would seem that this *newfound ability* may be one of those residual effects we spoke of earlier. Ling was a very powerful Were; I cannot begin to speculate what ramifications may result upon her death. As we all saw, this skill, which the sergeant seems to have acquired, first manifested with a *touch*. And now, it appears to be by *sight*—or perhaps *inner sight.* Of course, it may only be temporary; we shall see."

Turning to Frieda and Wilhem, Trey said formally, "I am so sorry. Please accept my deepest apologies. I meant no disrespect."

Wilhem and Frieda gazed at one another in silent communication and nodded to Trey.

"We accept. However, I must caution you," warned Frieda, "that should we meet elsewhere, or pass upon some road, you must not speak in recognition. We must be as strangers. Do you understand?"

"Yes, indeed! In my realm, we would call that *blowing one's cover*. It will never happen," he promised.

"Very well, then," rumbled the Guildmaster. "Time is of the essence; so, let us review the details of the plan and address any questions."

In less than half an hour, the plan was under way.

WHAT IS THIS? NOTHING but utter greyness, a dull swirl of featureless fog? I know this place. I've been here before. Maude, are you here? Am I dead?

. . . Oh, Ellen, you always ask that, don't you, sweetie?

. . . Maude? Is that you? Am I dead?

. . . Well, yes and no. Yes, it is me—and no, you are not dead.

. . . Then I must be asleep—and dreaming? No—I didn't fall asleep. That mage—Roland? He zapped me somehow. I'm unconscious—that's why I can talk to you.

. . . Very good, Ellen. What can you remember?

. . . I remember an arrogant woman—Ling? Yes, Ling! She demanded that I open a portal. Mark! Mark was there, and then . . . I don't remember anything

but sudden pain—that's all. But if I'm not dead, just unconscious, then I'm somewhere—my body, I mean. But, where? I'll have to wake up to find out, won't I?

. . . Right again, my dear. I suspect it might be best for you to awaken sooner than later.

. . . Why? Is something wrong?

. . . Isn't there always?

. . . But there are so many things I want to ask you. I can't help but think that the opportunities to do so are slipping away. I mean, I still read the journal—and I make my own entries. However, it seems I'm left with more questions than answers.

. . . You are quite perceptive, child; and you may be right in that my time here, in this place, may be coming to a close. As you know, there are others here, whom I avoid. I sense a certain anticipatory restlessness about them. I can say no more in that regard. The journal is important, as you well know. As counterintuitive as it may seem, it actually pleases me that you find more questions than answers. If you look deeply into your heart, you will realize that this is how it should be.

. . . .I think I understand. Without the questions, why strive for answers? Our curiosity would dull, and our creativity languish—how utterly boring life would be.

. . . Well reasoned, Ellen. You see? You already know this truth. But the time has come for you to depart this place. Others have sensed your presence—your life energy—and are drawn here. They must not find you—or me. You must awaken, and be wary. Your situation was perilous before; it may not have improved. No, do not offer any argument! You must not delay! Go now!

"GUNTHER, WE HAVE THEM!" Triona gloated. "They have all taken refuge in a tower on the roof—no doubt the same one in which your mistress, the Lady Sabrina, is held."

Gunther's eyes blazed and fists clenched as he faced Triona in the dim hall.

"Good! We must see that none escape!"

"Oh, none shall," responded the glaistig. "You have sufficient troops now in position on the roof, and more will come as those annoying barrier wards on the stairwells weaken. The noose tightens!

"However, a handful of the Were still roam about; but we have no control over them. Apparently their leader, *Ling*, has left them to their own devices. She has reportedly not been seen in the last few hours."

Gunther scoffed in dismissal. "Ling is distracted. She seeks the Steward and is convinced that she is here. She even insists on taking some defenders alive and interrogating them—a waste of my time!"

"It matters not to me," Triona tossed off with a shrug, and then leaned forward with eyes agleam. "Now, as for this tower, I have found a way in through the water system; I shall slay all I find."

"No! Not yet! First, I must secure m'lady's freedom—then you may do as you please—but not until Lady Sabrina is free! Do you understand, Triona?"

The glaistig pouted coyly, but soon saw that such wiles were wasted upon the vampire lord. He was clearly obsessed with his mistress.

"Oh, very well." She shrugged in mild exasperation. "I suppose I can be patient for a bit longer. What have you in mind—a trade for that pitiful human I captured?"

"Possibly, yes. I know he is close to the Steward. Remember that Ling insists that the Steward is here in this realm; and that this realm has serious need of the Steward's services—the portals, you see. If this indeed be true, then our prisoner, or rather *hostage,* surely has some value as a bargaining chip."

"And if he does not?" Triona asked.

"It will not matter. There is the issue of my own vengeance—which I shall *not* be denied." Gunther scowled, a finger stroking his scarred cheek in an unconscious gesture. "I care not one whit that he is *marked by her.* In fact, I think he need only be alive. Perhaps a few moments alone with him would suffice. "

Triona said nothing in response, simply tilting her head and smiling blandly; but her thoughts were far darker.

Gunther, I have underestimated you. You are a far more dangerous fool than I thought. To deliberately run afoul of the Lady Leanan is most unwise—well beyond stupid—even among the undead. On the other hand, it is indeed tempting to taste the blood of one who has stirred Leanan's fancy. What a delicacy that must be! A perilous thought, indeed—oh, but it adds such spice to the thrill! Yet, perhaps there is a way. Yes, and you, my blindly obsessed friend, would be held to blame.

"Gunther, would it not be best to offer an unharmed hostage in trade?" she asked reasonably. "Consider this; it may be wisest to forgo your revenge for the moment; allow it to simmer in patient anticipation. Remember, the return of your lady, as you keep reminding me, is your first priority."

"Enough!" he snapped. "I am well aware of my goals! You would do well to focus on the problems at hand!"

"Indeed, m'lord. As it happens, I have a plan."

Gunther fixed her with his baleful eye. "I am listening."

"Remember your high station, m'lord. Allow me to handle the negotiations on your behalf. I have certain skills in that regard; perception can be critical in the art of negotiation. Any desire you harbor for vengeance must be hidden. Your entire focus must appear to be on the safe return of your mistress, the Lady Sabrina. Whomever we must negotiate with must not be aware of any other agenda."

"I am quite capable of negotiating on my— "

"Of course you are, m'lord," Triona interrupted soothingly. "But the commander of an invading army would not be expected to stoop to such trivialities—it would be unseemly, a sign of weakness. Moreover, in the grand scheme of things, would it not be fitting that you, as a high-ranking vampire lord, have a *herald* speak for you?"

"A *herald?* Oh yes, I see—it *is* fitting," he conceded, his ego obviously flushing with pompous presumption. "Very well. You shall serve as herald and speak for me. Let us go."

ELLEN SWAM SLUGGISHLY upward through the weakening vestiges of cloying unconsciousness. She felt the last tendrils of Roland's hastily cast spell dissipate and fade, its strength now depleted. Becoming more aware of her surroundings with every steady heartbeat, she could hear voices, speaking softly yet laden with concern.

". . . it was but a simple task; it took less than an hour with Frieda's help. Tell me, how is she?"

"I think she stirred a bit just now. Do you think we should send for Gallenius?"

Stacy! That's Stacy's voice! Where am I? Lying on a bed? What happened?

"He is still busy with Mark and Trey," rumbled the deeper voice.

Miska! He's here, too! I've got to wake up!

Forcing her eyes open, Ellen squinted at the two forms hovering over her, licked her dry lips and managed to croak a request.

"Wa-water . . . p-please . . . "

Hands gently assisted as Ellen raised her head and shoulders and propped herself up on one elbow.

Sipping gratefully from a cup Stacy handed her, Ellen drained the cup.

"Ellen, are you all right? How do you feel?" asked Stacy anxiously. "More water?"

Miska took the cup for a refill.

"Thanks, I . . . Stacy, you're okay?"

Stacy smiled. "I'm fine—and you?"

"Uh, I'm okay . . . Where are we?"

"Here, have some more water, and I'll tell you . . . Right now, you're in the Citadel, in a tower on the roof of the Ministry—you know, the administration building. It's a long story. There's a lot more to tell you; I'm not sure where to begin."

"We are under siege," announced Miska, "and many details will have to wait. The sooner you can move about the better. We may have to evacuate."

"Under siege? Evacuate? Where is everyone else?" Ellen demanded as she sat upright, already thinking about transiting them out of Storm Haven to safety.

Stacy and Miska exchanged a pained look, but said nothing.

"Tell me, please—tell me now," Ellen insisted.

"Mark and Trey are with Gallenius. They had an encounter with *that woman*—Ling. They needed, uh, some medical attention," Stacy explained.

Miska stared at her, his eyebrows raised, but said nothing.

"And Hawk?" Ellen pressed.

Miska and Stacy shared another uncomfortable glance before the big man responded.

"We do not know where Hawk is. He went missing several hours ago when he and Trey were searching for a suspected vampire. He has not yet been found, but—"

A commotion from outside, somewhere on the broad flat roof of the administration building, interrupted Miska's explanation; the big man strode to a window.

Stacy helped Ellen to stand and steady herself. Both women froze at Miska's hissed curse.

"Damn the gods! They have Hawk!"

"What?" Ellen lunged for the windowsill.

Below them, the rooftop cistern lay bathed in amber torchlight. In the center of the pool, dwarfing a tiny island, stood a majestic willow tree, soundly rooted in the depths of the water, its languid limbs undulating sinuously in the night breezes, a deceptively calm backdrop to the drama unfolding beneath its indifferent canopy.

A silver-haired female figure in a loose green and black robe stood astride the cistern's chest-high wall. Gesturing gracefully with her right hand, she spoke to half a dozen guardsmen who had cautiously approached to within ten yards of her and held their positions, weapons at the ready. Her left hand tightly gripped the tousled hair of a kneeling man. Blindfolded, his hands bound behind his back, he was perched precariously atop the wall.

"Are you sure that's Hawk?" Stacy asked, peering past Miska's shoulder.

Before he could answer, Ellen stilled both her companions with a gentle touch. Closing her eyes, she sent her awareness forth and probed the group below.

It took only a moment, but drained a good portion of her depleted energy reserves, leaving her mentally exhausted. Nonetheless, confirmation birthed a confusing clash of emotions; relief and fear thundered through her heart like an undisciplined brace of runaway chariot horses. She gasped involuntarily.

"It—it *is* Hawk! I-I sensed, um, latent traces of a fading spell of some kind. But he seems to be okay, and he *is* aware—although he's tied up and can't see! We have to get closer! I can't hear what's going on from here!"

“Look!” Stacy pointed. “Isn’t that the Guildmaster? What’s he doing?”

“I don’t know—let’s get down there!” Ellen urged. “Now! Let’s move!”

They quickly made their way to the lower level, only to be stopped by a pair of guardsmen at the door to the roof.

“Halt! Forgive me, m’ladies, m’lord. The Guildmaster ordered that no more follow him. We are to stay within the tower.”

Before any argument could be offered, Gallenius’ voice sounded from behind them. “Stand down, Corporal. The Guildmaster intended that no more *guardsmen* follow him. The Steward and her companions are not so constrained.”

Turning, Ellen saw the tired mage approaching, anxious concern etched upon his face.

“Lady Ellen, I am pleased to see you. How do you feel?” he asked solicitously.

“I’m fine, Gallenius,” she responded urgently, “but I have to get out there—that’s Hawk!”

“Yes, it is—and we shall *all* go. But you must wait a moment for Mark and Trey—they are on their way. Be warned; there is, no doubt, some foul treachery in play here. I have taken certain precautions, which will require that Mark and Trey be present.”

“They come now,” rumbled Miska, pointing over Gallenius’ shoulder at the two men hurrying toward them.

“Ellen! You’re all right?” boomed Mark, opening his arms to envelop her in a hearty hug.

Gallenius pulled the anxious guard aside and spoke quietly. “Stand easy, Corporal. I understand your concern, but there has been a change in plan.”

Gallenius spent a few more moments with the guard and then returned to the companions. Cautioning each to display no emotion and maintain a stoic demeanor, he led them single file out onto the roof, keeping mostly to the shadows.

AS THEY NEARED THE Guildmaster, who had ventured no closer than the guardsmen would allow, the companions could more easily hear the conversation.

". . . hardly an unreasonable request—and we can put this unpleasantness behind us," the woman remarked placidly.

"Perhaps," conceded the Guildmaster, "but you have not addressed my request that your forces quit this realm."

"A subject that the great Lord Gunther would gladly broach upon the return of the Lady Sabrina. He would consider such a gesture a manifestation of your purported goodwill," Triona countered sweetly.

The Guildmaster gestured offhandedly in response. "And I presume that would include, as a reflection of your lord's *goodwill*, the release of the poor bound innocent who now kneels at your feet?"

"Oh? Do you mean *this* man—called the Lord Hawk, of the Realm of Man, the beloved of the Steward of the Grand Portal of the Realm of Man? I believe my Lord Gunther may be so persuaded. But alas, I do not see the Lady Sabrina. Nor is she among those who now approach from the tower. Hmm, have you some treachery in mind?"

"Not in the least, m'lady," assured the Guildmaster. "These are my advisors, those with whom I must consult in regard to your proposal. If it would put you at ease, I shall invite our guest, the Lady Sabrina, to join us. Is that acceptable to your lord?"

"Indeed so. Let it be done," Triona acknowledged.

"Just so. Now, if you will excuse me?"

Turning his back to Triona, the Guildmaster walked several paces away and waited patiently for Gallenius and the companions to gather around him.

Ellen had eyes only for Hawk, and would have rushed to him had not the Guildmaster demanded her full attention.

"Lady Ellen," he whispered urgently, "I am pleased to see you are well. But you must listen to me—this glaistig does not know who you are, and she must not learn! It is clear she knows that Hawk is dear to the Steward, but not precisely *who* the Steward is. So, you must not react to what you see—do you understand?"

"Y-yes, I understand." Her heart was racing; she could *see* Hawk, only a stone's toss away, bound and helpless. With a great effort of will, she tore her gaze from his kneeling form and stared at her clasped hands in frustrated acquiescence.

The Guildmaster turned to the mage. "Gallenius, what is our *guest's* condition?"

"She is weak, not having fed; but she is generally compliant and tractable. She promises no trouble—especially if she expects to be released."

"Very well. Have her brought forth, with the dignity she would expect, relative to her noble station."

"Wait a minute," interjected Trey. "Are you seriously going to release a prisoner because a *terrorist* has taken a hostage? Where we come from we don't even *negotiate* with terrorists! If they find their tactics are successful they just repeat their crimes—kidnapping, hostage taking, and even murder—over and over again!"

"I wonder if your partner, Hawk, feels the same way at the moment," Gallenius rebutted.

"I *know* he does," Trey responded, nostrils flaring.

"Calm down, Sergeant. Gallenius, please do as I asked," the Guildmaster said evenly as he gently pushed the mage toward the tower, and then took Trey's elbow.

"Sergeant, I understand your position; that is the way you are trained in your home realm. But we are not there—we are here. You must trust me!

"The Lady Sabrina has personally done us no harm, and thus, we intend her none. True, we have inconvenienced her somewhat, but it was never our intention that she remain here in Storm Haven, as a prisoner or otherwise. At some point we would insist that she leave and return to her home realm of Shadow—voluntarily or otherwise—*deport her* is the phrase you would likely use.

"So, now we have the opportunity to send her back to her own kind *and* free Hawk, thus solving two problems at a single stroke. We only need to let it appear that we have been outmaneuvered in these negotiations."

"Okay, I get it—but I still don't trust them," Trey growled.

"Nor should you—that is why you and Mark now wear those gemstones about your necks."

"Guildmaster, I don't mean to interrupt," Mark said, concerned, "but I'm sensing that this, uh, *glaistig,* was it? She's concealing something; her intentions are *not* as she wants you to believe."

"I expect as much," admitted the Guildmaster. "But we need only play this out a little longer. The sunrise will be upon us within the hour. It is they who are running out of time—not us."

Moments later, Gallenius returned escorting the Lady Sabrina; two guardsmen accompanied them, walking discreetly a pace behind.

"Ah, the Lady Sabrina is here," noted the Guildmaster. "You must all remain alert, and stay *here*—within reach of Mark and Trey."

Stepping toward the cistern wall, where Triona waited, the Guildmaster extended his arm and said, "As you can see, the Lady Sabrina now joins us. If this pleases your lord, shall we now exchange our guests?"

Triona looked over her shoulder, and acknowledged someone unseen. "As you wish. If the Lady Sabrina would walk to her left, to the far side of the cistern wall."

At a nod from the Guildmaster, Gallenius stepped back and made a sweeping bow to Sabrina and gestured in the direction Triona had indicated.

Sabrina's eyes darted from side to side as she held her head high and strode regally forth, with as much noble bearing as she could muster in her weakened state, until she rounded the cistern wall and entered its deep stygian shadows.

AT FIRST SABRINA THOUGHT she was alone; suddenly Gunther had her in his arms. She shuddered from shock, weakness, and surprise.

"M'lady, m'lady," Gunther gasped, nearly overcome with relief.

"Gunther . . . I—"

"Quickly—come with me!" He tugged her deeper into the shadows and through an unseen doorway.

"Light!" he demanded, and the sound of flint and steel echoed in the dark room.

Sparks showered and winked out as an oiled torch flared to life. The flame revealed a man-at-arms standing over a bound and gagged man, bruised and barely conscious from a severe beating. With hardly any visible effort, Gunther snatched the battered prisoner to his feet and held him out at arm's length, examining him as one would a side of beef.

Satisfied, he grunted, "This one will do."

The man-at-arms paled as he fixed the torch in a wall sconce, executed a short bow, and quickly left the room.

Turning to Sabrina, Gunther thrust the captive forward. "M'lady, you are weak—you must feed!"

Weak as she was, Sabrina smiled and gazed at Gunther through half-lidded eyes. She considered the offered victim, allowed her eyes to close, and savored the scent of abject fear rolling off the unfortunate man in literal waves. Yes, she did need to feed; this man would do nicely.

She seemed to glide effortlessly forward almost as if floating, and seized the prisoner's gaze with her own—his eyes widening in fear and anticipation. In the next instant, she had his head brutally pulled back over his shoulder, as her fangs hovered over the pulsing vein of his neck. She traced the blood vessel with the tip of her tongue. Her victim shuddered in pleasure, then blanched in excruciating pain as her teeth sank into his throat.

Sabrina's eyes found Gunther's. She felt something in that moment—something akin to gratitude—but it quickly passed. Her eyes rolled up in her head as she drank deeply.

However fleeting her subtle reaction, Gunther had noticed. He stared into the sightless whites of her eyes, and smiled.

SEVERAL PACES FROM the cistern wall, the Guildmaster addressed Triona. "I trust your lord will be pleased. Now, if you will release the young man at your feet, as agreed . . ."

The glaistig scoffed and twisted her wrist, wrenching the man's head upward. She looked down into his blindfolded face, and then back to the Guildmaster.

"This one? Oh yes, do try to come and get him." She cackled. "My Lord Gunther has indicated that he has *other plans* for this one!"

Ellen bolted forward—ignoring Gallenius' choked warning.

Miska and Stacy, throwing caution to the wind, sprinted after her!

Mark and Trey would have joined them, but Gallenius grabbed them and whispered a harsh command.

As Ellen ran toward the wall, she locked eyes with Triona.

The glaistig smiled wickedly as recognition dawned. Never taking her malignant gaze from Ellen, she slowly pulled Hawk's head back until he lost his balance, pitching over backwards into the cistern's murky waters.

For an instant, time seemed to stop.

Rage flared in Ellen's heart! Just as she was about to lunge at the glaistig, a huge hand slammed down on her back, flattening her upon the broad flagstones of the roof. Sucking a desperate breath, she heard the swift passage of crossbow bolts over her prone body, and shuddered at their lethal proximity.

Miska, rising to one knee and mumbling urgent apologies, started to pull Ellen up. But Stacy, running hard, leapt up and sprang off the big man's shoulders, aiming a flying side kick at the glaistig.

However, Triona was not so easily attacked. She deftly sidestepped Stacy's kick and whirled around delivering a two-footed kick of her own that caught Stacy in the back. There was a flash of cloven hooves; the impact sent Stacy thudding into the willow's massive trunk.

Ellen caught her breath and peered warily over her shoulder as she rose. She saw Mark and Trey holding up something in their outstretched right hands, standing to either side of the Guildmaster and Gallenius.

Shimmering blue and green light danced upon their palms, coalescing into a bubble-like shape that encompassed the four men. Crossbow bolts and arrows struck the shield-like surface and fell clattering to the flagstones.

Grumbling ominously, Miska rose to his full height and advanced on the glaistig, heedless of the barbed dangers zinging through the air around him.

Dancing along the top of the wall in stuttering, mincing steps, Triona cackled and spat, teasing the advancing big man mercilessly. She was nevertheless careful to stay out of his reach, and relished in his furious frustration.

Ellen could only think of Hawk—helpless, bound, and surely drowning! Without another thought, she scrambled up the wall, estimated where he had fallen in, and jumped into the murky water.

"No!" Miska shouted, in futile desperation.

Triona lashed out with a vicious kick that opened a gash on the side of the big man's head.

He reacted with blinding speed. His swiping backhand knocked her sprawling along the wall, upending her robe over her head—exposing her goatlike legs.

Ignoring the crumpled glaistig, Miska pressed a hand to his bleeding scalp, leaned over the wall where he had seen Ellen disappear and plunged his other arm in the water. He felt nothing in the murk; the cistern was far deeper than it appeared. He pulled himself over the wall and slowly slipped into the water feetfirst, probing for a bottom that he couldn't find.

There was a frantic scrambling sound as Triona got to her cloven feet, a murderous scowl on her face. Spying Miska in the water, her expression hardened ominously.

She advanced on him, slowly at first, but was soon running, her mouth opening in a silent scream of rage and fangs sprouting from her drastically distended jaws.

"Keep the glaistig from the water!" shouted Gallenius.

With an inhuman screeching howl, the vampire leapt in an arc that would put her on Miska's shoulders in the next instant.

That instant never came.

Miska looked up to see Triona suspended above him—shock and utter surprise etched upon her horrid visage. Thin whips of willow limbs wrapped completely around her squirming body; she slowly began to rise, hissing and spitting, into the night air.

Miska's gaze followed the line of tree limbs until he saw Stacy lying against the trunk, her battered face pressed against the rough bark and one hand placed lovingly against a thick root. Peering through half-opened eyes, she smiled at Miska and gave him a *thumbs up* sign.

Smiling back, he returned her sign, took several deep breaths, and disappeared beneath the dark surface of the water.

A QUIET STILLNESS SETTLED over the roof, or perhaps it was only in Stacy's mind. Gallenius and the Guildmaster were still within the protective bubble emanating from whatever Mark and Trey held aloft.

Feeling somewhat *displaced*, her thoughts wandered, her curiosity mildly intrigued.

. . . gemstones from a dragon's hoard, perhaps . . . holding spells, surely . . .

. . . But . . . Hawk . . . Ellen . . . and now Miska—gone . . .

Her mind grew foggy, her eyelids heavy, and darkness claimed her.

CH 13

ELLEN SHUDDERED AS the chill water closed over her head. Opening her eyes was a futile effort; she could see nothing in the murk. The cistern's depth was deceptive; she swam downward, her arms thrust out before her, in search of Hawk. She quickly realized she would not find him like this. So, shunting her rampant anxiety aside, she deliberately calmed her racing heart and opened her awareness.

She found him, a fathom below her, and descending. Nor was he alone; a handful of smaller entities were tugging him downward.

Nixies—water sprites!

The certainty of that sudden thought surprised her. She had no idea how or why she knew that information; however, she knew it to be true. But her distraction was short-lived; someone, or something, was behind her—pursuing her.

Miska!

No sooner had recognition dawned, then his huge hand found her ankle and grasped. Stifling an instant of panic, she deliberately patted the back of his wrist twice, and then tugged him in a downward direction.

Thankfully, he understood and released her.

Mustering her resolve, she resumed her descent. He followed.

For just a second, she thought she had lost track of Hawk; she found him with her awareness, still descending, but now much deeper. Holding her breath was becoming unbearable. Her anxiety for Hawk flared anew—he was *helpless, bound and blindfolded.* He would surely drown!

Instinctively knowing that she would never reach him in time, her mind raced. In an instant of inspired desperation, she drew enough energy to create a transit globe, and cast it just below him.

She *felt* Hawk disappear within the orb.

Without warning, she found herself sucked into a swirling vortex. Tumbling out of control, weightless in the chaotic maelstrom, she lost all sense of gravity and direction, as helpless as flotsam in a flood.

Slamming onto a bed of wet leaves, she sputtered in a torrent of rushing water splashing around her. An earth-shaking *thump* and a gurgling groan announced Miska's equally graceless arrival somewhere behind her.

Damn! The portal is still open—the cistern is draining through!

With deliberate intent, she willed the portal closed. The cascade of dark water abruptly stopped. Wiping her eyes, she peered into the night. The waning moon offered just enough pale illumination to see.

A handful of small female forms, slender creatures no more than knee-high, arose unsteadily from the soggy ground and gasped at the disappearing water, now soaking into the forest floor. Their heads twisting about frantically, the nixies suddenly fled, scrambling into the night.

Ellen blinked and saw only a ring of stark trees and deeply shadowed forest beyond. Tall colorless grasses lay bent in every direction, no doubt from the sudden deluge; two sodden men lay unmoving in its wake.

Crawling to the nearest, she found Hawk and snatched off his blindfold. He did not react; his eyes remained closed. He just lay there, motionless.

Clasping her hands to either side of his face, she stared frantically at his drawn and ashen visage. Fear and panic rose within her heart and might have overtaken her had not a large hand gently come to rest upon her shoulder.

"His heart . . . still beats . . . but he does not breathe." Miska sputtered, gasping for air. "You must do it for him . . . I will see to his bonds."

Her awareness snapping into focus, she knew what to do—standard CPR rescue breathing. As she patiently forced her breath into Hawk's lungs, his body convulsed and he coughed up a mouthful of foul water. After a few gagging coughs, he began to breathe on his own, sucking in great gasps of air.

She sat back and ardently gripped his hand as he came up on one elbow and tried to speak.

"Wha-what hap-p—what happened?"

"I . . ." she began, but found that words failed her. Tears of joyful relief welled in her eyes, and she bit at her lower lip. She couldn't speak; there was simply too much she wanted to say.

Fortunately, Miska was not so afflicted and interrupted pragmatically. "Not now—no time! Miss Ellen, where are we?"

"Uh . . . um, sorry, in the Realm of Were, somewhere. I couldn't very well send us home—not with those nixies pulling on Hawk. I couldn't let them loose there. This was the only other place I could think of in a hurry. Is this a problem?"

"I do not think so. We cannot linger here—we have to get back to Storm Haven."

She nodded in agreement and squeezed Hawk's hand. "Hawk, look at me!" She released his hand, cupped his chin, and looked deeply into his eyes. She had to be sure he was all right. She stroked his wet hair away from his face. "Are you okay? Do you need some time to recover?"

Hawk rolled his shoulders and rubbed his wrists. "I'm stiff from being tied up, but I think I'm okay. I understand we need to *go back*, but where to exactly? I was blindfolded, so I don't even know where I was."

"You were—no, we *all* were on the roof of the Ministry Administration building," she explained, and turned with open hands to Miska. "But how can we go back there? There was a battle going on—we could wind up right in the middle of it!"

Miska pursed his lips. "No, that would not be wise . . . I know! We can go to a place I know to be safe—close, but not too close. We will still have to . . . "

As Miska's voice trailed off, Ellen was about to ask for a more specific description of this destination when the big man's hand went up in a signal for silence. Ellen and Hawk froze as Miska slowly turned his head about and delicately sniffed the night air.

Leaning forward he whispered, "Do not move, make no sound—we are not alone."

Cautiously moving only her eyes, Ellen scanned the area, but saw nothing. Nor did she hear anything, no normal night sounds at all, no crickets or insects of any type—*that* wasn't right. In fact, that alone was sufficient to alarm her.

Opening her awareness, she expanded her scope beyond the nearby trees, and became aware of a number of entities stealthily approaching from different directions.

"I count six, at various distances, but all around us." She slowly pointed to her left. "The closest one is in that direction. I don't think they're friendly."

An errant cloud slid over the face of the moon and the night reasserted its dark dominion. As the cloud drifted past the waning lunar beacon, a languid pool of pale argent revealed a form standing at the edge of the trees.

It was a woman, her features shadowed by a thick shock of tawny hair tightly curled around her head like a dusky halo. A spotted pelt drooped across one shoulder, and dangled to mid-thigh. She took a single step forward and stood more fully in the weak light. Around her neck, on a thin leather loop, hung a round wooden amulet festooned with a roughly cut, ruddy-hued stone that refracted the spare moonlight like a corrupted infection. A lifeless nixie hung limply from her hand.

Miska silently rose to his full height to confront her.

Her smile was feral, her voice fluid yet husky with the trace of harshness.

"My, what interesting prey we have found, my sisters—an easy hunt, indeed."

"No prey, here," rumbled Miska ominously, "unless, it is to be *you!*"

That seemed to surprise the woman, who took half a step back and reappraised the big man before her.

Ellen sensed three more women coming up through the trees behind them. She urgently whispered, "Now, there are *nine!*"

Miska grunted in acknowledgment, but remained facing forward.

Without taking her eyes from the strange woman, Ellen helped Hawk to stand.

The movement drew the woman's attention, and for an instant, she and Ellen locked gazes. Ellen was startled to see a pale green luminosity reflected deep in the woman's eyes.

The interloper returned her focus to Miska, then glanced into the shadows beyond the surrounding trees, and seemed to regain a measure of confidence. She casually tossed the dead nixie aside and squared her shoulders. With slow and deliberate motions, she brought both hands to her chest, picked up the amulet, and held it forth while beginning a monotone chant.

Miska immediately bristled, took a step forward, and announced in a booming voice, "Hear me, fools! I am called Miska, of the Ursus Clan—your pathetic magic has no effect on me! Depart at once! Fail to heed my warning at your own peril!"

The woman balked, and dropped the amulet back to her chest. Turning her head from side to side, she shouted in a strange language. One by one, the other women stepped forth from the shadows, completely surrounding the companions.

"Then, so be it, Miska of the Ursus Clan," she uttered gutturally. "The Hy'dae Tribe fears no lone lion—or bear! We need no spell to take such prey—nor are mere humans any challenge."

"How are you called?" demanded Hawk, brazenly stepping forward and surprising his companions.

"Who dares to ask—and why?" the woman retorted, as she made a subtle gesture and a number of her women slipped back into the shadows and dropped to the ground.

"Know me as Lord Hawk," he responded confidently, executing a slight yet polite bow with his hands behind his back. "And I would know the true name of the life I may be compelled to take."

His bravado clearly had an effect on the woman. She bristled and sneered, her hands curling into claws.

"What?" she spat venomously. "You dare to ask for my true name? What manner of pitiful sorcery is this?"

Miska caught an alarming scent and urgently whispered to Ellen, "Some of them are changing! They are too many—we should go!"

"*Changing?*" She was momentarily confused; but realization dawned. "Oh no! What are they?"

"Were-hyenas—all females. This tribe is no more than a matriarchal pack; they are very dangerous! We must leave this pla—"

"I will eat your *heart!*" The woman screamed, taking a lunging step toward Hawk!

However, her movement was a feint. The real threat flashed in from the side, slashing its slavering jaws at Hawk's stomach in an effort to disembowel him.

Hawk whipped his arm around, a small pistol having materialized in his hand. He fired twice from the hip—right down the throat of the onrushing beast. It twisted in midair, biting in writhing agony at its own gut as the silver-filled hollow-point bullets burned through its stomach. The huge speckled form tripped, crumpled with a howling whimper, and lay still.

From the shadows, another hyena leapt for Hawk's throat. The detective deftly stepped to one side and shot it once behind the ear. The beast dropped like a stone.

Another woman, in mid-metamorphosis, with distended face and inhuman teeth, charged in a loping two-legged run and tried to grasp him, but Hawk swept one of her bandy legs from beneath her. She went sprawling at the feet of her pack leader, who disdainfully kicked her away and screamed a command over the growing din of growls and excited yelps.

"Hold, my sisters—this one is *mine!*"

The rest of the pack paused and backed off, slowly forming a tighter ring around the companions. The pack leader paced with deliberate intent, slowly back and forth, her unholy eyes never leaving Hawk's own.

"Miska," whispered Ellen, "Take my hand and don't let go. Think about that safe destination—keep it firmly in your mind. When I tell you, grab Hawk with your other hand and pull him with us."

Miska nodded, and adjusted his stance.

They watched in morbid fascination as the woman dropped to her hands and knees and began to shake violently. A thick steam began to rise from her body and coalesce into a cloud-like opaque mist, as small snapping and stretching sounds emanated from within. A sick musky scent fouled the air.

HAVING SEEN SHAPE-SHIFTING metamorphosis before, Hawk was neither impressed nor entranced. Instead, he firmly planted his feet shoulder-width apart, brought his Glock Model 27 up in his favored two-handed Weaver stance, settled his breathing, and waited for his target to appear.

He had just decided that the present situation could be best addressed by the Mozambique Drill—a *double-tap* to the center of mass and then one to the head—when he was jerked backward quite violently, caught up by a massive arm, and suspended well off his feet for an instant. The wind was all but knocked out of him.

There was a moment of dark weightlessness; then Ellen was suddenly there, whispering in his ear.

"Put the gun away—we're safe. We're back in Storm Haven. And by the way, just where did *that* come from?"

Released by Miska, and back on solid ground, Hawk stepped to one side, took a couple of deep breaths and stooped to secure his pistol.

"Ankle holster—they never thoroughly searched me. I never found the right circumstances to try to use it, especially since they kept me blindfolded, with two or more guards on me."

"Well, I'm sure glad you had it. Those hyenas were pretty *nasty*." She shuddered.

"We were fortunate, indeed," agreed Miska. "They were too many; it could have gone badly."

From somewhere nearby, in the occluded darkness, came another voice, much deeper, and louder. "What ho? Look here, my brothers! It is our good friend Miska!"

"Hello, Gronk," rumbled Miska. "I thought we might drop in on you."

"Ah, you are welcome, of course," Gronk replied genially, stepping from the darkness. "Now, the Lady Ellen we recognize—"

"Yeah, we've met," interjected Ellen frostily, "under less than ideal circumstances."

Gronk shrugged. "Regrettably, our previous encounter was unfortunate; such can be the nature of mercenary life—no hard feelings, m'lady. We bear you no ill will. We no longer serve the Were."

Ellen scowled, but nodded and kept silent.

Gronk pointed to Hawk. "Who is this?"

"Why, this is my good friend, Lord Hawk," Miska replied happily, as he clapped Hawk on the shoulder.

Looking up in the dim moonlight as the last trace of cloud slid past, Hawk could see that the huge troll stood even taller than Miska.

"Well then, well met, Lord Hawk. I am called Gronk; my brothers and I are in service to the Counselor."

Counselor? Hawk was becoming more confused by the moment.

Were these the trolls that Mark bought off—or rather hired? They're far more intelligent than I expected.

He looked to Ellen for an explanation, but she was warily approaching the faintly glowing portal she had just employed in their hurried escape.

"Oh, by the way, Gronk," said Miska impishly, gesturing over his shoulder with his thumb. "We might be followed. So, anything that comes through that portal—before the Lady Ellen closes it—you may eat."

THE HEALER, A GREY-haired woman of infinite patience, leaned over Stacy and fit the sling around her patient's neck. Stacy only winced once as her right arm was gently placed in the sling. Her dislocated shoulder was back in place, but it throbbed with a vengeance.

Mark hovered annoyingly close to her bedside, unnecessarily crowding the healer.

"Mark, would you be a dear," Stacy asked sweetly, through a slight grimace, "and go look out the window and tell me what's happening? Are they still by the cistern?"

"Oh yeah, sure, of course," he mumbled, as he took the hint and shuffled over to the windowsill, where Smokey sat watching the roof below with casual feline interest.

The healer and Stacy shared a small knowing smile.

"Well, they're still there, still talking, but their voices are lower now," he reported. "I can't quite catch everything they're saying."

"Who are we talking about?" asked Ellen, stepping into the tower room.

"Ellen!" squealed Stacy as the healer tried to restrain her. "Are you all right? What about Hawk and Miska?"

"We're right here," announced Hawk as he and Miska followed Ellen into the room. "We're all fine."

Mark swept his cousin up in a hug and mumbled, "How did you all get here? We saw you go in the water—and then there was this *huge* whirlpool. What hap—"

"Whoa!" Ellen grinned widely and pushed back from his embrace.

"Easy there, Mark, let me go now. That story will have to keep for a bit," she explained as she went quickly to the window and peered out. "The fighting stopped? Is that—is that *Queen Mab?* And who else? What's going on down there?"

The room was silent. Stacy and Mark shared a concerned glance.

Picking up Smokey and cradling him in her arms, Ellen turned and faced her cousin. "Mark, what's going on? Tell me—tell me now."

"Yeah, it's Queen Mab. She showed up, right after I brought Stacy here; and then the fighting stopped. She's not alone; Lady Leanan and Lord Addecus came with her, along with an elfin mage who Gallenius says is called *Gaspar* or something—"

"They came looking for you," interrupted Stacy.

"Me?" asked Ellen incredulously.

"Yeah," agreed Mark. "Something about closing some portals. But no one has told them that you, uh, weren't here, exactly."

"What? Why not?" Ellen probed.

Mark shrugged. "We don't know. That was the Guildmaster's call. But, were I to hazard a guess, I suspect it was so as to not diminish his negotiating position—remember he wants to end the conflict and get the invading troops out of this realm. And for some reason I can't really explain, I get the sense that he expected her, Mab, somehow."

"Okay, now I'm really confused." Hawk scratched his head.

"No, wait," Ellen said contemplatively, as she absently scratched Smokey's ears while staring into his wide and mysterious eyes. "Mab hasn't actually *seen* any of you, right? I think I may understand the Guildmaster's strategy; but, that would depend upon . . . Yes, of course—that's *got* to be it! I have to get down there, right away!"

"What? Then, I'm going with you," announced Hawk.

"And I, as well," echoed Miska.

"Me, too!" added Mark.

Ellen deposited the cat on Stacy's bed, and held up both hands. "Listen to me—I need to go down there *alone*. You all will just have to trust me. And Miska, you especially must not be seen—remember this Queen Mab is the former Lady Diere. Need I say more?"

"But I don't see why—" Mark began, but Ellen cut him off.

"No, I'm sure you don't—nor is it necessary right now that you do. Please, don't argue—not now! You really should stay with Stacy. How soon is sunrise—anybody know?"

"Sunrise, m'lady? In about half an hour, I should think," offered the kindly healer, who had been silent until now.

Ellen pursed her lips and sucked through her teeth. "Then there's no time to lose. Please, you must all stay put and not be seen. I'll be back as soon as I can."

"But—" Hawk began.

"No buts—gotta go!" With a quick kiss on Hawk's stubble-rough cheek, Ellen slipped through the doorway and was gone.

Stacy chuckled. "You may as well get used to it, Hawk—your girlfriend's got a mind of her own, *and* a stubborn streak."

GALLENIUS WAS GROWING concerned. The Guildmaster had launched into a painstakingly detailed recitation of the proposed terms of Were and Shadow troop withdrawal; Queen Mab's impatience was becoming more obvious by the moment. Her mage, Gaspar, stood at her shoulder and rolled his eyes in bored disdain. Lord Addecus and Lady Leanan stood to one side behind the queen, at a subtle yet telling distance from the oily elfin adept. Rows of Shadow and Were troops stood in ranks several paces beyond.

There had been little time to discuss any sort of plan; so much had happened so quickly.

Moments after Ellen and Miska had disappeared beneath the waters of the cistern, Mark rescued Stacy from the base of the willow. With her in his arms, he made for the tower.

Without warning, a sickly-hued transit globe appeared on the roof of the Ministry. The Dark Elfin Queen herself stepped forth, followed by her entourage. Queen Mab immediately ordered that the Were and Shadow forces were to cease fighting the Storm Haven defenders. Lord Addecus and Lady Leanan enforced compliance within their respective troops.

Mab then demanded to speak with the Guildmaster.

Supported by only a handful of uninjured black-clad guardsmen, hastily called up from Storm Haven's nearly depleted reserves to serve as an apparent *honor guard*, the Guildmaster began a discussion with the Dark Elfin Queen that had evolved into a protracted negotiation session.

Gallenius sensed that the Guildmaster was stalling, but he did not know why. He did fully well understand that they would be at a serious tactical disadvantage should hostilities erupt anew.

As it happened, thanks to Padraic, they'd had good intelligence that Mab was most likely going to make an appearance—but they had not known *when*. She had come sooner than expected.

Gallenius had great faith in the Guildmaster, whom he knew to be a master strategist. However, he was considerably less than confident in these present circumstances.

With a subtle jolt, like a small static electrical charge, he sensed a deft probing at the metaphysical wall of his carefully crafted mind shield. It was, no doubt, a sly incursion by that sinister mage of such ill repute, Gaspar. Gallenius knew he must guard his thoughts—doubt and worry were the enemies here. Negative energies such as those would not only weaken his resolve, but his defenses as well.

Hearing footsteps approaching, Gallenius reinforced his mental shields and shunted aside the subtle yet insidious tendrils of Gaspar's dark probes. He turned to see Lady Ellen walking through the shadows toward him. His eyes widened in surprise, but he quickly held himself in check. He had no way of knowing how she had done it—but she was here!

Leaning toward the Guildmaster, Gallenius cleared his throat and said, "Please forgive the interruption, m'lord. The Lady Ellen joins us."

The Dark Elfin Queen's head snapped up and she looked past the Guildmaster. A storm of angry pique briefly flared in Mab's eyes, but she quickly regained her composure, apparently confident that her façade was intact, her slip unnoticed.

She was wrong; Gallenius had seen.

"AH, GUILDMASTER, MAGE Gallenius," announced Ellen. "I thought I'd join you. Greetings, Your Majesty, it's so nice to see you again. I do hope I'm not interrupting."

"Not at all," conceded Mab drolly. "In fact, you were the topic of conversation a few minutes ago."

"Indeed?" responded Ellen wryly. "My, my—I thought my ears were burning—well, no matter. Guildmaster, I trust you have had the opportunity to articulate my position in regard to the complete and unilateral withdrawal of Were and Shadow forces from Storm Haven—*before* any consideration, much less discussion, in regard to the disposition of certain portals on Olmus, might be had?"

"Precisely, m'lady." The Guildmaster bowed slightly. "In fact, I was just enumerating the proposed details of troop withdrawal, as we had so recently discussed."

"I have not the time for this!" exclaimed the queen. "I am here at the request of Were and Shadow to arrange for the closure of those two portals! Steward, you *shall* do so! Er, ahem, I mean to say, Steward, will you do so—or not?"

Gaspar grinned and rocked back on his heels.

Leanan and Addecus stared at Mab in shocked silence and shared a worried glance.

With a subtle nod to Addecus, the Sidhe stepped forward.

"Majesty, perhaps it would be beneficial if Lord Addecus and I were to further explain the circumstances to Lady Ellen," Leanan suggested reasonably. "Matters might thus be *expedited*."

"Then do so! Stop wasting my time!" Mab declared in a huff, any semblance of patience evaporating like a puff of steam.

Leanan and Addecus stepped off to one side where Ellen joined them.

"Ellen, please," pleaded Leanan, "I—*we*—want nothing more than to withdraw our people from this realm of Storm Haven. However, there is no way to do so without your help—you know this is true.

"Of a greater concern for us are the portals in the realm of Olmus that remain open into each of our home realms—they are potentially disastrous! You know there is a long history of animosity between Were and Shadow. We have a very slim chance here to begin to mend that breach. Addecus and I have taken the first steps; but, we are doomed to fail if those portals remain open."

"It isss true," agreed Addecus. "You now hold the fate of ssseveral realmsss in your handsss—to include Ssstorm Haven. Make no missstake; deny Mab and ssshe will make it her life'sss goal to obliterate thisss realm and all thossse within it—even if jussst for ssspite."

"I understand, I really do," assured Ellen, "but now, you must trust me."

For a moment, silence hung heavily in the air.

"It would ssseem . . . " began Addecus, glancing to Leanan.

". . . that we have little choice," finished the Sidhe with a barely perceptible shrug and resigned sigh.

Returning to her place beside the Guildmaster, Ellen spared him a sly smile and addressed the Dark Elfin Queen.

"Majesty, in answer to your question, here is what I am willing to do. Just outside the Citadel, I will open a portal to Olmus. All Were and Shadow forces are to use this portal to transit to Olmus. From there, the troops may return to their home realms through the existing portals. It will be left to the respective leadership of the Were and Shadow forces to maintain a peaceful withdrawal with respect to each other.

"When I am satisfied all such forces have departed Storm Haven, then, Your Majesty, you and I will go to Olmus. There, you will release whatever sorcerous hold *you* have placed upon the portals that now connect Olmus to Were and Shadow, and I will close them as agreed. Then, we will go our separate ways. Is this acceptable?"

Leanan and Addecus looked at each other and slowly nodded their heads. However, Mab's head was tilted toward Gaspar who was whispering urgently in the queen's ear.

She waved him off and turned to Ellen. "It will take some time for the forces of Were and Shadow to transit from Storm Haven to Olmus—a day at least."

Gallenius leaned near Ellen and whispered in her ear. She nodded and faced the queen.

"They should be able to do so by sunset, this coming day," Ellen insisted.

Mab's eyes narrowed at Ellen's tone, but Addecus and Leanan both nodded in the affirmative.

"Very well; it is agreed," acknowledged the queen, looking down her nose haughtily with her chin jutting forth and the corners of her mouth curling down in mild distaste.

"Now, I have other matters to attend to. I shall return here at sunset. Be prepared to keep your word, Steward. I shall leave the Magus Gaspar to observe in my absence. You may work out the details with Lord Addecus and Lady Leanan."

Without waiting for assent, Mab spun on her heels and nodded to Gaspar. An instant later, a transit globe appeared, its sickly colors shimmering in the torchlight. The Dark Elfin Queen stepped through the unsavory event horizon, and disappeared. With a subtle *pop*, the ominous orb winked out of existence.

Gaspar appeared to be unduly pleased with himself and was about to speak, but Leanan stepped forward and casually cut him off.

"You were told to *observe*, Gaspar. That will not require you to speak unless asked to do so. Now stand aside while Lord Addecus and I confer with Lady Ellen and the Guildmaster."

As Gaspar stepped back, a furious scowl on his face, Ellen could not help but smirk. Clearly the elfin mage was not well regarded by the Sidhe, or the Were Lord, who hissed in disgust. However, she reminded herself, it would be most unwise to discount or underestimate the threat that any Dark Elfin mage might represent.

"Lady Ellen, Guildmasssster, if I may," began Addecus. "I too mussst attend to sssome presssing mattersss in my home realm. Asss sssoon as my commander isss located, ssshe will oversssee the departure of Were perssssonnel."

"Forgive me, but would that be a were-panther called Ling?" asked the Guildmaster.

Addecus stiffened and nodded.

"Then I am sorry to inform you that she was among the casualties," the Guildmaster said softly.

"No—that cannot be. That isss imposssible." Addecus' brows knit and his tongue flicked in and out in agitation.

"On the contrary, I assure you it is quite true. Would you see proof?"

"Proof? Y-yesss . . . I mussst."

"As you wish." The Guildmaster gestured to Gallenius.

The mage walked into the shadows and returned with a guardsman, who carried a simple box of rowan wood in his arms. Stopping before Addecus, Gallenius looked to the Guildmaster, who nodded once. Gallenius opened the container and withdrew the macabre trophy, holding it up by the hair for all to see.

Addecus stared into Ling's sightless eyes, and swayed slightly. Leanan reached out, placing a hand on his arm and gently squeezed. He straightened and took a deep breath, as Gallenius returned the head to the box.

"May I?" Addecus asked, in an appeal to the Guildmaster.

"Of course." The Guildmaster gestured for the guardsman to relinquish the box.

Addecus took it reverently and held it close to his chest.

"Thank you," the Were Lord replied wearily. "Under the circumssstancesss, I will asssk Lord Novusss of the Lupine Clan to ssserve in the capacity of acting commander, and oversssee our troop withdrawal. I trussst you find thisss acceptable?"

"Yes, of course, I fully understand. And, you have my condolences, Lord Addecus."

"My apologies, Guildmaster," interjected Leanan, "I do not mean to interrupt, but I must depart as well—sunrise will soon be upon us. I am prepared to leave Baron Von Kestel to act as my proxy, as I must take the Lady Sabrina and Lord Gunther with me."

"I understand, m'lady," said the Guildmaster, who then gestured to Ellen. "That is acceptable—provided of course, the Lady Ellen concurs?"

Ellen stood stunned—staring at the rowan wood box held in Addecus' arms—until the Guildmaster cleared his throat.

"Ah . . . You *do* concur, Lady Ellen?"

"Uh, yes, yes, of course, I do," agreed Ellen, tearing her eyes away from the box and pushing aside the unbidden questions roiling in her mind.

A sudden crackling in the air drew everyone's attention—Gaspar was trying to craft a transit spell.

Seeing their eyes upon him, he abandoned the attempt and the lingering dark energy dissipated. Shrugging his thin shoulders, he opened his palms to the group.

"You said you had to leave. I was just preparing a transit spell—"

"No one asssked you to do anything!" Addecus hissed.

"Indeed," added Leanan. "We will depart through the portal that the Steward will open to Olmus as agreed—not another dark gate of dubious origin."

"Gaspar," intoned the Guildmaster, "I will tell you only once; attempt no more sorcery in this realm."

The elfin mage's face took on an ugly cast and he ever so slightly narrowed his eyes; nonetheless, he remained silent.

"Lady Leanan, if I may?" Ellen pointed up at the willow tree. "The glaistig, is she not of Shadow? Will you not take her with you?"

For a long moment, Leanan studied the suspended vampire, still tightly wrapped in the willow's limbs.

"Ah yes, Triona of the Glaistig—indeed, that is her *true name.* I had almost forgotten about her. True, she is of Shadow. However, it is my understanding that she has brought harm to someone whom you hold dear, someone who bears my mark.

"I also understand that Gunther is not without some responsibility in this regard; you may trust that I shall deal with his poor judgment accordingly.

"However, Triona is another matter. I believe she has cast her lots quite poorly; consequently her fate is set—and sealed."

"I don't understand—what do you mean?" Ellen tilted her head.

Glancing up once more, Leanan paused, and arched a lone elegant eyebrow.

"I can see that she is well placed indeed—to enjoy the sunrise. Let her do so. Shall we go?"

CH 14

AS THE AFTERNOON WANED, Ellen stood on the front steps of the Ministry Administration building. Shielding her eyes, she gazed westward toward the lowering sun. It would set within the hour, the appointed time that Queen Mab had declared she would return. Ellen thought it wise to be at the newly opened portal before Mab arrived.

"Excuse me, Lady Ellen?"

She turned to find the Guildmaster standing in the doorway.

"Oh, hello Guildmaster, I was on my way to the portal site."

"As I surmised, my dear. Might I walk with you?"

"Of course, I'd be happy to have your company. Shouldn't you have an escort of guardsmen?"

"No, I have no need." He chuckled. "The guardsmen have been busy enough confirming that all the Shadow and Were troops have departed through the new portal you opened to Olmus, and that none remain in or around the Citadel. But might I ask, why you are alone? Did not your companions wish to accompany you?"

"Oh, they sure did—but I had to insist that they *not* come. I thought it might be better if Queen Mab doesn't know they're even here. At least, I have a strong feeling that's the case. It's like, I just . . . I don't know—I can't really be more specific."

"You need not be," he assured her. "To trust one's instincts or intuition is most often the wisest course, especially when dealing with a Dark Elf. And, if it eases your mind, I do not trust her either."

"Yes, I know. But something's bugging me; why did she leave—earlier, I mean? I would have thought this issue was sufficiently significant to warrant her full attention."

The Guildmaster paused slightly before responding. "And I would agree—assuming, of course, there was nothing more pressing on her mind."

Ellen grinned mischievously. "Aha! I knew it! You know something, don't you?"

"I suspect we do." He snickered, and then theatrically cleared his throat.

"Harrumph . . . It has come to our attention that Queen Titania of the Light Elves has been insisting—although to be perfectly honest, mercilessly *pestering* may be the more accurate term—upon a ceremonial meeting of the two elfin queens. Actually, it is a traditional requirement in the case of a newly ascended monarch; both elfin rulers must formally confirm the Elfin Accords."

"Elfin Accords?" Ellen echoed inquisitively. "What are they? I've never heard of them."

"The accords are a group of mutual agreements between the two elfin realms," he answered, and then added an afterthought. "You should know that there was not always a clear division between the Light and Dark Elves."

"You mean they were . . . like, one race?"

"Precisely, although you must understand this was very long ago—many millennia before the founding of the Council. They all lived in the same realm as distended clans and tribal groups, a world much like your home realm was tens of thousands of years ago.

"Their environment was bountiful and pleasant; ambient energy was abundant for the shaping of small magics. But the realm began to cool; the winters, usually mild, began to grow increasingly harsh, and last longer. The other seasons shrank, until any vestige of warmth in the normal yearly cycle had all but disappeared."

"You know," Ellen mused aloud, "if I recall my basic meteorology, that weather pattern sounds a lot like a normal cycle of environmental progression for a given planet, usually caused by variations in its orbit or the tilt of its axis. I know my own earth—uh, my home realm—has gone through changes like that. There's ample geological evidence to support it."

"Indeed so," the Guildmaster confirmed. "In meteorological and geological terms, you could speculate that they had entered an ice age. However, they did not understand it; and that was the beginning of their problems."

"How so?"

"We believe they lacked the ability to creatively conceptualize any explanation beyond their collective historical experience. We know that their social structure was rather strictly defined and fraught with taboos; curiosity outside the generally approved acceptable parameters of the magical arts was strongly discouraged.

"A hierarchy of accomplished magic users had evolved, even among and within the distended social groups. They consistently sought to more firmly establish and perpetuate their presumptive *higher* status. Now, as is often the case, those in charge were determined to maintain whatever level of control they enjoyed, despite any climatic upheaval."

"That certainly sounds familiar," she remarked wryly.

"Indeed . . . However, this was still a distended social network with no comprehension of the cyclic nature of global climate variations.

"Frightened, superstitious, and distrustful, the tribes and clans blamed one another for their misfortune, arguing and accusing each other of tampering with the magical forces of their world. Unfortunately, this led to true attempts at sorcerous manipulation of the environment—wind and weather, tides and currents. A number of the more adept sorcerers—some acting independently and others collectively, albeit typically at cross-purposes—managed to stumble upon a method of affecting the planet's rotation.

"Their thaumaturgy, steeped in their fledgling comprehension of the mysteries of astrology, more so than astronomy, led them to mistakenly think they were simply controlling the sky. The end result was that the planetary rotation stopped—quite suddenly—but the molten planetary core did not. The kinetic energies of the core's inertial forces began to rip the world apart."

"What? How did they survive?" Ellen's mind reeled with horrible images of death and destruction.

"Most did not. Those who did were rescued before the planet was completely torn asunder."

"Rescued? How? And more importantly, by whom?"

The Guildmaster shook his head.

"How, and by whom, indeed . . . Aye, therein lay the real questions. The answers depend upon whomever you might ask. Some say the dragons rescued them; others say the Old Ones. In truth, no one really knows, not even the elves themselves. It is, at best, a muddled tale within their lore. Any who may have known for certain are long dead."

"But they *were* rescued," Ellen prompted. "Does anyone know how?"

"Well, yes, in a manner of speaking, although there will always be some degree of speculation," he cautioned. "It appears that whoever it was showed the surviving elves how to craft transit globes, directing them to realms in the *wild*. The clans and tribes were somewhat polarized by the time of the exodus, so for the most part they went respectively as two distinct groups to two different realms—"

"The realms of Light Elves and Dark Elves that we know today," Ellen finished.

"Quite so," confirmed the Guildmaster. "Although still somewhat competitive, and mildly antagonistic politically toward each other, the elves honor a set of accords agreed upon millennia ago that states, among other things, that they will never again harm their respective worlds.

"Of course, over the years, the accords have grown in scope to include the basic structure for the management of their realms, their aristocracies and noble houses, and in some more recent cases, their current trade agreements."

"I think I get it," Ellen surmised. "It's these trade agreements that lend urgency to this traditional meeting of the elfin monarchs."

"Exactly. If Queen Mab were to decline a *third* formal invitation to meet and ratify the Accords, then Queen Titania would have been within her rights, under Elfin Law, to declare the present trade agreements null and void, and demand full renegotiations. The Light Elves would then be in an excellent position to demand considerable trade concessions from their Dark counterparts.

"In fact, Queen Mab has yet to even name a Lord or Lady of Commerce. Thus, she would have to negotiate, on her own behalf, with some lesser noble of a Light Elfin House—a situation she would most certainly loathe."

"So," reasoned Ellen, as they passed beyond the walls of the Citadel, "Queen Mab went to this meeting with Queen Titania, essentially to ratify these Accords?"

"We believe so, among other reasons," he hedged. "At any rate, I anticipate that we may have confirmation soon enough. Ah, look there—I see Gallenius awaits us."

Just beyond Gallenius, in the center of a large field, lay the new portal, an opaque hemisphere of shimmering multicolored light.

A handful of guardsmen stood about it in a loose perimeter; none taking their eyes off a sallow man with a sour expression. Attired in the robes of a Dark Elfin mage, he stood apart from the portal, his thin arms crossed tightly and his chin pressed to his narrow chest, refusing to meet anyone's gaze—Gaspar.

"Ah, greetings Guildmaster, and to you, Lady Ellen," declared Gallenius with a demonstrative bow. "We believe the task is done."

"All the Were and Shadow troops have transited to Olmus, as directed?" the Guildmaster probed.

"Yes, m'lord, none remain in Storm Haven, as our Guardsmen have confirmed," assured Gallenius. "In fact, it appears that all those in Olmus have already transited to their respective home realms. Do you not agree, Gaspar?"

The Dark Elfin mage glanced up without raising his head or altering his demeanor and merely shrugged. "I agree. I await my queen."

The sun settled on the treetops of the western horizon, as if it would singe the wood into slow submission. Shadows grew long and the lingering light took on a softer golden tint.

Ellen tugged on the Guildmaster's sleeve. "I can *feel* it; she's coming."

A moment later, a dark transit globe formed nearby. A mildly unpleasant static charge crackled across the ground below the orb as it settled. The hairs on the back of Ellen's arms stood up. This was no ordinary transit globe; there was something tainted, almost foul, about it.

But Ellen had little time to wonder, for Queen Mab stepped forth. The sinister orb shrank and winked out of existence with a whiff of ozone and a muffled *pop*.

The Queen of the Dark Elves stood regally erect, resplendent in a russet and verdant gown clinging to her slim form. A large topaz ring graced her left hand; an equally stunning emerald captured the failing sunlight on her right.

Gaspar groveled obsequiously. "Ah, most esteemed and revered Majesty, I bid you welcome. Your servants await your command."

Ellen bristled at the implication, but the Guildmaster gently squeezed her hand, and thus forestalled any retort she may have offered.

With an air of aloof disdain, Mab simply ignored Gaspar, and turned instead to the Guildmaster and Ellen.

"I presume all is done as I have commanded. Steward, you are prepared to perform your role?" With an absent flick of her wrist, she continued before Ellen could respond. "Very well, it will just have to do. I will have a word with my mage, and then we shall proceed."

Turning her back on Ellen and the Guildmaster, Queen Mab strode away, stopping after a few paces. With barely a backward glance, she raised a delicate hand, snapped her fingers, and commanded, "Gaspar, attend me."

The elfin mage approached her and dropped to one knee with bowed head.

An elegant eyebrow rose as a slight smug smile flickered across Mab's face. She reached down and slid a fingernail sensuously along the length of his jaw, and spoke huskily, "Arise, my loyal wizard, and heed my words carefully . . . "

Neither Gallenius nor the Guildmaster and Ellen could overhear what was said, but Ellen did notice that Mab pressed something into Gaspar's hand as she whispered instructions in his ear.

Stifling a curse for not thinking of it sooner, Ellen relaxed to let her awareness expand and caught but a fleeting trace of Mab's thoughts.

". . . them all . . . Do you understand?"

A black shield of dark energy suddenly slammed down, blocking the Queen's thoughts from Ellen's perception. She rocked back on her heels, momentarily stunned; the Guildmaster unobtrusively steadied her.

"Lady Ellen, are you well?" he asked softly.

"Y-yes, I'm fine." She looked up to find Queen Mab staring at her, a fleeting flare of angry surprise fading in the depths of her violet eyes.

The queen deliberately turned and focused once more on her elfin mage. A moment later, she turned her back to him in subtle dismissal and announced, "Gaspar will wait here. Let us proceed."

Without another word, she walked to the portal, and disappeared within the event horizon.

Ellen started forward but Gallenius stepped into her path.

"Lady Ellen, you do not have to do this alone."

Looking into his worried face, she gave him a small uncertain smile. "Actually, I do—but I thank you for your concern. Don't worry about me. I'll be fine."

With a glance to the Guildmaster, who nodded, Gallenius bowed and stepped back. "As you wish, m'lady. We shall await you here."

With a hesitant wave for both of them, Ellen stepped into the portal to Olmus and vanished.

UNSEEN IN THE UPPER boughs of a tall pine along the eastern tree line, a stunted form squatted upon a narrow limb, committing all it had seen and heard in the vicinity of the portal in the field below to memory. It cocked its long pointed ears in all directions, but heard nothing other than the normal sounds of the forest. Certain that it was otherwise alone and unobserved, it stood upright, extending and stretching its broad leathery wings. With a last look at the portal, the diminutive gargoyle folded its wings and leapt into space, dropping like a stone in free fall. Mere feet from the ground, its wings flared, catching the air in one mighty stroke, sending the small spy swooping into the encroaching shadows of the deepening dusk.

GEORGE SIPPED THE TEPID ale and set the pewter mug aside. His attention was drawn to movement within the scrying orb, something other than the lengthening shadows of the slow sunset. Peering closely at the two figures in the depths of the globe, his eyes widened in surprise. He spun about, looking for the nearest servant. Two goblins were huddled in a corner gleefully dismembering a rat; George's face soured in disgust.

A taller form stepped into the chamber, bearing a serving tankard of ale, a veiled woman attired in the diaphanous costume of a harem concubine.

George smiled at the sight; of course, her garb had been his idea. For the moment, she would do for the task at hand.

"Stellara, fetch Daegon—right away!"

She stared vacantly at her master, bowed listlessly, and walked in resigned silence from the room.

George had spent most of the day staring into the orb, watching long lines of troops appear from a new portal and march directly into either of the two older portals on the field of Olmus. The troops who had previously been in Olmus had departed the same way much earlier.

It all led George to correctly speculate that these troops were returning to their respective home realms.

But from just where, exactly? Yes, indeed—where had they been and what had they been doing?

Daegon had come earlier that day and watched the orb for a while as well. He had readily agreed with George's assessment as to *who* the soldiers were, troops of Were and Shadow, but would not bother to speculate as to from *where* they had come. Besides, he insisted that he had other priorities—like draining Zerban of the last traces of any arcane knowledge—so, he left George to his observations.

However, the orb now presented ominous portents that could not be ignored. *This* Daegon simply must see for himself, George rationalized.

He could hear Daegon's grumbling before the alchemist even entered the chamber, obviously resenting the interruption.

". . . confound distractions . . . must get control of these damned bats."

The alchemist strode angrily through the door, with a pair of simpering goblin servants in his wake, and demanded an explanation.

"All right, I am here! Now what is so important that you must have my work interrupted? You know the bats are a problem; they are becoming more vicious and unpredictable! Three more of the Red Cap Goblins went missing last night. And now something has the bats all worked up. I'll have to—"

"Listen!" George interrupted and pointed emphatically to the orb. "Right now, you *have* to see *this!*"

Daegon pursed his lips, shuffled over to the globe, and peered deeply into its crystalline depths. His face hardened and his brow furrowed as recognition dawned.

"That is *Diere—the usurper!*" Daegon seethed through clenched teeth. He balled his fists as hatred burbled up from the depths of his being like hot lava, and flushed his cheeks with angry heat.

"Yes, and the Steward, Ellen Doyle," George added, oblivious to his mentor's ire. "That's a surprise in itself! But what are they doing *here?* Looking for us? Are they working *together?* Why *would* they?"

"What? How would *I* know?" grumbled Daegon in barely controlled irritation, locking eyes with George. "*You* are the one who watched the orb all day! So, tell me, *apprentice,* when did they arrive?"

Unbowed, George returned the alchemist's smoldering stare as he shrugged in answer. "A few minutes ago, from the new portal. It appears they're alone."

Just then, a winged shadow flashed over the scene within the scrying orb; neither Daegon nor George noticed.

But someone had; a frightened gibbering rippled through the goblins like a wave, and their eyes grew wide with fear. In the next instant, all four servants had scrambled from the room.

George stood there in stunned surprise, but Daegon, once again moderately composed, stoically observed the goblins' rapid departure, and tilted his head as one eyebrow rose in wry exclamation.

“Indeed? What now, I wonder? Such erratic beasts.” He scoffed dismissively, and gestured to the scrying orb. “Now, to the task at hand, hmm, let us watch.”

ON THE FIELD OF OLMUS, Ellen squared her shoulders as she faced Queen Mab.

“I don’t know what you did to these portals from Were and Shadow that stopped me from closing them in Storm Haven, although it didn’t stop me from redirecting them here to Olmus. Whatever you did, you’ll have to undo it now. And don’t bother to deny anything—I know it was *you*. That’s why we’re alone now, isn’t it? So no one but me will see you undo what you’ve done.”

Mab looked down her nose at Ellen. “I do not owe *you*—or anyone else—any explanations! You would be wise not to provoke me! Now be silent!”

Ellen resisted the urge to retort, and watched as Mab gestured to the portals and began a soft rhythmic chanting just below a whisper.

As the spell grew in power, Mab’s eyelids drooped and she swayed slightly. The portals began to glow with a sickly purplish light, veined with craggy black tendrils that pulsed with the Dark Elf’s heartbeat. With a burst of pressure, like a silent thunderclap, the putrid purple light flared and winked out.

The portals remained, seemingly unchanged.

The elfin queen straightened and took a deep breath. Turning to Ellen, she smiled smugly and made no effort to disguise the droll condescension in her voice.

“Now, I suppose you may proceed . . . *Steward*.”

Something about the way Mab spoke, and the way she stood there so haughtily, evoked a bristling anger deep within Ellen, but she fought to contain it.

It would do no good to let Mab know her words had any effect. Rather than let her emotions surface, she concentrated on the portals.

The conscious act of closing the portals to Were and Shadow took very little effort; it was merely the release of the constrained energy. But as soon as the portals dwindled and *popped* softly out of existence, Ellen knew something was wrong.

She could not move—not a muscle! Her heart still beat and she could breathe—only her eyes obeyed the commands of her mind.

Mab stepped into Ellen's field of view, mere inches from her face, and smiled evilly.

"Oh, I see you have discovered my little surprise! When I removed my wards, I left a *little something* for you. It *is* rather unnerving to suddenly find oneself so completely helpless, is it not? No, do not even *try* to speak—any such action is beyond you now. In fact, everything is beyond you now! I have waited a long time for this moment—and I *will* savor it!"

A fluttering of panic rippled in Ellen's stomach, but she pushed it down and took a deep breath. She had to keep her mind clear and her wits about her! Surely someone in Storm Haven would grow worried, and come through the remaining portal to investigate. She focused on maintaining her composure, and realized that Mab was still talking.

". . . of course, I did not expect such an opportunity to arise so soon, but it required no great preparation on my part. I suppose I can tell you now; Gaspar tried closing your portals, but failed. *This place* has some sort of strange energy. All he managed to do was have his spell rebound and knock him senseless. That was the moment I knew for certain that you alone could perform this task. And then, this potential opportunity presented itself. Rather clever of me, was it not?"

Ellen's eyes narrowed, but she could offer no response. Yet she couldn't help but think how typical it was of Mab to prattle on about herself—*what a colossal ego!*

"Oh, yes, you cannot answer—a *pity*, that." Mab's tone of mock concern dripped with sarcasm. "I am sure you are wondering if any of your friends will brave the portal and come for you. Would not that be *gallant?* I must disabuse you of that fantasy—they are likely all dead! And you shall join them soon enough! But first . . ."

Mab steepled her long fingers, gently rubbing her hands together while gazing at Ellen over the tips of her elegantly manicured nails. A vestigial beam of setting sunlight, briefly captured by the considerable emerald ring on the Queen's right hand, flashed in a sudden verdigris flare.

Ellen blinked, and with a start realized that Mab's left hand was bare. The topaz ring was gone!

Gaspar?

"If I had my preference," Mab droned on, "I would have you relinquish your authority as Steward, and its attendant powers, to me *voluntarily*, of course. But I suspect you would not choose to cooperate. So, I am prepared to *take* what I want!"

Mab held the emerald ring up before Ellen's face.

"Your fate lies here, within the gem, a set of spells that need only draw upon the strange energy of *this place*. It is very strong, the strongest I have ever felt. With it, I will strip you of your powers, your very essence of self, and enslave your soul! For I know your *true name!*"

Ellen's eyes widened in shock—could Mab actually do this?

"Ah, I see that struck home!" the Dark Elf cried gleefully. "Now, now, don't fret. You need not overly concern yourself, for you see, you will not survive very long, not long at all. Ah, what sweet irony, the final spell will be your doom, exactly as it was for my dear cousin, Celeste, the *late* Queen Mab LIV of the Dark Elves."

Mab laughed and cackled as she spun about, her arms flung out in celebration. She suddenly stopped in mid-twirl, right in front of Ellen, and assumed an expression feigned regret.

"Then, it will be my sad duty to inform the Council of your unfortunate demise, during your failed assassination attempt—upon me, of course.

"I am certain that without too much effort they can also be convinced that you had already succeeded in the murder of my predecessor, using the same method. It will then be made clear that the Realm of Man and the wild realm of Storm Haven have been deeply involved in a conspiracy to undermine and overthrow the legitimate authority of the Council by assassinating the rulers of its member realms. Furthermore, it will be strongly suggested that this foul conspiracy is no doubt responsible for the recent incidents of *necromancy!*

"Oh yes, I can see it now. The Realm of Man will be declared *rogue—expelled* from the Council! Like the Realm of Storm Haven, there will be no Council protections or interference."

Mab sneered gleefully. "The absurd prohibition against *hunting and harvesting* will be null and void—*once and for all!*"

Ellen was stunned; she was having difficulty comprehending the depth of Mab's plotting and vindictiveness. Yet, in a sinister way, the tale the Dark Elf could spin before the Council would make a sort of ominous sense, and was so potentially disastrous in scope that it chilled Ellen to the bone.

"And do you want to know the best part?" the queen taunted, leaning close to Ellen's ear. "With the Realm of Man gone, I will have solidified my control of the Unseelie Court and its voting bloc on the Council. I have plans in place to exert considerable influence within other realms as well. All of which means that I will effectively control the Council itself. Oh, yes! The dominant political power of the known realms will simply drop into my lap!"

Ellen would have shuddered, had she been so able, at the demented gleam in Mab's eyes.

A change came over the gloating queen; looking up, her eyes widened in surprise!

A sudden *whoosh* of air ruffled Ellen's hair and fluttered her clothing; she saw nothing in her limited field of view.

But Mab had seen something; she took a few halting steps back, stopped and stood her ground. Her expression darkened, taking on a furious cast. Her voice shrieked with invective.

"By all the damned gods! What is the meaning of this? You damned grotesque *abominations!* How *dare* you! The Council has *no* business—or *jurisdiction*—here!"

A shape moved on Ellen's left, into her line of sight.

A Sentinel? No, there were two—no, make that four Sentinels!

Ellen could clearly see the four hulking gargoyles standing around—*no, encircling*—the Dark Elfin Queen.

A deeply resonant male voice, its tone somber and heavy with authority, spoke from behind Ellen.

"My companions are *not* Sentinels; nor do they serve the Council. Heed my words, Queen Mab LV, nee the Lady Diere of the Dark Elves. I would advise *silence,* as it seems to me that you have already well overstated your case."

A short, broad-shouldered man stepped in from Ellen's right and stood before her. Dressed in a dark knee-length cloak, he stood no taller than her chin. White shoulder-length hair framed an open face with a closely trimmed beard. But it was his piercing ice-blue eyes and intense stare that commanded her attention. When he bowed with an easy grace, his cloak fell open to reveal a burnished cuirass of scale armor trimmed in gold.

"I am called Ignatius, Avatar of the Dragon Lords. My gargoyle companions also serve the Dragon Lords." His tone was now pleasant and rich, almost melodious, and yet, still firm and assured.

Ellen was at a loss for words—even if she'd been able to speak.

"Now, by your leave, Lady Ellen Doyle, Steward of the Grand Portal of the Realm of Man, I will dispense with this *inconvenience* that constrains you at this moment."

Ignatius simply snapped his fingers and an opaque wall of shimmering blue and green light sprang up around all of them, arcing overhead to seal everyone within the large dome.

Instantly, Ellen felt the spell that held her immobile fade to nothingness. She slumped, but straightened and steadied herself. She cautiously addressed the Avatar.

"I . . . I thank you . . . uh, is it *Lord* Ignatius?"

He smiled. "That would be appropriate, m'lady. Now, if you would indulge me, I have business with this Dark Elf."

MAB VISIBLY FLARED at the intentional slight, but she kept silent as Ignatius came to stand before her and looked up into her haughty, scowling face.

"Your Majesty, it has been decided that you will *not* perform any such sorcery as you have described—especially not in *this* realm. It is *not* permitted."

Her eyes blazed; for an instant, she considered argument—perhaps even resistance. But a surreptitious glance at the nearest glaring gargoyle was sufficient for her to maintain an advisable level of restraint.

The avatar pointed to her emerald ring. "To that end, I drain the enchantments now housed in that gem."

A bright green spark arced from the stone to his fingertip. The stunning emerald lost its luster, and lay in its setting like a dull piece of glass.

The scent of ozone hung heavily in the air. Mab stared at her now impotent jewel.

What sorcery is this? You dare! I will learn this—this trick. I am not without my own resources! You will come to rue this day!

Slowly lifting her head to emphasize her height advantage, she stared down her nose to confront the steady gaze of the avatar. With no small effort to constrain her anger and thus maintain her composure and bearing, commensurate, she firmly believed, with her perceived regal status, she posed a conundrum.

"For five hundred years the Dragon Lords have been conspicuously absent from the affairs of the Council and its members. Noninterference was thought to be a guiding principle. And now, you deign to *meddle* in the *personal affairs of royalty!* I find that *unacceptable! Why are you here?"*

Ignatius slowly shook his head, and with a sad, wry smile, muttered, "Are elfin memories truly so poor?"

"I am queen!" Her face distorted in rage. "You will answer me!"

Stepping back a pace, the avatar considered the elfin queen cautiously before he answered her outburst.

"You are correct, for the most part; the Dragon Lords do not interfere, *unless* it is in their interest. You shall perform no sorcery here—you should have known better."

Mab was truly surprised, but hid her confusion behind a façade of frigid silence.

What? I should have known better? What did that mean?

She had no idea what the avatar referred to; but, she was determined to find out.

"Your business here is concluded," Ignatius intoned, and with a casual gesture, caused the surrounding dome of dancing energies to fade and dissipate.

"I recommend that you take this opportunity to return at once to your home realm."

The Dark Elfin Queen radiated murderous anger; but, remained tight-lipped as she stalked away and summoned a transit globe.

She turned at the last moment and stared directly at Ellen with such a flash of unbridled hatred that her exquisite elfin features twisted into a masque of malice. Then it was gone, replaced by a placid expression and devious smile.

Mab disappeared into the globe; and then it, too, was gone.

ELLEN BLINKED, AND turned to the avatar. "Um, excuse me, Lord Ignatius?"

"Yes, m'lady?"

"What just happened here? I mean, I know what I saw, but *why?* You certainly saved me, for which I am eternally grateful. But you just stopped a very powerful Dark Elf—a queen, no less—and sent her packing! Don't get me wrong; I really liked that part! But, I just don't really understand what's going on here."

Ignatius pursed his lips as his eyebrows rose. He spent a moment apparently deep in thought, and then seemed to come to some sort of a decision.

"No, I suppose you do not. Very well, I can only offer a brief explanation, for time is fleeting."

"I would appreciate anything you can tell me, I assure you."

Pausing, he stroked his short beard and then made a broad sweeping gesture that encompassed the countryside.

"First of all, Lady Ellen, you must understand that this realm, Olmus, was a place of power, a very old and very dark power. Even now, there are lingering residual energies, still tainted by the dark touch of those who strode here."

"Who was that?" she prompted.

He looked up at her in mild surprise, and then answered softly, "I speak of the Old Ones, of course. This was once, millennia ago, one of their strongholds, a place of grief and death. In the struggle to defeat them, a terrible battle was fought here. There was much loss of life; but, the evil was at last defeated.

"However, great thinkers far wiser than most, caution us that such dark energy can never be completely eradicated; traces linger, hidden pockets accumulate, and random eddies of contamination flow freely and undetected. Some places hold more grim secrets than others. Any dark sorcery performed in such a place takes on a more sinister aspect than intended, or expected.

"It is believed by some that the practice ultimately strengthens the Old Ones, who long to return. This realm was once proscribed; but, that was long ago. Alas, it appears that the elves, too, have forgotten. Perhaps there are more in need of reminding."

Ellen nodded slowly. "I have heard of these *Old Ones*. Many think them only a myth."

"No myth, m'lady; nor is it wise to speak of them aloud—especially in this realm."

"Oh, yes, of course—I'm sorry."

"No apology is necessary, m'lady. But you should leave this place," he warned. "You are needed in the realm from whence you came. You should go now."

"I will—right away," she assured him. "Thank you, again."

He smiled. "I am happy to have been of service, m'lady."

She hesitated, as if hearing a faint and distant voice.

"Lord Ignatius, forgive me, but . . . I don't really understand *why* . . . But it occurs to me to ask; may I tell my friends what has happened here, and about you?"

"The actions of the Dragon Lords, and the tasks I perform in their name, are, for the most part, not to be spoken of. However, in this case, yes, of course, please do."

He smiled. "I appreciate that you seem to know the proper protocol, and did seek permission to speak of me. In fact, it might be best if you were to tell the Guildmaster first. But ultimately, all must be warned to avoid *this* realm."

"Then I shall bid you good-bye, m'lord," she smiled and deftly curtsied. "I have a portal to close."

Ignatius smiled in return, but his expression flattened. He stiffened and tilted his head as if he too listened to an unheard voice. Speaking evenly, but with clear urgency, he said, "You must hurry—things are not going well for your friends."

She paled and ran for the portal. The transition took only an instant.

She was back in Storm Haven—and right into a scene from hell.

CH 15

DEEP IN THE HIDDEN chambers below the ancient temple ruins in the Realm of Olmus, George had the presence of mind to remain silent while he and Daegon watched the events on the surface unfold through the scrying orb. But as the last gargoyle disappeared within an eerily strange transit globe, the New Orleans gangster could contain himself no longer.

"Okay, Daegon, what the hell was that all about?" he demanded. "Just who the hell was that guy, *Ignatius*—and why were he and those flying goons of his here?"

"You saw and heard as I did," Daegon replied thoughtfully, hand on his chin.

"Yeah, but I didn't see or hear anything once that fizzy blue-green dome went up." George pointed to the orb and shrugged. "So, what—"

"Nor did I," Daegon spat, cutting him off. "But methinks we heard enough, before and after the dome. *Think* for a moment; we have learned some valuable information. It is possible that a number of curious questions, with which I had been struggling, may well have been answered—"

"Yeah, like what?" George groused in interruption. "That Mab—Diere—doesn't like the Steward, Ellen Doyle? Hell, *I* could've told you that! But who was this avatar guy? And what does this all mean?"

Daegon winced at George's impatience.

"Indeed, it does appear that Diere bears some great animosity for the Steward, and clearly covets her position and power. Now, as for this 'avatar guy', as you so crudely put it, he claims to represent the Dragon Lords. I must admit that an escort of gargoyles, ostensibly *not* from the Council, does lend a certain amount of credence to his assertion. And if that is the case, dragons are not to be trifled with—if any still exist."

"What the hell do you mean? What dragons?"

Daegon sighed at George's ignorance. "Understand this, my apprentice, dragons are, or were, very powerful in their own right, and once held great sway with the Council of Realms."

"Oh yeah, I remember there was a Dragon Chair; but, it was empty."

"Indeed, so it has been for at least the last five hundred years."

"So, they're dead, right? Or does this avatar showing up mean they're still around?"

"Let us just say that I have always had my doubts. But be that as it may, I am far more interested in what he had to say to the Steward, this Lady Ellen. For example; he said this was a place of power, something I already knew. But that this was a bastion of the Old Ones, something I strongly suspected, is now confirmed. Now *that* explains, or at least suggests, a number of interesting possibilities about some things I have found here."

"What are you talking about?" demanded George. "Like what?"

Daegon cocked his head and pointed. "This scrying orb, for example—it was here when I found this place. I know it is very old. I have always wondered who crafted such a thing; and, then again . . ."

"And, *then again—w*hat?"

"Hmm? Oh, is this the only one?" Daegon pondered, stroking his chin.

Clearly George had no answer for that; his mind was already moving on to something else that had been overheard.

"Now hold on a minute. Didn't that avatar guy say that no one should come here, that this realm was to be avoided? Doesn't that work out well for us—I mean, with everyone being told to stay away? Doesn't that mean that our base of operations here is, and would still be, a secret, right?"

"Yes, that *is* true." Daegon nodded in acknowledgment. "Without the constant threat of uninvited visitors, I would be unhindered in ferreting out the secrets of this place, learning its mysteries, and—"

"That's fine, but we also gotta have something going on—you know, some *cash flow!* Get some people working for us—*earners.*" George smiled, his eyes bright.

"But, we already have that which we need; basic sustenance, servants, and much sorcery to learn," Daegon offered, clearly somewhat confused.

"Yeah, for the moment," George countered. "But, see, I'm talking about building a power base, controlling some *turf,* and any action on or around it."

"*Turf?*" Daegon echoed, perplexed.

"Yeah, I mean like our own kingdom or something, controlling all the commerce—having a piece of every pie!"

"But we are in an isolated realm in the wild, populated by only a few tribes of goblins and some wild beasts. There is no commerce to speak of. You would have to extend your reach into other realms," Daegon reasoned.

"Exactly," agreed George with an evil grin. "Well, weren't we planning to go to a few of these other realms in the wild, once I have a better grasp of magic?"

"True, but there is so much to learn *here,*" Daegon argued.

"No *buts*, Daegon. You just focus on the sorcery, and teaching it to me," George insisted, rubbing the knuckles of his fist into the palm of his other hand. "I'll take care of *earners*—and getting *organized.*"

MOMENTS AFTER QUEEN Mab and Ellen had transited from Storm Haven to Olmus, to finally close the 'back door portals' to Were and Shadow, the elfin mage, Gaspar, who had remained on Storm Haven per the queens' instructions, commenced the execution of Mab's treacherous scheme.

Calling down a blast of putrid purple energy from a roiling mass of unnatural clouds, Gaspar took the armed guardsmen standing about in the open field completely by surprise. A sorcerous fusillade of sable lightning scoured the immediate countryside; none of the guards in the vicinity survived.

At the onset of the attack, Gallenius had instinctively erected a focused metaphysical shield in an effort to protect himself and the Guildmaster. His quick action spared their lives, but they were both thrown violently to the ground.

Desperately maintaining his shielding, Gallenius reached out and frantically grasped the Guildmaster's arm. "Guildmaster! Are you hurt?"

"I-I am fine—only shaken . . . got my wind . . . knocked out of me . . . You must deal with this elf—quickly!"

"I will! You must stay down, m'lord! I shall lead him away."

Matching deed to word, Gallenius rose to a crouch, reinforced his shielding with a murmured spell, and then sprinted dozens of paces to his right. Certain that his movement had caught Gaspar's attention, Gallenius readied his counterattack and faced his adversary.

He would engage Gaspar formally—wizard to wizard. In stentorian voice, he called out a formal challenge.

"By the powers of Air and Earth, Fire and Water, I, Gallenius, Magus Primus of the College of Mages, do lay the charges of *oath breaking* and *sorcerous treachery* upon you! You, I name Gaspar, Magus of the Dark Elves. I hereby challenge you! I will now accept your surrender!"

Gaspar smiled in amusement.

"A *challenge?* My *surrender? Gallenius,* is it? You are a fool of the first rank to dare challenge me! I am going to enjoy this. I *accept* your pitiful challenge!"

Stupendous sound and flashing fury erupted as their opposing thaumaturgic energies clashed. The very ground shuddered with each concussive blow as assault and defense met in explosive instants of mutual oblivion. Deflected errant energies ripped at the earth and shattered boulders like hammered blocks of ice. It went on and on, without respite.

Dozens of paces apart, both wizards were frantically casting and deflecting massive blasts of energy at each other in thunderous cacophony and blinding flares of sorcerous light.

When the first reinforcing squad of guardsmen arrived, the field was already a surreal scene of devastation and horror. A handful of guardsmen rushed the Dark Elf in an effort to aid Gallenius, but were struck by a sinister bolt of Gaspar's vile energy. Held briefly in midair in the unrelenting grip of this dark sorcery, the heart of each man burst forth from his chest and burned to sudden ash before his dying eyes.

No one again dared to approach the battling sorcerers.

GALLENIUS APPEARED to be losing ground, steadily driven backward, toward the distant walls of the Citadel. Gaspar relentlessly pursued, too focused to notice the surviving guardsmen evacuate the slightly injured and badly shaken Guildmaster to relative safety beyond the field and into the woods.

As each mage positioned and postured for any advantage over the other, their confrontation inevitably brought them ever closer to the city itself.

HAWK AND TREY ARRIVED on the periphery of the chaos. Instinctively avoiding the dueling wizards, they made their way around the perimeter in search of the Guildmaster. They were shocked at the scope of the damage. Deep smoking gouges rent the tortured ground, and steaming chunks of sundered rock lay strewn about.

A hidden guardsman stepped from the trees and motioned for the detectives to follow.

Within the forest, they found the Guildmaster, arguing with a handful of guardsmen.

"No I am not leaving! My injuries are not severe—I am in no immediate danger. I will *not* quit the field—not while the injured need rescue! The wizards' duel moves away; so, let us rescue and treat the wounded, and recover our dead."

No one offered any further objection.

Trey and Hawk joined the guardsmen in their rescue and recovery efforts.

THE GUILDMASTER WALKED among the wounded, offering what encouragement he could. He then spent a moment of silence standing before the row of dead.

Hawk nudged Trey and asked, "Don't you think Ellen's been gone long enough?"

"I dunno, maybe. Why? What are you thinking?"

Before Hawk could answer, the Guildmaster demanded everyone's attention.

"Hear me! The wounded must be taken to the infirmary. However," the Guildmaster's gaze settled upon Trey and Hawk, "this portal must be guarded—lest another imminent invasion of shock troops is also part of Gaspar's treacherous plan!"

Hawk did not want to perform mere guard duty; he wanted to use the portal to go and find Ellen in Olmus. He felt she'd been gone too long. His gut churned—he just knew something was wrong.

He would have plunged through the portal but for Trey, who grabbed his arm and hissed in his ear. "Hold it, Hawk! I know what you want to do—but think about it first!"

"But Ellen! She's been gone—"

"Yeah, she has! So how long is it supposed to take, huh? Do you have any idea? No? Have a little faith in her, man! She can get herself out of any tight spot just like that!" Trey snapped his fingers.

"She's the Steward! You can't go chasing off after her every time she's outta your sight! Give her some credit—she knows what she's doing! She's got her mission, and we've got ours—right here, right now! The Guildmaster's got a point; we don't know what else this Gaspar bastard has planned. He may have screwed with the portal and you could blunder right into an ambush or a trap! Besides, you know it's not smart to blindly do anything—even follow your heart. Think, plan, and *then* act. Hell, I'll even go with you! But right now, let's be smart."

"Okay, you made your point." Hawk reluctantly acknowledged the inherent wisdom of his partner's words and complied. But it did little to assuage the ache in his heart.

"Come on, let's give these guys a hand," Trey urged, gesturing to a number of guardsmen hastily erecting a barricade of fallen tree trunks and debris.

No less concerned for Ellen, Hawk threw himself into the task; the abatis was soon completed. From that well covered position, he and Trey could maintain surveillance on the portal.

THUMBING OVER HIS SHOULDER, Trey said, "Hawk, check it out. It looks like the Guildmaster finally agreed with his guard escort. They're moving him back into the trees."

"Yeah, I don't know how much shelter the forest will really offer, but at least he'll remain somewhat hidden from any potential threat coming through the portal. You know—good concealment but not that much cover. Hey, where are those guys going?" Hawk pointed at four guardsmen following the path of the dueling wizards, albeit from a safe distance.

"They're probably going to try to assist Gallenius," Trey guessed, "if that's even possible."

Trey peered over the top of the makeshift barricade of fallen trees, some of which were charred and still smoking from the collateral damage of the wizards' duel. Small fires, shattered tree limbs, and great clumps of ripped earth littered the ravaged field. Clouds of wispy smoke and acrid steam gusted about, obscuring the area nearest the portal.

Trey knew that Hawk was frustrated, chafing at the bit to go in search of Ellen; and he sympathized. But a glance to his rear, where a macabre line of recovered bodies lay in a neat row, was sufficient to remind him of the wisdom of patience and planning.

Little time had passed when Trey spied a lone figure emerging from the roiling clouds of smoke and steam in the vicinity of the portal to Olmus.

"We've got company," he hissed to the others, and readied a shotgun.

"Hold your fire!" Hawk ordered, as he scrambled, heedless of caution, over the barricade.

"Is it Ellen?" Trey demanded, squinting into the smoke.

"I think so," Hawk tossed over a shoulder, as he hurried forward, and then exclaimed, "Yes! It's her!"

PEERING THROUGH THE smoke and steam, Ellen thought she saw someone running pell-mell in her direction through the debris-strewn field—Hawk!

He barely slid to a stop—nearly knocking her over as he swept her up in his arms.

"Ellen! I was afraid something bad had happened to you. What's this—tears? Are you okay? Are you hurt? Were you chased?" His words tumbled forth as he clenched her tighter and peered over her shoulder at the area near the portal.

"It's all right—I'm fine! Not so tight, okay?" She pushed free of his embrace. "Tears? All this smoke stings my eyes. But what's happening here?"

"It's Gaspar—he's turned on us." He pointed behind her. "Listen, the portal—do you still need it? These people fear another invasion; we've been watching for it. Can you close it?"

"Yes, of course—I'll need a moment."

She turned and faced the slightly shimmering sphere. Closing her eyes, she concentrated. The portal paled and shrunk, its light growing dull and listless, until it simply winked out of existence with a soft *pop*. Until that final moment, she hadn't realized she'd been holding her breath. Sighing, she leaned against Hawk.

"There, it's done."

"Are you sure you're all right?"

"Yes, now I'm fine. Now tell me about Gaspar. What happened here?"

As he hustled her toward Trey's hidden position, Hawk quickly explained how Gaspar had betrayed their trust, and commenced a devastating attack. It came as no surprise to Ellen—Mab had boasted as much, telling her that her friends were dead.

"Some guardsmen were killed; more people were hurt, some not too bad, including the Guildmaster—Gallenius managed to protect him. Gallenius confronted Gaspar, challenging him to a wizards' duel—it got ugly. That's what happened here." Hawk gestured in the direction of the Citadel. "They've moved off; but you can hear them going at it. Come on; Trey's behind this barricade."

Trey beamed upon seeing her. "Oh man, Ellen, we are so glad you're back—safe and sound! How did it go with Queen Mab? Is everything okay?"

She gave Trey a quick hug, knowing that for the moment she'd have to forestall any questions about her experience with the Elfin Queen.

"Yeah, for the most part—I can't go into it right now, okay? What about the Guildmaster? He was *hurt?* Where is he? Please, take me to him, right now! It's important! I'll explain everything later—I promise. But we've gotta hurry!"

THEY FOUND THE GUILDMASTER attended by a hovering healer in a small clearing just inside the forest. Seated upon a log, his staff across his lap, he was surrounded by guardsmen. He appeared to be in good spirits.

"Pah! My injuries are minor and irrelevant. I am greatly relieved that you, m'lady, are safe. Sit here, beside me. You are well?"

"I'm fine, Guildmaster, thank you." Ellen sat and courteously offered her report. "The troops of Were and Shadow have returned to their respective home realms; and, those portals are now closed. Queen Mab, she, uh, departed, as well. Upon my return here, I closed the portal to Olmus."

"Ah, good, well done. The boundaries of our realm are once again secure," he proclaimed in a weary yet hopeful tone, "and, we have you to thank, Lady Ellen."

Flushed with embarrassment, she grimaced. "I was only correcting my own mistakes. None of this would have happened, had I not trusted Queen Mab in the first place."

"Nonsense," he declared. "I know full well that you were compelled against your will, your loved ones threatened. But that is over now, and we are still very grateful for your assistance. You were not at fault, you understand?"

"I do. Please forgive me . . . I have this strong sense of responsibility—or maybe just a heavy conscience," she conceded, dropping her gaze. "But there *is* something else. Could I speak with you privately?"

"Of course, my dear. But, first things first; we must aid Gallenius. And if at all possible, take this elfin mage, Gaspar, alive. We will need to know whatever he knows."

The Guildmaster turned to a guard officer. "Lieutenant, where are they now?"

"M'lord, we understand that they are now within the walls of the Citadel. The fight continues unabated."

"Oh, no," cried Ellen. "What about the people?"

"Be at ease, my dear. You may recall that most had gone to ground or into hiding outside the city." The Guildmaster laid a calming hand upon her arm. "The rest, to include Lady Stacy, Lord Mark, and Miska, have been evacuated to the caves beneath the Citadel."

"Under the protection of Mark's trolls," added Trey with a grin. "Everyone's safe—except Gallenius. He had his hands full when we last saw him. We need to get to him, now."

"Go then," urged the Guildmaster. Then firmly gripping his staff and shunning any assistance, he expended considerable effort to pull himself up to a standing position, and deeply sighed. "I will follow as quickly as I can. Lady Ellen, would you walk with me?"

"Of course, Guildmaster." She stood, grateful that he had so deftly arranged such an opportunity to speak privately.

Hawk started to offer to stay as well, but Ellen squeezed his hand and stared into his eyes imploringly. She realized he likely didn't really understand, but hoped he was wise enough to relent.

"Uh, okay, be careful," he said, and kissed her quickly. With a lingering look, and just a trace of confusion, he followed Trey and most of the guardsmen into the night.

A FOUR-MAN GUARD DETAIL remained as a personal escort for the Guildmaster. He asked that they use a bracket formation, each pair staying several paces ahead and behind their charges—close enough for protection, but out of earshot.

"Now, Lady Ellen, you have my undivided attention," the Guildmaster noted. "Please tell me what merits such discretion."

Ellen took a deep breath and carefully related the events of her experience in Olmus. The Guildmaster listened attentively, nodding in understanding as they walked onward. His demeanor grew quiet and reserved as she described Mab's treachery in detail. He asked few questions, and kept his comments succinct in acknowledgment.

However, it was the recitation of Ellen's encounter with Lord Ignatius, Avatar of the Dragon Lords, and his intercession on her behalf, that stopped the Guildmaster in his tracks. As his head drooped and shoulders sagged, her words dwindled and her concern grew. Leaning heavily upon his staff, the Guildmaster's disquiet shaded his voice with the tinge of regret.

"So, it has come to pass, after all these years," he whispered, balefully.

"Uh, Guildmaster, are you alright?" Ellen asked.

"Ah, yes, of course." He slowly straightened up and squared his shoulders. "Please, forgive me, I was, um, *surprised.* I am quite all right. Now, this Avatar, Lord Ignatius, he had no problem with you divulging this information?"

"None! He was quite clear; he *wants* people to know, to be *warned!* Although he did suggest that I tell you first. But everyone must be warned about Olmus."

"I understand." The Guildmaster resumed walking with a steady yet measured pace. "But I think, under the present circumstances, it might be best not to tell anyone just yet. The reaction to a possible return of the Dragon Lords would be staggering and potentially unsettling news. Indeed, reactions could be *unpredictable* at best, perhaps even precipitate an unanticipated panic. If this information is not properly, um, *handled,* there could be serious, unwanted, and unintentional repercussions."

"*Panic?* Really? That hadn't occurred to me," Ellen admitted, matching his stride. "I'm still not sure I understand. But what about Mab? *She* certainly knows."

He chuckled. "I would not be overly concerned about the Queen of the Dark Elves telling someone that she was bested at any kind of sorcery, or by whom. Were anyone to learn of this, it would only diminish her status. That is something she firmly believes, and simply cannot abide. No, for the time being, she will see her own silence as her best course—otherwise outright denial must be her path."

"Well, whether *she* denies it or not, Guildmaster," Ellen declared in a grim tone, "that does not change what the avatar said—all should be warned.

"I have always believed that withholding information, especially from those who may be impacted, is never a wise course. It smacks of none-too-subtle manipulation of those very people, who may not be as prone to panic as some might speculate.

"You should know that I have every intention to fully inform *my* people as soon as I get the opportunity."

The Guildmaster shrugged. "I see. Very well, m'lady. In that case, I ask that you not do so until you are once again in your home realm, hopefully after we have dispensed with this matter of Gaspar."

Ellen cocked her head. "Out of respect, I will try to do as you ask—but, I make no promises."

"Hmm, so be it then," he acknowledged as the walls of the Citadel loomed overhead and they passed through the open gate.

SOMEWHERE IN THE CITY, sordid flares of corrupted light reflected off lowering clouds; booming crashes and muffled screams echoed off the warren of stone walls and cobblestone streets.

The wizards' duel raged on, in full force.

Following the escort's lead, the Guildmaster and Ellen carefully wound their way through the city and finally crept up behind Trey and Hawk's position near the darkened mouth of an alley. There, in the deeper shadows, the two men were huddled with a guard sergeant, anxiously gesturing in an animated, yet hushed, conversation.

Ever alert, the guard sergeant paused, peered into the dimness, and recognized the approaching Guildmaster. Bowing briefly, the sergeant offered a whispered report.

"M'lord, Gallenius faces the Dark Elf in the square at the end of this block. Our men are in well covered positions in the surrounding streets and alleys and are making careful observations; but there is no way to offer more aid to Gallenius at the moment. He appears to hold his own, but with each attack his defense seems weaker. The College of Mages has been fully committed; but even they have now tapped their reserves. I know not what more we can do, m'lord."

"Which is why," Hawk began to explain, hefting his MP5/PDW, "we were trying to get close enough to get a clear shot—"

The slightly exasperated guard sergeant cut him off. "And I was *trying*, m'lord, to explain to these gentlemen that we had already tried that—the attempt cost me two men!"

"Gaspar is no doubt shielded," surmised the Guildmaster. He gestured sympathetically towards Trey and Hawk. "Your firearms will have no effect—not even, I fear, with your silver-laden bullets. No, his defense is far too strong, and likely enhanced. Perhaps, if we knew its origin . . . Sergeant, has the College determined any other source of this augmented power?"

"No, m'lord, our captain is in contact via runners with the Mages of the College. He advised that they deem Gaspar's power to be as formidable as their own."

"Guildmaster, if I may?" interrupted Ellen.

"Yes, m'lady?"

"This may be nothing, but . . . Queen Mab was wearing two rings when she arrived here earlier this evening. However, when she and I were in Olmus, she only had one with a big emerald in its setting. I, uh, had a very good look at it. She boasted that it held some powerful spells—the other ring might, too. I didn't see the other ring—a topaz, I believe. I don't think she had it with her. Could she have given it to Gaspar?"

"Spells? I suppose it is certainly possible," allowed the Guildmaster, "if it is a gem from a dragon's hoard. Has anyone seen this ring—does Gaspar indeed have it?"

"No, m'lord, no one has reported seeing such a ring," answered the sergeant. "Nor do I think that anyone can get close enough to be certain."

"You know, we may not have to," suggested Hawk. "Ellen, can you do your *thing?*"

"Oh, yes, I can try. Just give me a moment."

Closing her eyes, she expanded her awareness—and was nearly overwhelmed by the strength of the clashing energies manifested by the dueling wizards. The chaotic surges of power lost definition and character in the maelstrom of the conflict; there was just too much confusion.

"I'm sorry, but I can't quite sort it all out," she explained. "I think I have to get closer—probably to the point where I can see them. Somehow, I think that will work."

"M'lady, it is far too dangerous," warned the sergeant. "These flashes of *foul light* are terribly bright; one of my men suffered blindness when unexpectedly exposed."

"That doesn't sound good," remarked Hawk with growing concern. "Ellen, maybe we could—"

"No, Hawk," she said firmly, cutting him off. "I can do this—in fact, only I can do this. Don't worry; I'll be fine."

"Guildmaster, you can't let her—" Hawk began to protest.

Holding up his hand, the Guildmaster interrupted, "On the contrary, I cannot stop her. She is certainly capable, as you well know. More importantly, I believe she is right."

"Well then, I'm going with her," declared Hawk, stepping forward defiantly.

With a shake of his head and a soft chuckle, Trey stepped forward a pace and announced, "I'm in, too." He grinned and shrugged at Hawk. "Sometimes, you just don't have time for a better plan."

Ellen would have objected, but the Guildmaster forestalled any complaint by raising his hands and declaring, "It seems we are all going to accompany her.

"Sergeant, please lead us to a position as close as possible, but where we may not be seen."

Lips thinned in silent disapproval, the guardsman sighed resignedly. "As you wish, m'lord, please, follow me."

CH 16

THE MUTED RUMBLES OF the conflict continued.

The sergeant led them into darkened buildings, through a series of corridors and chambers devoid of any occupants. They finally arrived at the front room of a candle maker's shop that faced the small public square.

Row upon row of hand-dipped candles hung in display, suspended in pairs by their uncut wicks from overhead hooks driven into the ceiling beams. More tapers lay like slim sticks of pale cordwood stacked upon lipped shelves along the walls. The heavy scent of beeswax and paraffin permeated the air, an ironically pleasant and soothing ambiance juxtaposed to the turbulent bedlam beyond the storefront.

The view through the windows was shocking. The dimly lit square was in shambles. A wellhead and its marble fountain lay shattered; an unchecked flow of burbling water stained the dusty cobblestones and muddied the raw earth. Many building walls were cracked and crumbling. Huge paving stones had been ripped up and strewn about. A number of small fires flickered amidst the dust and debris.

Flashes and flares of wretched light sporadically illuminated the candle shop's interior in stark relief. Subsequent concussion waves rattled thick window glass in loosened frames, and caused pairs of dangling candles to swing erratically. Shelf loads of fresh tapers rolled off balance and plummeted to the floor.

"Look not directly at the light!" the sergeant cried out in warning, as everyone hunkered down and did their best to shield their eyes.

Ellen attempted once more to discriminate between the energy signatures of the combatants, but her perception had improved only incrementally. The details escaped her, lost in the overall sorcerous pandemonium. Sensing her frustration growing, she deliberately tried to calm and clear her mind of all distractions, so she could focus.

Unbidden, a soothing and reassuring voice seemed to speak in her mind.

. . . You have yet to fully appreciate the spectacles, or what you really can do, haven't you?

. . . Maude? Is that you? What about the spectacles?

Of course, there was no answer.

Had she really heard her aunt? Or was it merely a memory swimming to the surface from the lowermost depths of her subconscious? Under the circumstances, did it really matter?

Fumbling in a pocket, she felt a flush of relief as her fingers closed on the small velvet bag holding the delicate eyeglasses. She was deeply grateful that some vague intuition had instinctively prompted her to habitually carry them with her.

Something else I should perhaps thank Maude for?

She put them on just as another putrid flash of light washed across the dust-coated windows; but this time, the intensity of the flare and the rumbling concussion that followed were strangely muted for her. It was as if the harshness had been filtered, somehow slowed down. In fact, everything seemed to be moving in slow motion; even her companions ducked and flinched in seemingly deliberate lassitude as the next protracted blast of light and sound seemed to gently rock the shop.

This is a most interesting effect. Hmm, attributable to the spectacles, I suppose.

She shunted her momentary fascination aside and marshaled her focus on the task at hand. Daring to peer out into the square, she could now easily see the two embattled mages. They, too, moved in decidedly slow motion. Swirling tendrils of energy arced around each adept in a rhythmically pulsing pattern that mimicked a slowly beating human heart.

However, she could now see that the individual energy signatures were markedly different. The one surrounding Gaspar had a distinctively darker aspect, a hungering impatience like a predator waiting in ambush. In contrast, the shimmering cloud of energy wrapping itself around Gallenius was lighter, somehow fresher, and building in intensity. A series of pale energy streams, barely discernible tendrils of support, flowed from unseen sources toward the senior Storm Haven mage and fed the coalescing energy field forming around him.

With a deliberate gesture, Gallenius shaped a spherical mass of pulsing energy and thrust his hands out at Gaspar, sending the roiling ball of sorcery across the scorched stones of the square.

Gaspar extended his left hand. Something glinted in his fist; a dark amber spark briefly flared.

The incoming spell slowed, faltered and stalled, like it had encountered a wall of soft mud. Suddenly turning in on itself, as if turning inside out in an agonizing parody, it then rebounded, a darkened mirror image of itself, and smashed mightily against Gallenius' hastily erected defensive shield.

The tiring adept staggered under the weight of the assault, but managed to stay on his feet.

Gaspar smiled evilly, and dramatically swept his left fist in a broad arc before him; a streak of blood-tinted amber light hung suspended in the air. Slowly it expanded and converted the residual energy from Gallenius' last spell into a freshened defensive shield, a barrier that strengthened as it faded into invisibility—but Ellen sensed it was still there.

Now Ellen understood; it all made a bizarre kind of sense. As she slipped the spectacles off, the world around her sped up to normal.

"Guildmaster," she whispered urgently. "I could see streams of energy flowing to Gallenius! Someone is helping him, right?"

"Yes, of course, the College of Mages—or to be more precise, the collective efforts of the assembled adepts. They send Gallenius their magic, in a manner of speaking."

"They have to *stop!*"

"What—*stop?*" echoed the Guildmaster aghast. "They cannot stop! Gallenius is already sorely weakened! At this point, it is their energy alone that keeps him fighting in this conflict."

"No! *That's* the problem! Listen to me!" She reached out and gripped the sleeve of his robe.

"Gaspar has Mab's topaz ring—I'm sure of it! Whatever spell it holds has the effect of using Gallenius' augmented magic against him! Somehow it twists and contorts the sorcery, sending it back *even stronger* to attack whoever originally cast it. I could *see* it happening. The twisted spell expends itself entirely on Gallenius; it goes no further. He can't take much more of this—he has to stop fighting! And the College *has* to stop sending any more energy—they're only making it *worse!* Don't you see?"

"But how then shall he defend himself?" asked the Guildmaster in deadly earnest.

"Good question," she admitted, releasing the sleeve of his robe, "but it can't be with magic—or at least not magic directed at Gaspar."

"Perhaps we can be of some service in that regard?" offered Trey, hefting the short shotgun, as Hawk grinned and unlimbered his H&K MP5 once again.

The Guildmaster cast a disapproving glance at the weapons and reminded them in a somber tone, "Please bear in mind that I need Gaspar *alive*. I would very much like to have the opportunity to question this elf, somewhat at length—if you don't mind."

"I'm sure you would," Trey acknowledged, "but certainly not at the expense of Gallenius' life! So, let me suggest an alternative. Suppose we were able to overpower or briefly incapacitate him without doing any lasting harm?"

"Hmm, that would be acceptable, I should think," the Guildmaster conceded. "But what about his shielding? Did it not already defeat the shotguns of our guardsmen?"

Trey and Hawk looked at each other with sudden concern; clearly they had overlooked that rather salient fact.

Ellen demanded their attention. "Listen! From what I saw, I think Gaspar's shielding is directional, to his front. If we create a distraction, you might be able to get to him from behind. And I mean a distraction *other* than Gallenius."

Another flash of sickly light and crash of crumbling masonry punctuated the night, in somewhat ironic emphasis, as Ellen continued.

"We're running out of time! Guildmaster, you have to tell the College to *stop!*"

"What about Gallenius?" Hawk asked. "How can we tell him what we plan to do—telepathy or something?"

"Aye, therein lies the rub." The Guildmaster sighed. "We can try; but that requires deep concentration, for sender and receiver. I fear that in his depleted state, he may not be capable of receiving such a message."

"Then we'll just have to work fast," Trey insisted with a shrug, "and assume he won't know what we're doing."

The Guildmaster nodded, gestured to the guardsman, and placed a small engraved brass and silver object in his hand.

"Sergeant, go advise your captain. Then take my signet seal to the College—this will confirm that you have come from me. Inform them that it is my wish that they are to cease the transfer of supportive magic to Gallenius—but they are to stand by in readiness."

"Here," said Hawk, pressing a small handheld unit into the sergeant's other hand, "take this radio so you can let us know as soon as they stop. To transmit, press this microphone button and speak normally; release to listen."

With another nod from the Guildmaster, the guardsman slipped into the shadows and disappeared.

"Now all we need is the distraction," Hawk mused aloud.

Trey held up two black canisters the size of narrow soup cans and grinned. "How about a pair of *flash-bangs*? These are our last two."

"Oh yeah, that'll work!" replied his grinning partner.

Muted rumblings from the square echoed through the shop as erratic bursts of failing light briefly flared and sputtered listlessly against the dusty windowpanes. Clearly Gallenius continued to weaken.

Ellen tried to remain calm but each passing minute seemed an eternity.

Finally, Trey's radio squelched to life; the sergeant's static-laden voice announced, "M'lords, the College is ready to stop support. Awaiting your command."

Hawk and Trey scrambled to positions near the damaged front door that was hanging by a single hinge, and readied their gear.

At the last moment the Guildmaster whispered, "Be careful! You must save Gallenius. I do prefer Gaspar alive—but not at the cost of any of you."

Trey nodded once, and keyed his radio's microphone.

"Now!"

HAWK AND TREY BOLTED through the doorway and charged into the roiling chaos. Each detective lobbed a flash grenade in the vicinity of Gaspar and then sprinted in different directions in an effort to circle behind him in a pincer maneuver.

The twin bursts of searing light erupted; explosive shock waves rocked the square, surprising both Gaspar and Gallenius, who had been totally focused on each other. Both mages were momentarily flash-blinded and disoriented.

Gallenius, now unsupported by the flow of energy from the College, stumbled back, tripping over a shattered paving stone, and staggered to one side—a serendipitous event that very likely saved his life.

Gaspar, reeling from the unexpected explosions, blindly lashed out using only his own personal power, darkly tainted, but nonetheless considerable. An angry sphere of virulent energy shot forth from Gaspar's outstretched hands at Gallenius—or rather, at where the wearying wizard had been standing but an instant before.

However, the foul spell did not entirely miss.

The sorcerous blast struck Gallenius' personal defensive shield a glancing blow, brutally knocking the weakened mage off his unsteady feet, and leaving him sprawled and crumpled like discarded raiment amidst the rubble.

Gaspar must have intuitively sensed an imminent threat, for he spun around, sending a searing beam of purplish light lancing out in a broad arc from the tips of the fingers of his right hand, shredding the shadowed night. Otherworldly fires sprang up wherever the foul-hued shaft alighted and began consuming everything, setting even the very stones of crumbling masonry to smoldering.

Trey saw Hawk dive for cover behind the remnants of the fountain and try to bring his sub-gun to bear. In this erratic light he doubted his partner would have any sort of clear shot.

Ducking a wildly lancing purple beam, Trey scrambled behind an unstable debris pile that mere moments ago had been the outer wall of a butcher's shop. Shotgun gripped firmly, he peered carefully around the shattered remains of a splintered window frame; but in the smoky murk, he had no clear shot either.

Gallenius, Trey thought, was somewhere off to the right of his position; but, he couldn't see him. Worse, he could hear movement from the other side of the square.

Gallenius is likely down; and Hawk's hunkered behind cover. So, that's probably the sound of Gaspar, still disoriented and moving.

But damn it, he's still deliberately lashing out with those bolts of dark magic. Or is he blindly reacting to unseen or imagined threats?

With any luck, Gaspar hasn't seen Hawk or me yet—we can still flank him, I hope.

STUMBLING ACROSS SHATTERED masonry, Gaspar steadied himself behind a broken column, taking advantage of its limited shelter to reassess the situation. His ears still rang; but his vision began to clear. He carefully peered into the chaos of the darkened square.

At first, he could discern nothing in the dim smoky haze—where was his opponent?

Muttering a simple spell, he waited as a disgusting breeze swirled up around him, clearing away some of the acrid smoke that had arisen in fetid clouds from the many small yet burgeoning conflagrations his violent sorcery had birthed. The tintinnabulation in his ears diminished to the point that he heard a lone pain-stricken groan.

Gaspar briefly spied Gallenius, prostrate and moaning, across the debris-strewn square, but a gusting cloud of smoke obscured his view once more. He pushed off from the shattered column and advanced in the direction of the crippled mage, a feral grin further distorting his scarred elfin features.

ELLEN WATCHED IN HORROR as their plan unraveled before her eyes. She had seen both Hawk and Trey go down. She could only assume that they had been injured—or worse. Her heart clenched.

And now, Gallenius was doomed!

She shuddered involuntarily, a reaction that went to the very root of her soul. Defeat and despair hovered in the rising smoke like gaunt scavengers sensing a freshly slain corpse. The chilling specter of death—or the essence of something even *worse*—loomed in that forsaken square.

She had to *do* something—but what?

Her thoughts raced, torn between an urgent sense of desperation and a growing moral determination to oppose the evil trying to overwhelm her. But it was all too much; the sense of loss was too great. Was death, however imminent, the final indignity, or were there unnamed horrors awaiting the sundered soul? Could she have dared to face what she truly feared, to be lost and alone—hounded by regrets and recriminations of wasted time and opportunities?

It was now too late. If this was to be her fate—then so be it! She'd rather fight than surrender!

The instant she decided she would not succumb to her fears, and accepted the challenge before her, a sense of detached calm came upon her.

A warm and familiar voice echoed through her mind, enmeshing her in memories that could not have been her own. Like a dam bursting, a hidden wellspring of inspiration poured forth, flooding her awareness with knowledge, comprehension, and insight. Overwhelming in its rich complexity, yet comforting and impossibly familiar, it just *felt right.*

. . . Welcome Ellen, you have come into your birthright.

. . . Maude? Oh my . . .

Stunned, and yet, somehow more fully aware, Ellen now knew and understood many things.

Armed with a confidence akin to madness, she entered the square.

TREY COULDN'T SEE GASPAR in the dimness. But then again, he realized, that likely meant Gaspar couldn't see him either. It would be wise to move.

As Trey worked his way through the unstable rubble, careful to avoid being illuminated by any of the small fires now growing in size and strength, his eyes caught a pattern of movement on the side of the square near the candle shop.

Someone is approaching—but who? Is that Ellen?

INTERSPERSED WITHIN the shifting coils of rising smoke and haze, Hawk could barely see the gaunt and grizzled shape of Gaspar—no doubt searching for the crumpled form of Gallenius.

Movement across the square snagged his attention.

Who is that? Someone else? Oh no! Ellen!

Icy tendrils of dread clenched at Hawk's heart.

Ellen's walking right toward Gaspar! What's she doing? Any moment now, he'll see her! She's gonna get herself killed!

Without further thought, Hawk scrambled to his feet and ran forward.

Suddenly he saw another dim form converging from the other side of the square.

Who? Is that Trey?

GASPAR GLOATED AS HE cautiously picked his way through the devastation, leaning forward and peering into the gloom in an effort to once again spy the fallen Storm Haven mage amongst the debris-strewn disorder.

ELLEN, OF COURSE, SENSED them all; Gaspar creeping through the smoke and haze toward what he thought was Gallenius' position, and both Hawk and Trey rapidly approaching.

Relaxing her gaze, she focused her calm and made her preparations.

Ellen knew that Gaspar could discover his prey at any moment. She could not—*would not*—let Gallenius come to further harm.

She cried out with all the determined resolve she could muster.

"Hold, Gaspar, Magus of the Dark Elves! I have business with you!"

GASPAR SQUINTED INTO the shifting acrid haze, not certain who had addressed him—knowing only that it was a female voice, one that spoke with confident authority.

Ever cautious around powerful and very often *capricious* females, he paused and very subtly held Mab's topaz ring slightly forward, pinched between thumb and crooked forefinger, as this mysterious woman drew closer.

A brief gust shredded the smoky curtain between them. *There!* She appeared to stand her ground, confronting him.

With a small start, he recognized her. *You? You should be dead!*

However, he managed to hide his surprise well, but not so his condescension.

"Well now, Lady Ellen Doyle. What business could you possibly have with me, Magus Primus to the Queen of the Dark Elves?"

"I am here to accept your surrender, of course."

Marvel and mirth warred across his visage before he burst forth in raucous laughter.

She stood stoically through his outburst, never taking her eyes off him.

"My *surrender?*" he croaked.

"Did I stutter?" she countered wryly.

"Surrender, indeed!" he repeated acidly. "My, how utterly *amusing!* Do you know that you are the *second* fool to suggest such an absurd thing this night? I assure you that the first has come to regret such folly—as shall you! But perhaps you merely jest, that such a powerful wizard, an adept of my standing, should defer to a mere slip of a trite human girl? I must say, I am quite surprised at your most unrealistic sense of humor."

"Do I appear to be laughing?" she replied tonelessly.

Like a darkening storm cloud gathering strength, his patrician features drew down in a mask of constrained fury. A pair of worm-like blue veins began to pulse at his temples; the tips of his pointed ears darkened with the flush of hot blood to match the livid scar flaring on his left cheek. Nostrils flaring, his breathing grew rapid and shallow. On the verge of losing his temper, a luxury he would now allow himself with deliberate intent, he smiled—a frightening sight.

In the forefront of his focused mind, he began to formulate a particularly pernicious spell that would render the Steward a mere shrieking shell, bereft of soul and true name, left to aimlessly wander the wastes *between* realms of the wild for eternity!

The sudden twin pains that flared in the small of his back almost didn't register, his mind so intensely preoccupied with the imminent spell.

ZZZAAAPPPP!

The subsequent jolt of 50,000 volts, administered through the pair of barbed taser darts, penetrated the very core of his being! Convulsive spasms commenced, his arms locking in vibrating rigidity with fingers outstretched in splayed extension, his jaws clamping mercilessly, and his teeth grinding. Finally the seizures abated; he toppled to his hands and knees, gasping and nearly spent.

Gaspar's mind reeled!

Ye gods! A spell of some kind, surely! But why had not the ring stopped it and sent it back twofold upon the spell caster? The ring! I-I do not have it! I-I must have dropped it!

Gaspar fought to muster his own considerable power to counteract the results of this strange spell. Within a few seconds he was making progress; the residual muscle spasms diminished and he rose unsteadily to his feet.

In the dim recesses of his mind he realized the attack had come from the rear; so, he began to turn.

IN A BLINDING RUSH, 240 pounds of former all-state fullback knocked Gaspar clean off his feet, and directly into a pale transit globe hovering just above the cracked paving stones behind him.

In the next moment, the globe shrank and winked out of existence with a soft *pop*.

"Trey, *damn it, man!* Are you okay?" shouted Hawk, as he rushed to his partner's side. He dropped the taser, letting the device, its bloody darts and trailing wires, clatter to the cobblestones.

"I-I'm all right," Trey responded, catching his breath, "I'm okay! In fact, I think we'll *all* be okay, thanks to Ellen. But we gotta find Gallenius! Go on, now—I'm fine!"

Ellen momentarily locked eyes with Hawk, both of their faces registering a flicker of relief, followed by concern. They turned as one to search for Gallenius.

Trey slowly rose to one knee and gently massaged a shoulder. It had been a long time since he had thrown such a righteous block and he couldn't help but smile.

You've still got it, old boy—but it takes quite a bit longer to get your wind back.

He started to stand, but the glint of an amber flash drew his attention; there, on the broken pavement, sat a gold ring with an obscenely large topaz. He paused for a second, thinking he should really join the search for Gallenius; but, years of training and experience came to the fore. So, he quickly withdrew some items, to include a compact flashlight, from a pocket. In the spare beam of light, he scooped up the ring with the tip of a pen and slipped it into a small evidence bag. He noted the time, date, and location of the recovery, and then initialed across the seal.

"Trey!" cried Hawk, waving his own lit flashlight in the air. "We found him—over here!"

Trey stood, pocketed the small bag, and then carefully picked his way through the demolished square toward his anxious partner.

GALLENIUS HAD BEEN seriously injured, and was now only semiconscious. As they hovered over the wounded mage, assessing his injuries, the Guildmaster and the rest of the guardsmen joined them.

"This isn't good," Ellen murmured as Hawk and Trey rendered first aid. "We've got to get him back to the Ministry, to the healers."

"Yeah," Hawk agreed. "I guess we can carry him."

Upon hearing Hawk's remark, a squad leader spoke up, "Your pardon, m'lady, m'lords, but we can see to that. Corporal, craft a litter at once!"

Within moments, Hawk and Trey had successfully managed to bind Gallenius' wounds and stop the bleeding. They stood back with Ellen as the guardsmen produced their makeshift stretcher, and efficiently attended to moving Gallenius.

The Guildmaster stood there in stunned silence, as if in a mild state of disbelief—and self-recrimination.

Ellen sensed his mood and gently pulled him to one side, out of the way—and out of earshot. There she urgently whispered to him.

ON THE WAY BACK TO the ministry, Gallenius slipped into a deep unconscious state—a dubious blessing considering the pain he obviously endured.

The finest of healers were summoned, and treatment rendered. However, Gallenius' injuries were quite severe; many felt he would not survive the night. And yet, to the surprise of some, he continued to linger on, his condition unchanged.

THE FOLLOWING EVENING, the mood was indeed somber when Ellen sought a late meeting with the Guildmaster in his private chambers.

"Ah, Lady Ellen . . . Please, come in and be seated. How may I be of service to you?"

"Actually, Guildmaster, I think it's rather that *I* may be of service. As you know, my friends and I must leave in the morning, at first light, and return to our home realm."

"I know." He sighed, leaning back in his chair, his gloved hands flat on the armrests. "You know you will be missed. And of course, you and your friends are always welcome here."

"Yes, thank you, we appreciate that. But what I came to say is, I would like to take Gallenius with me.

"I know you have fine healers here, and I'm sure they have done everything they possibly can. But I think—no, I *know* that my realm has outstanding medical practitioners, *doctors, specialists.* I just couldn't go, leaving Gallenius in that state, without exhausting every possible remedy at our disposal.

"Please, I mean no disrespect—not to you, this realm, or the healers here. I don't mean to offend, run afoul of your laws, or complicate the issue. It's just that I have to *try.* Do you understand?"

"I believe I do, my dear. Nor is the matter particularly complicated. Let me explain." The Guildmaster leaned forward.

"You see, it is not forbidden to seek something, be it medical assistance, or anything else, in another realm—provided of course, our administration is first made aware of the quest. In fact, a search for assistance with healing has never come up before. I suspect primarily because we do believe that we have excellent healers. Our innate caution should be understandable—remember that heretofore, our very existence has been a well-guarded secret. Well, suffice to say *that ship has sailed.* As I said, the only stipulation has always been that whoever would so venture forth must first seek permission."

"But that's the problem," she insisted, perched on the edge of her chair. "Gallenius hasn't regained full consciousness since he was hurt—he can't ask! But you could authorize it, on his behalf, based on the rebuttable presumption that he would ask, were he capable. And I can't imagine that you would be the least bit concerned about his discretion regarding any of Storm Haven's secrets."

The Guildmaster chuckled. "You certainly sound like your cousin, Mark, the *lawyer.* Has he been counseling you in this matter?"

Ellen smiled coyly. "Maybe a little. He offered to come and plead the case; but, I told him that I just wanted to talk it over with you. Of course, he did say that such a decision could set an important precedent in the administration of the realm, and that alone was worthy of *due consideration*. But I don't care about the politics—I just want to help my friend."

"As do I, my dear, as do I. You may consider such permission as granted. I shall ask the healers to prepare him for transit in the morning."

"Thank you, Guildmaster."

"It is I who should be thanking you," he admitted with a wave of his hand. "I must confess that it had not yet occurred to me that there were other options for his care."

"Oh, I'm sure you would have thought of it. You just have so much on your mind right now. I just hope—no, I *know* it'll help Gallenius. You know, of course, that if there's anything else I can do . . ?"

"Well, Lady Ellen, if you do not mind, I do have some questions."

"Of course, Guildmaster, what would you like to ask?"

He paused and straightened a bit in his armchair before speaking.

"I find this a bit awkward . . . You have not volunteered the information, nor has anyone else asked. You see, it is generally considered impolite to so question a Steward. But, in the interest of the security of the realm for which I am responsible, I am compelled to make this regrettably rude inquiry, um—"

"Go on," she said, hiding a smile, her curiosity piqued.

"Ah, when you crafted the transit globe that ultimately removed Gaspar from Storm Haven, where did you send him?"

"Oh, yeah, Gaspar . . . I regret that we weren't able to simply capture him as you would have liked, but he proved to be far too dangerous."

The Guildmaster slowly nodded. "Yes, I understand. And for what it is worth, I quite agree; he was far too dangerous."

Her palms open, Ellen shrugged. "So, rather than trying to kill him, I transited him to a realm where he couldn't harm anyone. And quite possibly, there was someone there who was better equipped to deal with the likes of him."

"Ah, I think I understand." The Guildmaster chuckled in appreciation. "You sent him to Olmus, in the hope that Lord Ignatius would deal with him."

Ellen smiled; he had the right of it.

The Guildmaster dropped his head. "And then you pulled me aside, when, I am sorry to say, I was not being very helpful as Gallenius lay injured.

"I know you deliberately distracted me, for which I am grateful. But more importantly, you urged me to have the College of Mages immediately reinforce the transiting wards on the entire realm to prevent Gaspar from making an uninvited return."

Ellen nodded. "True, however, not just him, but Queen Mab, as well. When I first opened those two portals at her insistence, I had no idea that I had also effectively managed to compromise your wards. Nor did I know how to go about fixing the problem when I subsequently learned about my terrible mistake.

"But when things couldn't seem to get any worse—when I had to face Gaspar . . . Well, let's just say I had a sort of *epiphany*. A number of things fell into place for me—quite a bit, actually.

"Anyway, as for your wards, somehow I just *knew* what had to be done. But only the College of Mages could do it; and, it had to be done right away! Only *you* could have directed them to accomplish that task, per the procedure I explained.

"I want you to know that I sincerely regret that I was responsible for all of this. I'm sorry that any of it ever even happened."

Waving his gloved hands in dismissal, he leaned forward as if to share a confidence. "I do not hold you responsible, Lady Ellen. Do not shoulder that burden.

"The weaving of the threads of fate is never solely one being's doing. To assume otherwise is either the utmost folly or blind hubris—I do not find you prone to either."

"Perhaps, but I'm only human. I know when I've made a mistake, and been burned. You can believe I'll not make the same one twice," she concluded firmly.

"Hmm . . . It is said that great heat tempers great steel," he commented softly. "And such resilience may yet be required of you. I fear that neither of our realms will ever be quite the same ever again."

She smiled. "That's too true."

"Let us turn our thoughts to other matters."

He reached for a tiny wooden box on a small ornate table by his chair, and opened it. Tilting it forward for her to see its contents, he posed another question. "What would you have us do with this? It is very likely the property of Queen Mab, you know."

"May I?" She held up the small evidence bag and studied the topaz ring within.

"Your thoughts?" he probed.

"Trey gave you this?" she surmised.

"Quite so, he even made me initial the seal, just below his own initials—something about maintaining a *chain of custody*, and insisting it is *evidence.*" He chuckled.

"Yeah, I suppose it would be. But as Mark would no doubt say, the jurisdiction might be an issue. If Trey wouldn't take it out of Storm Haven, he must believe that this realm is the appropriate jurisdiction. Have you asked Mark about it?"

"Yes, I did. He agrees that the ring should stay here. Furthermore, he proffered that it may be considered a 'spoil of war', since we *were* invaded, and

Queen Mab was at the heart of the crisis and most likely the provocateur. He even offered his services as an advocate, and would be more than willing to put the entire issue before the Council itself should Mab ever try to recover the ring."

She laughed. "Oh, I'll bet he would—anything for an argument! In truth, I would agree; the ring is now the property of Storm Haven. I am sure the College of Mages can find some useful purpose for it."

"No doubt they can, my dear. Very well, this issue is decided."

He extended the box for her to drop the bag within. Gently closing it, he returned it to the table, and stared blankly at the simple container as he unconsciously sighed.

"Is everything all right, Guildmaster?"

"As well as could be expected, I suspect. Would that this were to be the last of Queen Mab, and her twisted intentions, that we should be destined to endure. Alas, I fear that such are not the whims of fate—nay, for neither Storm Haven nor you, my dear, as the Steward of the Grand Portal of the Realm of Man."

He slumped in his chair. "Ah, I grow so weary of such continual strife, and tend to prattle on. Forgive an old man."

Sensing his melancholy mood, Ellen stood. "Rather you should forgive me. It is late, and I've kept you from your rest. You have been an excellent host and a good friend. But, I miss my mother; I'm ready to go home tomorrow. So, I'll bid you goodnight, Guildmaster."

He rose and bowed deeply in formal respect.

"Lady Ellen, I bid you goodnight and safe journey. Know that you are always welcome here. May you be well; and, may the fates be kind to us all, m'lady."

CH 17

ELLEN HELD THE DELICATE glass ornament out at arm's length, letting it dangle from her fingertips. She tried to visualize just where on the modestly decorated Christmas tree it ought to hang.

The last few errant rays of the setting sun passed languidly through the front windows of her Delafaire Farm home, refracting playfully off the faceted surfaces of the prismatic globe. Much to her delight, the reflections burst into bright multihued spots that danced like frolicking sprites across the deepening shadows, those dusky heralds of encroaching evening that would slowly claim the walls and ceiling of the cavernous ballroom.

Oh my! Am I ever in a poetic mood. Well, I do so like the holidays.

A small yet cheery fire blazed happily away in the nearest hearth, keeping the December chill at bay as she and her mother, Millie, puttered about, comfortably probing with familiar curiosity the depths of assorted cardboard boxes full of seasonal decorations. The Chows, Max and Sophie, slumbered on either side of the warm hearth like a pair of furry rugs, while the cat, Smokey, lay atop the nearby piano, contentedly sound asleep.

Of course, the southern end of the ballroom was simply the perfect place for the Christmas tree. Ellen and Millie had spent the better part of the day unpacking forgotten boxes and rediscovering cherished decorations from past Christmases. The hours passed most pleasantly, a wonderful experience, like sharing a special window into her childhood. Fortunately, these were all happy memories for both mother and daughter.

Millie stood up and stretched, wincing as she eased a cramp in the small of her back.

"Oh, I just remembered something. I've got to go to the kitchen. I'll be back in a bit. Can I get you anything?"

"No, I'm fine, thanks anyway, Mom."

Millie returned moments later, a paper-wrapped bundle in her hand. Peeling the paper back and thrusting the parcel toward her daughter, she grinned happily.

"Here! You've got to smell these! Aren't they wonderful? I found them in a drawer in the kitchen. I wonder if we can't use them—you know, in our decorations?"

"Candles?" Ellen looked at the delicate tapers. Familiar scents of paraffin and beeswax wafted up, triggering a distinct memory.

She lifted a pair by their common wick—still uncut—and studied the obviously hand-dipped pillars. An image of the chaos of that night swam forth in her mind; the damaged candle maker's shop, the shattered square wreathed in smoke from a host of smoldering fires.

She shrugged off the reminiscence, and responded casually, notwithstanding the disquiet the recollection had engendered.

"Yeah, they're nice; and they do smell good. I guess we could use them, but I don't think we ought to light them."

"Of course not, silly," Millie teased. "You know, people used to use lit candles as tree decorations—pretty dangerous, if you ask me. I just want to use them in other ways—you know, like on a wreath or a table setting."

"Oh, that'd be great; but, I still wouldn't want to light them," Ellen hedged. "I think they're too pretty to burn, don't you?"

"I suppose," Millie allowed. "I'll bet Maude used them, though. I found a couple that had been burned down to mere stubs in that drawer. Maybe she used them during a power outage?"

"That makes sense," Ellen agreed, but her curiosity was piqued.

As Millie delved once more into the boxes, Ellen focused her awareness on the candles. As she suspected, there was the lightest trace of a benign spell on the tapers, something altogether wholesome and comforting that fostered a sense of contentment. A small smile blossomed.

Once again, Maude, you surprise me. I'm not certain what you've done to these candles, but I know it was well intentioned. And I think I know just where you got them. For now, I think I'll keep this to myself—although I will definitely consult the journal.

Ellen placed the bundle on the mantle and joined her mother in unpacking the rest of the seasonal decorations.

As the late afternoon waned, Millie finally stood and announced, "Oh darn, I'm getting stiff again; I gotta take a break. It's almost time for me to get supper started."

"Want some help?" Ellen offered.

"No thanks. Why don't you keep looking for that little porcelain angel we always place atop the tree? You know it's been in our family for at least three generations. Why, it just wouldn't be Christmas without it, now would it?"

"Nope, sure wouldn't. Don't worry, I'll find it. I'm sure it's here, somewhere."

As she smiled and watched her mother make her way into the hall, an unbidden memory arose in the recesses of her mind. Hadn't Maude given that favorite angel figurine to Millie's mother long ago? It was one of the most treasured keepsakes Millie possessed, a tangible link to her own late mother.

For some reason, that thought bestowed a comfortable certainty and pleasant warmth in Ellen's heart. So, once more on her knees, she gladly resumed her eager search, unwrapping each ornament and decoration with a very childlike anticipation of an imminently rediscovered treasure.

In the bottom of a smaller box, swaddled in thickly wrapped layers of crinkly tissue paper, she found her missing angel. Smiling, she cradled the delicate figure in her hands and glanced at the bare pinnacle of the Christmas tree.

Now, of course, everything would be all right.

Her idle musing was interrupted by a familiar sensation subtly impinging upon her awareness. A transit portal had just opened—she was certain. It was close, somewhere nearby.

The dogs were suddenly alert and on their feet. Even Smokey had awoken. Still lounging on the piano like a sphinx, he held his head up, his ears erect and his eyes fixed upon the front hall.

Ellen stood up, the dogs staring at her inquisitively. Closing her eyes, she immediately knew that the portal had appeared on the front lawn. In the next moment, she knew it was already gone.

But someone had come through; the dogs must have known it as well. They trotted silently into the hall and faced the front door.

Ellen arrived at the door just as three soft knocks sounded on its surface. She glanced at the dogs for reassurance; they were still alert but not alarmed. Smokey hadn't even bothered to investigate. As she grasped the latch, she realized who had come.

With a mighty pull, she swung the door open.

"Padraic! How nice to see you!" She pushed the screen door open. "Please, come in. How are you?"

"I am fine, Ellen, just fine. And you?" He displayed a broad smile, pushed the hood back on his dark robe, and stepped into the hall.

"I'm good," she assured him. "Can I take your, uh, robe? Can I get you something to drink? My mother's in the kitchen fixing supper. Can you stay and eat with us?"

"I suppose I can stay for a little while." He shrugged off the thick woolen robe and handed it to his daughter. "I do so love your mother's cooking... What?"

Ellen stood there smirking, trying to control her sense of humor; but, she couldn't contain it any longer, and burst out in laughter. After a moment, she caught her breath and found her voice.

"Oh, my . . . I'm sorry, but what—what are you wearing?"

Taking on an air of mock superiority, he drew himself up. With an elegant flourish of his hand, he swept the air before his face and intoned loftily, "I shall have you know, young lady, that this is formal court attire of a prince among the Dark Elves. Yes, I have been elevated formally to the rank of prince consort—and sadly, have to dress the part when required, for um, functions of state and the like."

Biting her lips, she tried not to snicker.

He sighed heavily and continued. "Ever since I had to attend the initial meeting of the elfin queens at Briar Castle, Mab insists that my attire befits my, uh, station—and that it be consistently more flamboyant than that of Duke Briar, a renowned *clotheshorse*. Truthfully, I think she just likes to twist the knife, and flaunt me in his face at official functions."

"Well, that doesn't surprise me." Ellen chuckled. "Forgive me, but you look like a cross between a *Mardi Gras* float and a refugee from a renaissance fair! What's with all the gold braid on your jacket, and the pastel tights?"

Before he could answer, she spied his mauve ankle boots, complete with curled and pointed toe tips. She lost it once again, her unbridled laughter bubbling forth. She had to take several moments to regain her composure.

Even the dogs took to sniffing the unusual boots.

To his credit, Padraic just grinned and shrugged, taking the situation in good humor.

"I am pleased that you are so amused," he said drolly, "as I am sure your mother will be as well. But before we see her, I must speak with you privately. There are certain things you must know, um, before . . . "

"Before what?" she pressed, her humor subsiding.

Rather than answer, he looked down the long empty hall, and then into the fire-warmed ballroom. With a gesture toward the glowing hearth, he simply whispered, "May we?"

As if on cue, Max and Sophie turned and escorted them into the ballroom. The dogs then resumed their former positions on either side of the hearth.

Spying Smokey atop the piano, Padraic went over and scratched the cat behind his ears, earning an audible purr that resounded softly through the room. Padraic sat down on one half of the piano bench and gently patted the vacant spot beside him.

As Ellen joined him, he spoke in a low and guarded voice.

"Tis best we are not overheard. Where is everyone?"

"I told you. Millie's in the kitchen; and no one else is here right now. Stacy went with Mark to drop off some cases of our homemade jams and preserves down at Tippet's General Store. Then she and Mark are going to a dinner for his law firm in LaBorde. They made him a full partner, you know—anyway, they won't be back until late tonight. Miska is at the cabin. He lives there permanently, now. He'll be here in an hour or so for supper."

"And your boyfriend?" Padraic asked impishly. "He is well?"

Ellen smiled, a touch of color rising to her cheeks.

"Hawk is just fine, thank you—although, I haven't seen him all week. He and Trey have been working a strange case, something to do with *cattle rustling.* Livestock have been disappearing throughout the parish.

"But, now what about you, Padraic? Why the visit, now? We—well, I mean *I*—haven't seen you in months! But I know Mark has. So?"

"My apologies," her father countered, "but I have been rather closely watched of late. It has been only very recently that such scrutiny has lessened somewhat. Mab has become quite suspicious and paranoid ever since her encounter with the Avatar of the Dragon Lords on Olmus."

"She *told* you about that? No, she wouldn't have! How did you . . . of course—the Guildmaster!"

"Yes, I am well informed—but not, as you have surmised, by the queen. I did see Mark occasionally at the Council meetings, but opportunities to speak were few and far between."

"Wait a minute, Mark told me that he invited you to Thanksgiving dinner. We had a great time! Gallenius was still here, almost fully recovered. And we missed you—my mother even set you a place at the table."

"Again, I must apologize to you and your mother. I did receive his invitation, but I simply could not get away at that time. I did receive word of Gallenius' recovery and his subsequent return to Storm Haven shortly thereafter.

"Unfortunately, it is as I said; Mab has made it a point to parade me before the attendees of any and all Unseelie Court functions—hence my garb, commensurate with my elevated position."

She chuckled once more, this time in sympathy.

He reached into a pocket and withdrew a soft leather pouch.

"Lest I forget, these are for you, your mother, and your friend, Stacy."

She took the pouch and upended its contents into her waiting palm; three clear crystals suspended on delicate gold chains tumbled out. Spectacular gems, sparkling with a clear inner light, each as thick as her little finger and half the length. They were breathtakingly beautiful.

She gasped involuntarily.

"Oh, Padraic, this is so, um, *unexpected.* They're simply beautiful! Uh, Christmas gifts? Thank you! But, I don't have anything for you—yet."

"Christmas gifts?" he echoed, momentarily confused.

She watched his expression soften as he glanced at the partially decorated tree. A flood of recollections must have cleared his befuddlement, she reasoned.

"Ah, not quite . . . To be honest, Ellen, I had forgotten how important this Christmas celebration is in the Realm of Man. I always enjoyed the warmth and affection that was so pervasive here—even if it was only for a brief time."

"Well, we do have our redeeming qualities," she quipped, not unkindly.

"So I have always said," he retorted with an impish smile, and inclined his head toward hers.

"You know, it may surprise you to learn that there are festivals of some kind held by most cultures at this time of year in almost every known realm. Some celebrate the winter solstice, the renewal of the seasonal cycle, or honor some obscure deity; there are, of course, many other rationales. The giving of gifts, offerings, or even sacrifices, can be fairly common."

"Well then," she declared, "I think, whatever the reason, it's a good thing!"

"Indeed so! As for these crystals, consider them as Christmas gifts, if you like. These are very special; they will warn you of the presence of evil, and alert you to the presence of beings from realms other than your own, or the one you're in at that moment. Trust me that you will come to know the subtle differences. These can be most useful. I am sure you understand.

"I must ask one thing of you, though; none of you must wear these necklaces until after I leave. The benign sorcery held within will begin working the first time they are worn; and thereafter, they will only work for the first, and intended, bearer. I fear that my presence here may interfere with the initiation of those spells."

"I understand; we can wait. But that is not all you came here for, is it?"

He smiled knowingly. "Very perceptive, my dear. No, there are, as always, compelling reasons, and among them, a far more dangerous secret—one that you must now learn, for your own safety."

“Does my mother know, or need to know, this secret? Should I go get her?”

Padraic held up both hands and uttered most emphatically, “No! Although this may indirectly concern your mother, she is far safer not knowing, at least for now.”

“Then, just what are you talking about?” asked Ellen, her tone growing decidedly cool.

Leaning back against the piano, Padraic sighed. His hand fell upon a small stack of sheet music, and the top page caught his eye. He picked it up and studied the handwritten notations. He began to speak softly, a hint of melancholy laced within his voice.

“This is difficult for me. What I am about to tell you must never go beyond us—by that I mean you and I, and only you and I. Otherwise, both our lives would be in jeopardy—perhaps those near and dear to us, as well. I cannot emphasize enough how critical this is; do you understand? Am I clear?”

She saw a fierce intensity in his eyes that almost frightened her. However, she also sensed the depth of his sincerity and the fact that he was primarily concerned for her safety—even more so than his own. What could be so significant, so important?

She looked him in the eyes. “I understand. I can keep your secret. What is it?”

“*My* secret?” He rocked back, mildly chagrined. “Indeed, it is *yours* as well. Heed my words.”

“Go on,” she prompted, with a trace of impatience.

He waved the page of sheet music before her. “Do you remember this *music?* Actually, it is a spell crafted by Maude Delafaire. You found it when your mother and Stacy were missing. You were contemplating using it in the course of your search.”

"Yes, I remember. You warned me not to try, because it was crafted for some other intention—to find a lost love, I think. You said it wouldn't work, at least not the way I would have intended."

"Quite right! I'm pleased you remembered the warning. It was more a spell of *compulsion* than of *finding*. That was why Maude, reflecting upon the wisdom of such an act, never brought herself to use it."

"What does that have to do with this situation?" Ellen asked, confused.

Padraic laid the sheet of music down and smiled indulgently. "Please bear with me; all will become clear. You have met Queen Titania of the Light Elves, yes?"

She frowned. "Yes, you know I have. So?"

He leaned back and cocked his head. "Have you never wondered about a *king?*"

"Why, no, I never gave it any thought; but I suppose it would make sense. Is there such a king?"

He leaned toward her, and winked conspiratorially.

"Indeed yes, my dear, there is a king; his name is Oberon. But for him, Titania would not be queen—but that is another story. What is relevant, however, is that he has not been seen for centuries; so, Queen Titania alone has ruled the Light Elves and the Seelie Court, for all that time, with no other consort; or, at least so it has appeared."

"Is he alive—Oberon, I mean?"

"No one truly believes him to be dead," Padraic assured her. "Oberon is something of an enigma, if not a paradox; King of the Light Elves, consort to Titania, and yet someone who has little taste for the responsibilities of a monarch."

"Wait a minute—you said 'consort to Titania', right? You mean they're not married? But she's his queen, right? I'm confused."

Neither the irony nor the awkwardness was lost upon him.

"Ah, yes . . . Ellen, please try to understand. Marriage, per se, is for the most part a human construct, a socially sanctioned institution that is not overly prevalent among other races in other realms. It exists in form and function, I suppose, because people do bond and commit to one another. However, it is not always so labeled. Marriage, as you mean it, is thus somewhat rare in Faerie, but not unknown."

"Okay, I get it," she acknowledged, without mentioning the obvious, "and Oberon *is* of Faerie."

"Oh yes, that he is of Faerie is certain. But some say that he is not of full elfin or Faerie blood, and may even be half human. But no one really knows. Indeed, such speculation has traditionally been discouraged. It was said that he would take umbrage at the notion of such personal inquiries; most realized that it would not be deemed wise to offend the King of the Light Elves. No one knows the scope of his power. It was even whispered long ago that he could step in and out of the flow of time."

"What? Time travel? Oh, *come on*—is that even possible?"

Padraic shrugged. "Who really knows? I have never seen any such evidence. It may be no more than an ancient superstition. However, at one time there were those who sincerely believed that the very skilled could do so. Wiser thinkers feared the consequences sufficiently enough to craft immensely powerful wards of proscription to hopefully forestall any such endeavor. Some realms still maintain such protections—Storm Haven, for example. Although, I suspect it may be from long-ingrained habit or tradition rather than any specific threat of paradox."

Ellen nodded. "Oh yeah, I've heard of paradoxes with time travel, like the *grandfather paradox.* You go back in time and accidentally kill your grandfather—then you can never exist."

"Ah, yes, quite so . . . irony indeed." He rolled his eyes in chagrin.

"So, when was the last time Oberon was seen, and where?" She realized that was the sort of thing Hawk would ask; that pleased her.

"Hmm, good question. I truly do not know," Padraic admitted. "In fact, I do not know that I have ever seen him. Few even know what he looks like. He would frequently disguise himself and travel about the known realms incognito, having adventures and scandalous trysts wherever fate would take him—a bit of a rogue, you see."

A wry smile and sole arched eyebrow betrayed her recognition of the inescapable irony. She bit her tongue, lest she laugh aloud.

Obviously oblivious, he continued.

"As expected, any rumors of his escapades that reached Titania's ears did not endear him to her. While it is true that she enjoyed more and more power in his absences, she did not care to be made a fool in the eyes of the Faerie Courts."

"Oh, yeah, I can just see her in such a *snit*." Ellen smirked. "Please, go on."

"Ellen, do not underestimate her; she is not one to be trifled with, or embarrassed."

"Duly noted. I've met her, remember? Sorry, I didn't mean to interrupt. Do go on, please."

"Very well . . . Upon Oberon's return, after a particularly protracted absence, she demanded that he stop his epicurean practices, and do as she so bid. What happened next is unclear. It was whispered that he laughed in her face, turned his back to her, and left her chambers. Rumor holds that he has yet to return."

"He abandoned her?" Ellen shook her head. "I'm sure that didn't go over well."

"Not in the least. She forbade any mention of him and his activities. And worse, she surreptitiously sent her agents out to deal with—eliminate—any who may have, uh, *enjoyed his company.* Nor would she permit any *illegitimate* progeny of Oberon's *dalliances* to survive."

"Wait a sec," Ellen interjected. "Did Titania ever bear a child of Oberon's, an heir, a *legitimate progeny?*"

"No," Padraic admitted. "Therefore, she would see any and all of Oberon's progeny as illegitimate, and in her mind, a direct threat to her throne."

Ellen winced. "Wow, these elfin queens sure are paranoid about maintaining power—their thrones, that is."

"Indeed! Need I remind you how it was that the Lady Diere became Queen Mab LV?"

"Point taken," Ellen acknowledged. "This is all very interesting; but, what does all this have to do with us?"

Padraic picked up the sheet music spell and locked eyes with Ellen.

Her face paled. She reached out to take the page from his hand. Staring at the handwritten notes, her hand began to tremble.

"Oh, my . . . Maude." She gasped. "Does this mean that Maude . . . and *Oberon?*"

Padraic nodded slowly, and stared off into a private distance before speaking.

"Yes, they were . . . lovers, for a time. But as was his wont, he moved on. And although I suspect she was tempted, she never told him."

"She never told him *what?*" Ellen laid the sheet music down, her suspicions rising.

Padraic glanced around the room. Assured they were alone, he took both her hands and leaned in conspiratorially. "That she was with child."

"What?" Ellen exclaimed in astonishment, surprised to hear her vague supposition so clearly confirmed. Yet, in the next instant, all the major pieces seemed to fall into place, and she *knew!* Without a shadow of doubt, she *knew!*

He saw it in her face, and he smiled.

"Yes, Ellen, I am the bastard son of Oberon—Maude Delafaire was my mother."

Her eyes wide, she squeezed his hands. "Then, that means—"

"Yes, Maude was your *grandmother*," he finished, "and *you* are of the Old Blood—in fact, the blood of Faerie royalty flows in your veins."

"B-but . . . " Her breath hitched. An image of Maude's smiling face and the echo of her ethereal words . . . *you have come into your birthright* . . . hovered in her mind.

She pulled her hands free and came to her feet.

"I . . . I don't know what to say."

"Say nothing!" he insisted. He rose and grasped her shoulders. "No one must ever know! Both our lives would likely be forfeit should *either* elfin queen ever learn of this particular truth!"

"So, not even Oberon knows? Maude never told him?"

Padraic just shook his head. "Never, she assured me."

Ellen was too stunned to reply, staring at her impassioned father.

"Ellen, you must know that Mab would gloat and rub it in Titania's face! Titania would no doubt dispatch her assassins—no one close to either of us would ever be safe! Now do you see why this secret must be kept?"

"Yes, of course I do; but, does anyone suspect this—*this truth?*" Ellen asked, still trying to wrap her mind around this staggering news.

"No, not as far as I know." He dropped his hands, and resumed his seat on the piano bench.

"However, Titania is an overly suspicious sort. I do not trust her—nor should you. I know she has invited you to her court, but I could not let you accept such an invitation, or ever venture into the Realm of the Light Elves, without knowing *our truth*."

Ellen walked to the fireplace and rubbed her hands. She was suddenly chilled in spite of the warmth of the room. Her mind reeled in a sort of benign chaos, but threads of logic began to unravel from the tangled skeins of confusion and weave a pattern of vague comprehension. The fabric of events enhanced the developing tapestry and subtle truths grew increasingly evident.

"So, that was why," Ellen murmured in dawning realization, "why you . . . It was more than just the fealty issue when you warned me against accepting Titania's invitation when I first met her at the Council meeting. Does she suspect something?"

"It is possible, I suppose," he admitted, "but I have no proof.

"I think Titania may have once suspected that Oberon might have had a fling with Maude—one among many, to be sure—but her subsequent pregnancy was a well-kept secret. No one knows I am her son; however, a few know that you are my daughter. And, while I doubt that Titania knows that we are so linked by blood, it would be foolish to assume she will never learn of it. Never forget that Queen Mab is among those who know about us. What she may do with that knowledge, even out of spite, is anyone's guess."

Ellen blew a thin stream of air through pinched lips. "I can see why we shouldn't tell my mother any of this. It would only distress her, and no doubt put her in danger."

"Quite so," her father agreed. "There may come a time when I can safely tell her—and it will be *my* place to do so, but not now. It will surely upset her to know that neither Maude nor I took her into our confidence, despite that it was for her own good."

"No, I can understand that. I'll keep it to myself," Ellen agreed, despite feeling inherently uncomfortable at keeping something so significant from her mother.

She began to pace to and fro. "Oh man, this is all too much! This could change so many things. It's gonna take me a little time to adjust. What are you going to do now?"

"For tonight, I simply plan to enjoy your mother's fine cooking; but then, I must go to Mer. I have a favor, actually an outstanding debt of honor, to repay."

"Mer? The water world?" Her interest piqued.

"Yes, indeed. You should find the time to visit that realm. It is quite a delightful place."

"Sounds like a vacation spot—I just might do that, eventually. But there's still a lot that needs to be done around here."

"Here? Do you mean Delafaire Farm? I was under the impression that you had rather a lot of help, periodic visitors from some of the other realms, yes?"

"Oh, certainly," she answered with a broad smile, "and they've been great! Our gardens and orchards have been simply wonderful—almost too good. But I'm referring to the more mundane things involved in running a successful business in this realm. We're doing quite well. There's plenty to share with our *periodic visitors*, and still maintain the appearance of a moderately successful family farm."

"Ah, I understand all too well," he assured her, rising and executing an exaggerated courtier's sweeping bow, "about keeping up appearances."

She smiled and shook her head in amusement.

His expression sobered. "However, we can never relax our vigilance. There are those who would upset the balance of things in the blind pursuit of their own ends, and others who champion chaos for its own sake. Tomorrow is assured to no one."

"Enough of those dark thoughts," she chided. "This is Christmastime, the season of good cheer and goodwill to all. So, be cheery already! Come on!"

Taking her father's arm, they walked down the hall, the dogs trotting in their wake and Smokey slinking after them like the shadow of an afterthought.

Just as they reached the kitchen doors, Padraic paused, and patted her hand.

"You must forgive me if I seemed overly grave. I did not intend to sound quite so morbid. It is only that I am aware of such things. Of course, other bits of information come to my attention, from time to time, that give me pause. I find that strange, since I never used to worry about anything. Oh well, suffice to say it seems that we are indeed living in interesting times."

"Interesting times? As I recall, that's considered a none-too-subtle curse," she observed facetiously. "But I think you're just trying to warn me that things could always get more dangerous, aren't you?"

He could only grin and shrug.

"At least we shan't be bored. Now, let us join your mother."

(The tale continues in MER, Vol. V of THE STEWARD)

How can an entire realm suddenly be at risk,

and only a handful of perplexed people be aware?

How can organized crime threaten realms of the Multiverse

with such perverse and rampant drug addiction?

Is this a long-term strategy to create and control an immense black market,

or a far more subtle and sinister bid for ultimate power?

Perhaps even worse, will the steadily increasing frequency of necromantic incidents

herald a resurgence of roaming legions of ravenous deceased,

led by another Lord of the Dead?

Ellen Doyle, Steward of the Grand Portal of the Realm of Man,

there's a call for you . . .

About the Author

M.D. Ironz is the pseudonym of a former government official, based in an undisclosed location in North America, and now serving as a confidential consultant on matters of intelligence, security, and investigations.

www.ingramcontent.com/pod-product-compliance
Lightning Source LLC
Chambersburg PA
CBHW030540310726
48979CB00010B/1976/J

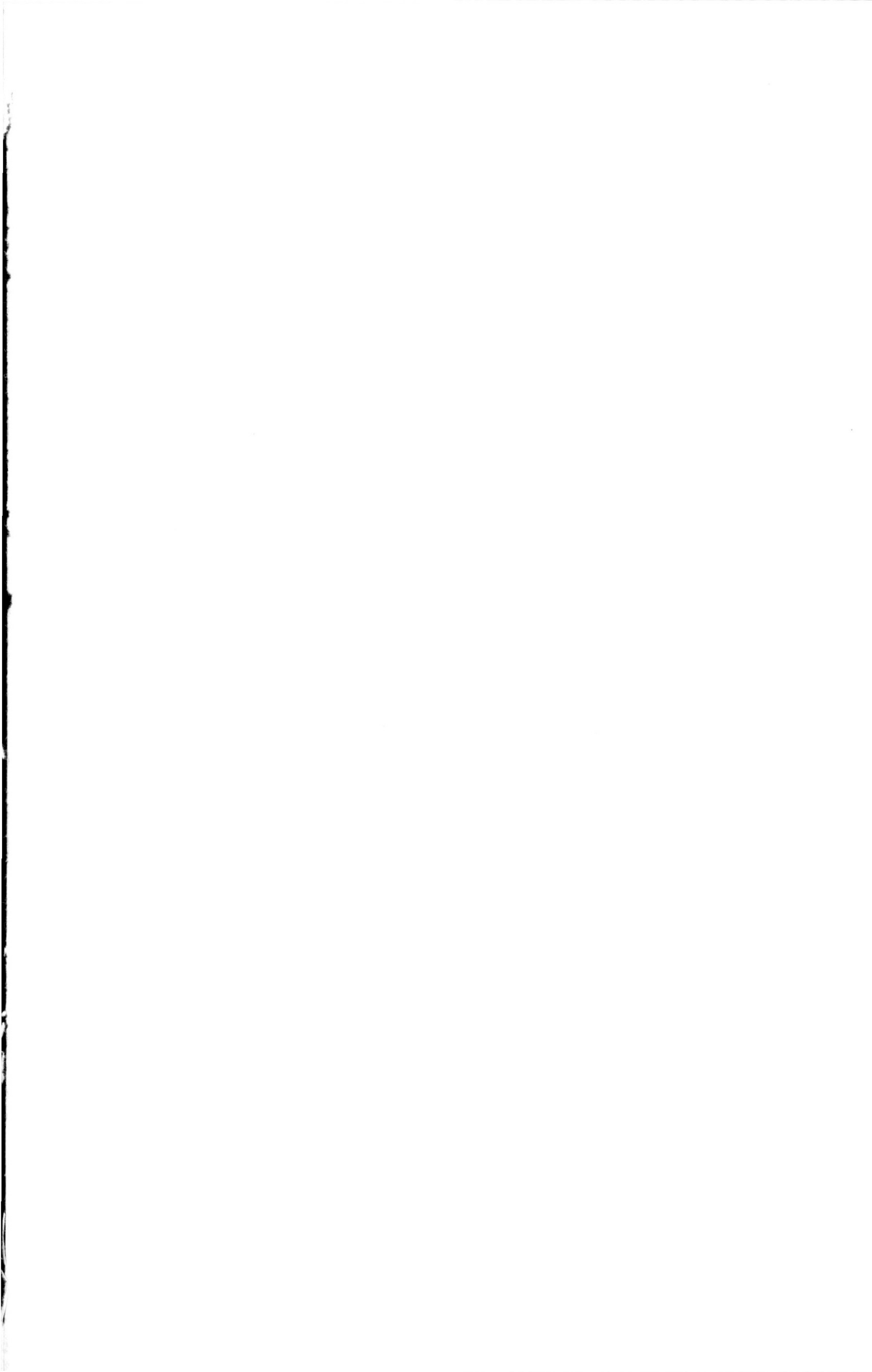